They'd met, the[...]

Now it lo[...]

back to[...]

and it's going to be

Even Better

Than Before

isn't it?

Wonderful authors
BJ James and **Anne McAllister**
bring you two intense, poignant
reunion stories.

Dear Reader,

Welcome to the sexy world of Desire!

We have three lovely volumes for you this month starting with two intense reunion stories in **Even Better Than Before** which features Anne McAllister's *A Cowboy's Promise* and another tale in BJ James's MEN OF BELLE TERRE miniseries called *The Redemption of Jefferson Cade*.

Our two heroines are **Under Suspicion** by rugged heroes in Elizabeth Bevarly's *The Secret Life of Connor Monahan* and Bronwyn Jameson's *Addicted to Nick*.

Finally, we have two wonderful stories with a fairytale twist in **The Nanny and the Boss** featuring *Wyoming Cinderella* by Cathleen Galitz and *Taming the Beast* by Amy J Fetzer.

Enjoy!

The Editors

Even Better Than Before

BJ JAMES
ANNE McALLISTER

Silhouette, Silhouette Desire and Colophon are registered trademarks of Harlequin Books S.A., used under licence.

First published in Great Britain 2002
Silhouette Books, Eton House, 18-24 Paradise Road,
Richmond, Surrey TW9 1SR

EVEN BETTER THAN BEFORE © Harlequin Books S.A. 2002

The publisher acknowledges the copyright holders of the individual works as follows:

The Redemption of Jefferson Cade © BJ James 2002
A Cowboy's Promise © Barbara Schenck 2001

ISBN 0 373 04763 0

51-1002

Printed and bound in Spain
by Litografia Rosés S.A., Barcelona

THE REDEMPTION OF
JEFFERSON CADE

by
BJ James

BJ JAMES

Her first book for Silhouette Desire was publishe[d]
February 1987. Her second Desire novel receive[d a]
second Maggie, the coveted award of Georgia
Romance Writers. Through the years there have been
other awards and nominations for awards, including
those from *Romantic Times Magazine*, Reviewer's
Choice, Career Achievement, Best Desire and Best
Series Romance of the Year. In that time, her books
have appeared regularly on a number of bestseller lists,
among them Waldenbooks and *USA Today*.

On a personal note, BJ and her doctor husband have
three sons and two grandsons. A small village set in the
foothills of western North Carolina is her home.

Prologue

The wilderness was his sanctuary. As a boy he'd come in search of solace. As a man he came for peace.

From his vantage among the trees, Jefferson Cade looked over a swampy Eden. A land few knew as he knew it. The land of his heart. One of strange, erratic temperament, as now. For even as he waited, its mood altered. Dormant air grew sultry. Moisture permeated each breath and burnished all it touched in a heated mist. The day, and the hideaway tucked among the limbs of the moss strewn tree, were held in the thrall of a lowcountry summer.

Far below the tree house, at the edge of a pond, a fish jumped, startling a fawn just dipping his head to drink. Jefferson smiled as the tiny creature danced away. A smile that vanished as he glimpsed the woman half hidden in the shadow of a palmetto.

Caught by her stillness, he waited. As she watched the fawn, he saw how much she'd changed, yet remained the same. When she'd first come from Argentina to live, to study, and absorb the graces still surviving in the quaint city of Belle Terre, she'd been a girl on the verge of womanhood. Now the tomboy who hunted, fished, and handled horses as well as any man, had indeed become a beautiful woman. And his best friend.

"Marissa." She couldn't have heard, yet her eyes lifted to his. And, as she came to him, he whispered, "Marissa Claire."

A half hour of silence later, Jefferson abandoned his pen and sketch pad. Moving to Marissa's side he sat on the tree house floor, wondering what trouble had drawn her to him.

This meeting had begun strangely. After a subdued greeting and a strained smile, she'd barely spoken. Conversation had never been necessary between them. Yet now her silence was unbearable.

Leaning on an elbow, he stared down at a beguiling woman who lay as if she were sleeping. But he knew her body language too well not to read the wakeful tension. As patience deserted him, he tugged a stray curl. "Hey, lazybones, want to go fishing?"

Reluctantly her dark gaze met his. Knowing the time for pretense was past, but not ready to speak, she looked away.

Jefferson had never seen her so distant. It was rare that she would call him at midday asking that he meet her here. Rare that she barely greeted him then withdrew. Something was wrong. "What is it, Marissa? Why did you ask me to come here?"

When her reply was only a shrug, he lapsed again into silent contemplation. She was Marissa Claire Alexandre. Merrie to all but him, for whom the name hadn't fit. An inexplicable perception he couldn't explain to any but himself.

Four years before, she'd come to Belle Terre. Sent from

the Alexandre *estancia* by a father determined to tame his daredevil daughter. Guided by Eden Cade, Marissa was to learn the ways of Southern ladies. Lessons she'd mastered perfectly, yet never lost her love of country life, or her passion for horses.

In the beginning their friendship was based on mutual admiration of their unique skill with horses. From that beginning came a deepening of common interests. As good friends became confidants, it was to him she turned in happy or troubled times.

But Marissa was only twenty-one, eight years younger than he. A disparity he never forgot, even as the remarkable girl became a remarkable woman—and Jefferson Cade, once forever immune, had fallen deeply in love with her. Deeply but in vain. In denial of all he felt, he survived by reminding himself the woman within the alluring body loved him as a friend.

Too soon even that would be taken from him. From the first, the plan was clear. Marissa would spend five years in her mother's homeland. Then she was to return to Argentina to honor obligations she neither explained nor discussed. Jefferson had learned to live with the inevitable. Time in hand was too precious to waste agonizing over the time to come. And if friendship was all he could have, he would be a friend in every need.

Besieged by desire, but setting the sorrow of it aside, he turned her face to him. "Hey," he questioned as he saw tears in her dark eyes. "What is it, sweetheart? How can I help?"

Marissa stared up at him, memorizing each handsome feature. She knew Jefferson had never understood the charisma of his smile, the power of his kindness. In all their years of friendship, he hadn't known of her dual dilemma. When he'd urged her to spend more time with classmates and teased that she would never find her Prince Charming in the wilds with him, he didn't understand she was promised to a much older man.

A promise she must honor. Though she'd found her prince where Jefferson said she couldn't, she would keep her father's word. And leave her heart in Prince Charming's keeping.

As always in his strong presence, she found her own strength. Catching his wrist, she pressed her cheek in his palm. "There's no help for a day that was preordained. I knew it would come, but not so soon."

Slipping the scarf from her hair, he smoothed dark, silky tresses with his fingers. "What day, Marissa?"

"The day I say goodbye."

He went totally still. "But you have another year."

"That was the agreement. But now it's different." Her voice broke. "I've been called home."

He wondered what agreement, but only asked, "When?"

Tears she'd denied flooded her eyes. "I leave tomorrow."

Jefferson tensed. Then he drew her to him, embracing her in futile denial. "Not yet. Not so soon."

Her arms crept around him, her head rested over his heart. She would remember this moment and treasure it. Someday she would tell the children she might have about this enchanting place, and of the man whose creation the tree house had been.

If she had sons, she would speak of his ruggedness, his adventures, and his communion with the wilderness. If she had daughters, she would tell them of the tenderness of a beautiful man, and would wonder if they looked into her heart and saw the truth.

But that lay in the future, that didn't begin until tomorrow. Until then, she had this one, last day with Jefferson.

His chest rose and fell beneath her cheek as it nestled

against the hard muscles. His hands at her shoulders moved her from his embrace. His shadowed stare moved over her face, lingering at her mouth, her eyes. Seeing what he hadn't let himself see before. Believing what he hadn't dared believe.

"Dear God," he whispered, with regret for lost time, lost love.

Marissa didn't flinch or turn away. For once, she wouldn't hide what she felt for him.

Jefferson's heart filled with hope. "Don't go, Marissa." Softly he spoke words he never expected to say. "Stay with me."

In his face she saw despair, honor, a friend's love. With a sigh she spoke the truth. "I can't. There is a man, my father owes him a great deal. In return, I was promised to him long ago."

"Promised to him?" Whatever he expected, it was never this. "Do you love him? Have I misread what I see in your eyes?"

Marissa felt the lash of his anger and forgave it. "I hardly know him. The betrothal was a business arrangement. He wanted a wife one day. It was decided I would be that wife."

"In return for what?" Jefferson's clasp on her shoulders seared into her flesh. "What do you get out of this arrangement?"

"I get nothing, Jefferson. But because of me, my father and mother can keep their life as it is."

"Your life and you were traded for wealth, to insure a lifestyle?" He spat the words. "Your father would do that?"

"For money, power, the lifestyle? Yes." Marissa was calm beneath his angry glare. "It's the way of the wealthy, bartering lives, love, even children. My father was desperate. My mother's health was failing. It was for her sake he negotiated this time in Belle Terre. In the bargain, I was to bring the expected graces to the marriage. And who better than Eden to teach me? Now, as a point of honor, my father is impatient to resolve the debt.''

''Honor?'' Disgust seethed in Jefferson. Disgust she didn't deserve. She loved her mother and her father. She was so young at the time, what choice was there for her? Deep in his soul, he understood. But understanding couldn't ease the anguish.

''Arranged marriages aren't uncommon in my land and families like mine. All my father has ever known is abundant wealth. As young as I was, even I could see the more extravagant the lifestyle, the less one can fathom living a lesser existence. In your world, the arrangement is despicable. In my father's, he has done his best for his family. I could defy him and refuse to honor his word. But, because my mother's illness is slowly debilitating and will likely continue for years, I won't try.''

Jefferson drew a breath. An unsteady hand caressed her face. Softly, he said, ''Then tell me how I can help you now.''

Marissa's lips brushed the heel of his hand. Her steady gaze held his. ''You could make love to me.''

His chest felt like a vise. If his mind reeled, now it spun into dementia. ''No,'' he heard himself say, though there was nothing he wanted more than to make love to her. ''You don't know what you're asking. You haven't considered the repercussions.''

''You're wrong, my dearest friend. I know exactly what I'm asking. I've considered every repercussion. What I'm expected to do, what I will do, is for my family.'' Touching his face, she let her drifting fingertips linger at his mouth. ''This, I ask for me.''

Curling her fingers into a fist, she stared at her hand, and thought of his. Strong, hard, roughened by calluses, yet beautiful. And even in passion his touch would be gentle.

"What crime is it to learn of love from a man who cares? What sin to want you, Jefferson? I do, you know," she whispered.

Jefferson clung to one last shred of sanity. "You…"

"Don't!" A fingertip stopped his words. "Don't tell me I don't know what I want, what I need. You haven't misread anything and I'm not asking for forever. But for my first time, I need to feel your hands on my body. Only yours.

"I can't change the path of my life. But I can survive it if you give me this to remember. If you pretend for a little while that you love me as more than a friend."

"No." Though he drew away from her and rose to stand at his full height, he meant only that he wouldn't be pretending. Marissa didn't understand. As hurt gathered the eyes, right or wrong, he knew he couldn't deny her. Or himself.

There was so much more he wanted to say, but he couldn't think. He couldn't be wise or pragmatic. He could only love her.

"Marissa." He called her name, only her name. Yet beneath the storm of emotions lay an unspoken question as his slowly extended hand offered her a chance to back away. His riveted look moved from his own roughened fingers to her face. As a bewildered frown marred her brow, he spoke again. "Take my hand, sweetheart. But only if you truly want me. Only if you're sure."

In a subtle change, hope shone in her eyes. "I'm sure, Jefferson." As she took his hand, her resolve was strong. "I've never been more sure in my life."

As clasped hands held fast, drawing her up to his embrace, he knew there were questions to ask. Warnings to give. But common sense was lost as he reveled in holding her. Then into his own silence, he breathed a surrendering word. A curse? A prayer? Not even Jefferson knew. The battle was done. There was no going back.

In the stillness he undressed her, and the discarding of each garment became an exquisite seduction. Each button slipped free, unveiling her body inch by inch, inviting a touch, a kiss.

When she was cloaked only in sun-spangled shadows and the dark cascade of her hair, he discovered she was more beautiful than he'd dreamed. More desirable. With a final caress, his hands fell away to attend the task of undressing himself.

When the last of his own clothing was cast away, seeing the apprehension of innocence, taking her hands in his, he brought them to his mouth. Lips and breath warming her cold fingers, he murmured, "Don't be afraid, Marissa."

Bringing her nearer, he bent to kiss the tender flesh beneath her ear. As she murmured an indistinct sound of pleasure, he let his fingertips stray over her throat and down. When his hands closed over her breasts, his palms teasing their tips, the nipples hardened, as his own body had, with desire.

"Don't be afraid," he said one last time.

Marissa's answer was a whisper as he drew her down to the floor. "Never with you, Jefferson." When his lips followed the path of his touch she cried again, "Never with you."

A virile man, Jefferson was far from innocent. He knew how to tantalize, how to excite, as he took Marissa with him from one degree of longing to another. Erotic forays discovered where to stroke, when to kiss, when to suckle, leaving her desperate for more, yet wondering how there could ever be. Then he tapped a secret well of unthinking hunger that spiraled into impassioned madness, intensifying every need.

Always before, he was the sole maker of madness. Once passion had sufficed. But with the coherent thought he could manage beneath her touch, he knew passion for passion's sake would never be enough again. And, as he found himself falling deeper beneath her spell, nor would anyone but Marissa.

He'd never wanted forever. He wanted it now. But in its stead, he would make for her a beautiful memory to take to a new life. And for himself, a dream. The only forever he could have.

Swept into the madness, a gentle man became more gentle. When she called his name in a voice husky with desire, there was no past, no future. They were only a man and a woman trembling on the edge of a world where neither had gone, and would never go again.

Drawing away, he looked down at her. "Even the making of a beautiful memory can be painful. But only once." Sealing his promise with a kiss, he came down to her, whispering, "Only once."

In a day bright and hot, a cry sounded as moisture laden air painted joining bodies in a sheen of gossamer. Then there was only a sigh of welcome as Jefferson went with Marissa into the last of rapture…while the world waited.

The splash wasn't enough to wake him, but it did. As naturally as breathing, he reached for Marissa. He was alone. In her place lay the scarf he'd taken from her hair. Sliding on his jeans, he moved to the ladder that led to the ground.

"No," Marissa called from the water's edge. "Don't come down, Jefferson. I don't think I could bear to leave if you do."

"Don't go," he pleaded, though he knew it was futile.

Marissa didn't answer. As he stopped short of the first rung, she turned to toss a stone into the pond. The water's surface was calm before she spoke again. "This day and this place have been magic. So I thought the pond could be a wishing well. It was greedy of me, but I've made two wishes."

"What did you wish, Marissa?"

When she looked up at him, her smile was bittersweet. "First I wished you wouldn't forget me."

Jefferson said nothing. It was a wish already granted. How could a man forget a woman like Marissa? "And the second?"

"The impossible."

"Maybe it doesn't have to be, sweetheart."

Her smile faltered. "You're wrong, my beloved friend. Though I've wished with all my heart, how could we meet again?"

A knife in his heart couldn't hurt as much. "Wishing wells grant three wishes. Will you wish again?"

"Yes." The stone was already in her hand.

"Will you tell me the last?"

"Not this time. Not this wish."

Jefferson didn't pry. And though he knew what would follow the splash of the last stone, he wasn't ready for it.

"Goodbye, Jefferson Cade." Her voice was soft, her words halting. "I won't forget you. I won't forget this day."

"Marissa." He waited until she turned back, until their eyes met. "If ever you need me...I'll come for you."

"I know," she acknowledged and turned away again.

He wanted to call out to her, to ask her again to stay. Instead, as silent as the wilderness, he watched her go.

At the far shore, she stopped and raised a hand. It was then the storm for which the land waited lashed out in a blinding bolt of lightning and a rumble of thunder. When the world was quiet again, the path was empty. Marissa had gone from his life.

* * *

Heavy rain was falling when Jefferson paused at the edge of the clearing. Through the downpour, his gaze sought the half-hidden bower where he'd made love to Marissa Claire Alexandre.

His sketch pad shielded by his body, a keepsake folded against his heart, he committed to memory this place. He would paint it, melding sketches and memories. Someday.

Rain fell harder, spattering over the pond like stones in a wishing well. "One wish is true, Marissa."

Lightning flickered, thunder growled. As quickly as it came, the rain stopped. As a mist shrouded the land, Jefferson waited for one more glimpse that never came. It didn't matter.

"I won't forget."

When he turned away, though the wilderness had been an abiding part of his life, he knew it could never be the same.

He wouldn't come again.

One

"Well, hello, handsome." The greeting, addressing the lone patron at the bar, was lilting and feminine. Teasing a favorite customer.

Setting his glass aside, a hand automatically going to his Stetson, Jefferson Cade smiled. A brush of his fingers tilting the tan brim accompanied a pleasant greeting as teasing. "Afternoon, Miss Cristal."

As she laughed in pleasure at the Western gallantry spoken in a Southern drawl, Cristal Lane slipped her arm through his. "What brings a Southern gentleman like you into town today?"

In this land of old ranches and older family names, with time measured in half centuries, if not centuries, Cristal was counted as new to Arizona. But Jefferson considered the remark conversation, not a question, for she'd owned the most popular saloon in Silverton years enough to know the spring stock show held annually in the town attracted ranchers from miles around. As it had drawn him from the Broken Spur of Sunrise Canyon.

But Cristal was also familiar enough with his reclusive lifestyle to believe the show, itself, would not merit one of his rare visits. As she silently signaled for the bartender to refresh the drink he'd hardly touched, Jefferson wasn't surprised when she suggested, quietly, ''Someone must be offering a spectacular horse to tempt you from your hideout.''

''Think so?'' Shifting his gaze from her, he nodded his thanks to the bartender, then folded his hands around the glass.

Her shrewd study drifted away to assess the needs of customers. Satisfied everyone was content, she looked again at the handsome Southerner, and inevitably at his hands.

As with everything about Jefferson Cade, his hands were intriguing. Weathered, callused, the hands of a working man, an artist. A mix of rugged elegance and gentle strength. One of the times he'd been in town and stayed late to walk her home after closing, she'd teased him about his hands. He'd only laughed when she'd called them fascinating, saying it was natural that any living, breathing female would wonder about his touch.

He'd asked what female? For in the four years since he'd returned to Arizona to work for Jake Benedict at the Rafter B, then Steve Cody at the Broken Spur, he'd done no more than speak a few pleasantries to any woman. Beyond the routine associations of ranching, he was happiest living his reclusive life.

''Do I think so? Yes,'' she murmured to his reflection in the mirror behind the bar. ''It must be one helluva horse.''

Her use of the rare profanity recalled a late-night talk when she'd ventured another startling opinion.

It must've been one helluva woman who spoiled all the rest of womankind for you, Jefferson Cade. She'd made the statement, then never mentioned it again. But he knew she was remembering the night and her words as her eyes probed his.

Jefferson held her gaze for a long moment, then turned his face away. A virile face maturity had made more attractive, and the new touch of silver in his dark blond hair only complemented. His mouth was solemn now. Beneath the brim of the Stetson, his downswept lashes shielded his eyes. But if his head had lifted and if his lips tilted in a smile that touched his eyes, it would still make an attractive man startlingly handsome.

He was immune, not a fool. He knew he'd caught the attention of a number of the female population of Silverton in the early days of his return. But he never acknowledged the most blatant flirtation with more than a courtly smile and a pleasant greeting. He became a master at making the most brazen feel he was flattered and perplexed by the advances, a gallantry that, at first, had an opposite effect than the one he wanted. But through the years, as even the most determined found him ever elusive, his would-be lovers became friendly acquaintances, if not friends.

Though she teased about his charm, Cristal's interest was platonic. As he recognized her honesty and wisdom, she became a close friend. A rare and trusted confidante.

"If not for a particular horse, you wouldn't be here, would you, Jefferson? There's nothing else in your life. You won't let there be, because of a woman." Cristal voiced a long-standing concern, exercising the privilege of friendship.

Only the narrowing of his eyes signaled this subject was off-limits. For once, Cristal wasn't to be deterred. "Do you ever get her out of your mind or your heart? This woman you loved and lost...do you ever stop thinking about her? Can you stop? Or do you spend each waking moment remembering how she looked, how she smiled, the way she walked? The fragrance of her hair?''

Jefferson didn't respond. Then, pushing away from the bar, his expression unreadable, he looked down at her. "What I'm thinking and remembering," he said as courteously as if she weren't prying, "is that it's time to see a man about a horse.''

Fingers at his hat brim, a charming smile, a low, "Miss Cristal," and she was left to watch him walk away. Long after he stepped through the door and disappeared into the crowd, no less concerned she stared at the space where he'd been.

"Cristal," a raucous voice called. "How about a song?''

"Sure, Hal." She didn't need to look around to recognize a regular customer. "What would you like to hear?''

"No preference, honey," he answered. "Just sing.''

With a last glance at the empty doorway, Cristal crossed the room. Despite the tightening in her throat, leaning over the piano player, aptly named Sam, she whispered in his ear. When he nodded, she looked over the room, her smile touched with sadness for a lonely man. "How about this one? An oldie for a friend.''

As the melancholy chords of the introduction ended, wondering what intuition dictated the old tune, she sang of a lady's choice to leave the man who loved her.

"Easy girl. Nobody's going to hurt you. Not anymore.'' In a soothing singsong, Jefferson coaxed the nervous mare from the trailer. As she stepped down the ramp, ears flicking in suspicion, he didn't blame her. Even for a high-strung filly who hadn't been mishandled, the unfamiliar surroundings and the noise of the stock show would've been excuse enough for being skittish.

When she'd come on the market as a difficult horse offered at a nominal fee, the most uninformed judge of horses could see promise. Which, given the bargain price, sent up a red flag that warned labeling her difficult was an understatement. Jefferson had driven to her home stable for a preliminary look, taking Sandy Gannon, foreman of the Rafter B and an expert judge of horses, with him for a second opinion. Both agreed the filly was of a bloodline and a quality Steve Cody would approve.

When the seller questioned who could tame the filly, Sandy replied that if Jeff Cade couldn't, then it couldn't be done.

"Let's hope Sandy knows what he's talking about," Jefferson crooned to the filly when she finally stood on the ground. The truth was, Sandy knew exactly what he was saying when he praised the Southerner. Before assuming duties at the Broken Spur, Jefferson had spent the last two of three years at the Rafter B as second in command. Though he'd made a show of grumbling over losing a good horseman, Sandy had backed Steve and his wife Savannah's choice.

Now, Jefferson had lived and worked in Sunrise Canyon for more than a year, loving each solitary day. "So will you, girl," he promised as he led the filly to a stall. "Some folks think it's lonely in the canyon, but it isn't. You'll see."

Realizing he was talking to a horse that would run with Steve's small herd, he laughed. A sound too rare in his life. "A stranger would think the loneliness has driven me bonkers. When it's driven me a little saner, instead."

His string of chatter elicited a low whinny and a nudge, and he knew his faith in the filly hadn't been misplaced. Stroking her, he murmured, "You'll be happy here, girl. One day soon, when we know what fits, we'll choose a name for you."

Slipping a bar over the stall door, he made a quick check of the other horses and stepped outside. After a long day and a four-hour drive across the surrounding Benedict land, it was good to steal a minute to watch the moon rise.

In daylight or darkness, the canyon was beautiful. When he'd come to Arizona as a teenage runaway he'd been too young and his life too chaotic to appreciate the stark magnificence of the land. Ten years later, when he'd left the lowcountry again—running away as an adult—he hadn't expected to find anything to equal the lovely land he left behind.

He was wrong. As an adult with an artist's eye, he recognized the different degrees of beauty, the different kinds.

The desert was his home now. Though he knew he could never go back, the lowcountry had been in his mind recently. Perhaps because, after years of neglect, he'd taken out his sketches and in the long winter darkness, he'd begun to paint again.

A painting waited now on the easel. The light wasn't so good in the renovated cabin, but it didn't matter. Painting was something he did for himself. A final healing, an exorcism.

Abandoning the soothing sight of the canyon in moonlight, he returned to the truck to retrieve his mail. No one wrote to him but family. Though he treasured the snapshots and letters, days could pass before he made a mail run. Given the size of the packet the postmaster'd had waiting for him, the time had been even longer.

Jefferson cared deeply for his brothers, and he was never truly out of touch. The family knew to contact the Rafter B in emergencies. Sandy would relay any messages by telephone or rider. No phone calls, no rider meant everyone was well and safe.

Tucking the packet under his arm, as the door of the truck closed, he whistled. Two clear notes sounded in the failing light, answered by a bark and the pad of racing feet.

As he braced himself, a dark shape launched itself like a bullet at his chest.

Letters scattered in the dust as Jefferson went down. A massive creature blacker than the night stood over him. Gleaming teeth bared in a grin, a long, pink tongue lapped at his face.

Laughing, pushing the great dog aside, Jefferson muttered, "If that means you're glad to see me, Satan, I hope you won't be quite so glad next time."

Satan barked and danced away. Normally with his sentry duty done, he was ready to play. This night, as if he would hurry his master to abandon the game by helping him to stand, the dog grabbed his hand between his teeth. The slightest pressure could have caused injury but, as with all creatures trained by Jefferson, despite his fierce look Satan was as gentle as his master.

The mock attack was a game, begun when Jefferson was new to the canyon and Satan a puppy with too much energy. Soon the dog should be taught the game was too dangerous. "Someone could misunderstand and put a bullet in your head." Jefferson cuffed him gently in a signal to let go. "Might bend the bullet."

Satan trotted away again in the prance common to Doberman pinschers everywhere. Stopping short, his dark eyes on his master's face, he made a sound Jefferson interpreted as canine impatience.

"Not funny?" Rising, the human side of the conversation dusted off his clothes. Gathering the mail, he declared in an understatement, "Considering that I would miss you, tonight's a good time to stop the game. As you obviously have."

In the gloom settling over the canyon, he almost missed one piece of mail. Satan's pawing interest, combined with the dull glint of its metal clasp caught his attention. Without both, the brown envelope would have blended with the shadowed Arizona dust. Perhaps to be discovered in morning light. Perhaps not.

Hefting it, he judged its weight. More than a letter, with only a blurred postmark. No return address. "What could this be?"

Satan barked and paced toward the cabin. "You're right," Jefferson agreed. "I should go inside and have a look."

Normally the Doberman refused to come inside. Tonight, he slipped past Jefferson when the door opened. Rather than stretching out on the hearth as usual in his rare sorties in the cabin, he streaked through the main room to the bedroom.

"Come away, Satan," Jefferson scolded as the dog scratched at the bedside table. "There's nothing here."

Nothing but a keepsake from his past, Jefferson amended as he herded the dog from the room. "Lie by the hearth," he directed. "After I check the mail, we'll have supper."

Satan obeyed, instantly. Containing his agitation, he tucked his nose beneath his paws. His dark eyes were white-rimmed beneath the pupils as he tracked each move his master made.

Jefferson sat at the table. Spreading mail over it, he plucked the brown envelope from the jumble. Satan whimpered. "Hey." Jefferson moved it left, then right. Only Satan's eyes turned, never leaving the letter. "What about this worries you?"

Jefferson believed animals possessed unique senses, perceiving more than the human mind could begin to conceive. Some would laugh, others would scoff at the idea, but he'd seen this anticipation too often in the wilderness to not believe it.

He'd seen it before in Satan when a rattler had crawled into a stall, striking a colt. Though little more than a pup, the dog had clawed at the cabin door, waking Jefferson, demanding his attention. Then he'd torn a pair of jeans as he'd dragged his master to the barn. Because of Satan, the colt was alive. Because of Satan, Jefferson opened the envelope with trepidation.

"What the devil?" he tore open another envelope.

When he moved past the surprise of discovering one unmarked envelope inside another, he almost pitched the whole package in the trash as a joke. Recalling Satan's reaction, he continued.

The next envelope, the last, bore a name. His name, written in a hand he knew. For one stunned moment he thought it was a cruel hoax. Next he questioned how it could be. When he drew out two sheets of paper, he knew it wasn't. The first was newspaper. The second a plain, white sheet torn raggedly from a tablet. One line was written across the sheet in the same familiar hand.

His own hand shaking, for longer than he knew, Jefferson stared down at it, tracing each letter, each word, with his startled gaze. Catching an unsteady breath, an unforgettable fragrance filling his lungs, touching his heart, he read the written words out loud. His own words, spoken just once, long ago.

If ever you need me…

A promise made. A promise to keep. But how?

The answer lay in the second sheet. A month-old newspaper article. "'The search for the plane of Paulo Rei has been terminated,'" he read, then read again. "'On board were Señor Rei, his wife, the former Marissa Claire Alexandre, and her parents.'"

There was more, a detailed description of the Reis and their lives. But Jefferson's voice stumbled to a halt. Papers fluttered to the floor. As his gaze lifted to the portrait over the mantel, he recited the only line that mattered in a lifeless voice, "'It has been determined there could be no survivors.'"

No survivors. The words were a cry in his mind. Words that made no sense. Trying to find sanity in it, he read his own words again. A promise only Marissa would know.

But a part of him couldn't comprehend or separate truth from fiction. Was it a charade? A ghoulish trick? Or was it real?

If it was real, why was it assumed Marissa had been on the plane? If it wasn't she who had sent the letter, then who?

His thoughts were a whirligig, going 'round and 'round, always ending in the same place, the same thought, the same denial. No one but Marissa could have sent the letter. It had to be. It must be. For, if she hadn't, it would mean she was dead.

"No!" Jefferson refused to believe. "I would know. The world wouldn't feel right without Marissa."

But how could he be sure? How could he know he wasn't persuading himself to believe what he needed to believe?

"Satan!" The name was spoken without thought or conscious volition. But as he heard it, Jefferson knew it was the way. Rigid as stone, the dog had watched. Now he came to attention, awaiting the command that always followed his name spoken in that tone. Jefferson smiled, a humorless tilt of his lips. Recognizing the stance, he gave the expected command. "Stay."

Certain Satan would obey, he returned to his bedroom. Opening the drawer by the bedside table, he drew out a scarf. A square of silk filled with memories.

Marissa's scarf. A memento of a day never forgotten.

How many times had he seen her wear it? How often had he thought how pretty the bright color was lying against her nape, holding back her dark hair? Why, when he wanted to so badly, had he never dared fling it away to wrap himself in the spill of silken locks?

How could her perfume linger so long, a reminder of the day he'd lived the dream he hadn't dared?

"The day I made love to Marissa."

As the floodgates opened, memories he'd never allowed himself to dwell on came rushing in wistful vignettes....

Marissa riding as only Marissa could, her body moving in perfect harmony with the horse.

Marissa with a rifle in her hand, the dedicated hunter who could track anything, but could never pull the trigger.

Marissa picking an orchid to celebrate sighting an eagle.

Marissa that last day. Sad, solemn, walking through sunlight and shadow to come to him. The wistful woman he'd loved for longer than he would admit, wanting him, as he'd wanted her.

Marissa, the innocent, teaching him what love should be. Wishing he couldn't forget her, and that they would meet again. Leaving with a wish unspoken, a secret he would never know.

Marissa, her hand raised in farewell, disappearing in the blinding furor of a storm.

"Dear God." Jefferson clutched the scarf. Every moment he'd locked away in the back of his mind was as fresh, as real as the day it happened. Though he truly couldn't forget on a subconscious level, he'd thought time had eased the bittersweet ache of mingled pain and joy. Proof in point, the portrait of Marissa hanging over the cabin's single fireplace.

The painting had been a satisfying exercise, one he believed had leeched away regrets, pain, longing.

"Fool." It would never end. Cristal's shot in the dark was more intuitive than he'd let himself admit. No matter the games he played, no matter how deeply he hid his head in the sand, what he felt for Marissa was too vibrant to tame into memory.

As the guilt that plagued him for his part in sending his

brother Adams to prison, never truly eased. Guilt that ruled and changed his life. Because of his teenage folly and what it had taken from Adams, he was never quite at home with his own family. His peace and refuge was the swamp. Then came the hurt of losing Marissa, and even the swamp was no longer a place of peace.

"Losing her made it all too…" Jefferson didn't have the right word. Nothing was quite enough. Lashes drifting briefly to his cheeks, he stood remembering regret, help-lessness. Pain.

"Too much," he whispered, understanding at last. He'd never analyzed the truth of why he'd fled the lowcountry the second time. He knew now it had been because of a morass of unresolved guilt and loss and grief. Arizona of-fered solitude, a different sort of peace. Here there was no one to hurt. No one to lose. No one he might fail. "Until now," he said softly. "If this is Marissa."

It was. He knew it in his very soul. But an expert second opinion wouldn't hurt. "Come, Satan."

With a surge of impatience, he barely waited for the dog to stand obediently by his side. Bending down, he held the scarf before the sensitive black nose. "Fetch."

The Doberman bounded away. Jefferson had barely moved to the doorway, when Satan returned. The page from a tablet was clasped in his mouth. Taking it from the sharp teeth, praising the dog with a stroking touch, Jefferson knew Satan's instincts, and his, had been vindicated. The scent that lingered on the scarf and the message was the same.

Marissa was alive.

Stunned, his mind a morass of grief and relief—relief that she was alive, grief for all she'd been through, all she'd lost—he couldn't think. Like a sleepwalker, he returned to the table and sat down. How long he sat there, staring up at Marissa's portrait, he would never know. Time had no meaning. Nothing mattered but that Marissa was alive.

"Why contact me, sweetheart? Why in such troubled times?" The sound of his own voice was a wake-up call. Suddenly, as with a man who lived by his wits, his mind was keen, perceptive, and considering each point and question. The most important was answered by his own promise. This was more than the call of grief.

If ever you need me… "I'll come for you," he finished. A promise recalled, but deliberately left unsaid.

Marissa was alive. Given the subterfuge of the message, she was in danger. She needed help. She needed Jefferson Cade. "But where are you, sweetheart? What clue did you…" His voice stumbled as he remembered the scrap of newspaper falling to the floor. Instinct told him he would find the answers there.

Minutes later, Jefferson was on the telephone that had gathered dust during his tenure at the Broken Spur. In rare impatience, he paced back and forth as far as the cord would allow while he waited for his call to be put through.

When Jericho Rivers, sheriff of Belle Terre, responded, Jefferson spoke tersely. "I'm coming to the lowcountry, to Belle Terre. I need to meet with you and Yancey Hamilton."

Jericho was known for his instincts and Jefferson was grateful for them now. Perhaps it was his tone, that he had called the sheriff rather than his own brothers, or simply that he was returning to Belle Terre, but for whatever reason, the sheriff only asked the particulars—when, where, how soon—and no more.

One step had been taken, leaving two more in the form of local calls. One to Sandy Gannon that would elicit no more questions than the call to Jericho. Jefferson trusted both men to do what was needed, when, and for however long.

The final call was to the airlines. The first stage of his arrangements was complete when he sat before a fireplace without fire. A letter had changed his brother Lincoln's life. Now a letter had done the same for his. Laying a hand on the Doberman's dark head, he muttered, "Sandy's sending someone to look after the ranch and you. But I'll be back, Satan. I don't know when, or what will have changed, but I'll be back."

On a windswept plain, a solitary woman walked through a waking world. Wind tore at her clothes and tangled in her hair, but she didn't notice. Had she noticed, she wouldn't care.

Once she'd been at home and happy in this sparsely populated land. A place of towering mountains and endless deserts, of sprawling plains and rocky coastlines. Once she'd loved the still beauty of wild places sheltered from the wind. Once she'd waited in wonder for that moment when birdsong heralded the incipient day, then fell silent in the breathless trembling time when the sun lifted above distant, wind-scoured hills and bathed the world in a shower of light.

Once she'd loved so many things about this land. Now as she walked, cloaked in a mantle of solitude, waiting for another day that would be no more to her than simply another day, her sense of aloneness intensified. There was no beauty for her grief-stricken eyes. No serenity in a serene world. Not for her.

Never again for Marissa Claire Alexandre Rei in this land called Silver by the first conquistadores.

"Argentina," she whispered as she paused in this sleepless hour, to stare at an untamed plain that in the half light had no beginning, no end. "A land of grief and loss."

A hand closed over her shoulder, its warmth driving away the chill of the wind. "Are you all right, little Rissa?"

His voice was deep and quiet, his English excellent and only a little accented by the speech patterns of Spanish, his first language. His touch hadn't startled her. Before he'd spoken, she'd known he had come to join her. "I'm fine, Juan." Her brown eyes, turned black in the paling of dawn, met eyes as black. "Fine."

"Who do you convince, *querida?*" he asked gently as his hand moved from her shoulder. "Yourself, or me?"

She laughed, a bleak sound. "Obviously no one."

"You walk now because you don't sleep," Juan suggested, moving with her as she began to walk again. "Not because you love the land at dawn as you once did."

Marissa didn't speak. She didn't look at this man she'd known all her life. The first to take her up on a horse, when he was in his teens and she was five. He was the first to instill in her a love of horses and riding. Juan Elia was a modern-day gaucho. A true descendant of Argentina's famed, wandering horsemen. With the coming of the *estancias,* the ranches, the wandering had ceased. Gauchos had settled down to work for the families of the *estancias,* as the Elia family had worked for countless years for her father's family. The life of the gaucho had changed, but the indomitable spirit hadn't been lost, nor the horsemanship.

Nor the loyalty that kept him here in a secret camp on the plain, rather than at home with his wife and three-year-old son.

"It isn't the same," she answered at last. "Nothing is as it was in the days when you brought me here as a young girl. When we rode like Cossacks over the plain."

"In the days when you wanted to be a real gaucho and wander the land?" Juan chuckled. "Before your mother and father sent you to the United States to become a Southern lady."

"Does growing up tarnish everything, Juan?"

He stopped her then. A touch at her cheek turned her to him. The sun was just lifting over the crest of a hill, in the sudden sliver of light his Native American heritage was visible in a face that had gown more handsome with time. "Death and guilt have tarnished this land for you. Deaths you couldn't prevent. Guilt you shouldn't bear."

"I was supposed to be on that plane."

"But, because of a sick child, *my* child, you weren't. You didn't send your mother and your father and your husband to their deaths, *querida*. Whoever planted the bomb did that."

"Because the plane disappeared off radar so abruptly doesn't mean it was a bomb." Marissa didn't want to believe explosives had blasted her husband's plane from the sky. Believing would lay the blame even more irrevocably at her door.

"*I* know," Juan said adamantly. "Just as I know who." Softly, he added, "As I know why."

"No." Marissa tried to turn away. Juan wouldn't let her.

"This is no more your fault than any of the rest. You were married to a man more than twice your age. If love was lacking, loyalty was not. You have no reason to accuse yourself.

"If a man of power covets all your husband has, his business, his land, his wife, the sin isn't yours. If he tries to coerce your husband to become a part of something evil, it isn't your fault. If this man decrees all you love and you must be punished for being honorable and loyal to the principles of a lifetime, it isn't your dishonor. If he carries out his threat in a way most horrible, the crime is his, not yours.

"My child lives because of your goodness. Your family died at the hand of an evil man. There is no connection."

"That a bomb caused the crash was a passing speculation, dismissed as quickly," Marissa reminded him.

"Yes," Juan admitted. "But there was the threat. And all who knew have been silenced. Or so he believes."

"Then, if Menendez should discover I'm alive, that would mean he would also have discovered you've hidden me and given me shelter. What more proof would he need to suspect you know everything? Then, my dear friend, your life would be at risk, as well." Fear trembled in her voice for this trusted man who was more like a cherished brother than a friend.

"No, *querida*," Juan soothed. "To the world, I am merely a gaucho who lived and worked on your father's *estancia.* Who would suspect an enduring friendship begun between a girl of five and a boy of sixteen? Who would believe such a grand lady as Señora Rei helped to bring my long-awaited first child into the world. Or that the name he bears is in her honor?"

"But if they should…"

"You will be gone from here long before that could happen. And when you're gone, we'll be as we were. My Marta, Alejandro, and I," he promised. "And you, Rissa? You will be safe."

Marissa brushed a forearm across her brow as if she would shield eyes that had known too many tears. "Will Jefferson come? After so long will he remember a promise? Will he care?"

"If he is even half the man you spoke of, he will remember, he will care, and he will come."

"We can't be sure he got a message passed through so many hands. If he did, was it too cryptic? The article on the back of the newspaper may mean nothing to him. He might not read it."

"He will read it, *querida.* He will read each word over and over again. Because he knows he must understand, he won't stop until he does. He will see the marks and make

words of them. Then, he will come to the *estancia,* and
Marta will do the rest.''

   ''After that can you be safe, Juan? You or your family?''

   ''Yes,'' he assured her as he smiled at a secret thought.
*We will be safe and you, Marissa, will be in the arms of
the man you love, at last.*

Two

***

"**W**hat the hell is this about?"

If Jefferson expected an answer, the buffeting thunder of the helicopter would have made it incomprehensible. With it, the pilot who had introduced himself as Rick Cahill and a friend of Jericho Rivers's, though courteous and efficient, was closemouthed. His eyes, cold steel, never wavered from the sky.

As he'd watched the helicopter fly fast and low through the canyon at dawn, Jefferson had known it was in the hands of an expert. When the monstrous machine touched down as gently as a dragonfly, he suspected the pilot could fly anything, anywhere.

"With his eyes closed." The growled assessment drew the pilot's attention. A riveting gaze turned. A lifted brow as black as shorn, curling hair, was the only variant in a calm expression.

Leaving his silence unbroken, Jefferson answered the

question in those keen eyes with a shrug and looked away.
But not before he wondered again at the strange turn of
events.

Within hours of opening Marissa's cryptic message, his
ordered life had spiraled into quiet chaos. Plans made, air-
line reservations secured, the ranch bedded down for the
night, he'd been packing a duffel when the telephone rang.
Alarmed, he'd answered abruptly. The caller's voice was
familiar, stunned recognition came with Billy Blackhawk's
official preamble and statement of the purpose of his call.
Though the sheriff of Silverton was far from a stranger,
Jefferson would have questioned the message he'd relayed,
were it not for his mention of Jericho.

Even then, he'd found it difficult to forego questions. But
on the strength of Jericho's name and Billy Blackhawk's
reputation, he had. Billy's promise that everything would
be explained when he arrived at an undisclosed destination
didn't ease his wariness. An astute judgment warned that
questioning Rick Cahill would be useless. Preserving the
silence between them, Jefferson stared out the window.
That the helicopter was capable of astonishing speeds was
evident. As they flew toward the sun and deeper into the
day, one color of the earth segued into another in the blink
of an eye.

When the chopper landed on an isolated airfield, Jefferson assumed it was to refuel. Instead, Cahill tossed the
duffel to the tarmac, signaled his passenger should follow,
and climbed from the cockpit.

In a ground-eating jog, Cahill approached the hangar.
With a scarred hand, he signaled Jefferson to wait while he
entered a small door and disappeared inside. Sooner than
anticipated, the hangar doors rumbled open, and Cahill
stepped out, a grin turning the steel of his eyes to smoke.
"We made it."

"Made what?" Jefferson asked as he joined Cahill.

"This destination, undisturbed. Which we hope means no one traced the letter to you or the Broken Spur."

"Undisturbed." Blue eyes narrowed. "By whom? Why?"

Cahill's grin faded. "The same people who shot Paulo Rei's plane out of the sky. *Why* can be better answered when we reach our final destination."

Shuddering in renewed horror, Jefferson kept silent.

"The crew will be back shortly. To return the chopper to its owner, now that its maintenance is finished." Another grin ghosted over the pilot's lips. "We should be gone before then."

"In that." Jefferson spoke of a small jet. "Which, I suppose, has been sent for maintenance that will never take place."

"Actually, the jet is for sale. The prospective buyer has taken it for a test flight and evaluation."

Jefferson nodded. "Too bad he isn't going to buy."

"Yeah." Respect gleamed in Cahill's eyes.

In the air, Rick Cahill was less guarded, but just as intent. While the jet streaked toward the east and a clandestine meeting, Jefferson thought of a plane the world assumed Marissa was aboard. And that Rick claimed had been blasted from the sky.

Questions teemed in Jefferson's mind. They went unvoiced. When the jet was traded for another helicopter, time zones had been crossed and daylight had burned away like a candle. But the terrain was green and mountainous now. He needed no answers to know this was the last of a convoluted journey.

Rick flew with the same skill and concentration, skimming through mountain passes as he followed the snaking path of a river. At a waterfall he banked and climbed, then dropped into a valley crisscrossed by creeks and a river filled by another waterfall. The tin roofs of two buildings gleamed in the sun. The helicopter hovered, then set down with an ease that recalled the canyon landing.

Jericho was there, flanked by Simon McKinzie whom Jefferson had met only once. Tall and massive, a lean Goliath whose mix of French and Native American heritage was evident in his chiseled features and gleaming black hair, the sheriff should have dwarfed the older man. But on the strength of that single meeting at Jericho's wedding, Jefferson had discovered no one could overshadow the silver-haired, bull-shouldered McKinzie. A man who wore the mantle of honor and authority as naturally as most men wore their own skins.

Yancey Hamilton, once Belle Terre's bad boy and now a man with mysterious and powerful associations—associations that prompted Jefferson's call for his help—waited a little distance away. Ethan Garrett, except for Simon the most unexpected element in this mix of different and unique men, stood by Yancey. Yet, on second thought, Ethan—who was the brother of Jefferson's own brother's wife and a man given to protracted, unexplained absences—fit perfectly in this mix of competent, enigmatic men. Men, Jefferson knew in a glance, for whom danger was a way of life. And honor their reason for being.

"Quite a welcoming committee," he observed. "Because of the Argentine connection?"

"Is that a question?" Rick asked.

"An observation, Rick."

"That's what I thought. You know everybody?"

Jefferson's gaze returned to the impressive gathering. "Except for Mr. McKinzie, I thought I did. Now I'm not so sure."

Rick rose from his seat. "They're still the men you knew, but you're about to see another side of all of us. The side Simon McKinzie saw when he recruited us for The Black Watch."

* * *

"Gentlemen." Simon McKinzie addressed the men gathered in the office of his mountain retreat. A place where The Black Watch came only rarely. Even more rarely, civilians, as he considered those not a part of the clandestine government organization that he had formed by order of a past president, and had solely controlled in the many years since. "Summing up. According to his ongoing dossier, in aspiring to become the next drug czar of the world, Vicente Menendez was determined to buy certain connections in Argentina as an alternate route of distribution through virgin territory. He chose an older man, thinking he would be more vulnerable. But, Menendez didn't reckon with the integrity and iron will of Paulo Rei. Nor was he prepared for a woman as spectacularly beautiful and accomplished as Rei's wife.

"Señora Rei would be remembered by all of you as Merrie Alexandre. To all but Jefferson. To whom, I'm told, she has always been Marissa Claire, her true, given name. Then, there's Rick, of course, who hasn't met the charming lady. A condition we should rectify, hopefully and soon. Any questions, thus far?"

No one spoke and Simon continued. "Mcnendez assumed, for a price, not only would Rei's honor be for sale, so would his young wife. We suspect that in underestimating his prey, Menendez revealed more of his operation than was prudent. Before he had understood Rei was a man whose honor was priceless, as was his wife's loyalty. After the brief suspicion of a bomb, we have reason to believe that fearing exposure and infuriated by Señora Rei's rejection, Menendez ordered their plane shot down over the sea.

"This was purely speculation based on the suspicions of an informant. Until Jefferson called Jericho, we had no reason to think Marissa Rei was alive. Even if we had, we wouldn't have known where to look for her. Now we do.

Because Jefferson recognized the need for secrecy, we just might succeed.''

"So, we're going after her.'' Playing devil's advocate, Rick Cahill locked stares with Simon. "Why?''

"Because she's an American citizen, born in America of an American mother. Because Menendez is also an American, one who destroys lives for profit. Because I want him.'' A cold stare turned colder. "Does that answer the question?''

Without waiting for a response, Simon looked at his men. Each of whom possessed unique talents, unique abilities, and infinite loyalty. "So we go?''

"We go.'' Rick spoke first. A surprise to no one, including Jefferson, who had learned many surprising things this day.

The land was rugged and breathtaking and vast. The sturdy horse he'd been provided was an excellent mount. The trail he rode was not difficult if ridden with concentration and caution. At his back, but beyond sight, lay the Alexandres's Argentine *estancia,* an oasis in the heart of a plain. Ahead, the Patagonian Alps, a part of the continent-spanning Andes, sprawled like sleeping giants. That the woman who was his guide knew the land and its irregularities was immediately apparent. Jefferson's only chore was to follow and keep Simon's timetable.

So, ever cognizant of the hour, he followed and worried about what he would find at their destination. And what would happen to the good people who had helped Marissa when she and he, and Simon's men of The Black Watch were gone.

Go with caution to the Alexandre estancia, *to Marta Elia, wife of the foreman. Horses and a guide will be provided. The rest we leave to you.*

The scant message that brought him here was a brand in

his mind. One he would never forget. As he would never forget Marta Elia and her husband Juan. Marissa's allies who offered secret sanctuary to a friend with no concern for the trouble they might bring down on themselves.

"If Menendez finds out...if he finds them..." Jefferson didn't want to think of it. Instead he fixed his gaze on Marta's back, and on little Alejandro, her three-year-old son, who clung like a limpet to her waist. When she'd ridden into the copse of stunted trees where she'd directed him to wait, he hadn't expected she would be his guide, nor that she would bring the child.

At first, given the obvious need for both speed and secrecy, he was disturbed by the boy's presence. But he needn't have been. Alejandro had ridden for hours beneath the blazing sun and had never complained. As the terrain gave way to a series of small rocky hillocks to climb and descend, the trail required more attention. But not so much that Jefferson didn't wonder how it would be to have such a son. Or perhaps a daughter.

He would have been startled at a thought so foreign to what he expected his life to be, if Marta hadn't slowed her horse and announced quietly, "We are here, *señor*."

The plain was still and quiet but for the hum of the ever-blowing wind. Nothing moved in the empty expanse, and for all the hours of their ride, the mountains seemed no closer. The stark beauty Jefferson had found in the land was only cruel and harsh as fear closed about his heart like an icy fist.

Had Marta made a mistake? Was this not the rendez-vous? Or had something gone wrong? Menendez?

"Marissa." A shudder shook Jefferson's lean, hard frame. Her name was a strangled whisper caught in the wind. And not even the blaze of the sun could warm him.

Then the bulky figure of a man was rising from an overgrown outcrop of stone where there should be none. He did not wear the celebrated ballooning pants of the gaucho. But his shaggy, dark hair just visible beneath his flat brimmed hat, his handsome features and demeanor left little doubt that he was one of the renowned horsemen of the Argentine pampas.

He carried no weapons but the tools of his work. Yet Jefferson didn't question that he was a man who would protect what was his, or that his name was Juan. A shattered breath later, Marissa stepped from the curtain of scraggly vegetation that rimmed the stones, and out of Juan Elia's shadow.

"I'm here, Jefferson." Her voice was music.

As he heard her, Jefferson's labored breath caught in his lungs. His mouth went dry, even as his heart lurched in an uneven rhythm. A woman so different from the woman he remembered, but still so beautiful, waited beneath his startled stare.

Her long brown hair had been cut shorter. No scarf held the sleek, sophisticated mane in check as it brushed the line of her shoulders. Beneath the low-tipped brim of a hat similar to that of her companion's, her face was angular and too thin, revealing bone structure that promised lasting beauty in happiness or grief, old or young. Her eyes were shadowed and veiled as she held his gaze.

On a glance he had seen that she was too slender, too worn by her ordeal. Trousers of dark leather clung to her long legs and brushed the toes of her boots, making a tall woman seem taller, a slender woman, more slender. A lighter vest hung open over a soft shirt and brushed the belt buckled at her waist.

Marissa, dressed as he'd seen her hundreds of times. As strong as he knew she would be. Resting an unsteady hand on the pommel of his saddle, vaguely aware that Marta, Juan, and even Alejandro watched him, and waited, he asked, "Are you all right?"

Her eyelids swept down, shielding her eyes from his. Her lashes brushed the line of her cheekbone. But neither they nor the shadow of her hat could hide the toll of tragedy.

Then, as a strong woman rediscovered her faltering stamina, her lashes swept up. As her dark gaze met his again, her somber lips tilted in a wavering smile. "I will be," she said in barely more than a whisper. "Now that you're here."

Now that you're here. The words he didn't know he'd waited for, spoken in the voice of the cultured woman. But with the wistfulness of the girl he'd first loved.

In a fluid dismount, Jefferson was out of the saddle and on the ground and Marissa was in his arms. "You're safe now, sweetheart," he promised against her hair as her hat went spinning in the wind and the dust.

Burrowing deeper into his embrace, her forehead against his shoulder, Marissa breathed in the familiar scent of him and reveled in his gentle touch. The scent she'd never forgotten. The touch that filled her dreams. "I was afraid you might not care. That you wouldn't come."

Moving her away only a little, a knuckle beneath her chin lifted her face and her gaze to his. "I promised, Marissa. Remember? If ever you need me…"

"I'll come for you," she finished for him as he intended she should. "And now you have. I should never have doubted a promise made by such a special friend. No matter how long ago." Her laugh was low, a trembling sound, and there were tears on her cheeks. "First Juan and Marta, and now you, Jefferson. Friends risking your lives for mine. It's more than I deserve. You're all so much more than I deserve."

"No." Jefferson gathered her back to him, to hide the tears he couldn't bear to see. "Never more than that."

As he held Marissa, Jefferson was aware that Juan and Marta had moved away. Stealing rare moments for themselves even as they were giving reunited friends time alone. But only a little time, for in the distance he heard the rhythmic throb of a helicopter. The percussions of the blades grew closer and louder each passing minute. Though he didn't want to let her go, there were duties to attend. Decisions to be made.

Releasing Marissa, but taking her hand, he went with her to Juan and Marta as they stood by the mass of stones. It was then Jefferson realized that rather than random rubble, they were part of the ruins of a structure. A home once, perhaps. One, he suspected, that served again as shelter.

Shelter for Marissa in the weeks since the crash of Paulo Rei's plane. But what shelter would there be for this small family? Who would be their allies? If danger threatened, how could those who would repay their kindness help? Jefferson knew the collective answer to his question. Simon and the men and women of The Black Watch would offer and insure sanctuary for the Elias as the Elias offered sanctuary to Marissa. So would Jefferson Cade.

Addressing Juan and Marta, he spoke into the escalating cacophony. "The men for whom we wait are coming. There will be room in the helicopter for both of you and your son. It won't be safe here if it's discovered Marissa wasn't on the plane and that you helped her.

"If you come with us, Simon assures safe passage into our country. With that, I promise a home and work for Juan with my brothers in the southeast. Or, if he chooses, with me in the west. Above all, we pledge you will be safe."

Juan had turned to face Jefferson and Marissa. With Alejandro in his arms, his eyes dwelt on the face of the young woman he had known all her life. "Marta and I understand the danger. We have from the first."

"Then you know it's impossible for you to stay." Jefferson met a dark gaze that took his measure.

"Do you understand the danger if we go, Señor Cade?" Juan countered, as he put his son down to play.

"You're afraid that if you and Marta and Alejandro disappear there will be an investigation. Possibly raising suspicions that could lead to speculations about me." Marissa's hand grew taut in Jefferson's as she saw beyond grief and guilt to the magnitude of what her friends had risked to help her.

"Any investigation will bring outsiders to the *estancia, querida*. People who will question, perhaps too skillfully. And someone will remember you were here, helping Marta with Alejandro's illness when it was thought you were on the plane. The time and place and circumstances will be investigated, and someone will realize the value of what he or she knows." Leaving the rest of his warning unsaid, Juan drew a harsh breath.

"Menendez has already proven his influence and his power. Someone will talk. For money, or in pain. Then he will search for you." The gaucho's darkly weathered face was grim. "The rotten threads of his ugly empire reach far and wide. His thugs know how to make the most unwilling speak. Wherever you are he will find you. And if he cannot take you, he will kill you, Rissa."

"That's the chance I prefer. The chance I would gladly take. Looking over my shoulder, waiting for Menendez would be easier than living in fear of what could happen to you and Marta, and to Alejandro." Marissa looked from Juan to Marta, to Alejandro who played quietly in the dust. "He's the child I couldn't have, I won't risk losing him."

"This is our country." Juan was adamant. "The *estancia* has been my home. If we stay, no suspicions will be aroused. The only newcomers will be those who inherit what your father left. We will be as safe here as anywhere, once you're gone."

"You don't think someone might remember, as you say,

and talk to the new owners?'' Jefferson drew Marissa back to him. With his arm resting across her shoulder, he discovered the brush of the tips of her hair against his wrist had the power to tantalize, even in times of crisis.

''We are an isolated people, caring little for what happens in the world beyond the plain. The news of the crash and the suspicion of a bomb came first to me. Marissa was already in hiding before I spoke of the deaths to anyone. For all those of the *estancia* know, she had gone to join her family on the plane.

''Later, on the occasion of my visits here, Marta made sensible, believable explanations.'' Juan's look met Jefferson's, daring him to doubt Marta. ''As she convinced the curious you were an American journalist seeking a story, Señor Cade.''

''It's too flimsy, Juan. You can't trust that no one will question the timing.'' It was naive of the gaucho to believe he could protect Marissa so easily. But Jefferson realized he couldn't convince this most stubborn man of it. A man who didn't want to uproot his family and turn his back on the only way of life he'd ever known any less than he wanted to see Marissa hurt.

Recognizing that as a stranger he couldn't sway this stalwart and uncompromising man, Jefferson bowed out of the argument, hoping Marissa might succeed where he could not. With a subtle pressure on the curve of her shoulder, he relinquished the debate to her.

Marissa stood silently as she considered what her lifelong friend and protector must be feeling. When she spoke, her voice was steady, her tone low. ''Then you've decided, and nothing can sway you. You won't go.''

''No, *querida*.'' Juan's arms were crossed over his chest, his feet planted firmly. As firmly as his resolve.

''What about Marta?'' Marissa tried one last ploy.

''Marta wants what I want, as always.''

Marissa only nodded. She'd always known Juan and Marta shared a love unlike any she'd ever known. That they seemed to feel the same and think alike on almost every issue.

Almost. Moving beyond Jefferson's touch, Marissa stepped closer to Juan. She was tall, he was taller. Her head tipped back, dark eyes held his. "Then I stay, too."

"No!" Jefferson objected. "You don't know what you're saying." He would have brought her back to him, back into his arms, but with a raised hand, she warded him off.

"I know very well what I'm saying. I'm staying here to protect my friends as they protected me. And to watch Alejandro grow up. If that means going to Menendez, then I will." Turning to him, she smiled a regretful smile. "I'm sorry, Jefferson. More than you can know." Her voice faded and faltered.

She looked away. At the ground, at the sky, anywhere but at Jefferson. Then, with her composure restored, she continued. "If I could change what Menendez has done, I would. But I can't, any more than I can leave the people who've done so much for me, and mean so much to me, to suffer the consequence of my defection."

"You're going to strike a bargain with Menendez?" It was Juan who was first to make sense of her hushed words.

She wouldn't deny what couldn't be denied. "If I can."

"Marissa, selling her body and soul again, for someone else." Jefferson's tone was bleak and bitterly mocking.

"Ask yourself what you would do, Jefferson." She looked from one man to another. "And you, Juan, would you not make a bargain with the devil to save someone you love?"

Jefferson had no answer. None except that he would do what he had to for Marissa. As the helicopter came closer, he made his decision. "It's settled then. If one stays, we all stay."

"You're wrong." Marta, who had only listened, lifted her son from the ground to settle him against her breasts. "My husband thinks with his heart, not his head. We go. All of us."

Then she addressed Juan. "We have no one here. You have no family. I have none. We don't know who will be the new owner, or if we will be happy. And if someone wants to talk about Marissa and the plane, they will whether we're here or not. This is a chance for Alejandro. One we must take."

Juan said nothing as his look turned to his son whose eyes were droopy with fatigue. Finally his dark gaze met Marta's. "You're sure, my love?"

Marta was steadfast and unwavering. "I'm sure."

Her answer was almost lost in the drone of the helicopter making its landing approach. A much larger craft than the two Jefferson had traveled in days ago. One meant to accommodate more than two added passengers.

"Come." Catching the reins of Marta's horse, Juan beckoned to him. "We must unsaddle the horses and set them free."

As Marissa went to calm her mount and Juan's, already unsaddled and ground tied in a cluster of misshapen, wind-pruned trees, Jefferson stripped both saddle and blanket from his mount. Then, bridle in hand, he waited while Juan led the other three horses to his.

In a shout Jefferson said, "We shouldn't leave anything behind. I don't know what suspicions it might raise if the saddles and bridles were found here. Or even if it would matter at all. But it would be best if no one had reason to suspect this land had been a recent campsite of any sort."

"Then what do you propose?" Juan asked.

''That we take everything. Saddles, bridles, blankets. Anything connected to the Alexandre *estancia*.''

The chance of more conversation was swept away in a lowering clamor. With a grim flash of teeth, Juan slipped the bridle from his mount and Marta's and set them free. Jefferson was only a second behind with his horse and Marissa's. The animals might return to their home pastures, or roam the plains. But grass and water would be plentiful wherever they wandered.

While the men had released the tethered horses, Marta and Marissa had cleared the area. Leaving no trace of the weeks she'd spent in the tumbled ruins that were once a home.

The helicopter hovered and waited. Close enough that Jefferson could see Rick Cahill was at the controls, as he'd expected. Yancey Hamilton and Ethan Garrett were standing guard, armed and ready. A testimony of Simon's grave concern.

The touchdown was to be brief. Only long enough to take on passengers and gear. With a hand from Yancey, Marissa, Alejandro and Marta were boarded, while Ethan took the saddles and other paraphernalia. Next was Juan, and finally Jefferson.

''Ready?'' Rick called above revving engines.

Giving a thumbs-up, Jefferson agreed. ''Take her up.''

Flashing a smile, Rick complied. As the nearly fully loaded chopper lifted off, the windstorm of the blades swept the plain clean of any footprint or proof that either man or woman or child had ever been there.

Jefferson looked across the craft at Juan and Marta, and Alejandro. A silent child, as brave as his parents.

As he brushed a hand over dry, burning eyes, the last person he saw was Marissa. With a tired sigh, he smiled.

If ever you need me…

A promise kept.

Three

Debriefing.

A strange word for a peaceful valley. But no more strange than the way this began. No more strange than now.

After another journey, a long, convoluted flight from the Argentine plain, and a restless night spent in Simon McKinzie's retreat, Jefferson stood at the edge of a jagged precipice beneath a gnarled evergreen. The valley below was calm, with no hint of troubles and danger that had been dealt with, or the threat of more to come. For hours he had studied this bastion. Because of what he'd seen, he felt no concern as Marissa walked the lakeshore. Or that Alejandro played with the youngest of the Canfield boys and their half-grown Doberman pups under the watchful eye of Raven Canfield. Simon's beloved goddaughter, mother of the Canfield children.

Jefferson's first time in the valley had been too short, too intense to allow time for more than business. He'd been too intent on the letter, and the message encoded within the newspaper article, to be observant of more than obvious facets of the land. He could think of little beyond the simplistic marking of partial words. Marks readily apparent, but only to one keenly interested in every aspect of the message. Only to one who understood the handwritten recollection of a promise, and realized the mistake in the news report. One who knew there must be more.

In retrospect and better informed, Jefferson recognized the frightening risk the letter represented. He understood the gamble that in the right hands the message would be discovered. In the wrong, tossed away in disinterest. A desperate gamble. Thank God, one that had worked in all its simplicity.

Chance. Much had been based on that happenstance and the thread of good fortune woven into tragedy. Chance, good fortune, good friends. But it wasn't over yet. Jefferson knew it would never be as long as Menendez and his minions walked the earth. Ruthless, corrupt, worshiping power and wealth.

Had Marissa known how prophetic her words were when she spoke of looking over her shoulder? he wondered in one moment. The next, he realized that she knew better than anyone. In a rush of anger for all she'd lost and endured, there was passion. The thrill of awareness that began like a whisper, touching his heart, his mind, his body. Until every sense was held in thrall, remembering a look, a smile, the heat of her hand in his. Until his arms ached to hold her, and his mouth hungered for her kiss. Until he wanted to lay the world at her feet, a better, safer place.

For want of a better world, he would make their part of it the best he could. If she must look over her shoulder... ''I'll be looking, too,'' he promised. ''For as long as it takes.''

As he spoke, his attention moved over the valley. The

safest of places with a gathering of men who risked their lives for Marissa and her friends. Who would again, if they must.

This, he'd discovered, was the other side of the men he knew. Men with qualities and strengths Simon recognized and drew to him. As the first McKinzies recognized the strengths of the valley and made it their home. A land nearly as impregnable as it was beautiful. A haven for Simon. With David Canfield, the first recruit of The Black Watch, to guard it in his absence.

"Canfield." Jefferson considered the quiet, rugged man. Retired with honor and always the standard for all who followed in his footsteps. Big footsteps but, he'd discovered, with big men filling them. Thoughts of Canfield led naturally to Raven. His lovely, dark-haired wife, whose heart was as big as any footstep. A heart that embraced Marissa, the Elias, and especially Alejandro, welcoming them into her home.

Jefferson smiled as he thought of life spent in the McKinzies's valley. For with Simon, he was learning the unexpected was the norm. But if the gallant lady who had lived most of her life with the McKinzies was perturbed by helicopters or strange men and women arriving at her doorstep, it hadn't shown by so much as a flutter of her long, dark lashes.

Shortly, the helicopter should return with the last member of The Watch Simon had summoned. Then they would get on with the rest of their plans, and their lives. Until then, Jefferson worked off the restlessness that kept him from sleeping, eating and being congenial company, by exploring the valley. And, he admitted paying homage to truth, guarding Marissa.

"What are you thinking?" he wondered from his distant watchtower as she walked along the shore lost in another world. Once she would have reveled in the scent of Raven's wildflower garden. Now she passed it by without a glance. An eagle's cry echoed above the valley. In another time she would have searched the sky for a glimpse of it. Now she didn't seem to hear.

He'd expected a tumult of emotions now that her circumstances had changed. Grief and, in part, the guilt Juan had addressed. But this emotion was more powerful and much deeper. Given this silent withdrawal, it was something she plainly intended to deal with alone. Just as plainly, whatever it was that weighed so heavily on her mind and her heart, it was consuming her.

"What is it, Marissa? What hurts you so, and how can I help?" Even as his own words fell into the silence hovering far above the valley floor, he knew there was little he could do. Little but deny his desire, forget the ache in his heart and body, and watch from afar. As now, he would watch, he would keep her safe, he would wait. Then, one day—if that one day could ever come—he would speak to her with his heart, not his voice.

A trill of laughter caught by a breeze drew his attention to the boys. The Canfield boy, whose name was Dare, was several years older than Alejandro, but in their game and on this clear, sunny day, age didn't seem to matter. On the fading note of laughter, Jefferson heard the sound he was expecting. A sound that had become more than familiar in a matter of days.

Time to go. Time to weigh issues and make decisions. Another skilled and unique agent had arrived. It was Yancey who had flown the chopper out of the valley before dawn. With instincts and skill rivaling Rick Cahill.

Jefferson wasn't surprised by this newly revealed accomplishment of a lifelong friend from Belle Terre. He'd decided, short of treason and conduct unbecoming a gentleman, nothing of Simon McKinzie or his Black Watch would surprise him.

Now, as he left the precipice and moved down the mountain, he wondered who would come and go in Simon's scheme of operations. His part as initial contact done, Jericho had returned to his duties as sheriff of Belle Terre. The new man, or woman, would take Simon's plan to the next step. Rather than speculate who that person might be, Jefferson wondered if Yancey's flight was as convoluted as his had been with Rick.

"Bet on it, Cade. With safety and stealth the order of the day, how else would the leader of The Watch have it?"

Though he made the trip down at a rapid pace, by the time he reached the valley floor, Yancey Hamilton had set the chopper down and cut the engine. It was Billy Blackhawk, who unfolded his massive body from the "duck and run" beyond spinning blades.

There was no time for surprise as Blackhawk's hand enveloped his. "Jeff." Half Apache and a match for Jericho in size, the sheriff of Silverton said sincerely, "Glad you made it."

"You, too," Jefferson drawled in return. "And just when I thought I couldn't be surprised."

Blackhawk grinned. "Just wait, there will be more."

"Yep." Yancey flung an arm around Jefferson's shoulder. "Never doubt it. Simon's full of tricks."

Poker-faced, Jefferson muttered, "Not just Simon."

By unspoken consensus, along with Juan and Marta, the men who regathered in Simon's office left the two seats closest to Simon's desk for Marissa and Jefferson. As he held her chair, she looked only at his hands, never at his face. Certainly never his eyes. As she caught her lower lip briefly between her teeth in a familiar gesture he hadn't seen in so long, he feared she would flee. Not from the office, not from the gathering, but from him. Instead, after a tense interval, she took the seat he offered with a husky "Thank you, Jefferson."

While Jefferson took his seat beside and a bit in back of Marissa, Simon spoke. "Ladies." As he turned to Marissa, then Marta, eyes that could freeze an antagonist with a single glance, were warm, even smiling. "I commend you.

"And you, gentlemen." Not so warm, not so smiling, he spoke to his chosen. And to Jefferson and Juan. "From the beginning you've made wise, intuitive choices." A massive hand lifted, blunt-tipped fingers splayed. "Beginning with Señor Elia's recognition that Señora Rei should be shielded from public notice until the truth of the crash was determined."

One finger folded into Simon's palm.

"Then Señora Rei, or if I may, Marissa?" Simon paused, all eyes turned to her. Including Jefferson's, and he was struck by her regal posture, the utter control with which she faced Simon. A veneer that had slipped on the plain, firmly in place again.

As she neither blushed, nor faltered, but nodded with a subtle smile, Jefferson realized Marissa Rei was two women in one. The courageous woman who refused to leave her friends to face the unknown in her stead. And, as now, the woman who had learned to hide her emotions— whether pain, grief, or concern—with cool control and uncompromising grace.

"Marissa, then," Simon agreed and returned to his habitual enumeration with his hand still raised. "Second was Marissa's plan to have her messages to Jefferson pass through the hands of several trusted college friends."

A second finger folded into a broad palm, but Jefferson didn't notice. His attention was riveted on Marissa. A Marissa he was seeing for the first time. Understanding for the first time. Yet one who had been there all the while.

She was the woman of strength who was part of the

young daredevil—a girl sent away from her own country, who made the new country home. The woman of courage who was part of the horsewoman who challenged any horse however frenzied and tamed it. She was the compassionate woman who was part of the huntress who was never ashamed of a heart too tender to harm any creature. She was the devoted woman in the daughter who had sacrificed, and would sacrifice, her own life and love for family and friends.

She was the daredevil, the horsewoman, the huntress, the daughter. And the woman they had made of her had been his friend.

Just once, she'd been his lover. With his brilliant gaze never leaving her, not caring who might see and read what was in his face, he vowed she would be again.

"That's the lot." Simon finished his enumerated praise with the last point made, the last finger fisted. A known gesture to longtime associates. It would become familiar to the rest. "Which brings us to the present and where we go from here.

"Marissa, Juan, Marta, it's most important you stay hidden for a while. How long, I can't say. But we need time to prove our suspicions and to corner Menendez. Until we do…"

Marissa clasped her hands tightly in her lap. "I understand. I'm sure we all do."

"Belle Terre, or the horse farms and plantations nearby are out of the question. You could be recognized. Unless there's another suggestion, I'm offering my home here." With a look at David Canfield, who stood by the door, Simon continued, "David will be here to serve as your bodyguard, along with Juan. More guards will be posted at points along the route into the—

"Jefferson," Simon interrupted himself. "You have a problem with this? I assume that's what the scowl means."

"No problem. Just that this isn't what I expected. I thought…I assumed Marissa would go to the Broken Spur with me. It's isolated, but surrounded by land that's patrolled. No one in the country would know her. Recognition would be a long shot."

"Good!" Simon exclaimed. "I hoped you would volunteer. In fact, it was for that reason I asked Billy to join us. Now the choice is up to Marissa and to Juan and Marta. But before you make your decision, I'll let Billy tell you what protections he can offer and will have in place."

Billy Blackhawk walked to a bare wall. Pulling down a map from a cornice, he began to explain. "Isolation and anonymity. This valley and the canyon offer both. The difference is space and manpower. Because Sandy Gannon keeps a close eye on Jake Benedict's empire, riders for the brand patrol this area constantly. An added man or two here, here, here—" a tanned finger tapped strategic corners of the map "—shouldn't cause suspicion.

"Added to that, Jake just acquired a small operation here." Another tap on the map, then with a slow sweep of his arm, Billy indicated a straight line intersecting the borders of both a thin strip of existing Benedict land, and the Broken Spur. "As the crow flies, the ride would be no more than an hour at an easy pace. Sandy has sent out word that he's looking for a tenant who knows cattle and horses and can tend the ranch and the land."

Billy looked then at Juan and Marta. "I've spoken to Sandy, the job's yours, Elia, if you want it." Big hands, strong and graceful at once, made a gesture of finality. "That's it. All that's left is the decision."

In the hours and days since Jefferson had come for her as he promised, Marissa had retreated within herself, dealing with a storm of grief and guilt, and unexpected emotions. She hadn't thought beyond each minute. She hadn't considered that life couldn't go on exactly as it was. "It didn't occur to me, I didn't think—'' Breaking off, she shook her head, shedding her lethargy. ''In different circumstances I would prefer the valley. But that could bring danger to Raven's children. To be honest, I don't consider the Broken Spur a suitable choice either. But if there's nowhere else then…''

Lifting a weary shoulder, she said hoarsely, ''I'm sorry, I'm not making sense. I think I must defer to those of you with better knowledge of the situation.''

''Jefferson?'' Simon laid the decision on the table.

Marissa had made it clear she didn't want the Broken Spur. But Jefferson had no intention of letting a third option crop up. ''I'm scheduled to manage the ranch for at least another year. It's a two-man operation, with one man in residence, I would appreciate having an expert horse trainer like Marissa on the premises.''

''In other words, you're offering the pretty lady a job,'' Yancey drawled in his best Southern accent.

''Why not?'' Jefferson grinned. ''She's a good hand.''

Marissa looked from Jefferson to the Elias. ''Juan?''

Juan, in turn, looked at his wife, who nodded. Then his solemn gaze returned to Marissa. ''We would choose the ranch Señor Gannon offered. Alejandro would like it if you were close.''

Marissa drew a long, considering breath, though there was nothing to consider. This was an opportunity such as Juan never could have expected in his own country. But if she didn't go to the Broken Spur, he wouldn't take it. She couldn't let a sudden deluge of grief and guilt deny these good people who had denied her nothing. Not even their lives.

''Then it's settled,'' she said in a voice that hid her fears for herself and for Jefferson in the days to come. ''We go to the Broken Spur, and to Jake Benedict's new land.''

* * *

The meeting dispersed shortly after Marissa's decision. Simon had made it clear he applauded her choice. And for the record, Yancey, a very silent Ethan, and Rick agreed. Billy Blackhawk had been clear on his choice from the first.

The three who had been most actively and dangerously involved stood in a group on the porch. They each turned from the view of the lake at moonrise as Marissa approached them. "Gentlemen." Her greeting was quiet. As each turned to her, with a gesture, a smile, or a nod, she addressed them separately. "Rick, Ethan, and Yancey, I can't begin to thank you for what you've done and what you've risked for my friends and for me."

When they would have protested, claiming it as all in a day's work, a day when nothing really unfortunate happened, she would have none of it. "The risk was there, a risk that could have meant your life, yet you took it willingly for people who were little more than strangers."

"Not quite, sweet Merrie," Yancey reminded her. "If I hadn't helped, half of Belle Terre and all the Cade brothers would have lifted my scalp. If they found it out."

An in-law of the Cades, of sorts, by way of his sister's marriage into the family, Ethan chuckled. "Yancey has that right. Rick isn't that familiar with Belle Terre or he would understand, as I came to understand in a short time, that the male half of the population of that most illustrious Southern city was head over boot heels in love with Merrie Alexandre. If we'd let anything happen to you, we would have that posse to face."

"I second that," Jefferson said from the shadows beyond the small circle of uniquely trained and accomplished men. Head over boot heels was an apt description of himself as well. And the years of separation hadn't changed what he felt.

Marissa turned to him, her expression calm, but with something unfathomable in her eyes. "Jefferson, I didn't see you there.'' She was flustered, unsettled. But, as quickly, she regained the monumental poise he'd just witnessed in the meeting. ''I should be thanking you as much as these gentlemen. Perhaps more, for setting in motion the chain of events that brought Juan, Marta, and Alejandro to safety with me.''

''Would you have me do otherwise, Marissa?'' Jefferson asked, speaking as calmly and as quietly as she had spoken. But any who knew him would have heard the thread of tension, the taunting, questioning satire. ''When you sent the letter, did you for one minute think I could *not* do what I did?''

He left unsaid that for him four years was an eternity in days, hours, weeks and months. But even an eternity couldn't erase his memories or ease his heart. Just as her strange attitude might hurt, yet still altered nothing. ''I don't want your gratitude, Marissa. In fact, gratitude is the last thing I want.''

His face was grim as he turned away. He would have left her then in the company of Simon's men, but Billy Blackhawk loomed before him with Simon only a step away. Their private discussion finished, both had come to join the gathering on the porch. The final plans concerning Marissa and the Elias had been resolved before the meeting adjourned, leaving time for pleasantries.

Jefferson was no more in the mood for pleasantries than for gratitude. He needed space, solitude. Time to organize his thoughts, to gather the willpower to curb his desire and his need for Marissa. Before, he hadn't thought past the message or considered the future. All he could think was that she was in trouble and she needed him. Worrying about how he would fit in to her life and she in his, hadn't been an option.

Neither was hurting her, but he had. Damning himself for flinging her gratitude back in her face, he stood in the gathering twilight, with twining currents of the heated air of the day and the cool of the night swirling about him. Of all the scents woven among them, it was her scent that caressed his skin. Her scent he breathed. Of all the looks that glanced at him, then looked away, it was her somber questioning look he saw.

He couldn't bear another minute. As conversation dwindled to a halt, he addressed Simon and Billy. "If there's nothing more to discuss that's pertinent to our plans, I'd like to take a walk by the lake before turning in."

He didn't wait for an answer. With a tilt of his bare head, he left the porch and crossed the stepping stones that led to the lake. At his back the buzz of conversation began again, before him there was the tranquil mountain lake.

Tranquillity that escaped him as he strolled the worn path. Laughter drifted over the water, a moment of returned camaraderie in the wake of tension. Farther along as drooping limbs of hemlock and pine surrounded him, he heard the pad of a footstep and the scrape of a claw against stone behind him.

Turning, he recognized the female Doberman, only because she was the smaller dog. "Jazz." Curling his hand around her cropped ears in a gesture the dog obviously enjoyed, he asked, "What are you doing out here alone?"

"Jazz isn't alone, Jefferson." Marissa skirted the limb of a hemlock. "She came with me." Pausing, gathering her courage she asked, "Would you mind if we walk with you?"

Jefferson hesitated only a half second. "Of course not." Normally he would have taken a woman's arm, even her hand, but tonight with Marissa, he simply walked in silence by her side. A quarter of the way around the natural lake fed by a waterfall and artesian springs, beyond the spill of light from the cabins, she stopped him with a light touch at his wrist.

When he halted she was waiting for his attention. "I'm sorry, Jefferson. I shouldn't have called on you. But I thought that after the years, I…we…" Curious at the sudden, faltering silence, Jazz nuzzled her hand. The hand that had touched him. Finally she continued. "I shouldn't have dragged you into this."

"Who else would you ask, Marissa?" Her hair was silvered by moonlight. She was light and darkness with eyes like midnight. And he was cold and cruel. Something he never believed he could be to any woman. Especially Marissa.

Something he wouldn't be. Certainly not to Marissa. Touching her face, brushing a wayward strand of dark silk from her cheek he tucked it behind her ear. "You were right to reach out to me. I didn't know how right until I met Simon, and his men. I'm sure there were others who would have tried. College friends, even others in Argentina. But would they have had Simon's resources, or men like Yancey and Rick and Ethan? Could they have offered a valley such as this, or a friend like Raven?"

"Or like you," she added softly.

"My part in this?" A small gesture encompassed the valley, the towering mountains, the security. And most of all, though it was hidden by the foliage of trees and laurel and rhododendron, Simon's home and the men who gathered there. "Purely the luck of a telephone call. I had no idea how to begin, or who to contact, so I called Jericho and asked for Yancey.

"I knew from past situations that he had mysterious and powerful connections. Since he can be anywhere in the world at any given time, I knew that if anyone could find him, it would be Jericho. That call was the beginner's luck of this."

A shrug of shoulders that had grown heavier and stronger through the years dismissed his part in her deliverance.

"The rest, God willing, is history. Tomorrow the future begins."

Marissa stared at him. She was taller than average, but still looked up at him. His face, tilted down, was in shadow. But in the silvered gold of the rising moon, his rough clothes were no longer the sensible jeans and boots of a horseman, but the mantle of a knight's armor. Though the once turquoise-banded mane was cut short and silver that owed nothing to moonlight dusted the darkened blond of his hair, he was still the Prince Charming she had thought she would never find in the swamp.

He would be that modern-day prince, that kind knight. In the swamp, on the plain, in a valley or a desert, in her heart. For that was the sort of man he was. The man he would always be.

"Tomorrow," she whispered, and clenched her hands to keep from touching him again.

Hearing the unsteady note in her voice, Jefferson framed her face with caressing fingers, gently raising her gaze to his. "Don't be afraid, Marissa. We'll do all right together at the ranch. Nothing will hurt you there." Then, remembering his curt words on Simon's porch, he murmured, "Nor will I."

"I'm not afraid, Jefferson. Not anymore. And never of you." As he looked down at her, his face was still veiled in darkness, but she knew it would reflect the tenderness in his touch. A touch that made her want to tilt her lips into his palm, to trace the gentle power there with her kiss.

Want that turned to searing pain, and to shattering guilt, as she remembered another kind and gentle man. *Paulo.*

"I should go." Backing away, one hand reaching out to caress the sleek and elegant head of the Doberman, she looked at the mountains that were only black and deep purple shapes lying beneath a darkening sky. She looked at the bright glitter of the lake as it gave back the light of the moon in countless ripples. She drew a deep breath, savoring the scent of honeysuckle and evergreen. Blended with it, the crisp, clean scent of sunshine and fresh mountain air that lingered on Jefferson.

For this moment she could almost imagine a different world where grief and guilt could never dishonor love.

"Marissa?"

She heard his concern, and only then realized that she was staring at him. "It's nothing." She evaded the truth and added the sin of lying by omission to her long list of guilt. "Tomorrow will be a long and busy day. I'll leave you to your walk and your thoughts." She meant to go, to flee from the churn of her emotions. But her conscience wouldn't let her. "I am sorry for what I've done to your life. For the danger I've put you in.

"Perhaps there were others I could have called on or turned to. But the truth is, I didn't consider anyone else. Without regard to what helping me would mean, or how it would disrupt your life, I thought only of you." Her head bowed, she stared at the ground, but saw Jefferson as he'd been that last day in the tree house. Tall, handsome, a golden man with eyes like sapphires. Her best friend, her gentle teacher, a tender lover. The man she couldn't forget.

Her head came up, she looked into the shadow of his face. "I wanted you, Jefferson."

Not sure how to interpret her words, Jefferson stood like carved darkness as he watched her walk away. "Don't be a fool, Cade," he muttered. "Don't read into this what you want it to be."

He was her trusted friend. It was natural that she would want him…to keep a promise.

A long while later, Jefferson retraced his steps, returning to the clearing. Simon's house still blazed with lights. The Canfields's was dark. He hoped that meant Marissa slept. She would need her rest for the journey tomorrow.

"Jefferson." Stepping from the gloom of a copse of pines, Raven fell into step beside him. The clasp of her hand at his elbow brought him to a halt. "Would you listen to someone who understands what Marissa is facing and has felt as she feels now?"

He knew from Yancey that Raven had lost her family as horrendously as Marissa had, but at a much younger age. Remembered hurt was there now in the reflected light of Simon's windows. "If that someone were you, Raven, I would listen to anything."

A nod acknowledged she understood he knew her history. Her smile was bittersweet. "Go carefully. Be as patient as Jericho says you can be. Treat each day as a separate accomplishment. Don't rush her, but don't let her heap guilt on herself.

"Most of all remember, through no fault of yours, you're a part of her guilt. If she lashes out or turns away from you, it will be for what you represent, not you. Wait for her then."

"What guilt am I to Marissa, Raven? I don't understand."

"She hasn't confided in me. I will only speak of what I see, Jefferson. Grief, guilt. The belief that, in some way she's responsible for the deaths of her husband and parents. Or that she could have prevented the tragedy. Most of all, she thinks it's wrong to feel, to care, especially to love again."

"When you lost your parents and your brother, did you think it was wrong to feel anything but guilt, Raven?"

She didn't reply for the length of a trembling breath. When she answered she was calm. "At first, I did. I hated the world. But I hated myself the most—for living, for feeling when my family never would again. But Simon had come for me and he brought me here to his mother, Rhea.

Together they wouldn't let me *not* survive. They wouldn't let me not be whole.''

"You think I can do that for Marissa?''

"Yes.'' She was adamant. "More than anyone, for I think you've felt the same in your own life. I suspect you still do in some ways. Just go carefully. For your sake and Marissa's. In the end, you might be surprised what you reap in helping her.''

"You speak from experience,'' Jefferson suggested softly.

Raven didn't bother dissembling. "David was troubled when Simon sent him to the valley. I was as recovered as I could be as a solitary woman. Together we found our way to the love and life we share today. It can be the same for you, Jefferson.''

"If I go carefully,'' he finished for her.

"Yes.'' A smile offered encouragement. "Now I'll leave you to think and rest. Tomorrow promises to be a long day.''

She was at the steps of her own home when he called out. "Raven, how will I know what to do?''

"That's the simplest part of all. Follow your heart, Jefferson Cade. Always and forever, follow your heart.''

Four

Jefferson brought his truck to a stop by a hangar, recalling another such structure that had housed the small jet flown cross-country by Rick Cahill. So much had happened, so much had changed, it didn't seem possible that the first flight had been only a little more than a week ago.

Slightly jet-lagged and weary from all that had transpired in those days, he looked at his watch. Mentally running through the agenda he'd been given, he was pleased. "Perfect timing. But what else would Simon McKinzie expect?"

Realizing that he was talking to himself again, instead of the horses and Satan as he was wont to do on the Broken Spur, he pushed open the door and swung to the ground. With the sun at his back, his stare searching the sky, he wasn't surprised when he heard the plane a second before he saw it. "Perfect timing again."

As Simon expected. The phrase rattled, unbidden, through

his brain. It was, he'd discovered, the code of Simon's men. Doing what the man who had drawn them to him required. Not just because it was what they'd been trained to do. But because it was what they wanted. For Simon, for themselves. Most of all for the safety of their country and its citizens.

For people like Marissa.

Jefferson paced, suddenly anxious. Though he knew this part of Simon's proposed itinerary would be executed as meticulously as his part had been. Proving his trust and easing his concern, in a matter of a few more minutes, a small corporate plane touched down and taxied almost to the hangar.

Jogging onto the runway, Jefferson waved at Yancey as if he were accustomed to seeing his friend in the pilot seat of first one aircraft and then another. When it came to The Black Watch, one quickly became accustomed to many things. And learned to expect anything and any hidden skill among its men.

When the passenger door opened, Jefferson was there to help Marissa. His hands spanning her waist, her body sliding against his like a caress, he set her down on the tarmac. Keeping her close within his embrace he recalled another time, another caress. Another land. As his fingers lingered over her ribs and with the fullness of her breast almost touching his chest, he smiled down at her. "Welcome to Arizona, Marissa."

"Thank you," she murmured and stepped out of the steadying protection of his arms with the aplomb of nobility.

Not sure if she was thanking him for sparing her the leap to the tarmac or the welcome, Jefferson turned to Yancey who circled the plane with a clipboard in hand. "Good flight?"

"When you're flying a sweet baby like this—" with an

easy move, Yancey tossed the clipboard inside the plane and secured the door Marissa had exited "—it's always a good flight."

"Another case of maintenance that won't happen? Or another plane that's not for sale?" Jefferson drawled.

"This sale is legit." Yancey grinned as he leveled an approving gaze at the sleek craft. "I'm delivering it as a favor to Patrick McCallum, a friend of Simon's."

"The Scottish financier." It wasn't a question, proving Jefferson's surprise quotient. "And strictly a favor?"

"Yes. Though there's a history there. One of Simon's own—a lady sharpshooter, to be exact—rescued Patrick's little daughter from a religious zealot. Patrick and Simon have also worn the Scottish kilts at more than a few of the same gatherings of the clans." Yancey grinned again and slid an arm about Marissa. Bringing her to him, he kissed the top of her head. "If it worked for The Watch that I had this beautiful traveling companion, Patrick will only be delighted."

"You know McCallum, too," Jefferson suggested.

"Our paths cross," Yancey admitted. "Now and again."

Stepping back from Marissa and offering a hand to Jefferson, his grin vanished. His brilliant green gaze held Jefferson's. "Our Merrie's all grown up now, so you two take care of each other. Watch your step, Jeffie."

"Count on it, Yance." There was warmth in the handclasp of old friends, and memories recalled in names of the past.

Patrick McCallum's new plane was in the air, a diminishing speck of silver flying into the sun that rode high above the horizon when Jefferson turned again to Marissa. "We have hours of driving before we make the canyon. We should go."

"Right," she agreed and would have taken the luggage

Yancey had left on the tarmac. Jefferson was there before her.

"After you." He waited until she turned, then together they crossed to his truck. Matching her long stride, he finished setting her bags in the bed of the truck in time to take her arm as she climbed into the passenger seat.

Marissa tensed, but didn't jerk away, and for the second time thanked him politely. When her door was closed, then his, she found being shut away from the world with only Jefferson was too intimate, too tempting. Though the truck was hardly the tree house, and Arizona's barren beauty bore little similarity to the lush lowcountry, memories came rushing back.

Memories that left her floundering, not sure what she felt, or should feel. Tension mounted and wore thin. A keening awareness scraped at raw nerves and crackled between them. An awareness as charged with emotion as it was unacknowledged.

Marissa's way of dealing with what she couldn't resolve was to huddle against the door, keeping her face toward the window. For hours she watched the stark and splendid vistas they passed by. In those hours she tried to block everything from her mind except how the play of changing light brought new and different grandeur to this vast land.

Jefferson turned twice and angled and skirted box canyons and washes countless times. Eventually the truck always headed due west again. Some roads were paved, some loose gravel, some hard-packed dirt. The first was nearly deserted. The last, totally deserted. Unless one counted a cow or two. Or the occasional small herd of horses. Twice she glimpsed a rooftop, then again a windmill. Another time, a small oil rig constantly churning. Each meant people. But none were visible.

"I should have known," Jefferson said, at last, in a voice rusty from disuse and dust.

Marissa didn't look away from the window, or from the sprawl of unbroken, empty land. When Jefferson thought she wouldn't break her interminable silence, she stirred and shifted, long legs stretching in the little space allowed. Though he concentrated on potholes and bumps and billowing dust, he could feel her gaze on him.

"What should you have known, Jefferson?" Her question was the first she'd asked. The first time she'd spoken since they left the private airfield.

Making the most of this break in her silence, he kept the conversation going. "I should have known Simon was too cautious to allow you to arrive by a straightforward, conventional route. The man thrives on intrigue. But, thank God he does."

"Yes." With that agreement, she resumed her mute study of the Arizona landscape.

"Yes?" He wanted to hear her voice more than an answer.

"I beg your pardon?"

"Yes, Simon's cautious? Yes, he thrives on intrigue? Or yes, thank God he does? Which is it, Marissa?"

She laughed. A husky, unconsciously seductive note. For a modicum of time, her tension eased. "All of the above."

"Yeah." He flashed a grin—for a beautiful woman, a father's daughter, a loyal wife. Even he didn't realize it was his first real grin in days. "Good call, sweetheart."

As she looked away, her hair fell from its center part to drape over her cheeks. Absently, with both hands, she raked it back, her fingers threading through it like a comb. Jefferson was fascinated by the way it fell so orderly to her shoulders once more. He was fascinated by the way the gesture lifted her breasts against the taut leather of her vest. Even with a road that demanded unwavering attention, it was hard not to steal a second glance at the curve of her narrow waist as it flowed into the slender line of her hips and thighs.

Except for concerned glances, he'd kept his gaze resolutely forward for the duration of this roughest part of the drive. But he'd been fiercely aware of everything about her from the moment she'd walked away from the plane.

Once they were sealed in the small cab of the truck, he sensed more than saw every move. Every slow, controlled breath that lifted her breasts against the vest.

He was aware of each rare and restless shift of her long legs. On the plain she'd worn leather. Today, new denim. Part of Raven's purchases made during a quick trip to Madison, a small college town near the valley.

The denim had been faded and softened by an artificial aging process. It was Simon's directive that Marissa's clothing not attract attention by marking her as a tenderfoot going Western with a new wardrobe.

"Didn't work."

The words were no more than a breath, his lips barely moving in a quirking smile. The worn, aged look that was supposed to make her blend like a native, drawing no inordinate attention to her, hadn't come close to the effect Simon wanted.

Instead the supple fabric clung to her lean body in ways that made a man enjoy watching her move in that gliding stride of taller, lithesome women. The dark red shirt, though slightly faded, too, was the perfect foil for her dark hair and tawny skin.

With her boots and hat and open vest, she could fit on any ranch. But she was too damn beautiful to go unnoticed.

Fighting the familiar surge of desire, gripping the steering wheel, Jefferson drove in silence. Leaving Marissa to her thoughts. Deliberately turning his to the trip home.

Home. This venture proved that after four years Arizona

had become home. And after the time away, it would be good to be back in the canyon. Good to see Satan again.

Perhaps that eagerness contributed to making today's journey interminable. The first part of his route from Simon's valley had been complicated. With secret stops and switches. Until the last, a commercial flight from Belle Terre. It was then he'd discovered his original tickets had been used, rather than canceled. Anyone curious enough or interested enough to make note of his arrival, or to check the point of origin of his flight, would assume he was returning from a visit with his family.

After he'd left the canyon with Rick, Billy had driven the truck to Phoenix. Leaving it in long-term airport parking gave credence to what the sheriff hoped would be the natural assumption that Jefferson had returned to the lowcountry for a few days.

Once he'd collected the truck from the airport, as instructed, he'd followed a circuitous route to the private landing strip to meet Marissa. Which left this final drive.

"Tired?" he asked as she sighed softly.

"Maybe a bit." The admission was made with a half smile.

"After weeks on the Argentine plain, the trip to the valley, then to the ranch, how could you not be? But I suspect it's more than a bit." Reaching out, his fingertips brushed briefly over her wrist. "But it won't be long now."

At his touch, memories she'd struggled to ward off wouldn't be denied. Bittersweet memories that made her body yearn for the touch of his weathered, brawny hands. Hands that were beautiful in their strength and tenderness. Gentle hands that could tease and seduce, leaving a trail of sweet, wanting flame with each caress. Knowing hands that incited needs and desire beyond imagining.

No one had ever touched her as Jefferson had. Never before. Never in the years since. Once she would have said that hadn't mattered. That the life Paulo had given her was enough. That freedom, education and his wise guidance compensated for the absence of vigor and passion. Then on the plain and in the valley, as she'd watched Jefferson through half-shuttered eyes, she'd known all she'd tried to believe was a lie.

Now, as she saw those powerful, virile hands guiding the truck skillfully over nearly impassable terrain, she remembered what she'd never truly forgotten. She understood that for as long as she lived she could never forget those roughened, beautiful hands, that could soothe and gentle the wildest of horses, had soothed and gentled an innocent young woman as he taught her the sweet secrets of passion.

"Hey, pretty lady. Penny for your thoughts."

Startled, ridiculously afraid he'd read her mind, she pressed her hands against the sudden rush of heat that burned her cheeks. Regaining her composure, when she faced him the guilt for her disloyal admission of the shortcomings of her marriage to Paulo had begun its ugly taunts.

Ungrateful, selfish, cold. An adulteress in heart and mind, if not her body. A wicked woman who lusted for another man when her aged, benevolent husband had been dead only six weeks.

Puzzled, risking a look away from what had deteriorated into a body-battering track, Jefferson reached across the cab to trail the back of his hand over her cheek. "I didn't mean to upset you, sweetheart. I'm not sure what I said or did, but I'm sorry."

"Don't! Please don't!" Lurching beyond his reach, Marissa huddled against the door. Her hand gripping the handle as if she would flee if she could. But was any place far enough? Her breath was labored, the harsh sound of it filling the stunned silence of the truck. Gradually as it calmed, she released the handle and clasped her hands in her lap. Her posture was rigid, her eyes shadowed when she whispered in a voice brimming with regret, "Don't be sorry, Jefferson. Not for anything. But, please, don't touch me again."

The sun had slid behind the mountains, and though he could just barely see her face, he stared at her. Even in darkness he could comprehend her rigid posture, the wooden expression and interpret their message. "Marissa, sweetheart…"

When she flinched at the endearment, his teeth clenched, his lips closed over questions he would have asked. Clutching the steering wheel harder, he stared through the dusty windshield, while he wondered how his life and hers would go from here.

He wanted to apologize for whatever sin he'd committed, but he knew she wouldn't listen. He wanted to brake the truck, to haul her into his lap and kiss away her pain and grief. Her fear.

But his endearment was offensive. His touch abhorrent.

Yet she hadn't minded that he touched her on the plain. Nor in the valley. What changed? What was different?

Separate silences settled over them as the truck continued its slow, bumpy path, its lights joining with moonlight to guide them. Marissa returned to her vigil of the land. If she'd really seen it, she would have discovered yet another facet of this endlessly changing terrain. But she didn't notice as she tried to forget what a fool she must seem to Jefferson.

After a searching look seeking answers, but finding her stiff and remote, Jefferson kept his eyes on the road ahead. But his thoughts were not as riveted on the road as his glaring stare.

Please, don't touch me.

Don't touch me.

Her cry was like an omen, a knell, sounding in his mind. At first, he'd thought he was mistaken when she'd drawn away so abruptly. But when he moved past the shock of her reaction, he knew it would take worse than a simpleton to misunderstand.

She couldn't bear to have him touch her. He had discovered this new Marissa was a quiet woman. Perhaps, withdrawn in her grief, even more quiet than usual. But until just now he hadn't sensed her loathing of the feel of his hands on her.

Loathing of him? Or of what he might want from her?

Then he understood. Even though it had been judged the safest of places for her, she hadn't wanted to come to the Broken Spur. Because that meant she would be alone with him. With her friends around, as Juan and Marta had been on the plain, or in the valley with Simon and his men never very far away, she was comfortable with him. At least comfortable enough to function.

"But never when we're alone." Jefferson didn't realize he'd muttered out loud through gritted teeth, until she finally faced him, a questioning frown drawing down her brows. "It was nothing," he assured her. "Just thinking."

"What were you thinking, Jefferson?" That she was insane? An ungrateful bitch? Was he regretting that he'd ever received her message? Didn't he have reason to, given her strange behavior? "It must be that I'm an ugly, insensitive person. Awful. Rude."

Her hands still clasped in her lap, her fingers twined over each other with a brutal force. "After you've done so much for me, stopping your life in midstride, abandoning your responsibilities…you must think I'm terribly ungrateful."

"You couldn't be ugly if you tried, Marissa. Or awful, or rude. And I don't want your gratitude." Pausing for breath, he recalled he'd said almost those exact words to her in the valley.

I don't want your gratitude, Marissa…in fact gratitude is the last thing I want.

"But that doesn't matter now." A jackrabbit bounded across the road. Braking and swerving to avoid it, he waited until the truck returned to an even keel before he continued. "The important thing is to get you settled in at the ranch. Then, within the next two weeks to a month, Juan and Marta will be moving to Jake's new property."

"Two weeks to a month. It seems as long as forever." Thankful for a change of subject, Marissa fought the urge to babble out her appreciation for this opportunity for Juan. Jefferson was indirectly responsible, but he wouldn't want her thanks for the Elias any more than he wanted it for herself. "I'll miss them, especially Alejandro."

"You love that little boy, don't you?"

She didn't answer. Then, her gaze locked on her tortured hands, she whispered, "As I would have loved my own son."

Jefferson heard another layer of grief in her voice. And he wondered if her life of wealth and influence had been so wonderful after all. Suddenly, he realized Señora Marissa Rei was a woman of secrets. Pain-filled secrets.

The need was there to touch her. To ease hidden hurts. Instead he settled for platitudes. "I know you didn't want to come here. But it's for the best. Once you've settled in and we get you on horseback, you'll find time flies in the canyon.

"And you *will* like it here, Marissa. I can promise you that, at least."

"Here?" Curious in spite of herself, she sat up straighter. Though she'd stared out the window hours on end, in the last miles her eyes had been blinded by thoughts turned inward. Now, gaze darting, she strained for a glimpse of the range she'd heard so much about. "We're on the Broken Spur?"

"Not quite, but at any second we will be."

"Then this is Benedict land." Even that was intriguing. She'd heard much of the Rafter B, and the Benedict empire.

"We've traveled across it for nearly four hours."

"That long? His land covers that great distance? Then it rivals some of the greatest *estancias* in Argentina."

"It's big," Jefferson agreed. "If Jake could've had his way a few years back, it would be bigger. And he would have what he's wanted for a long time. Steve Cody's Sunrise Canyon."

"Obviously he didn't get it." It was good to speak of something other than her own troubles, and the unthinking hurt she'd caused Jefferson. "What went wrong?"

"It shaped up to be quite a fracas. Then it wasn't."

"Because?" Marissa prodded when he said no more.

"Because Steve came away with all he ever wanted. The Broken Spur and Jake's daughter, Savannah."

"Savannah Cody. Savannah Benedict Cody, currently in England with her husband and their daughter Jakie." Marissa laughed softly. A sound as rare in her life now as it had been in Jefferson's. "A fairy tale come true."

"Not a fairy tale," Jefferson said. "A love story come true. Sure Steve ended up with the ranch and the woman he loved. But if he'd had to choose…"

"He would have chosen Savannah," she supplied, and was certain she was right.

"No contest."

"It turned out wrong for Jake Benedict, but right for everyone else."

"In the end, it was right for Jake, too. Thanks to Sandy Gannon and a baby called Jakie." But that was a story for another time Jefferson decided as he let the truck glide to a stop. He turned the key and stepped out. Crossing to her side, he opened the passenger door, careful not to touch her. "Come with me."

When she stood beside him he went with her, leading

her across rough and rugged ground to a precipice. Without taking her arm, as it had been drummed into him all his life he should. Old habits of Southern gentlemen died hard, but he was learning.

He hadn't planned to arrive just as the moon struck the stream, turning it to a ribbon of silver, but he had. A globe of cold fire, its light filled the canyon where the grass was belly deep and only a few horses grazed, waiting for the rest of the herd to come from a pasture deeper in the canyon.

A barn huddled a little away from the stream. Beyond a grove of aspen, the house that had been no more than a cabin, lay in darkness. The hand Sandy sent to fill in had finished the day's chores and returned to the Rafter B for the night.

His gesture swept over the entire vista. "Welcome to Sunrise Canyon and the Broken Spur, Marissa. The home of Steve and Savannah Cody. And—for a while—yours as well."

She was quiet as she looked from one side of the canyon to the ridge of the precipice where they stood. Far longer than it was wide, and with water plentiful and good grass, it was a natural corral. Perfect for horses and for a woman who loved them. Perfect, Jefferson was certain, for this woman who needed a place to heal. A refuge, not just from the man who posed the threat, but from herself and what she believed. What she feared.

Jefferson hoped the healing had begun when she looked up at him and smiled. A small smile, a gentle lift of the corners of her mouth. No more. But for the first time, there was pleasure not tinged with hurt and grief.

Turning back to look again at the canyon, she was still smiling. "It's beautiful, Jefferson."

"Yes." As he agreed he knew it was right she'd come.

* * *

Viewed from the canyon floor, Steve Cody's land was no less spectacular. As she stood by the truck, Marissa turned in a slow circle. "It's no wonder Jake Benedict wanted this. No matter how much land he might have, any cattleman would want this. But I expected the operation would be larger."

"It could have been. At first, even though the land was a gift, money was a factor. Steve did all the work himself, unless a neighboring cowhand happened by to lend a hand now and then."

"One of them called Jeffie?"

"I pitched in a few times. So did Sandy Gannon. For that matter, even when they were at war with neither admitting what they felt for each other, so did Savannah."

"You make it sound more and more like quite a love story."

"Yeah." Moving away from her because he couldn't stand so close and not touch her, Jefferson searched the gloom beneath a tree. "There's someone I'd like you to meet."

"Here?" The house was dark. The stables, quiet. No unexpected arrival disturbed the grazing horses. "Now?"

"Here and now. His name is Satan. I think you're going to like him. I know he'll love you."

"He." Her head tilted. But as in the valley by the lake, his face was in shadow. Softly she repeated the unusual name. "Satan."

Finding pleasure in the verbal fencing that recalled their time together during her years at the university in Belle Terre, Jefferson grinned. "Satan."

"How many legs would Satan happen to have?" Before he could answer, she stopped him with her hand up, palm facing him. "No, let me guess—four."

"Good guess."

"Satan's a male name. Would he be in the barn?"

Propping a forearm against the truck, Jefferson loomed over her. His fingers nearly brushed a curling tendril at her temple, before he thought to draw them back. It would be so easy to succumb to the desire to slide his fingers through the dark wealth of her hair. But she'd laid down the rules of her stay, and he would abide by them, even if it killed him. "Satan can be in the barn, at times. But not usually."

"Not a Cody stud," she ventured. "Not a horse at all."

A slight tilt of his head and a drawl acknowledged she was on target. "Not a horse."

"I don't think you're a cat man." With narrowed eyes, she considered that. "Not unless it was a bobcat." A shake of her head set her hair stirring against her shoulders and the scent of it surrounded him. "But not with horses. And that leaves…a dog."

Jefferson answered with a shrill whistle. After two sharp trills, Satan's deep bark rumbled, then he whimpered as the pads of his massive feet pounded the red earth.

Because Satan was the color of night, Marissa saw little more than a black shape hurling itself at Jefferson. As man and beast went down, she heard laughter.

When the wrestled greeting ended and Jefferson had cuffed the great dog affectionately on its massive head, he got to his feet. A little out of breath he made the introductions. "Marissa, meet Satan."

Fearlessly delighted, she was down on Satan's level immediately. Crouched in the dust she was eye-to-eye with the magnificent creature. "Hello, Satan." Petting fingers stroked the long Doberman jaw. "I'm glad to make your acquaintance."

Jefferson tensed while Satan shivered and danced in place. But as Marissa continued to croon to the Doberman, he realized that the massive dog looked like a puppy falling under her spell. By the time she rose to stand next to him,

Jefferson knew the Dobie had fallen completely in love with her.

A common male occurrence, he thought wryly as he watched them form a mutual admiration society. "If I can tear you away from each other, it's time to show Marissa her new home."

Together they walked to the cabin. Marissa and Jefferson, with Satan between them. When Jefferson opened the door, Satan waited, determined to enter, but only after his new love.

Jefferson knew Satan had just acquired himself another human. From this day, he would be Marissa's constant companion, her protector. Added insurance that wouldn't hurt at all.

When he'd shown her to her upstairs bedroom, Satan was by her side. With her permission, he was still there when Jefferson returned to the first floor and his own bedroom.

Where long into the night, he lay sleepless, thinking about Marissa, the woman who was only a forbidden touch away.

Five

"**O**uch and be damned!"

Angry at himself for his carelessness, Jefferson dashed blood from his hand and returned his attention to the strand of barbed wire he was repairing. Where his attention should've been all along. "Except." he muttered taking a bandanna from his hip pocket to bind around his palm when the furrow across it bled profusely.

"Yeah, *except*." Except he couldn't keep his eyes off Marissa. The bandanna slipped, and he bit back another oath.

She'd been in the canyon two weeks. And for two weeks they'd kept a careful truce. By tacit agreement, they didn't discuss her life or his life, the past, the present, the future. Nothing more personal than the responsibilities that were part of ranch life.

"Tiptoeing, like strangers." With that low growl, his gaze lifted again to Marissa. Admiring her, and her spirit.

She'd certainly assumed a healthy share of the workload that was involved in the daily routine of ranching, and raising and training horses. Beginning with her first day in the canyon. When he expected she would sleep late, or at least rest, she was the first up and moving about the kitchen as if she'd never been tired, much less exhausted. As if she were quite at home on the Broken Spur.

Jefferson remembered that odd little lurch he'd felt when he'd stepped into the kitchen that first morning. Whatever he might have expected to discover it wouldn't have been a beautiful woman just taking a pan of biscuits from the oven. Five minutes later, he'd been seated at the table, a cup of coffee in his hand and a plate filled with bacon and scrambled eggs set before him.

"Earning my keep. It's the only way this is going to go," she'd told him when he protested. The pleasant words and a determined look ended that discussion effectively and forever.

Each day thereafter, breakfast was on the table promptly at five-thirty. Before he left the house, leftovers of bacon or sausage or whatever, were wrapped and ready for a lunch on the move. As he'd told her was his custom. Supper was never fancy, but she had a way of making plain fare not so plain. It was plentiful, and always ready at the end of each long grueling day.

Through it all, they observed a careful truce, and he never touched her. "Tiptoeing." How else could they go? How long?

When the blood had been stanched, or at least slowed to an ooze, he wrapped the bandanna more loosely around his palm, looped it clumsily with his right hand, then held the cloth with his teeth to secure a knot. Satisfied the makeshift bandage would suffice, he glanced one more time at the corral where Marissa put the new filly through the first paces of her training.

Marissa in action was a sight to behold. But Jefferson needed to concentrate on his own set of chores, for beholding the sight of her had led to his confrontation with the barbed wire. Turning away, thankful this was the last broken strand, he made quick work of it. Between the resounding strikes of his hammer, he could hear her low croon. He couldn't distinguish the words, but he knew by rote the string of constant instruction and praise she chanted as she taught the filly the first of a number of skills.

When the repair was finished, Jefferson gathered his tools and stowed them in a small toolbox. Stretching the ache from strained shoulders, he glanced at the sun, judging the time. Almost noon, time to knock off for lunch. The day that had begun early and would run late, was hot and would be hotter in an hour or so. The filly shouldn't do much more. But he wouldn't interfere. Marissa was as aware of the dangers of overheating as he.

And as he, she was inclined to take better care of the horses than of herself. Conscious of his own formidable thirst, foregoing the thermos he'd tucked into the toolbox, he crossed to the stream where the water ran clear and deep before separating into two branches. One meandered through fenced pastures. One veered past a grove of trees, then by the house.

He'd discovered that at this exact spot, the water was sweetest. Kneeling on one knee in the shade of an overhanging cottonwood tree, with his good hand he scooped up a palmful and drank. Thirst quenched, flinging aside his hat and the bandanna, he cleaned his wound, then splashed his face and head. As the cooling liquid sluiced down his arm and his body, he found his gaze returning to the corral, seeking out Marissa.

The corral was empty. As he'd known she would before long, she'd completed this training session, then had taken the filly to the barn. His hand rebound, returning to the fence, he gathered up the toolbox, mounted his ground-tied mare and cantered to the barn. To her.

"Good girl." Marissa petted the filly as she combed and curried her. "You're a pretty thing. Smart, too. Not to mention a bloodline that ranks with the royalty of horses. Gitano or Black Jack, or both, should get excellent colts on you."

The scuff of a boot heel, the whisper of cloth against cloth, caught her attention. Looking toward the barn door, she saw him standing there. Her hands went still. Her crooning faltered. Silence amplified by the tramp of horses and the creak of wood was broken only by the thunder of her heart. "Jefferson."

With sunlight at his back, he was only a dark figure. His hat was tilted over his forehead, shading an already shaded face, yet she felt the weight of his stare. Broad of shoulders, narrow-hipped, he was lean and strong in jeans that hugged his thighs before being drawn over boots with worn heels bearing a star.

There had never been anyone like him. There couldn't be. Inexplicably nervous, clasping the currycomb, she rested her hand on the filly's neck. "How long have you been there?"

"Not long." Long enough to see the gentleness in her as she cooled the horse and groomed it. She'd made a pet of every creature on the ranch. Including Gitano, Steve's Spanish stallion. And especially Black Jack, Savannah's mount—half wild, half mountain goat, all horse, the stallion had been moody and had moped around missing Savannah. Until Marissa had arrived.

"Where's your shadow?" He referred to Satan, the most besotted of the lot. Next to Jefferson Cade, he amended.

"He must have grown bored while I worked with the pretty girl." Laying comb and brush aside, she led the filly into a stall and closed the door. Facing Jefferson again, she explained. "He scurried off a little while ago. Chasing a roadrunner."

Jefferson chuckled. "He never learns. But if he should catch one, he wouldn't know what to do with it. I doubt bird or feathers are his favorite food."

"Has he ever caught one?"

"Never. Doesn't matter. The chase is the fun of it for Satan." The animals, always their safest subject. Something to keep his mind diverted from what he wanted. *What he wanted*... In an ungoverned impulse he asked, "Have you had lunch, Marissa?"

The abrupt shift surprised her. Frowning, she searched for an idea of the time and drew a blank. "Is it time already?"

"Past time." He moved closer. "It's also past time I checked the herd deeper in the canyon. Since you haven't seen more than the main part of the ranch, I thought you might grab a biscuit and ride along. There's a nice spot for a picnic."

Marissa had wanted to ride through more of the canyon. She'd wanted to ride with Jefferson. She'd wanted it for a long time. As he waited for her answer he moved closer, gradually becoming more than a dark familiar shape. He was color and light, wickedly rugged, wickedly handsome. She could think of nothing but Jefferson. There was only here and now, with the past and its grief and guilt forgotten in the thunder of her heart. But if he had work to do, she shouldn't hamper him. "Maybe you'd do best alone."

"It isn't wise to leave you." With his uninjured hand, he pushed his hat back. His blue gaze was more than brilliant. More than riveting. "Even with Satan on sentry duty."

"I see." Disappointment she tried to deny constricted her throat. He'd asked out of obligation. Not because he wanted to ride with her. But why should she expect it would be different? She'd treated him more like an enemy than a friend. The fault was hers, yet he'd borne the brunt of it.

She'd allowed it with her silence. But how could a woman thought to be a wife and widowed such a short time explain the need, the awakening of long-dormant desire so soon after her husband's death? Wouldn't the man she lusted for feel disgust for one so unfaithful, even if only to an arrangement and a memory?

"Marissa?"

He moved closer, questioning her silence. Bringing with him the fragrance of the out-of-doors to mingle with the scent of hay, horses and leather. The fragrance and scent that never failed to bring him to mind, no matter where she was. A pleasing scent that made her wish for… No! She spun away, turning her back on him. She mustn't let her mind wander where it wanted to go.

Laying the bridle aside, she reached out to take the saddle from the rail where she'd left it. Jefferson was there before her and she could only watch as he took it to the tack room.

Seconds later, he was back, looming over her, jogging her memory with his presence as much as his words. "The ride, Marissa," he prompted. "Would you like to go into the canyon?"

"I…no." Her eyes were downcast. Then, for no reason she could explain and casting caution aside, reversing her choice, she lifted her gaze to meet his. "Yes." Her voice was steady, her tone emphatic as she reached deep for the courage that had sustained her through other times of her life. Some as difficult. Others far more. "Yes, I'd like to ride with you, Jefferson."

Jefferson made no comment on her change of heart as he reached for a pair of bridles hanging outside the tack room door. "I'll get Black Jack and The Lady from the pasture. The Lady is Savannah's favorite next to Black Jack, and as surefooted as the stallion. I'll have them saddled and waiting when you're ready."

He was transferring the bridles to his left hand when Marissa gasped. Forgetting rules she'd laid down for herself and for him, she caught his wrist. "Jefferson!" Her eyes were riveted on the bandanna soaked in red. As she brought his hand with its bloody bandage closer, there was horror on her face. "What happened?"

"Got bit by a stubborn strand of barbed wire." Lifting a shoulder in dismissal, he smiled ruefully. "Goes with the territory. There are days that if I met the man responsible for inventing the damnable stuff, I'd shoot him."

"Stop it." She was frowning and cradling his hand in hers. "Don't make light of this. Surely you know an injury like this is dangerous and no joking matter." Then the desperate, worried questions poured out. "Have you had a tetanus vaccine recently? How deep did the barb go? Did you clean it? You could get an infection, or worse. Why didn't you tell me? I could have helped. I would have. Surely you know that."

When her worried tirade died more from lack of breath than questions, a pleased, deliberate grin curled Jefferson's lips. "Are you all done fussing over me? If you are, I'll explain."

"I've just begun fussing, as you say. But I'll listen to your excuses." She swept a doubtful look over him. "If you have any."

Her fingers still circled his wrist, as if he might run from her. When the last thing Jefferson wanted was to run. Standing compliantly in her grasp he addressed her questions in perfect order. "I know an injury such as this is nothing to blow off. I had a tetanus vaccine last year, providing immunity for several years. The barb didn't go deep, so much as it grabbed and ripped."

He caught a breath. "I cleaned it in the stream because, of course, I know it could become infected. I didn't tell you because I didn't want to interrupt your session with the filly.

"And, yes," he finished softly. "I knew you could help, Marissa. I knew you would."

"But you didn't ask."

"I'm a big boy, now, sweetheart. I've lived here alone for over a year, and I was taking care of myself pretty well even before then." The endearment hadn't been intentional. But once spoken, it felt natural. Better yet, this time she didn't flinch. His grin grew. Hope for better days rippled through him. "Maybe I've been too alone for too long," he added thoughtfully. "If you'd like to fuss a little more, be my guest."

"I intend to." Practically dragging him to the house, the dangers of living a lonely, isolated life were too clear to her. Too frightening. A horse could throw him, or roll on him. A snake could bite him. A rock could tumble from the rim of the canyon.

The mental tabulation of dangers would have grown, but with the falling rock, they arrived at the steps of the house. When he had been marched up the last stair and directed to sit at the kitchen table and wait, he sat at the table and waited.

There were first-aid supplies in the pantry off the kitchen. In no time, she was back. Dumping what she'd collected on the table, she left him again to fill a basin with warm water. With a towel and soap, she returned to the table. Sitting catercorner from him, her knees brushing his, she untied and unwrapped his hand, groaning. "The wire did a number on you."

"It snapped." The terse explanation was enough. Both were familiar with the rapid recoil of wire that lost tension.

"In that case, it's fortunate that this is the worst of it." She went to work on his wound. First, soaking his hand. Then bathing it with soapy disinfectant. "I don't want to hurt you."

"You won't, sweetheart." His voice was deep, a whisper.

Gradually her hands ceased moving. Then were still, cradling his. When she lifted her head, she found him waiting for her. Brown eyes held blue. Seeking. Perhaps finding.

After a time, he smiled. "You never have, you know."

Marissa couldn't respond. She didn't know what she felt or what she should say. Yet she didn't look away until Jefferson turned his hand clasping hers. Soberly, but with humor glinting in his eyes, he murmured, "Think I'm gonna to live, doc?"

Snapping back to real time, she said, "You might. After I paint this with antiseptic, and if you keep the bandage clean."

"That stuff stings, but I'll try to be brave."

"I'm sure you will be." Her tone was serious while his teased. "You always have been."

She was winding the last length of gauze around his palm when he commented on her skill. "You know what you're doing, don't you, Marissa? If I'd needed stitches you could have done them."

It wasn't a question but she answered. "I've studied medicine. Mostly obstetrics, to help on the *estancias*. Though practicing was never an option, I completed my studies…" Her voice broke, yet she continued her explanation. "I had completed the course. The trip was to be a celebration. When Alejandro fell ill, I planned to join Paulo and my parents later."

Jefferson wanted to take her in his arms. He wanted to

hold her and make her believe that with her or without her aboard, the plane would have crashed. And none of it was her fault. But it wasn't something he could make her believe with one embrace, one denial. It needed time, and that time was not now. Instead he addressed her studies. "You studied to learn, but never to practice. Your husband's blessing didn't quite embrace a career."

"He was very much of the old school where women were concerned. But he was a good man, Jefferson. Generous to a fault. Kinder and more forgiving than I deserved." The bandage was finished, the tape in place. There was no more reason to touch him. "Whatever sham our marriage might have been, Paulo was kind and forgiving, and always supportive."

"Kind, forgiving," Jefferson mused quietly. "You've used those words twice, almost in one breath."

Marissa didn't explain. "He was that sort of man."

"But you didn't love him." It had taken time to figure it out. But it was the only answer for her behavior. He met her startled look, seeing an answering regret in her expression. It would hurt to speak the words. Yet, like a festering wound, it would hurt more if she didn't. "Did you love him, Marissa?"

Color drained from her face, the pallor turning her eyes lightless black and bottomless. "Of course I loved him." Her voice shook and there was grief in the sound. "To know Paulo was to love him. Everybody who knew him loved him."

"Everybody loved him. You loved him." Her father's friend had been good to her. In her words, kind. For that, he was grateful. Marissa was a caring woman. She would respond to Rei's kindness. But Jefferson went with his gut feeling.

"You loved Paulo Rei." A clock on the mantel ticked

off seconds before he finished. "But you weren't in love with him."

Marissa stood hastily. Her chair tilted but righted at last. With competent hands only a little unsteady, she gathered up the first-aid supplies and repacked them into the kit. When that was done to her satisfaction, she took the basin to the sink to rinse it. Next she returned the kit to the pantry.

As he followed every move she made with interest, it wasn't difficult to imagine her serving as an over-trained medic working among the people of far-flung *estancias*. Something he suspected, she would prefer over an official medical practice. She was good. Damned good. But she hadn't answered his question.

She'd just stepped from the pantry, when he spoke again, taking up his conversation where it had broken off. "Were you, Marissa?" She stopped in midstride, her face still pale, her eyes still dark with grief. "Were you ever in love with Paulo Rei?"

She drew that long breath she needed to gather courage. "No, Jefferson." Her voice was calm. Too calm. "I was never in love with Paulo. Ours wasn't that sort of relationship."

That, he knew instinctively, was a great part of her guilt. A sham; she'd called her marriage a sham, and described it as not *that* sort of relationship. There were questions he would ask. But not now when she was so distraught. Rising from the table, he flexed the fingers of his injured hand. "Thank you for this, Marissa. It feels better already. If you're still interested in that ride?" Pausing, he waited only for her slow, silent nod. "I'll saddle Black Jack and The Lady. We'll be ready when you are."

Marissa tarried, wondering what she'd done. Long after his footsteps faded from the porch and the steps, she returned to the pantry to scavenge its shelves for an impromptu picnic.

The trail was an uneven track ever climbing, snaking past boulders and clumps of scrub and sparse cacti. As Marissa followed Jefferson, she could see that it was a route constantly changing. The soil was a mix of crumbling detritus, sandlike soil, or hard packed red earth. Some parts of it were wide, easily navigated, others were narrow, with jutting rock formations threatening a knee or ankle. But the threats never came to pass, thanks to Jefferson's guidance and softly called warnings.

When the idea of this ride had first been presented, she hadn't voiced her questioning of his choice of Black Jack over Gitano. Now, the black horse proved Jefferson's wisdom.

Black Jack was the most surefooted horse she'd ever seen. With The Lady coming in a close second. Only Satan, ranging ahead of them was surer. The filly she had worked with all morning hadn't been exposed to the trails, but there was something about the way she moved. "She could do this."

Jefferson turned in the saddle. "Something wrong?"

Realizing that she'd spoken her thoughts, Marissa shook her head. "Just thinking out loud."

"Care to share?" Beneath the brim of his hat, his eyes were stunning, as blue as the unclouded sky.

Eyes that could make any woman shiver in anticipation of the thoughts that clear steady gaze inspired. But certainly none she could, or should speak of. "I was thinking of the filly." Not quite a lie, not the full truth. "There's something about the way she walks. I can't explain it, but my intuition says she will make an excellent mountain horse. At least as good as The Lady."

Jefferson respected Marissa's horse sense. As much as

anyone he knew short of Sandy Gannon, Steve Cody, or Jesse Lee. And Savannah was no slouch. He wouldn't presume to second-guess any of them. Especially Marissa. Threading his reins through his gloved fingers, he leaned on the pommel of his saddle, his gaze keeping hers. "When you think she's ready, we'll bring her into the canyon. It's a good test for mountain horses."

"When she's ready," Marissa agreed. "If I'm still here."

Jefferson tensed, Black Jack responded to the change in his bearing by dancing restlessly in place. With a touch of a hand and a softly spoken word, the stallion was calmed.

Marissa watched as he stroked the horse. As his long, gloved fingers moved over Black Jack's sleek, black hide, there was gentleness in the stroke that controlled more than force or power. That was his way. As natural to Jefferson as breathing. A power greater than brute force.

His brothers had been brawlers. Known as boys, then men, who never instigated a controversy but were always standing in the end. Jefferson's one foray into battle ended with Adams Cade going to prison. Marissa knew Jefferson had been barely in his teens when he'd taken it upon himself to avenge an insult. He was too young, too inexperienced, to handle the issue. Adams had gone after him. What happened then lay shrouded in mystery for years.

Though she'd heard gossip, she'd been too young also. And too new to Belle Terre to understand all that happened. Except Adams was locked away and Jefferson banished himself in the swamp. In time the truth was revealed, Adams was exonerated.

All was forgiven. Except by Jefferson, who had never forgiven himself. In the time they'd spent together, pals, best of friends, roaming the land, this was the one subject of which he never spoke. Though it changed his life irrevocably, causing him to exile himself from his brothers, he had never explained.

She knew the truth. That the oldest and the youngest of the Cade brothers had truly saved each other that night. She'd never heard it from Jefferson's guilt-ridden perspective. She'd never questioned him, she never would. But she realized now, on a dusty trail far removed from the Carolina lowcountry, that she very much wanted to hear the story in his own words.

Then she would understand this good man. Because they were so alike. Because they both bore the brunt of tragedy, maybe in understanding Jefferson, she could understand herself.

She watched his fingers trailing over Black Jack, soothing the spirited creature. He'd done the same for her that final day in the swamp. He'd given her the accord she'd sought, courage to do what she must. He would again, if she'd let him.

His hands were magic, their caress a gift of courage and peace. His gift, honed by tragedy. Given to all but himself.

Dust that billowed in a red cloud beneath the stallion's hooves began to settle. The upheaval was finished, when Jefferson spoke again. "There's one bad patch left on the trail. But from there, barring a new slide, or a collapsing rock formation, it should be downhill and easy the rest of the way."

Black Jack stamped a foot, eager to move on. The Lady responded with a toss of her head. Jefferson smiled, reading the message they sent. "Ready?"

"I'm ready." She wasn't quite sure for what, or when. But something inside her was changing, shifting. Something that couldn't be hurried. "Or I will be." Her words were quiet, lost in the clatter of hooves on rocky ground. "One day. Soon."

* * *

Confident of her ability, and The Lady's, Jefferson set Black Jack into a gallop. With dust flying again, they rode in silence, enjoying the moment. At the crest of this last rise, the trail began a sharp descent. Twisting, nearly looping back on itself, it descended again into the protective shade of canyon walls. Brush thrived and thickened, nearly blocking the narrow, little used trail in places. And as they moved deeper into this secluded part of Sunrise Canyon, the sound of tumbling water was a welcome intrusion into the quiet of the trail.

One strand of wire stretching across the trail turned the arroyo into a natural corral. Jefferson's quick dismount, a shift of fencing, then when she'd ridden past it leading Black Jack, the reconnection of wire, and they were in. Secure in a tiny world of every color of the spectrum. A feast for the senses.

"Take a look around," Jefferson suggested. "I'll check the horses, then meet you by the stream." He looked down at her, struggling against the compelling urge to touch her. Against the need to kiss her. With his look tracing the shape of her mouth, he asked, "Have you worked up an appetite?"

"Yes." Her answer was automatic. But she discovered she was looking forward to eating, as she hadn't been since the day her family died. "I'll set out what I put in the saddlebag. I'm sorry it isn't more. Where would you like it?"

"Anything will be fine. Anywhere you choose will be fine." Backing away while he could, he hurried to the horses. Leaving her questioning the sudden edge in his voice.

In this tranquil place, after a challenging ride that should have worked off lingering tension, he seemed ill at ease. He was striding past boulders that would hide him from her sight, before she turned to the stream to seek out a place for a picnic.

The site she chose was shaded by the spreading limbs of a cottonwood. There were only biscuits and bacon from the morning, along with a thermos of the strong, black coffee he liked. With another of the cool, sweet water from the stream for her. Makeshift fare, spread on a tattered blanket. But neither he nor she were prone to great feasts in the middle of a hot, dusty workday when it was thirst, not appetite that needed quenching.

When she finished, she sat down to wait for Jefferson's return, and a sense of peace surrounded her as she listened to the whisper of a breeze in the cottonwood. A perfect accompaniment for the babble of the stream. Jefferson's footsteps sounded behind her, but she didn't turn. With her gaze ranging this unexpected place, she murmured, "This is beautiful."

"Yes," he said simply. But he only had eyes for Marissa as he came down beside her.

"The horses?"

"No problems. The grass here is good, but we should consider moving them in a week or so."

We. He spoke to her as his partner. "Will we need help?"

"They've done this enough that they know the trail. One hand could do it. Two makes it easier. But that's enough."

"Hungry?"

"Am I?" He laughed, a rare husky sound touched by strain. Dear heaven, yes he was hungry. Hungrier than he'd ever been or thought he could be. He was too hungry here in this secluded paradise. But not for food. "Yeah," he muttered. "As a bear."

"A bear?" Her speculative gaze ranging over him not helping his situation, "A wolf maybe, or a tiger, or even the bobcat like before. But I could never see you as a bear.'' The beginning of a smile faltered as she saw the bloody bandage on his left hand. ''Jefferson, you're bleeding again!''

''It's nothing.'' Her fingertips barely brushed his wrist when he jerked away. ''Don't! Don't touch me, Marissa. Not here. Dear God, not now.''

Her hand hovered between them, then dropped to her knee. The flush of color the ride had brought to her cheeks faded. The pleasure she'd found in this wild and wonderful place that matched the aura of the lowcountry vanished. ''I suppose I deserved that.'' Her voice was raw, brittle. ''I'm sorry.''

Wishing he'd bitten his tongue rather than spoken to her as he had, he searched for a way to make her understand.

''After the way I behaved on the drive to the canyon, I can't blame you for not wanting me to touch you, Jefferson.''

''Not wanting you to touch me? Is that what you think this is about?'' He wanted to lift her face to his. But he dared not. Instead, he said, ''Look at me, Marissa. Look in my eyes, see for yourself and believe that I want your touch. See and believe that I want far more. More than you're ready to give.''

''You're not angry about what I said?'' Her dark eyes searched his, and saw no condemnation.

''I was never angry. Puzzled, yes. Then, after a while, I understood. You've a long way to go in resolving your grief. But, just so you understand, I want you, Marissa. I want your touch, your kiss. I want the love, and yes, the lust. I want it all, Marissa. Everything. But not before its time.

''I don't want to rush you, sweetheart. But if that day in the swamp didn't mean what I thought it meant, if you didn't love me then, tell me now.''

There it was. Dragging in a long breath, Marissa closed

her eyes. Shutting out everything, but the one thing she couldn't deny. Right or wrong. Reprehensible or not—the truth. "I can't."

"Can't?" he prompted gently, patiently, leaving countless questions unasked.

She turned to him, staring up at him. "I can't tell you that you were wrong. I can't tell you I didn't love you."

Forgetting his hand and breaking rules that no longer applied, Jefferson reached for her then. Folding her into his embrace as she came willingly to him, he held her. "That's a beginning and enough for now." His lips brushed her hair as he whispered a promise. "We'll work it out. Maybe sooner, maybe later, but we will work this out.

"All of it," he added grimly as thoughts of Menendez turned his tenderness to anger.

Six

"**A**h-h." With that groan of relief, dusty, soaked with sweat, body stiff and refusing to obey, Marissa fell out of the saddle. More a gangly landing than her usual easy dismount. Her legs nearly buckling, with another groan she straightened, discovering the exhilarated pleasure in every taut, aching muscle.

Her day had begun as days always began on the ranch. Awake by five. Breakfast by five-thirty. In the barn tending and feeding horses by six. Next a session with the pretty mare she'd begun calling Bonita. A session that had run long today. Not because the surefooted horse was having difficulty, but because Marissa sensed her agile and cooperative mount was enjoying the routine. Bonita was proving to be a unique horse. A hard worker, a quick learner. Patient. A mount that shared a rapport with its rider.

When the session ended the sun was high, the early summer temperature soaring. It was time. Time to ride again with Jefferson to the *ciénaga*. This, he had explained at the end of their first trip farther into the land of the Broken Spur, was the name Savannah Henrietta Benedict Cody had given that distant part of the canyon when she was still a young girl. A very young girl called Hank, not Savannah, who found it a respite from the often impossible burden of being Jake Benedict's only child.

The most isolated part of the canyon would never by any stretch of the imagination truly be a marshland. But, for Marissa, in mood and spirit, the Spanish name fit.

She'd come away from it the first time with the beginning of a better perspective. Nothing concrete. A change sensed rather than understood. A cornerstone for building toward a new outlook, a new life. A paradoxical feeling of history repeating itself as Jefferson shared the healing serenity of a desert paradise as kindly and gently as he had in the lowcountry.

The first ride in had been a time of exploring the canyon. A part of a normal workday coupled with the pleasure of discovery. Today had been strictly labor. As a team they'd worked together, Jefferson and she, driving the herd pastured there back home.

Though the roundup was strenuous, keeping the horses on the trail as a whole hadn't been difficult. But there was always the wanderer that would stray past an outcropping of boulders or through a copse of brush. Or straight up an impossible incline. But The Lady was always willing to follow, and Satan helped.

Through the day, Marissa whistled and called until her throat was parched. She'd stretched and strained, riding her stirrups until her legs trembled. Her hat and her hair, drawn back in a ponytail, were covered in a film of red dust. Her face was marked and streaked with that same dust mingled with sweat. When she clenched her teeth grit ground between them.

As she stripped the saddle from The Lady and led her for a short drink, she was as hot and exhausted as her mount. As she took off her hat, dragged the tie from her hair and wiped the back of her gloved hand over her forehead, she'd never felt so good.

Leaving the horse to rest, she walked to the corral fence. Leaning against the top rail, she watched the new herd mill among the old. A result, in part, of her efforts. Bodybattering, unglamorous work. She laughed, a contented sound.

"A pretty sight, isn't it?" His own mount unsaddled and watered, Jefferson had come to stand beside her. He was as dusty, perhaps as exhausted, but in him there was a glow of fulfillment. Together they watched the herd.

Standing beside him at the end of a day of accomplishment made the concerted effort even more satisfying. Turning her gaze from the herd, absorbing the look of him— the dark blond hair, streaked with silver and barely visible beneath his hat. Broad shoulders made broader by work and life and time. A lean torso, flat belly, powerful thighs and long, muscular legs, all blending into an arresting and beautiful man.

It was all a part of Thomas Jefferson Cade. A man who had come for her when she needed him. Who shared this moment with her. "I can't think of anything or any place prettier."

"Rough day?" he asked, though there was no question in his tone. "Have I demanded too much of you, sweetheart?"

Sweetheart. He called her that routinely now. But she'd never gotten accustomed to the endearment. Even in her grief and guilt, a warm sensation never failed to settle in the pit of her stomach. Though she'd learned to keep her hands and gaze steady, with that single word, he made her serene demeanor a lie.

"Rough, but good." Brushing a sweat soaked strand of hair from her cheek, she saw his concern. "You haven't demanded too much of me, Jefferson. You never have. It feels good to be useful. I rode often when Paulo and my parents were alive."

"But, as the wife of a wealthy man only for pleasure," he finished for her. "Rarely grueling work like this."

"No." The Lady had come to snuffle at her shoulder. Marissa stroked the mare and sighed a contented sigh. "Rarely like this. Of course there were occasions when I got away to the *estancia.* Beyond prying, watchful eyes, I rode less sedately."

"Especially with Juan."

"With Juan I could be myself. Rissa, as he has called me since my fifth birthday." Her hands clenched one over the other in painful remembrance. "My mother's illness had just been diagnosed. My father was wrapped up in her and in his business problems. I was always in the way. An energetic child who was too much for an ailing mother and a busy father.

"My father decided to channel the energy into a new passion. Horses was the obvious solution. Juan was young, but the best rider on the *estancia.* I was given into his care on that day."

"Not a bad choice." Jefferson had never met the Alexandres and he could never forgive them for bartering their daughter for wealth and security for themselves. But in their self-absorption, they'd given her a lifelong gift in Juan.

"Even with Juan's help, I wasn't the perfect daughter my parents needed," Marissa continued her reminiscence. "In my waywardness, I was a burden. But never for Juan. He expected no more or no less of me than that I be who I really was. He knew me as well as I knew myself, and understood me better than anyone else."

Her head turned, her eyes lifted to Jefferson's, seeing again the man who was everything she ever wanted. Everything she'd been denied. There was an ache in her voice for things lost as she whispered softly, "Better than anyone, except you."

Jefferson didn't move, he didn't respond. Though it took every iota of his willpower, he didn't reach for her. He didn't draw her into his arms, shushing her, soothing her anguish as he would have with any other hurting creature. But this was Marissa. As painful as her revelation must be, as painful as it was for him to let her endure this, it needed to be said.

When it was done, from the exorcism of guilt and pain would come healing. In silence that was agony, he waited.

The Lady butted Marissa's shoulder again. With leather-clad fingers moving in slow strokes over the horse's nose, she began again. "When I returned to Argentina to marry Paulo, no one but Juan understood that I needed to stay busy. Like the blind seeking light, or the renegade seeking peace, I needed drudgery. Grinding, grueling labor that punished my body and numbed my mind. He understood that only then could I find an ease for grief that wouldn't go away."

"Were you grieving for us, Marissa?" Jefferson's own gloved hands were fisted to keep them at his side. She was a strong woman, her troubles were her own to bear. Troubles she'd hidden from the world and him. Their last day in the swamp had been the first crack in the dam of hidden emotions. Today was the second rift in that wall.

A small leak in the dam she could deal with. A leak and a stiffened spine were an equal match. Comfort and tenderness could be her undoing. A deluge, with one pent-up emotion tumbling over another, and another, could be too much. Too much, too soon.

Going against every ingrained instinct, but certain he was

right, Jefferson held himself apart. But not aloof. He could never be aloof where Marissa was concerned.

Black Jack whinnied, calling to the horses in the pasture. Drawn to the stallion, The Lady trotted away. Marissa's hand drifted to the splintered railing. As she clutched it, leather served as protection against stabbing splinters of wood.

The land was quiet. Only the stream, cleaving the lull as it cleaved the canyon, raced along its banks, babbling in whispers, catching light in ripples as it went. The canyon would be a canyon without water. But what it brought to the land made it a better place. As loving Jefferson made her a stronger woman. One who could do what she must, for all but herself.

The thought surprised her. She'd never seen her life in that light before. She'd seen only her own shortcomings. Condemned no one but herself for emotions she couldn't control.

"I grieved for both of us. For what we discovered too late and could never have. Then, there was guilt." Turning, with her back to the fence, her body nearly touching his, she looked up at him. Her eyes, normally unfathomable darkness, were spangled with light as they studied the lines of his face. "I spent years wallowing in guilt because I couldn't love Paulo. A good man, a man of old values, guided by old standards. Who with my parents, counted on Marissa Alexandre being the dutiful daughter as they denied her the most important choice a young woman can make. The man she would love and spend her life with.

"You asked me to stay." Tears threatened and were denied. "Like a fool, I didn't."

"Never a fool, sweetheart." Jefferson couldn't let her assume another burden. "You were what you were expected to be. Your father was desperate." He didn't know how desperate a father must be to do what Alexandre had done to Marissa. But it was too late to judge. "You made the choice any caring daughter would make, bearing the brunt of your father's mistaken business ventures and their need to sustain a lifestyle."

The perfect daughter. She'd used the words herself. Subconsciously condemning her shortcomings. What only *she* considered failures. This, Jefferson thought, explained decisions she'd made in the past, and the unwarranted blame.

"You weren't perfect, Marissa. But out of love you made selfless choices. Adams made the same sort of choices and bore the same sort of consequences for me."

Marissa wouldn't look at him. Instead, she stared down at the ground. Freed from its binding ribbon, the fall of her dark hair tumbled over her shoulder, veiling her face. He knew she was wrestling with the sense of what he was saying.

Sliding off his gloves, letting them drop where they would, Jefferson risked a touch. With a bare finger at her chin, he lifted her face to his. "In an act of love, you married a man you didn't love. In another act of love, Adams took the blame for a blow I struck in a brawl I instigated. You both went to a prison of sorts, for someone you care for."

"Marriage to Paulo wasn't a prison, Jefferson." She wouldn't paint the marriage black to excuse herself.

"No?" His finger moved from her chin, skimming the line of her jaw to the sensitive spot at the corner of her mouth. At the slow caress, she shivered, but didn't speak or move away. Years had passed since he'd discovered the wonderful response. But a hundred more could pass before he forgot. "I suspect that if the two of you compared notes, you would find strong similarities. In some ways, Adams's prison offered more freedom."

"Don't make me a martyr. I never suffered in my marriage."

"Perhaps not. But can you deny you were the sacrificial lamb on the altar of riches?"

She was silent. How could one argue with the truth?

Jefferson's knuckles moved over her lower lip, then her chin and the line her throat. Unfurling his fist, he stroked the base, measuring the rush of her heart in the tiny hollow. His voice was deeper when he spoke again. "Adams was deprived of his freedom, and I can never forgive myself for the years my senseless act of bravado and vengeance took from him. But even prison didn't take from Adams what marriage took from you."

Marissa understood, then, what she hadn't thought to consider before. Jefferson was speaking of her body. Of the mating of a husband and wife as expected within marriage. But her marriage to Paulo Rei was never based on normal expectations.

For that she was grateful to Paulo. No matter what else he wanted of her, none of it had been physical. In this bargain, he had been kinder and more generous than she'd expected.

Such a man deserved to be mourned by a celibate wife.

But Jefferson had been kind as well. He deserved the truth. Moving a little, only enough to break physical contact, she admitted what she'd once thought she would never speak of to anyone. "My marriage to Paulo wasn't that sort of arrangement. We were…" With the halting of a confession that would be shocking, she searched for the right words to make this easier. But, she discovered there were no such words. No easy way.

She had never lied to Jefferson. At the same time, she hadn't been as honest as she should have been. It was time he knew the truth. All of it. When her lashes lifted and her eyes sought his, he saw more pain than he'd ever seen before. "Paulo and I were never intimate. Our marriage was never consummated."

Nothing she could have said would have shocked him more. No man in his right mind who was married to a woman like Marissa would be content in a platonic relationship. "That's impossible."

With a shudder, he bit back his doubt. Marissa wouldn't lie about this. Which meant she wouldn't have lied to Paulo Rei either. "You told him about us, and the day in the swamp."

"Yes." She wouldn't equivocate about something as important as what she must tell Jefferson. "All he asked was who my lover had been. Then he confessed that during the time I had spent in Belle Terre, a medical condition caused him to be impotent. There couldn't be the sort of union and the children he'd planned, but he still wanted the marriage. With no recriminations, no demands and only one restriction—that there be no other lovers.

"The greatest surprise of all was that he offered to release me from the agreement completely and he would forgive my father's debt anyway." A shoulder lifted in regret. "But there was the matter of the questions and gossip. Perhaps a scandal I didn't want my mother to face. Then, there was my father's honor."

"Damn his honor!" Jefferson snarled. "What honor is there in any of this? Except yours, when you kept the agreement?"

Marissa's gaze held his, in her pale face, her eyes were bleak. "Haven't you done exactly the same sort of thing for your own father, Jefferson? Haven't you made costly sacrifices in pride and peace of mind for Gus Cade? Don't most children at some time in their lives? Tell me which of your brothers has not."

His anger died on his lips. How could he fault such courage and wisdom? He wouldn't spoil the time they had, brooding about time lost. "You're right. We won't speak of it again."

"Perhaps we should," Marissa began.

Though he wanted to hear the rest of what she had to say more than anything, with a finger at her lips, he stopped the revelation. "Listen. Someone has gotten past the guards."

With that warning, neither moved. In the dusty corral, with only the shuffle of restless horses breaking the quiet, Marissa strained to hear what Jefferson heard. At first, there were only the noises of the ranch. Then she could distinguish the sound of a car or a truck, negotiating the precarious incline into the canyon. Someone who was driving recklessly.

It was the scrape of metal against rock that captured Jefferson's reluctant attention. Reluctant only for that frozen instant. With a second scrape, he was galvanized into action. "Marissa, I want you to go to the barn."

"No." She had no intention of running for cover, leaving him to face whoever and whatever this was alone.

"I'll be fine." He'd caught a glimpse of the vehicle. "I recognize the car. It belongs to a friend. A very close friend, one I trust. But there's no need in taking a chance she's not alone." He turned her toward the barn. "You've only a minute and one more turn before we're visible from the road. Hurry."

Marissa hurried. Jefferson scaled the fence, and went to wait for Cristal Lane in front of the house.

"Hello, handsome." As Jefferson closed the door of Cristal's convertible, she rose on tiptoe to kiss his cheek.

"Hello, yourself, Miss Cristal." With a concerned check of her tires, he leaned against a glossy red fender a layer of dust couldn't dim. "What brings you so far from Silverton?"

"You make it sound as if it's been a long time since I came by to visit." A long red nail traced down his throat to his chest. "When I was here just…" Eyes as green as new, sweet grass laughed up at him. "Well, I was here sometime not so long ago."

"Three months ago," Jefferson supplied. "You were worried because I hadn't been into town in a while. Instead of celebrating your third twenty-ninth birthday with patrons of the saloon, you drove this wicked machine across Benedict land bringing your celebration to me. To find out how I was."

"Oh," Cristal said. "Can't a disreputable saloon keeper spend her own holiday with a friend without ulterior motives?"

"Yes, she can," Jefferson agreed reasonably. "But she shouldn't. Not when there are better opportunities in town."

Slender shoulders moved in an elegant shrug. A coil of windblown auburn hair fell over her cheek. "Maybe I'm not looking for opportunities. If I were, name me one in Silverton."

Jefferson raised an incredulous brow. He could name a half dozen or more. And one in particular, who didn't know yet quite what to think of this supposedly shady lady whose heart was pure, bigger than the world, and twice as tender. "So," he said, "I take it you were worried again."

"Okay." Color flooded Cristal's tawny cheeks, turning green eyes greener. Exasperated that she was so transparent, she threw up her hands. "You got me, handsome. Billy said you'd been home for a visit. I wondered how it went."

"How would you expect it to go?" Billy had done his work well. The surprise was that he'd chosen Cristal, the one person in Silverton least likely to gossip. Especially about Jefferson Cade. "Or did Billy tell you that, too."

"Okay, so Billy Blackhawk didn't tell me anything." Cristal came to lean against the car beside him. "The truth is the great Apache hardly acknowledges me with more than a scowl. You'd think I was the prerequisite fallen woman and he the dedicated sheriff waiting for a reason to run me out of town.''

Jefferson chuckled and ruffled her tousled, auburn mane even more. As the chuckle grew into a laugh, he threw an arm around her shoulders and dropped a kiss on the top of her head. ''Last time I looked Billy was only half Apache and he *was* sheriff of Silverton. I don't think either's due to change anytime soon.''

''Half Apache by blood. All Apache in mind-set. He's hated me since I came to town. Stubborn, too gorgeous for his own good...'' Cristal searched for proper castigation. When it escaped her, she sighed. ''... bullheaded, gorgeous *creature.*''

Jefferson laughed. ''When are you two going to decide what you're going to be when you grow up?''

''Decide?'' Cristal scowled at her favorite friend. ''What's to decide? We hate each other. It's in the genes. The age old clash of the stalwart lawman and the bawdy lady.''

''You're repeating yourself. Same song, second verse.'' He stroked her hair, taming it. ''If you and Billy hate each other, I hope someone hates me as much some day.'' The comment was tongue-in-cheek and utterly serious. ''Not Billy, of course.''

An elbow in his ribs took his breath away. Cristal muttered, ''That was a dumb thing to say.''

''Which part,'' he asked when he could speak again.

''All of it.'' With an exasperated gesture, Cristal raked a hand through her hair, undoing Jefferson's taming.

''Ah. You're that sure, are you?''

''As sure as my name is...well, what it is.''

Jefferson chuckled then. ''Tell me that when you two finally decide if you're going to be friends, foes, or lovers.''

''That's a no brainer. I just finished saying our magnificent Blackhawk has absolutely no use for me. Or I for him.''

"Perhaps the gentleman protests too much. And the lady.''

Cristal stared at him. "You've gotta be kidding." Another look turned into a frown. "You're not kidding.''

Recognizing a lost cause, Jefferson shifted subjects. "What I'm doing is wondering what really brought you here.''

"Belle Terre, like I said. Jasper and Billy were talking in the post office about your trip. I eavesdropped.''

"Ah." If Billy wanted word of his supposed trip to Belle Terre to filter through the territory, Jasper Hill, veteran postmaster, inveterate gossip, was the one to do it. "I suppose Jasper decided that's why my mail was accumulating.''

"Actually, he was wondering why your brother, Adams, would be writing you here while you were visiting him there.''

"If Jasper's reading postmarks, he needs more to do.''

"Billy told Jasper he would bring the mail out later this evening. After Billy left, I decided it was time I took an afternoon and evening off to visit my favorite lowlander. So, here I am, Silverton's newest mail deliverer. Or something.''

"So now you've seen I'm in one piece and healthy and you're still lingering. Something else on your mind, Cristal?''

"I'm waiting to be introduced to your lady friend.''

"My what?''

"Your lady friend. The tall brunette who dashed to the barn as I came down the grade. You might also explain the good-looking cowhand patrolling the road by the rim of the canyon. I know all Sandy's men, remember. Almost as well as Sandy.''

"With your hell-for-leather driving, I'm surprised you see anything but dust." He was stalling. Cristal was too sharp and he didn't know how to explain. He chose diversion, while he gathered his thoughts. "How did you get past the new cowhand? Why would you think he's patrolling the canyon rim?"

Cristal's green gaze flashed to Jefferson's, seeking answers in their shuttered depths. "Why else would he stop me, asking what business I had on Benedict range, or the Broken Spur?"

"So, you showed him the mail, claiming to be the carrier."

"Well, yes." Her shoulders lifted again in a "what else could I do?" sort of twitch. "Isn't that what I am, today?"

"Today and the only day," Jefferson observed dryly. "But I see it worked. He let you pass."

"Well," Cristal drawled, hedging more than a little.

"Let me guess, Ethan didn't let you pass."

"Ah, so that was Ethan." Her face brightened. "I'd seen him in town, always going or coming from Billy's office. But then, cowhands are always in and out of there, resolving one problem or another. I didn't know until today that he worked for the Rafter B. I must say the name fits. He certainly looks like an Ethan, all stern and broody. And when he gets here, I suppose, angry."

"In other words, with the accelerator on the floor, you left Ethan in the dust." Jefferson wanted to shake her for being so foolhardy. "You could've been shot."

Cristal's laugh was low and husky. "No one shoots the local bawdy lady, especially when she offers to share the cookies she's brought to a friend."

For the second time in less than a very few minutes, the sound of an engine rent the usual peace of the canyon. "Ah, that's surely Ethan, now." She was smiling in anticipation of a good row with a handsome, dangerous man. "He must've had a vehicle stashed somewhere out of sight. Quicker than a horse, no doubt.

"Why don't you run along to the barn and fetch your guest. Then when Ethan finally makes it down the incline, we can have lemonade and cookies while you both explain."

Jefferson was moving away from Cristal's car, ready to greet another visitor. When he recognized the truck that traveled only a little more carefully than she had, he laughed, though grimly. "I hate to tell you this, Miss Cristal, but I think you're the one who has some explaining to do."

"For visiting an old friend? For bringing cookies? Surely Ethan will understand. Or he will when he takes his first bite." Cristal had come to join Jefferson in the dirt track that served as the road. Now she stopped short as she recognized the truck.

"Oh dear," she muttered. "I don't believe that's Ethan."

"Somehow, I don't either. Not with a star on the door."

"Oh dear," Cristal had time to say again before the truck skidded to a halt. Dust was still billowing like smoke around them, when the door opened, then slammed shut, and a dark-haired, grim-faced golden-eyed giant bore down on them.

"'Oh dear' is right, sweet Cristal." Sarcasm dripped from Billy Blackhawk's greeting. If it could be called a greeting. Stopping before her, with barely a glance or a nod for Jefferson, massive hands fisted on his hips he glared down at her. "Well?"

Billy was known as a man of monumental patience. A man who never seemed to hurry, even when he did. Part Apache and all stoic, he rarely revealed either anger or frustration. Today was obviously an exception. In the rare times he flashed his attractive, but genuine smile, his teeth gleamed in contrast to his naturally dark skin. The dimples that smile revealed were intriguing, at odds with his magnificent, rough-hewn features.

As he stood toe-to-toe with her there was no monumental patience, or any patience at all. There was no smile, no dimples. If he was forever stoic, forever didn't include this day.

Offering her best smile in place of his, one that brought most men to their knees, Cristal looked up and up. From the button in the center of his shirt, to broad shoulders and a stubborn chin, to dark eyes blazing gold fire. What she saw in that beautiful glare made her smile wobble. Obviously Billy Blackhawk wasn't most men. With a touch of bravado and her own hands resting at her own hips, she drawled, "Well, what, Blackhawk?"

"Why the hell are you here?" Billy never cursed. Never.

Jefferson's brows shot up, but he stayed neutral and out of the fray. From where he stood, despite the disparity in size, they were evenly matched opponents.

"You don't curse, Billy, so stop. Gentlemen don't curse a lady. Anyway, it won't intimidate me." As if she would match him in stubbornness if not size, Cristal scowled at the sheriff.

"I didn't think it would. And I do curse when I'm as angry as I am now. Lady or not." Billy's broad hand swept up, powerful fingers threaded through her hair, gathering it at her nape. What could have been a brutal jerk, was a gentle tilt of her head. Golden eyes boring in the depths of her green gaze, his tone turned deadly calm. "I asked what you're doing here, Miss Lane."

"A minute ago, I was Cristal."

"Yeah, well, that was a minute ago. I'm calmer now."

"This is calm?"

"I said calmer. Which, for the moment, means I've decided not to break your beautiful neck."

"In that case may I suggest we all go inside out of the hot sun?" Marissa had come to stand by Jefferson. "Then we can explain some things and make some decisions."

Billy ceased glaring at his nemesis and faced Marissa. His hat was suddenly in his hand, as it hadn't been before. His demeanor was calm, on the surface. "If you're worried this was a grave breach of security, Marissa, don't be."

He directed their attention to the rim of the canyon where Ethan sat, rifle at the ready. Spaced along the only entrance to the canyon, were two more riders. Each with weapons as ready. "By my order, any unidentified intruder who doesn't halt on command, will be fired on.

"One of those riders is a crack-shot called out of retirement. She can shoot an earring from your ear, never drawing blood. Unless she wants to." Rounding on Cristal, the only one who wore earrings, Billy's calm tone vanished. "As for you? You're damned lucky Ethan had seen you in town and recognized you."

Not to be outdone, Cristal tilted her head to meet his gaze. "Is that why you're angry, Blackhawk?" she asked thoughtfully. "Were you afraid I might be shot by mistake?"

"Yes," he growled and took her arm, leading her less than gently to the house. "But only because it would deny me the pleasure of wringing your neck."

"Why, Blackhawk, I didn't know you cared."

"Don't flatter yourself, Cristal Lane."

"Don't worry. I won't."

Following behind them, Jefferson twined his fingers through Marissa's. "Sounds like love."

Marissa's heart was in her eyes. "I hope so. Someday."

"Count on it," he murmured and squeezed her hand.

Seven

No one ate cookies.

With tension and easing tempers still ragged, no one remembered he or she was thirsty. The interior of the house was cooler. If only by a little, at least there was that. With that degree of physical comfort, in this taut moment, Marissa remembered her surprise when she discovered the difference the sliver of shade cast by the near canyon wall could mean.

Once the house had been a cabin, its single room serving as kitchen, living space, and sleeping quarters. With the Cody's addition of a bedroom wing and a second floor, its functions changed. Though still the heart of the house, serving two purposes rather than three should have made it seem more spacious. But in the charged atmosphere, Marissa felt the walls closing in on her.

She suspected the others felt the same. Cristal Lane had taken a chair by the fireplace. Billy Blackhawk stood like sculpted stone, his back to the mantel, Cristal at his right. The kitchen table where Marissa sat by Jefferson, on his left.

The shadow of the vermilion bluff had crept farther across the canyon floor, enveloping the cabin in an ever deepening cocoon of dusk. No one thought to turn on a lamp. No one cared. In dusky light, Marissa considered the woman across the room. A woman Jefferson had teased as she'd rarely known him to tease.

It was good to hear the lighthearted exchange. But when he'd drawn the red-haired beauty into his arms and kissed the top of her head, envy, even jealousy, had pierced the watcher's heart.

She'd scolded herself for being a fool and not realizing that in four years Jefferson would have special friends. Even lovers. Then the sheriff had arrived, and she'd seen how it was between Cristal Lane and Billy Blackhawk.

She felt it now, an almost tangible part of all that charged the air. A cataclysmic emotion that couldn't remain static, and one day must spill over into hatred or love.

Marissa let her gaze dwell on Cristal who sat so rigid on the sofa, tangled in things she didn't understand. Then, in somber, uneasy silence, drawing her gaze from the vibrant woman only a little older than she, she turned her attention to the sheriff. Dour, stern, he bore little resemblance to the Billy Blackhawk who had come to Simon's valley.

His grim mood was due as much to the fact that it was Cristal who had been involved in today's events as the distress her rash act had caused. Anyone entering the canyon as she had would cause concern. But in this case, there was an extraordinary animosity.

They were like magnets. Billy and Cristal, repelling each other in personal friction, in turmoil. But turned on the right track, they would be drawn to each other, more powerfully than now. Too powerful to resist. Then they would build the enduring bond of strong people. And...lovers?

Unconsciously Marissa sighed and, resting her hands on the table, wound them restlessly over each other. Without word or sound, as naturally as if he'd been doing it forever, Jefferson laid his hand over hers, folding them into his clasp. Turning to meet his gaze, she was warmed by his tender support.

Their relationship in Belle Terre had begun gradually, building from common interests into friendship. Then into love. A voiceless love that deepened into a strength as quiet. It was, in contrast, as gentle as Cristal and Billy's was explosive.

But Marissa knew that if she could get past the doubt that scored her soul, this impasse would resolve itself. When she believed again in what her heart told her, she and Jefferson would find their way as lovers. Then, unencumbered by doubt and grief, the embers of their passion would be incandescent.

Engulfed with the meteoric heat of desire for that day, she turned her hand within his grasp and struggled to find her way to peace, and to him. Fitting her palm to his, slowly her fingers curled, keeping Jefferson the little while she could. Her clasp was desperate, wanting. In a glance she found his gaze riveted on their joined hands. As if he felt the touch of her searching look, his arresting blue regard lifted to her face and to her eyes. When Marissa thought she would lose herself in their brilliant blue, he caught a long trembling breath. A smile, slow and beguiling, shone in their mesmerizing depths.

And her eyes burned with tears for the lost years.

"I suppose there's no help for this."

The words rang in her mind. No help at all, Marissa agreed. Then she gave her attention to Billy Blackhawk, who had spoken the prophetic words.

"It's done and nothing can change what's happened." Billy reiterated a totally different thought. His narrowed eyes flicked from one person to the next, his frown grave. "Cristal has discovered Marissa's here. An unfortunate happenstance, leaving us to make the best of it we can. If you're in agreement, Marissa and Jefferson, it might help her to understand the urgent need for secrecy if she knows why."

"Which brings up another problem." Jefferson's concern was evident to Marissa in the unconscious pressure of his hand over hers. "Every person who knows the circumstances behind Marissa's being at the Broken Spur adds to the danger. Knowledge in this case could be life-threatening. It would be simpler if we asked Cristal for her silence and her word that she won't speak of today. The less she's involved, the safer for all of us."

"Exactly, Jefferson, if Cristal is satisfied with that. If she will promise us her cooperation," Billy agreed. In contrast to his agitated behavior by the corral and his anger with Cristal, he was totally in control. He didn't tug at the cuffs of the perfectly pressed shirt of his immaculate uniform. He didn't rake a turbulent hand through his burnished hair—black as night and drawn back from his forehead to be controlled at his nape by a leather thong. Much as Jefferson had worn his years ago.

Marissa realized Billy Blackhawk wasn't a man given to excessive displays of emotion or wasted motion—except in face-to-face conflict with Cristal Lane. When addressing the threat of danger, he became the consummate professional, cooler and calmer and grimmer with each second.

She hated the subterfuge, the emotional tumult she'd brought into the lives of all she touched. Now the circle was growing.

Lingering tears welled in her eyes, clung to her lashes. She willed them away and refused to look at Jefferson as she felt the weight of his concern. She had to speak, to tell them this couldn't be. That she couldn't allow the risk they were taking.

"Don't, Jefferson. Don't, Billy. I can't do this anymore. Too much has happened, too many people have been hurt or killed because of me. I didn't realize the scope of this, or the effect it might have on any who were involved."

Pausing, she slid her gaze from Billy to Cristal to Jefferson. "I want it to stop, here and now." She'd taken her hand away from Jefferson's. Free, lost without his strength, but determined, her joined fingers clenched in her lap. "At first light tomorrow, I'll leave. Then no one else will be hurt."

Jefferson had sensed this building since she'd stood with him listening to the sound of Cristal's car barreling down the incline. He knew how it felt to be responsible for drawing innocent people into danger. He was well acquainted with the helplessness of watching matters spiral out of control. He understood heartache, and self-inflicted bitterness.

He knew the hurt. He felt it now, in empathy for Marissa, the only woman he'd ever loved. The only woman he could love. Heart aching, he fought a battle with himself, even then he barely resisted reaching out for her. To comfort her, to remind her none of this was her doing. Instead, keeping a careful distance, he asked, "Where would you go, Marissa? What would you do?

"For the love of God, sweetheart, tell me how I live with myself if I let you face something that isn't your fault alone?"

"You can live with yourself, Jefferson, because it has nothing to do with you. You wouldn't have been a part of this if I hadn't—" Marissa's voice broke. The downward sweep of her lashes to hide her emotions revealed how she hated the weakness.

"I wouldn't have been a part of this if you hadn't called

in a promise made long ago on a rare day in the lowcountry,'' Jefferson finished for her. ''But you're wrong, my love.''

''You wouldn't, if I hadn't been weak.'' Cristal and Billy ceased to exist for her. There was only Jefferson, and she must make him understand she had to go. ''You're a man who keeps promises. No one knows that better than I. If I hadn't—''

''If,'' he interrupted softly. ''The world and life are full of questions. We can always second-guess ourselves with that damning word. If I hadn't made the promise. If I hadn't loved you. If your father hadn't sent you to Belle Terre and Eden. If he hadn't given you into Juan's care long before that. If Juan hadn't taught you to ride like a gaucho.

''If your father hadn't promised you to Paulo Rei, none of this would have happened. That's the most damning of all.''

Jefferson dared to take her hands, to open her whitened fingers and lace his own through them. As he continued his hushed monologue there was no one else in the room for either of them now. ''How many of that list could you have changed?''

''One.'' Her answer was a whispered breath. ''The one that mattered. The one that drew you into this, Jefferson.''

She looked across the room made welcoming and comfortable by another woman who had to choose between her father and the man she loved. In greater wisdom Savannah Benedict had chosen love over duty. Wisdom a young Marissa hadn't learned.

Marissa's gaze settled on Billy, the giant of a man whose eyes were as black as his hair. Eyes that watched her as he listened, the scowl he had turned on Cristal replaced by a neutral expression. She knew he would never regret helping her, but she regretted the need. ''If I hadn't reached out to you, Jefferson, your life wouldn't be in turmoil. Cristal wouldn't be in danger. Billy wouldn't be worrying over me, over you, over Cristal.

"If I leave, she won't have to be told any more. She can return to Silverton and go on with her life like this day never happened. She'll be safe. All of you will be safe."

"As Jefferson asked, where would you go, little one?" Billy spoke at last. As tall as Marissa was, the name would have been absurd coming from anyone but him. "How will you hide yourself from this man who has informants everywhere?"

"Everywhere, Billy?" she mocked, but her voice was soft.

"Money talks. Even as he hungers for more, the man in question has plenty." Billy still hadn't moved, he hardly seemed to blink an eye. He could stand for hours and not move, not blink. He had. As part of a ritual of his father's people. "What he wants, he takes. What he can't have—" Pausing, as the hard look left his face, he emphasized softly, "What he can't have, he destroys."

Marissa remembered Menendez's sly advances, touches bordering on insult, yet not quite. She remembered the final, lurid proposition. A sickening ultimatum. Menendez was a monster.

"A destroyer." She didn't realize she'd spoken out loud until she found Jefferson and Billy, and Cristal waiting.

"When he couldn't buy Paulo, his business, or his wife—" her lips curled in contempt "—Menendez destroyed him and, he believes, the little toy he lusted after.

"He *believes*." Marissa faced Jefferson. "That's my protection. As long as he's sure he succeeded in silencing us, he won't look for me. No matter his far-reaching influence, no matter his fortune, what he isn't looking for, he can't find."

"And if the plane is found?" Billy asked.

"It won't be." There was still grief in her voice as she assured the sheriff. "It went into the sea."

"Maybe." Billy's gaze held hers. In the first of twilight, his Native American ancestry even more apparent. "That was speculation. It doesn't mean the plane won't be discovered somewhere, someday. By someone."

"Then I'll deal with that when it happens."

"Wherever you are, Marissa?" It was Jefferson who asked. Jefferson who wouldn't keep her from leaving if she insisted. But she wouldn't go alone.

"I'm sure Simon can suggest a reasonably safe place. If not, I can find one myself."

Jefferson didn't ask if she would consider Simon's valley. That question had been irrevocably resolved weeks ago. The questions he asked were much more discouraging. "How will you live, Marissa? What will you do to keep body and soul together? I know you have money of your own. But the first penny you touch, Menendez will know you're alive."

"He'll find you," Billy added, going for the jugular with the truth. "The first indication that someone who has denied him and who poses the greatest threat to his grand plan still walks the earth, the search will begin. He won't stop until he can control you. Or when one of you is dead."

His black eyes holding Marissa's, compelling her to listen, to think, to believe, Billy's voice was grave and very soft when he murmured, "There are some things worse than dying, Marissa. Vicente Menendez is a master at inventing ways to make you wish you had been on that plane."

Fighting back a shudder and tearing her gaze from Billy's, Marissa stared down at the cherry tabletop. "I know what you're trying to do. I know why. Don't think I don't appreciate that you care, Billy. But it changes nothing.

"I have to go." Her head came up, her gaze touched on each of them. Cristal, vibrant and so very alive, but thoughtful and quiet. Billy, grim, concerned, a man of wonderful contrasts.

And Jefferson. Dear Jefferson, more rugged, older and harder now, but still the Prince Charming she'd found in the lowcountry. Her prince, her lover, her only love. She would do what she must to keep him safe. "When I go, foolhardy or wise, I'll have to take whatever consequences come my way. And whatever chances."

"You would risk your life, your freedom, or both for those you care about." It wasn't a question. And for once, Billy's stoicism deserted him.

Marissa didn't respond. Now it was her gaze that held Billy's captive. "Wouldn't you?" She didn't need an answer. He couldn't know she'd read his answer in his eyes when he looked at Cristal. "It seems only fair, doesn't it?"

"When you all get through deciding what's best for everyone, including me, do I get a say in this?" Cristal's serene comment was soothing music in taut silence.

As if with the power of a look he could compel her to understand, Billy didn't look away from Marissa. His voice was a low, impatient growl. "Be quiet, Cristal."

"I will not. I've been quiet long enough. Too long." Before he could rebuke her, she was on her feet, standing before him. Challenging him as if he didn't tower over her. As if one controlling clasp of his huge hands couldn't send her reeling back to her seat. If he should dare. But everyone in the room knew he wouldn't, especially Cristal.

"Why should I be quiet, Blackhawk?" she challenged though her tone was the calm contralto of before. "Tell me why, if you can, when it was my blundering that caused all this."

"Perhaps because two blunders don't make a right," the sheriff suggested.

"Oh, good grief." Cristal groaned. "Don't tell me you've added speaking in fractured clichés to Apache, and an oh-so-perfect English. Perfect for being perfected at Oxford, no less."

As she dropped that little-known bombshell on him, she moved closer, but only to stand before the mantel. Her eyes lifted to the bare wall where Jefferson's painting of a young and beautiful woman had hung when she last visited. The occasion of her third twenty-ninth birthday, as he had reminded her in a lack of gallantry he committed only when he teased.

Cristal realized now the portrait she had admired was a painting of a very young and beautiful Marissa Rei. Except she'd been Marissa Alexandre then. When questioned about the painting and the model, Jefferson said little but that if the painting was beautiful it was because the woman was beautiful. He'd spoken no more of his model except to say she was once a dear friend.

"Very dear." Cristal interpreted the remembrance. But she had suspected even then that the young woman in the painting was far more than a friend, more than dear. Perhaps the woman who had taken his heart when she chose to leave him.

But now the portrait was nowhere in sight, and the woman, who was more than a friend, was back in Jefferson's life. If anyone deserved a second chance, it was this strong but gentle man who would likely love but once.

Turning on the heel of a stylish boot, Cristal stood with her feet apart, bracing for a battle. In a shaft of light falling through a window, she was elegance in black leather pants, black vest, and a russet blouse that made her look as if she belonged on the fashion runway, not in a saloon in Silverton.

Unmindful of the picture she made or that she took a reluctant Goliath's breath away, she regarded each member of her captive audience. When it seemed she wouldn't speak, she broke the unsettling silence. "For once in his life, our illustrious sheriff is right about me. I did blunder into this. I thought I was visiting a friend. The last thing I expected in our quiet cattle country was to walk into the midst of clandestine affairs. The last thing I wanted was to make life difficult for anyone.

"I don't know what this is about. But not knowing doesn't keep me from caring what happens to the people involved."

She cast a look at Billy Blackhawk, green gaze met black and lingered. Cristal was first to look away, but only because she had something that very much needed saying. "I can deduce enough to know that Jefferson and Marissa have a history. Perhaps there was an affair."

She was skirting too closely to personal matters. Billy made a sound and a move as if he would stop her. Cristal ignored him. "But I really think not. Or else neither of you would have allowed the years of separation. I can't know what happened in the interim, except that Marissa lost her husband and her parents. For that, I'm truly sorry. I know, too, that she's in trouble. Trouble that brought Jefferson rushing to the rescue, with Billy not far behind. I know someone called Menendez is involved, and that he's a rich and vicious man.

"Beyond that, I know very little. But I can tell you this, Billy and Jefferson, you both underestimate Marissa." An open palm held up toward Billy stopped the comment he wasn't going to make. "You act as if she's fragile. Grieving? Yes. Carrying unwarranted guilt? I imagine so. But fragile? Never."

Saving the most important for last, Cristal faced Marissa squarely. Her hair was dark fire and her features contoured by pale light and darkness as the day grew older. As she accused, her voice lost its scolding tone. "As for you, young lady."

Marissa waited, silently. Though they'd barely been introduced, and then not officially, an instant bond of respect had leapt between the two women, like the rare meeting of different yet kindred souls. A frisson of jealousy had become respect and she very much wanted to hear what this woman who knew the land and these men far better than she had to say.

Seeing how intently the younger woman watched her, how quietly she waited, Cristal realized that what she said could be the resolving factor. Perhaps her judgment could be the catalyst that decided whether this fugitive from tragedy and menace left the canyon, or if she stayed. If she listened and if she cared half as much as Cristal suspected, Marissa would never leave Jefferson again. "You misjudge us. Billy. Me. Especially Jefferson. Whatever danger you might have brought to the canyon, it would never be more than these men, or even I can handle.

"Maybe neither of us has been through what you have. But we've each had our own losses and our own troubles. Our own trial by fire. We lived through it, we survived. And in the end we became stronger people. So will you, Marissa."

"How can you know that, Cristal? On less than an hour's acquaintance, how can you say what I will be?" Marissa had studied this rare woman, and she'd listened. She speculated that there was the wisdom of misfortune in her words.

"I know you, because I know Jefferson. I know because I know the kind of woman he would be drawn to. The sort it would take to turn him into a brooding loner. Half the single female population of Silverton is in heat for him. Some not so single. None subtly. Yet in four years, he's never been tempted.

"He wouldn't become involved simply for the sake of his masculine or even sexual gratification. And he isn't the sort to settle for a second-best love. He couldn't. He's waited four years for you. And if you think Jefferson Cade could let the woman he loves walk out of his life a second time for any reason but that she doesn't love him in return, lady, you don't know your man.

"Here in the canyon you both have security and the protection of those three riders Billy pointed out to us. And you have Billy, himself. If you leave the Broken Spur, Jefferson will leave with you. He'll go wherever you go, Marissa. Into any danger. I promise you."

Marissa was too stunned by Cristal's blunt assessment to think. She really wanted to look at Jefferson to judge his reaction. But she dared not. Not yet. "I don't want to bring harm to anyone, and I don't want to be a burden."

"Danger is Billy's business and Jefferson won't be lacking when the chips are down. As far as being a burden, or intruding on Billy's time, don't worry. He needs more to do," Cristal asserted. "Then he wouldn't have time to irritate me."

Billy Blackhawk groaned softly, but said nothing. Neither did Jefferson. Cristal was obviously on the right track and neither wanted to interfere.

"As for me," Cristal continued. "I'm stronger than I look. And I'll be all right. Billy might very well like to break my neck himself at times. But he would kill anyone else who tried.

"That's my two cents and change. I can't make up your mind for you. I can't make you stay. But I hope I've given you something to think about. Remember this hasn't been just your loss. It was Jefferson's, too, since the day he lost you. Now that you've found each other, don't waste time grieving over a past not of your making. I hope you'll stay, for Jefferson, and for me."

"For you?" Marissa hadn't expected this.

Cristal laughed. A genuine laugh that lightened the tensions pervading the room. "Hey! I need a friend and an ally. Who wouldn't dealing with these two? Now, I've had my say. I'm out of breath, and I'm heading home. I need to be in Silverton in time to close the saloon."

With a hug for Marissa, a kiss for Jefferson, and a sassy wave for Billy, Cristal was gone. Only seconds after the last of her footsteps sounded on the stairs, the powerful engine of her convertible roared through the canyon.

"Who is she?" Marissa asked as the sound faded. "How did she become so wise?"

"No one knows very much about Cristal." Billy offered the answer. "She arrived in Silverton one day. Liked what she saw and decided to stay. She's a good listener, but she rarely talks much. Today was the most I've heard her say at once in the five years she's been in town. For all any of us know of her past, she might as well have been born the day she arrived in Silverton."

"You've never run a background check?" Jefferson asked, though he knew all he needed to know about Cristal.

"I could," Billy shrugged. "But I won't stoop to invading her privacy without due cause. Despite our conflict, she hasn't given any cause. Now, if you both will excuse me." He reached for his hat, which had rested on the mantel since he entered the house. "I have work to do, and you two have decisions to make. Jefferson, I've a couple of things to discuss, if you'll walk with me to the car."

Sundown had long passed. Ruby cliffs turned to deep purple, then utter black. Long shadows casting puddles of darkness over the canyon had been swallowed by the night. A silver moon rode low in the sky and from the pasture a night bird called.

The supper no one wanted was done and Marissa sat on

the top step of the porch, with only Satan as her companion. The massive Doberman was given to wandering away for small chunks of time, but he always wandered back. Always to Marissa. He seemed to sense when she needed him and when she didn't. Tonight he lay as close as he could get, his head rested on her thigh as he slept.

This should have been a pleasant time, a time of accomplishment for one who had reveled in the long hours in the saddle herding the canyon horses to home pasture. But as she stroked Satan's head, Marissa could think of nothing but what Cristal had said.

"Then, lady, you don't know your man," she whispered the last of the most stunning statements.

"She's right, you know." Jefferson stood at the bottom of the steps, watching her in the moonlight.

After supper, with the untouched food put away and the kitchen in order, while Marissa excused herself to go upstairs to soak her aches, he'd gone to the barn to check the horses close to foaling. For one this would be the first foal and the mare was restless and frightened. Marissa hadn't offered to help for she needed to think. And no one was better at soothing a skittish horse than Jefferson.

"I didn't hear your footsteps." She looked down at him. Now that the sun had gone and he no longer needed the protection of his hat, his head was bare. Though his hair was wet and darkened, streaks of silver still gleamed in moonlight. His shirt was open, his belt unbuckled. She knew then he'd bathed in the creek. The vision of how he would look standing naked in water reflecting a thousand moons sent shards of desire spiraling through her.

Suddenly insecure and uncertain, she said the first thing that came to mind. "You cut your hair."

Jefferson didn't smile at the inane remark. "A long time ago. But so did you."

His face was in shadow as he looked up at her, but she

knew his intense blue eyes were watching every nuance of every expression. "It was easier shorter."

"Yes."

Her hand stopped stroking Satan. Her eyes strained to read what was in his face. But there was nothing she could distinguish. Drawing a long breath, she whispered, "Is it true?"

Jefferson didn't pretend that he didn't understand what she was asking. "It's true."

"You've waited all these years for me?"

His head inclined a bare inch. "Until I heard from you again, I didn't realize I was waiting. But, yes, I have."

"You won't let me walk out of your life a second time?"

"Only when it's safe, and if you don't love me." His hand was on the banister, but he made no move to climb the steps to her.

"In return?" Marissa stared down at the lean shape he projected in the dark. "Cristal said in return."

"I love you, Marissa. I have for longer than you know."

It was simple declaration. And more beautiful for its simplicity. There were tears in her eyes, but this time she didn't blink them away. "Four years is a long time to wait."

"I would wait longer. Forever, if need be."

"If I ask you not to leave the ranch, would you stay?"

"Not if you go."

Clasping her hands at her shoulders, hugging herself, she murmured, "Even if I don't love you?"

"Even then," he admitted, adding softly, "But you do love me, Marissa. I saw it on the plain. I saw it by the lake in Simon's valley. I've seen it here. I'm a part of every breath you take, every beat of your heart. As you are in mine."

Her tears spilled at last, leaving tracks of wonder on her face. "If I stay?" she whispered hoarsely. "What happens then?"

"What do you want, love? Tell me and I'll try my best to make it happen. I'll do whatever it takes to make you happy."

Marissa made a sound that was almost laughter. "You make me happy just by being Jefferson."

That small sound released him from his self-imposed restraints. With agile grace he climbed the steps to sit beside her. Gathering her in his arms, with only the lightest of kisses brushed across her forehead, careful not to go faster and further than she was ready to deal with, he held her. And together they watched the night.

Neither knew how long they sat in the darkness. Neither cared. But after a time, she relaxed, curling into him. Breathing a sigh of longing, she murmured his name. And Jefferson stood, his arm outstretched as he whispered unforgotten words from the past. "Take my hand, sweetheart. If you truly want this. If you truly want me."

Marissa's trembling fingers met Jefferson's strong clasp. Satan whimpered, but slept on as his master swept the woman for whom he'd waited a lifetime into his tender embrace.

Eight

Hands joined, fingers twined with Jefferson's, Marissa walked with him through the house. She wore a long, loose dress of a thousand tiny pleats reaching from shoulders to toes. A gift from Raven that had quickly become a favorite in those evenings she normally spent in her room after a soothing bath.

But tonight, the walls of her room had also seemed to close in on her, driving her from its confines. To the porch, to the night. To Jefferson.

The pressure of his clasp drew her to a halt, spinning her to face him, setting the thousand pleats rippling about her. Catching her free hand, then drawing both to his lips, between small kisses trailed over her knuckles, he whispered, "Did I tell you how beautiful you are tonight?"

"Am I?" Was it vain, she wondered, to want to hear him say the words? To revel in them. Treasure them.

"Since the first day I saw you." Opening her fingers one

by one, he linked them around his neck. Drawing her body
to his, he smiled down at her. "My brothers, Lincoln and
Jackson, and I had come to Eden's Inn. And there you
were, just coming from the garden. Your long hair wild and
tangled from the wind, a basket of flowers in your arms.

"Over what seemed like blossoms of every sort found
in the lowcountry, and of every color, you looked at me
like some enchanted creature. I'd never seen anyone like
you. Or felt for anyone what I felt for you."

"I didn't know. I didn't understand. Not then."

"You weren't supposed to know, sweetheart. I was eight
years older and you had your whole life ahead of you.
Though not the life I expected. But that's the past." Slowly,
with her arms still linked at his nape, and his at her waist,
he began to move in the smooth, gliding steps of a waltz.
"Do you realize that in all those years, we never danced
together? I never held you in my arms, until it was too
late."

"It isn't too late now," she murmured, and leaned her
head against his shoulder, giving herself up to the silent
music guiding his steps. As naturally as if they'd always
danced together, her body matched the tempo of his.

In moonlight falling through a window, bodies close,
hearts keeping time, Jefferson danced with his love to
strains of music only they could hear.

After a time, his steps slowed, his lips traced over the
satin skin of her temples, then her ear. Softly, on a breath,
he asked, "What do you want, sweetheart?"

Her head came up, her eyes met his. "I want you, Jefferson. I want forever. However long forever can be."

"Yes," Jefferson agreed hoarsely. A single word that
said everything. Then he was lifting her into his arms, striding to his bedroom. A single lamp burned by his bed. In
its pool of light he set her on her feet.

When she swayed against him, he made a desperate

sound and bent to kiss her with the hunger of years. His mouth was gentle and demanding, devouring and giving at once. As her lips parted, his kiss deepened. His tongue caressed hers. His hands spanned her waist, urging her closer.

Marissa's fingers glided up the column of his neck, damp strands of his hair threaded through her fingers as she cupped her palms around the back of his head. She wanted to keep his mouth, his kiss, his intimate caress. She couldn't drink deeply enough of him. Or get close enough.

His long, lean body was her bulwark. Her support. Her haven in the storm.

He made her whole.

Curling her fingers, catching fists of his hair, she drew him away. Denying herself what she wanted most, to say what she must. "Jefferson," she whispered as he looked down at her, a look she couldn't fathom on his face. His eyes, catching the little light, held the question he didn't voice.

"I'm sorry." A tremor sounded in her soft words.

She was so close, every nuance of her breathless words seemed to flow over him like a touch. Two words that would set the course of his life. Keeping her in his embrace, he asked gently, "What is it, sweetheart?"

"I'm sorry for the years. For the hurt. I'm sorry for so many things." Bowing her head, she touched her forehead to his shoulder again. As she caught that ever-familiar calming breath, her breasts touching his chest, she shivered, returning her gaze to his. "I'm sorry I didn't have the wisdom and strength of Savannah Cody, or the vision of Cristal Lane."

"And now?" Jefferson's palms skimmed slowly over her ribs, then her back, coming to rest at the curve of her shoulders. His splayed fingers touched her nape, her hair, her throat. His thumbs strayed over the line of her jaw to the corners of her mouth. Her lips, when he traced their shape, were still moist from his kiss. "Are you sorry now? For this?"

Marissa's look moved over his face, touching every feature, seeing the strength, the love. "Only for the lost days, the lost hours, the minutes."

"The seconds," he finished for her as his mouth took hers in another kiss, and another, as with his tender touch he made her forget about sorrow. About grief. "Time doesn't matter tonight. Tomorrow's a new day, a new start, a new life."

"Together," she whispered softly against his throat as she stepped from the circle of his arms. The slender column of her dress swayed as she moved. The ripple of pleats molded her body and danced around her ankles. With a shake of her head her hair tumbled down her back.

Jefferson had only a second to realize that as her breath came in uneven shivers her unfettered breasts strained against the pleats. Then, with the graceful crossing of her arms and the stroke of her palms, the dress was gliding from her shoulders and her arms, baring her body inch by glorious inch.

When the supple garment lay in a forgotten pool at her feet, she didn't speak. She didn't move. Marissa, an entrancing woman. A woman who knew what she wanted, and believed at last there was no guilt in the wanting.

Jefferson's body shook, his chest rose and fell in harsh, uneven rhythms. His eyes never wavering from her, he shrugged from his shirt, kicked aside his boots. As quickly the rest of his clothing followed.

He was fiercely aroused and he wanted her, needed her desperately. But not yet. Despite the heavy throbbing demand, he wanted to claim her first with his eyes and his touch. As a blind man who must see with his fingertips, he traced the line of her brow, the contour of her cheek, lingered long at the pulsing, fragrant hollow of her throat.

Then his quest moved lower, discovering her breasts were a perfect fit for his cupped palms. As he cradled them gently and leaned to taste first one taut nipple, then the other, his gentle suckling was rewarded with her quaking sigh. Her body swayed and the sigh became a low cry as his questing caress trailed over her midriff to her waist. Then down her hips to clasp her buttocks as he had her breasts, drawing her to him, at last.

She was beautiful, as beautiful as in his memory. She was tawny grace and long, lean elegance. A temptress, an awakening wanton. A mystery to unravel again and again. A treasure to hold, to keep, to protect. Forever.

Then she reached for him to work her own sweet magic. Setting his heart pounding in a wild erratic rhythm, she was the siren whose silent song was her touch. A touch that left nothing undiscovered, nothing unworshiped. In the space of a shivering gasp, he was beset by torture that was as artless as it was provocative. As beguiled as it was beguiling. A madness drawing him ever deeper into the storm.

She was wonder and agony that had him crying, "Enough. Dear heaven! Enough."

Then he was sweeping her into his arms to take her, at last, to his bed. A bed that once had known the passion of other lovers, yet in his time had been solitary—but no more. Even as he regretted laying her on a bachelor's utilitarian counterpane when she should have silks, he knew she must understand this couldn't be just one night. Or two, or even a dozen.

Not once he made love to her. For when he did, he knew he couldn't let her go a second time.

Brushing her hair from her face, he stood looking down at her. "I've dreamed of this." His voice was hoarse, strained, as he struggled for the last of his control. "I want you more than anything. More than life. But only for forever.

"Tell me now, Marissa. Tell me what you want. Say the words. I need to hear the words."

Lying so quiet with her taut, shallow breath hardly a ripple in the stillness, she met his look. As he had kissed her and caressed her, in a smoky whisper he had called her beautiful over and over. But he was the one of true beauty. Rugged, masculine, virile beauty. His face less pretty and more handsome with age.

His body had grown leaner and harder and strong. His features bore the mark of sun and wind. But he had weathered the onslaught well. The frown lines, the crinkles and creases only served to make him more intriguing. The darkening of his skin defined the power of brawny muscles. Hours in the saddle kept his stomach flat, his hips lean, and corded his thighs with muscles.

He was a man who had chosen to live in a harsh, unforgiving land, yet had never succumbed to the harshness.

He was all she hoped. "Forever isn't long enough."

"No?" he asked, his voice rough with need.

"Not nearly." She laughed softly as she took his hand. "But if you promise to love me as I love you every day of forever? Then forever's a promise I'll take, and give in return."

"So will I." Jefferson smiled as he came down to her. And as his body joined with hers, as the ease of heartache began in the healing of love, into the enchanting fragrance of her hair he murmured, "Forever, indeed, my heart."

Long into the night he made love to her and she to him. Sometimes with whispered words. Sometimes with wandering caresses and gliding kisses. Sometimes in the raw and intimate hunger of joined bodies, gleaming with the sheen of the sweat of exertion, seeking to be closer, deeper.

Kindling again and again the flames that licked at them until the firestorm swept them over the edge into mind-shattering rapture.

Just before dawn, they fell silent and still. Too weary to do more than whisper the last of countless words of love. Too weary to move, it was in a lovers' embrace that sleep claimed them.

At dawn, Marissa rose, plucked her dress from the floor and tiptoed from the room. When she stepped onto the porch and into the cool predawn air, she slipped on the dress and sank to the top step to watch the canyon wake. There was light on the horizon, turning the sky and the canyon walls astonishing colors, long before the sun truly rose.

Marissa didn't know how long she'd sat without moving, falling in love with the canyon all over again, when Jefferson's footsteps sounded behind her. Even as she looked up, he was bending down to sit beside her. His chest and arms were naked, and only jeans covered his lower body.

''Mornin', darlin','' he drawled in his best Southern accent. ''I missed you when I woke up. Then I decided that maybe you were running for cover.''

Smiling, Marissa didn't rise to the teasing challenge. ''Never running. Only enjoying the morning.''

Jefferson's palm at her chin turned her face to him. His blue gaze studied her carefully, looking for any hurt he might have inflicted with a passion that, in retrospect, seemed too strong even to him. ''Don't play games, sweetheart. Did I hurt you? When I was thinking straight again, I was afraid…''

Marissa's hand came up between their bodies, her fingers folded over his mouth, stopping his words. ''Last night was beautiful, not painful. Loving me could never hurt.'' She smiled then. ''I'm a little tired, pleasantly achy, and I've never felt so wonderful in my life.''

He laughed then, a low sexy chuckle. His fingers slipped from her face to her hair, ruffling it as he planted a chaste kiss on her forehead. He couldn't really kiss her. Not if he meant to keep from tumbling her back on the porch and taking her again.

"Too tired to take Gitano and Black Jack for a ride later?" His fingers left her tousled hair to skim over her lips. If he couldn't kiss her, at least he could touch her. "I have a surprise for you."

"A surprise?" Her breath came in short, little gasps as the touch of his fingertips on her tender lips sent sensations racing to the most achy part of her body.

"Don't ask, for if I tell you, it won't be a surprise." Rising from the porch, he held out his hand. "In the meantime, how about a swim and a bath in the stream?"

"A swim?" Marissa couldn't remember anywhere the stream was more than hip or waist deep.

"There's a place beyond the pasture where the creek is fed by a small waterfall. For electricity, Steve put in a small generator and harnessed the power of the fall. Then, he did some excavating, adding irrigation and landscaping to create a small lake as a special gift to Savannah."

In her weeks in the canyon, Marissa had never had any inkling there was more water than the two streams she'd seen. "Is that where you bathed last night?"

"No." The barest move of his head accompanied his denial. "I was saving the lake for a special occasion. This one."

Giving him her hand as her assent, she rose to stand beside him. "How do we go? Walk? Horseback?"

"Neither, my love." Jefferson was laughing as he tugged her down the steps. "We go by the cowboy's second-best steed."

"The truck," Marissa supplied. Then, her gaze raking down his body, she wondered out loud, "If we're both going as we are, it should be interesting if more unexpected visitors arrive.''

''Doesn't matter.'' His grin teased. ''If anyone dares intrude, I'll just have Satan eat them.''

''Right.''

Then there was no time for more and he dragged her to the truck. The pleated dress swirled and danced around her legs while the supple fabric played touch and tell, teasing the sensitive points of her breasts. When he helped her into the truck and climbed in beside her, she knew he should've looked ridiculous dressed in only jeans and Stetson. But the truth was he looked like nothing but what he was, magnificent, sexy, and all male.

''Ready when you are,'' he said, his fingers hovering over the key already inserted in the ignition.

Marissa knew he was giving her one more chance to back away. One last chance to avoid the lovemaking that would be an inevitable part of their interlude by the lake. ''I'm ready now.''

The drive was slow, uneven, a wonderful adventure. Marissa saw a different view of the canyon. At first sight, from the rim, it had appeared cloistered, closed in by the very walls that protected it. From the floor, the canyon was a veritable mix of ecosystems. Her first look at the waterfall that fell an incredible distance into a small cul-de-sac, and she realized she had seen it all along. But from the distance of the house and barn, she had never recognized it as a fall, assuming it was another quirk in striations of rock walls that were constantly unique.

When Jefferson brought the truck to a halt, he waited a minute to let her take in the wonder Steve had created for his wife. ''Amazing, isn't it?''

''More than amazing.'' Marissa looked from palms to

ferns tucked in shady alcoves, to brilliant tropical flowers. "But no more amazing than Sunrise Canyon, itself."

"The secret is water, sweetheart. Men have been known to kill for it in this land." Gripping the steering wheel, he turned from her. "That was a part of why Jake Benedict coveted the canyon for most of his life. Likely he still does. Even though it belongs to his daughter and her husband. Offer a man gold or good water out here and only a fool would take gold."

"Steve Cody was no fool," she ventured. "But how did a down-on-his-luck rodeo man come to have it at all?"

"It was a gift. Steve saved a friend's life at the risk of his own. A fellow rodeo man and an old nemesis of Jake's who had better things to do than battle the old man."

Marissa heard respect in the name. *Old man.* "You like him. Jake Benedict, I mean."

"I do." Jefferson's attention seemed to be riveted on the tumbling fall of water, yet his mind was on the past, when he was a young runaway looking for a home. "He can be a son of a bitch. But he goes after what he wants fairly. As Savannah did."

"Savannah wanted Steve?"

Jefferson laughed. "Eventually." Opening the door, he crossed to Marissa. When she stood beside him, he said, "Despite the temperature, the water will be cold. A lot of dynamics figure into the reason, but I like Savannah's best."

"Which is?" Marissa was beginning to realize how fond Jefferson was of Savannah Cody, as well. She hoped someday she would meet and know the legendary woman.

"She thinks, quite simply, the water outraces the sun."

"And, therefore, is never warmed by it."

Jefferson nodded, turning to her. "Ready to skinny-dip?"

* * *

The water was as cold as he'd warned, but invigorating. Even restful. Later, sitting on a grassy bank covered by a bath sheet Jefferson had taken from his truck, Marissa soaked in the heat, finding peace in a manmade desert oasis. A gift of love. A secret trysting place for that love.

Jefferson sat beside her, a towel draped at his waist. "Nobody intrudes. Which isn't surprising since few people know it's here. This was Savannah's place. Steve wanted her to have the freedom to do whatever she wished here."

"Like this?" With a turn of her face and a tilt of her head, she touched her lips to his shoulder. With the lave of her tongue, she felt the heat of the sun on his skin and the clean, exciting taste of him. When he went still and tense, she laughed wickedly, letting her breath cool the moisture left on his shoulder by her tongue.

In a swift move he turned to her, his hands at her shoulders bearing her down on the velvet of the sheet. A low growl rumbled in his throat as he muttered, "Or this."

Then his hands and lips were everywhere. Stroking, petting, seeking out new, maddening, undiscovered responses of her body. Adding them to the old, blending old with the new. Sending sensation after sensation rocketing through her.

Jefferson's long legs tangled with hers. Using their muscular power he turned, lifting her high above him. Then gradually he lowered her to him. There was a fierceness in her now. And she was sweet and hot as she took him, riding him like the Cossack she'd been named. Wanting even more, she leaned over him, her fingers in his hair, her breasts a caress of their own against the hard plain of his chest.

When the first nuance of release fluttered through her, with incredible strength he surged upward, matching her rhythm with powerful thrusts. When she cried out, in his own final passion he gathered her to him and held her through the euphoria.

In the return of serenity, as she fit so perfectly in his arms, he found peace he'd never expected to know again. She was the light in his darkness. Perhaps his way back to all he'd lost.

Then, with one hand tangled in the spill of her hair, the other flung across her body as if he would watch over her and keep her forever, Jefferson drowsed in the heat of the day. When he felt her relax in the abandonment of sleep, he slept as well.

"Wake up, sleeping beauty." Jefferson leaned over her, loving the way she woke. Quickly, completely, but with a dreamy, remembering look in her eyes.

"Jefferson." As she looked up at him, she touched his face, her palm cupping his cheek, her fingers curling at the tender skin at his temple. "Good morning."

"It was, wasn't it?" He laughed softly and kissed the tip of her nose.

"Was?" Her fingers slipped into his hair, loving the shining blend of silver and deep gold.

"Nearly." He tilted his head to kiss the tender line of her wrist. "It's almost noon."

"Then we have hungry horses."

"No, Sandy Gannon has seen to them. I spoke with him about it last night." There was no one Jefferson trusted more than the foreman of Jake Benedict's Rafter B. He would trust Sandy with his life. And if all else failed, with Marissa's.

She laughed, suddenly. She'd forgotten the nearly un-used telephones in the house and the tack room of the barn. "You planned this, and here I was thinking it was spon-taneous."

"Let's just say, I hoped." Leaning closer, kissing her

eyes, her nose, then lingering at her mouth, he murmured against her lips, "Any complaints?"

Marissa's answer was to tug at his hair, bringing his kiss closer, deeper. When she let him move away, the laughter in her eyes was enticing. "Does that answer your question?"

"Oh yeah." He grinned down at her, savoring the easy camaraderie of lovers who, for one short and passionate interlude, lived together in a world apart. "If I had the stamina, I would show you exactly how much. But alas."

When he left the rest for her to remember, she laughed again and ruffled his hair. "Poor baby."

A look he couldn't fathom flickered over her face. It came, then was controlled so quickly, he would have missed it if he hadn't been watching closely. In a dreaded moment he feared it was grief and unmerited guilt for loving him in every sense. "Hey, sweetheart, what is it?"

"It's nothing." A minute shake of her head accompanied the denial. As she saw his need to be assured she had accepted the past as something she couldn't change, and that her grief for her parents, for Paulo, was finally without guilt, she smiled. "It truly is nothing, Jefferson. Except, maybe I'm a little sad that days this wonderful were so long coming for us."

"They're here now, to stay. And each will only get better," he promised. "As soon as—" Breaking off, because he didn't want to sully this place and this morning with the name of danger, greed and murder, he changed the subject. "I have another surprise, if you're up to another ride. This time on horseback."

"Black Jack and Gitano," Marissa recalled.

"Want to try? It won't hurt the young horses to have the day off, and Sandy has seen to the rest of our chores. While we're gone the riders on the rim will watch over the ranch."

"We're riding out of the canyon?"

"Yeah." He grinned again. "There's something I want to show you."

"Another lake?" she drawled.

Rising to his feet, he scooped up his towel and secured it around his waist again. Then, he turned, his hand reaching out to her, waiting for hers. "Not another lake," he assured as he drew her up and back into his embrace for a quick kiss. "But something I think you'll like even better."

As the crow flies, the trip would have been much shorter. There was even another faster, more direct route. Because Jefferson didn't want to tax Marissa any more, so she wouldn't be staggering from fatigue, he led her across easier terrain. Along the way, he pointed out interesting rock formations, birds and animals, and plants. Especially the cacti. A common thing in Arizona, a rarity on the plains of Argentina. Finally at the rim of a low bluff, he reined Gitano to a halt.

Leaning on the pommel of his saddle, he smiled as Marissa came to join him. With a wave of his hand, he offered his surprise. "As promised. Today and weeks ago."

Below the rim, a little distance away, a weathered cabin sat at the far end in a small cul-de-sac. There were two corrals. One attached to a barn as weathered as the house. Another by a trickle of a stream. There were no animals, no people. Yet on this hot day, smoke drifted from the chimney. Someone cooked.

Marissa turned from the scene below, her eyes sparkled. "Jake Benedict's newest acquisition." It wasn't a question and she didn't wait for an answer. "Juan, Marta, and Alejandro. They're here."

"Two days ago. One to travel in, one to settle down." Seeing her so happy twice in one day made it a great day for him. "Shall we ride down, say howdy and welcome to Arizona?"

"Yes. But first, thank you."

Shifting in the saddle, Marissa reached across Jefferson. Clasping a hand at his nape, she brought him down to her kiss. Her lips were soft, giving, sweet. If this was gratitude, he knew he could never have enough of it.

When she moved away, he knew the kiss had had the same effect on her. "You know something, sweetheart," he began in a roughened voice. "This bonfire of ours is turning into an eternal flame."

"Would you have it any other way, my love?"

"No," he admitted when he could breathe again. She had never called him anything but Jefferson, and in rare times, Jeffie. The endearment, spoken in sudden gravity, added to the hope that burned in his heart. "Never any other way."

Jefferson touched her face, his eyes filled with desire. Then he remembered that people who were special to her waited for this day as eagerly as she had. He satisfied himself with a feather light tap on her lips. The promise of other kisses. Then, smiling, he gathered up his reins. "Shall we ride, my love?"

"She looks happy." Juan didn't smile, but there was relief in his voice.

"She is." Jefferson didn't look away from the small house, or from Marissa. She sat on the steps with Marta. Alejandro sat in her lap, chattering, gesturing, more animated than he'd seen the child. Neither she nor the boy had let each other go from the moment she'd rode into the yard to hail the house.

Though their conversation didn't carry to the barn or the corral where Jefferson stood with Juan, their laughter did. The trill of the boy's happy giggle blending with Marissa's contralto with such regularity, made it clear the reunion was a joyful return of old habits. In what once would have seemed to him to be rare exuberance, Marta was clearly expounding on this new home. A home she could never have expected before.

But for all the elation in this time, it was Marissa who held Jefferson's exclusive attention. Marissa and Alejandro.

This small, handsome child with his dark, dark hair and eyes as dark could've been her child. And, as she bent to kiss his cheek, or ruffle his hair, laughingly accepted another of many hugs, only a blind man wouldn't see that the love was as strong.

Tearing his gaze from her, he spoke to Juan. "Marissa has worried about you. Knowing you're all safe and close is the best of it." With a thumb, Jefferson tilted back the brim of his hat. His sky-blue eyes returned again to the woman and child. "Especially Alejandro."

"There is a special bond between them," Juan agreed. "There was no doctor when he was born. Just Rissa. He wasn't positioned properly for the birth. In the greatest patience and with only what she'd learned in the stables, she turned the infant. For me, it was a miracle."

The gaucho's hands closed tightly over a splintered rail. "If not for Rissa, I would have lost them both."

Jefferson nodded. He could understand, for he'd witnessed her skill at River Trace, his brother's horse farm. If the fates were kind, he would witness it again on the Broken Spur.

If they were kinder still, one day she would have children of her own. His sons, his daughters. No, he amended, our sons, our daughters.

He hadn't let himself think that far into the future before. But standing in the heat and dust, hearing her laugh, seeing the love on her face as she held a child, Jefferson knew he wanted a life and a family with Marissa.

A life, a family, and forever.

Nine

"**T**ired?"

Marissa didn't lift her chin from her folded hands, or turn from the darkening and ever fascinating sunset. Regretting the concern she heard in Jefferson's deep voice, she answered, honestly, "Of course." Then to ease his mind she smiled her assurance. "But pleasantly so."

Quiet returned to the porch again. Only Satan, sleeping by her side, scratched at the wooden floor as he chased some elusive creature in his dreams. For once hardly aware of the dog's antics, from her place on the top step Marissa watched the end of day in continued preoccupied silence.

Jefferson stood only a pace away, hipshot, shoulder braced against a post. He was oblivious of the time or the canyon and the shadows that crept across its walls. His attention and his world revolved around the woman huddled at his feet.

Riding back from the Elias's new home, she had grown

quieter. The joy of the day had been replaced by a mantle of melancholy. He assumed it was the sadness of saying goodbye to her friends, even for a little while. A grief he thought would ease. But the rest of the day and evening had been no different.

Supper was another fiasco that neither of them wanted. Now she'd sat for nearly an hour, silent and brooding. Whatever it was that had sent her into this mood, he had to understand. To help, if he could. Sitting down beside her, with an arm around her shoulder, he asked, "Are you thinking about Alejandro?"

Nodding and lifting both hands, with the heel of her palms, she squeezed her temples as if she would push her thoughts away. In a continuation of that same motion, with her fingers she combed her hair back from her face, before clasping her hands again as tightly as before.

The clean scent of her surrounded him, tantalized him, as strands of her falling hair brushed the back of his wrist. Hair that smelled of sunlight. Dark hair, as dark as the boy's.

It was strange that since he'd seen them together again, all thoughts seemed to lead to the black-eyed child. Marissa's thoughts, as well, he suspected. "He's on your mind even more now that he's close. It's obvious how much you love him."

She didn't speak for a while. Easing the clasp of her hands, reaching across her body, she laced her fingers through his. "I think of him. Constantly. I always have. But tonight is different. Tonight Alejandro is a reminder of something I should tell you. Something I should have told you long ago."

Jefferson felt the sudden clench of premonition in his gut. The grip of his fingers over hers was unconsciously fierce. "Then now is as good a time as any, isn't it?"

"As good as any?" she whispered hoarsely. "I don't

know. But it's the best time we have now.'' Turning in his embrace, her solemn gaze held his. Her breasts rose and fell in one long, unsteady breath. ''There was a baby, Jefferson. Our baby, conceived that last day in the tree house.''

Pausing she waited for his reaction. Anger, disgust, regret, anything. When there was none, when he sat as still as death, waiting, she continued her revelation in a somber, lifeless tone. ''When I knew, I went to Paulo again. This time, he released me from our final agreement and all my promises. I was making arrangements to come back to you. Then, for no apparent medical reason, it was over. Too soon to know if our child would be a boy or a girl, it was gone.''

''Then there was no reason to come home to me.'' Though he spoke of things other than the child, the hurt, the loss, colored his voice. In his tone there was the grief of unspoken words.

Sliding her hand from his, she framed his face between her fingers. ''There was always reason, my love. But—''

''*But*,'' Jefferson interrupted with a grimace. ''*If*. There's always one or the other, isn't there?''

''For us, so it would seem.'' She wanted to hold him and comfort him, but the look in his eyes, the tension in his face, warned it was too little, too late.

''What was it this time? No.'' With an abrupt, humorless laugh he stopped any explanation she might make. ''Let me guess. Does it go something like this…the discovery that you were expecting the child of another man, a stranger, caused such a furor your mother became even more ill.

''So ill that when our baby was lost, you had to stay. To be the dutiful daughter again,'' he finished, bitterly. Bitter for her, never with her. For he understood how the Alexandres worked. Understanding their sort and their selfishness wasn't difficult. Even without knowing them. "All for that precious lifestyle that was your price to pay."

Marissa hoped that someday she could make Jefferson understand what was abhorrent to him was an accepted practice among the people who moved in her parents' social and economic circle. She hoped he would know and believe that they thought the arrangement they made had given her the best of her world. In time, perhaps, he would, but not now. Not yet. She need not waste time or breath trying until he was ready to understand.

"My mother's heart problem had taken a severe toll on her in my absence from home. Before I realized I was carrying your child, news of the wedding was widespread. She was really too frail to cope with the scandal of a broken betrothal."

"But she would have had no choice but to cope, if the baby hadn't miscarried? Is that what you're saying, Marissa?" His face was still grim. His voice roughened by pain.

Marissa looked away, gathering her composure. When she turned back to him, there were tears in her eyes and on her cheeks. "I loved my mother. But in choosing a life, my choice would have been our child and you."

Groaning softly, Jefferson reached for her. "I know, sweetheart. I could never doubt that."

Folding her closer, with her head on his shoulder and her face nestled against his throat, he embraced her. Even now, he could feel the pain thrumming in her. Not for the first time, he realized how strong she'd become. The choices she'd had to make were enough to bring the strongest to their knees.

But not Marissa Alexandre.

She had walked out of his life a young woman of clear but untried principles. She had returned to him a woman tested by grief and tragedy. A woman who would walk by his side in the worst and the best of times. A woman to treasure. To love.

For the gift of that woman, Jefferson could even forgive the Alexandres for the time she had been taken from him.

"The baby, our baby, is part of the reason you studied medicine and obstetrics." His fingers glided over her hair, smoothing it. His touch was comforting in the absence of anger.

"I wanted to keep what happened to me from happening to others."

"Juan says you have already. With Alejandro's birth."

"That was good fortune. It was too early in my studies for any real medical knowledge to come to bear. Fortune and dire determination Marta wouldn't lose her child as I had."

She had found her way through grief with strength and a goal. He believed now her mood was a reaction to the resurrection of memories. Memories provoked by a dark-haired child.

"Alejandro is a bit more than three?" he ventured.

She had relaxed beneath his soothing touch and tensed a little again at his question. "Only a bit. If our son or daughter had been meant to be, he or she would be the same age."

"She," he insisted. "I prefer to imagine our baby was a little girl as pretty as her mother."

Leaning away from him, solemnly Marissa searched his face. "You aren't angry that I didn't tell you before?"

"There's nothing to be angry for, sweetheart. All I feel is sorrow for what we've missed." With the pad of his thumb he wiped away the spill of her tears. "And regret that our lost baby never knew what a generous and wonderful woman her mother is."

A low cry sounded in her throat. In the last of twilight,

her eyes were luminous. "You really mean that, don't you?"

"I've never doubted it. Not even when I was struggling to forget you. The more I struggled, the more I proved it couldn't be done. You were—you are—unforgettable."

"And when I reached out to you?"

"I knew I was a goner." As he kissed her cheek, his breath was warm against her skin. "I don't know how your letter found me, but I'll be eternally grateful it did."

She laughed for the first time in hours. "That part was easy. My final letter came to you from Eden. The original packet was a series of letters within letters. With the exception of their separate instructions, I asked that each send it intact to the next person. When it came to Eden, I asked only that she send it to you if she was certain you would want to hear from me."

"And my beloved, first sister-in-law knew I would."

"Perhaps, if she'd known what I was asking, what I was drawing you into, she wouldn't have sent it on."

"She would have. But I'm glad she didn't know. I'm glad none of your helpers know. You took a chance trusting that they would each do what you asked."

"They were good friends, and my only avenue. There was no other choice."

"Then it's truly all's well that ends well?"

"If it ever ends. If we can ever lead normal lives again. If those who have helped me here can have their lives back." Her face was suddenly bleak when she looked to the rim of the canyon. "What are they thinking now, the riders who stand guard? Are they missing their families? Someone special they love? Where do they sleep? When do they sleep?"

"Jake Benedict has a line shack nearby. A step above what you would see in movies, but still a shack. They're accustomed to rough quarters. Even Valentina, I imagine.

Billy's plan was that they would work in overlapping shifts at night. That way one would sleep while two patrolled. But, I figure they're as familiar with catnaps as with rough quarters."

"Rough quarters, little sleep, away from home and family. I have to wonder, Jefferson, what I ever did to deserve such care. And how long can it go on?"

"You deserve it because every citizen deserves protection. It can go on as long as needed. But Menendez will make a mistake sooner or later, and Simon and his men will have him."

"I've wondered how Juan and Marta's disappearance was handled. Surely someone questioned how they could be there one day, and gone the next."

"Ah, sweetheart, never underestimate Simon. A wonderful job opportunity arose for Juan. So wonderful time was of the essence. So wonderful Juan sent a crew to the *estancia* to collect his belongings and make his goodbyes."

"You think that story will be believed?"

"After seeing Simon in action, do you doubt that he will see to it that it's taken as gospel?"

Marissa smiled then. "Not really. In fact, there were times I had trouble remembering he isn't Superman in disguise. Or that he isn't infallible."

"Maybe not. But he's as close to both as possible."

Her short trill of laughter held the sound of conflicting emotions. Abandoning this digression, she spoke again of what was in her heart. "I've wondered how you would feel, what you would say when I told you about the baby. I imagined every reaction."

"And?" With the back of his finger he drew a caress from her forehead to the tip of her nose, then to her lips and her throat. The gentle exploration ending at last at the cleft of her breasts just visible within the opening of her shirt.

"I've discovered I love you more than I thought I could." Her voice was husky, her eyes languorous, in response to his intimate quest. "Far more."

"Enough to stay with me when this is done and be my love?"

"I would be your love, your mate, your everything, Jefferson. And stay as long as you want me."

"Then I want forever. And babies. Especially a dark-haired, dark-eyed little girl who looks exactly like her mother."

It was a dream. She was too happy. Happiness this extraordinary couldn't last. But she could pretend for Jefferson. "A boy first," she whispered as she touched her lips to his. "Every girl should have an older brother."

"To keep the wolves from her door." Gathering her to him, he scattered kisses over her face. "A brother to keep her safe, as Juan kept you safe, until a lover comes along."

"As you came for me, Jefferson."

"About those babies, sweetheart. Considering that I wasn't exactly prepared for making love, and considering our track record, we might have made another baby already." He had never asked about birth control. For a faithful woman with an elderly husband in name only, there was no reason.

"How would you feel if there was another baby so soon?" Her expression was a mix of hope and anxiety.

"Like this." Touching her only with his lips, he trailed kisses over her forehead then down the first of the path his plundering finger had taken. One kiss, then another skimmed over her arching eyebrows. "And this." Kisses closed her eyes, and with the tip of his tongue he caught the last of tears shimmering on her lashes. "And just in case we haven't already succeeded, this."

His mouth, when it touched hers at last, was gentle, sweetly seductive, moving again and again over the line of her lips. Teasing, but making no effort to be more. Until, at the end of her restraint, it was she who clasped his nape to keep him, her mouth opening to his in silent need for more. As the intoxicating magic of his response spun through her like delicious flames, she sighed in mournful regret as he drew away.

"There's a better place for this, sweet Marissa."

"This?" She saw the teasing in the quirk of his lips, but knew that with the teasing, he was serious.

"Making love. Making a life with you. Making a baby."

"Is that truly what you want, Jefferson?"

"It's what I truly want, in that order." His smile faded. "If Menendez finds us?"

"He won't." Jefferson willed it to be true.

"But if he should, and it goes bad?"

"Then we will have had this much."

Then he was rising to stand over her. His callused hand reaching down, waiting for her. The instant her hand touched his, he brought her up to him. Up for one more kiss, one more caress before he walked with her to his bedroom.

Jefferson was up first the next morning. Though exhausted and mindless from the night, he had willed himself to wake early. A skill he'd perfected years ago in the wilds of the lowcountry. He was dressed and had just begun planning Marissa's surprise when the rumble of Satan's rare bark reverberated over the yard, then was lost in the thunder of galloping horses.

He was reaching for the rifle he kept loaded and ready by the door when he recognized a familiar voice quieting Satan. An insistent rap pierced the predawn darkness and Juan Elia called for him. Wary of a trick, Jefferson flicked off the light. Easing back a shutter, he peered at the porch and into the yard.

In light of a moon half as bright as day, he saw Juan by the door. Ethan Garrett and Valentina Courtenay, Simon's crack shot called from retirement, stood by their mounts. As he moved to the door, Marissa stepped from the bedroom, dressed and wary.

"Who is it?" There was no panic, only alarm in her voice.

"Juan, with two of the guards from the rim." Jefferson was terse, his gaze holding hers a second before he opened the door. No one thought of greetings as Juan moved past him to Marissa. Moving as quickly, the rim riders were close behind.

"He has him. Menendez has Alejandro. I don't know how, but he does," Juan blurted without preamble, his eyes black holes in a colorless face. "Alejandro wanted to ride with me to check the fences," he explained before anyone asked. "When Marta went to wake him for breakfast, the window was open and he was gone."

A crumpled scrap of paper fluttered from Juan's fist to the table. "This was on his bed."

"A ransom note," Ethan Garrett supplied, familiar with the circumstance. "Menendez will trade the boy for Marissa."

As pale as Juan, Marissa reached out to take his hand, struggling to stay calm. "How long ago did this happen?"

Valentina crossed to Marissa, laying a comforting hand on her shoulder. Though she was much smaller, no one who watched how she moved, or saw the look in her eyes would think her smaller stature indicated lack of strength or ability. "Marta found the boy was missing a little more than an hour ago.

"Wisely, Juan drove the ranch truck as far as he could. Then he switched to horseback when the terrain was impassable for the truck, saving time. Rick and I intercepted him at the last mesa. This was our first inkling of trouble, but we'll find the boy. I give you my word." With a tilt of her head, she met Juan's black gaze. "Both of you."

"You saw no one else?" Marissa asked.

"No, I'm sorry. All we have to go on is the note. But we'll find more." Though Valentina's words were infinitely gentle, they rang with assurance. "Juan and I rode ahead, Ethan came to take his shift and joined us along the way. Rick will be here shortly with Marta. Then we can pool our thoughts and make plans."

The last of Valentina's speech was lost in the jangle of the telephone in the bedroom. The room was eerily quiet. All eyes turned to Jefferson when he reappeared in the doorway.

"Simon," Valentina suggested. "And madder than hell."

"Simon." Jefferson acknowledged. "With an informant's tip and a warning that Menendez is on the move. Madder than hell that it's too late doesn't touch it."

"What's the word?" Ethan asked. "How did this happen? Who knew where Juan and Marta were?" His golden-brown eyes turned to Marissa. "How did he know he could get to you through the Elias?"

"For that matter, how did Menendez know Marissa is alive?" Even worried for his son, Juan was concerned for her.

"Simon's sources report Rei's plane went down in a ravine, virtually intact. Rather than the sea," Jefferson explained. "Proving the theory it was shot down or sabotaged. Not a bomb. One of Menendez's suspected informants found the aircraft. He could've known for days Marissa wasn't on board."

"Which put him days ahead of Simon, giving him time to use Juan to find me. But how did he know about Juan at all?"

"There's a little girl on your family's *estancia*." Jefferson spoke directly to Marissa, dreading what he must tell her. "Her mother brought the girl to you for treatment at the same time Alejandro was ill. The little girl is missing the tip of a finger now. It would have been more if the mother hadn't talked."

"Maria. Her name is Maria. She was a playmate of Alejandro's," Juan supplied hoarsely. "If Menendez would mutilate a three-year-old girl, what will he do to my son?"

"Nothing," Valentina declared vehemently. "Because we're moving on it at first light. We're going to track this animal down and neutralize him before he knows what hit him."

"The note says he will contact us by noon. Instructing where to meet to exchange Marissa for Alejandro." Juan crumpled his hat in his hand, his face stark. "If we make a misstep..."

"We won't." Valentina snatched the note from the table. Crushing the paper in her fist, she tossed it aside.

Jefferson saw in her eyes that she knew Menendez would never let any of the Elias live. But there was one chance. "How do we know this is Menendez? Perhaps he sent his men, but didn't come himself. With Simon on his trail, it would be dangerous for him to enter the country at all."

"Menendez will be there." Ethan had said little. When he spoke, his rage was glacial and that much more ominous. "He likes to inflict his revenge in person. Marissa refused him. He won't tolerate refusal."

"You don't think he intends to let Alejandro go," Marissa spoke so softly her question was barely audible, "do you, Ethan?"

Ethan didn't respond at once. Silence sweeping through the room like a cold wind, was answer enough. After a time, he shrugged. "I wish I could tell you differently, but I've seen his handiwork too many times."

"Ethan's knowledge of Menendez is one reason he was

assigned to this case. And why we're going to jump in first.''

''How do we get that jump, sweet Valentine?'' Rick Cahill drawled the fond name as he stood at the door with Marta by his side. In the tension, no one noticed their arrival. Now, with a word and a squeeze at her shoulder, he freed Marta's riveted concentration, sending her into Juan's arms.

''We have the edge in Ethan who knows how Menendez thinks. Added to it there's Billy Blackhawk's word that we have one of the best trackers in Arizona in Jefferson.''

''Speaking of Billy, where is he?'' Rick asked.

''He's on his way. Simon called him before he called here.'' Jefferson briefly caressed Marissa's shoulder. ''He and his deputies will stay with Marta, and Juan, and Marissa.''

''I'm going with you,'' Marissa stated as a matter of fact. Her tone said implicitly she wouldn't be left behind.

Jefferson still tried. ''Sweetheart, you can't.''

''Yes, Jefferson I can. I will. Our best bet could be to negotiate with Menendez. Without me, what is there to negotiate?''

''No.'' He was adamant. ''There must be another way.''

''She's right, Jefferson.'' Valentina resolved the argument. ''Don't underestimate your lady. She's done well so far. She'll do well in this.''

Considering the matter settled, Valentina turned to other concerns. Addressing each with an assurance that left little doubt that she'd done this before. Jefferson remembered a comment Yancey had made. *One of Simon's own—a lady sharpshooter, to be exact—rescued Patrick McCallum's daughter.*

Yancey's words reverberated in his mind. Cold comfort now that the situation was real to him. But he looked at

Valentina Courtenay with renewed respect, and with gratitude for setting retirement aside to come to Marissa's aid.

"All right," he muttered but only to himself. For he knew Marissa's decision was irrevocable. Standing together they listened to Valentina's plan.

Keeping low to the ground, Jefferson dodged by the Elias's ranch buildings and fences, then disappeared into an outcropping of rock. He was dressed in leather the color of the land. His hat had been replaced by a band around his forehead to catch the sweat. His boots, set aside for quieter moccasins.

He blended so well with the terrain and moved so quietly, he stepped on the small mesa before anyone knew he had returned.

"Well?" Valentina wasted no time seeking his report. No one listened more intently as he described what he'd found. When he finished, she was silent, mulling over what he'd said. "You think there were only three of them?"

"Menendez and his two bodyguards," Ethan suggested. "He doesn't go anywhere without them."

"There were only three, and they were headed toward an old mine shaft on the far boundary of the property. Not many people know or remember it's there," Jefferson said grimly.

"Which would suggest Menendez had inside information." Valentina's gaze strafed over the men she worked with. "Any suggestions on the informant?" With an abrupt gesture, she set her question aside. "We can deal with that later. For now, Alejandro is our first priority. Marissa? If we need you?"

"I'm ready. For anything, for Alejandro."

"I expected as much." Turning a look at Jefferson, Valentina smiled and reminded him again, "She's your lady, and worthy of you. As you are of her."

Turning to Ethan and Rick, she said, "Let's get this guy. For Marissa's family. For Alejandro. For Simon. And for all the kids who might someday take drugs brought to this country by Menendez."

Jefferson wasn't wrong. Neither was Ethan. At more than two hours before the noon contact, Menendez and his two bodyguards were hunkered in the little shade provided by the rotten framework of the ancient shaft.

The heat would be horrendous. A fact that made Jefferson more fearful of Menendez. A man of his power had to be eaten alive by the bitter need for revenge to endure such conditions.

"Are you sure about this, Valentina?" he asked.

She was assembling her rifle. When she looked up, her steady gaze met Jefferson's. In that moment he knew he'd never seen a woman as cool, as calm. Until he looked at Marissa.

Valentina's confidence was contagious, and Marissa had absorbed her share. She understood her part in this, and what she must do. Jefferson didn't know he'd shivered until Valentina gripped his arm.

"Jefferson, doubt makes for mistakes. We can't afford either. If we don't believe this can be done, we shouldn't try at all. If one doubts, we all fail." Snapping the rifle case shut, taking up the weapon again, she looked at him. "What will it be?"

"We do this," Marissa answered. "There's no other way."

Jefferson wanted to keep her from the risk she would take. Instead he stood taut with worry.

"I love you, Jefferson." Not caring who heard, she stroked his face. "I want a life with you. A life free of worry, and most of all from guilt. I want babies like Alejandro. I want him to grow up with them. To be an older brother. None of that can be if we don't do this.''

''You aren't afraid to do this, my love?''

''Yes. But I'm more afraid not to do it.''

Jefferson nodded that he understood, because he couldn't speak the words. And he'd never loved her more.

Marissa's fingers slipped from his face to his hair. Drawing him down to her, she whispered against his lips. ''Kiss me for luck, and let's get this done.''

With a groan, Jefferson drew her closer. His kiss was desperate, as if with the power of his love he could keep her safe. As harsh as it was, it was the sweetest kiss he'd ever known.

She stepped away, their hands clasped a second longer. ''Whatever happens, take care of Alejandro. Promise me that.''

''With my life.'' Because the child was more than Juan and Marta's son, because he was the embodiment of the child she lost, Jefferson vowed she wouldn't lose him again.

When he turned, Rick and Ethan were no longer on the mesa. He knew they'd gone to take up their post. Rigid and unmoving, he watched as Marissa climbed down to her assigned place.

Then there was only Valentina. Everything hinged on her.

''Make it count, Valentina.''

''I intend to, Jefferson.''

''You're pretty confident.''

Her eyes held his. ''There can be no doubt in what I do.''

''Have you ever missed?''

Grief scored her face briefly, then was gone. ''Once.''

''Why?''

As before, her eyes met his. ''A split second of doubt.''

"What happened?"

"In my hesitation, the man I loved took a bullet."

"But you got the shooter."

"I got him."

"The man you loved, what happened?"

"He died, in my arms." There was pain in her voice. "I won't hesitate today, Jefferson. I won't miss. And nobody's going to die. At least, none of us."

She said no more, and too many agonizing minutes to count later, Jefferson was in place. Moving like a ghost, he sprawled in heated dust above the mine shaft. He could see no one. That Ethan and Rick were in place he had to trust to their expertise.

That Valentina could see what she must and could do what she must he trusted to God and Simon.

A child whimpered, a frightened, pitiful sound carrying over the expanse between the mesa and the mine shaft. Then Marissa appeared, calling Menendez's name, taunting him.

A tall, dark man stepped into the open with Alejandro in his arms. Vicente Menendez with a pistol at the boy's head.

Ethan called out from the side of the shaft as planned. Menendez began to shift instinctively toward him, then froze, suspecting a trap. In the second that followed, in sequences too rapid to register except after the fact, all hell broke loose.

A shadow, where no shadow should be, vaulted from a ledge toward Marissa. In tandem, a single shot reverberated through the stillness. A second that could have been its echo whined in ricochet after ricochet. Marissa falling beneath the shadow was the last thing Jefferson saw as he leapt into chaos.

As quickly as it began, the furor ended. The land was still again. The quiet broken only by a child's cry.

Ten

There was laughter in the ranch house of the Broken Spur. Laughter and celebration, for Juan and Marta Elias's son had been returned to them. Still a little clingy, a little frightened and confused, but unharmed and truly safe at last in his mother's arms.

A reason for celebration and laughter. But as he sat at the kitchen table with the others, a heavy weight bore down on Jefferson, sucking the laughter from him. Dampening the elation.

While the others talked, questioned, theorized, he sat solemnly, listening. A part of the team in body. Detached in mind.

Valentina's shot had been true, as she promised. And as she promised, none of them had died. Except Menendez.

His bodyguards had been disabled and by now were under arrest. For, on a signal from Valentina, the second phase of the plan had been set into motion. With Juan and Marta

Elia no longer needing protection, Billy had left the ranch for the mine shaft.

Without the intimidation of their leader, Menendez's men were talking loud and long, telling however much about his singular operation anyone wanted to know. As a sheriff who had fought against drugs all his life, Billy wanted to hear chorus and verse of their revelations while memories of the price of Menendez's crimes was still vividly etched on their minds.

In the flush of success, no one thought past returning Alejandro to his mother. Which Marissa had done a while before. In that time, Alejandro had been bathed and redressed in clothing Marta had brought, to have something of Alejandro's with her.

Now, as the boy sat in Marta's lap stealing shy smiles at him, Jefferson knew their part had ended. Except for the explanations and the rehashing. Jefferson wasn't sure he wanted any part of revisiting all that happened at the shaft. Not when memories of Marissa falling and the whining scream of an endlessly ricocheting bullet ambushed his thoughts at every turn.

But as he heard the questions and saw the need to know written on Juan and Marta's faces, he knew reliving that awful time was inevitable. And as Valentina began to speak, he understood it was an exorcism of sorts for the parents.

"Juan, Marta, Marissa and Jefferson." Valentina looked at each of them before continuing. "Though bringing Alejandro home to you was our chief purpose, we've done more today than save a child. We've toppled what could have become the largest illegal drug operation in the country. We did it by taking a single man out of the equation. For Menendez was a one-man operation."

Jefferson was startled to hear Valentina speak the conclusions he'd drawn from watching Menendez in action, and from hearing the babble of his henchmen. Given her skill, her unique understanding of the people involved and of the situation, he could almost believe she had plucked his thoughts from his mind.

If she had, it wouldn't surprise him. Valentina Courtenay was an intuitive woman. From the time of Juan's arrival, once she heard his frantic revelation, she'd taken charge. Anticipating every move, down to the last detail. Even Marissa's part.

Marissa. He fought back a shudder as his gaze found her with Satan at her side. Satan, who had disobeyed him for the first time since he was a pup. Ignoring a command to stay at the ranch, trailing behind in hiding. With that rare sense of animals, becoming the shadow in the melee at the mine. Her shadow every minute since. As she stroked the Doberman, and in the celebration, the risk she'd taken was forgotten. But never by Jefferson.

Feeling the force of his stare, taking her hand from Satan and abandoning her regard of the Elia family together again, she met his gaze with luminous eyes. As her attention strayed over his features, carefully, cataloging his hurts, sensing his malaise, her expression grew tender.

Jefferson saw the tenderness, he saw the love, but his heart was too encased in ice to respond. If beauty was only in the eye of the beholder, in his eyes she was the most beautiful woman in the world. The first darkening of a long bruise reaching from her forehead, down her temple, to her cheek—a mark of her courage—made her more than beautiful.

Yet he couldn't return her smile. Even as he ached to touch her, he couldn't reach across the table to take her hand.

He could only replay the memory of his paralytic horror at the sound of the wild shot taken by one of Menendez's bodyguards.

Beyond that gut-wrenching moment of despair for Marissa, he had little memory of what he'd seen or done. His body became a mindless machine, doing what it must. He barely recalled that he'd leapt into the midst of the ambush and in one continuous motion had snatched Alejandro from Menendez. Even as the drug czar was collapsing against him, Jefferson wasn't aware of the blood.

It was only a nightmare, until Alejandro locked tiny arms around his neck and buried his tear-streaked face in his throat.

"How?" he asked when all seated at the table fell silent. "How did this happen? With Simon's care and his planning, aside from little Maria and her mother, how could Menendez find Juan and Marta? Who was the informant?

"This should have been foolproof." Suddenly furious, he pushed back his chair and stood, not caring that the chair banged against the wall, scarring the wood. "What damned good were all our precautions when Menendez saw through them like gauze?"

"Call it bad luck or fate, but what happened was the same thing that comes into play in most screw-ups," Valentina answered calmly. "We don't know what went wrong, Jefferson. But I suspect the one thing we can't control, a chance encounter. Perhaps something as innocent as an offhand remark to the wrong person at the wrong time."

"If it was a chance remark, what would it matter?" Marta asked, struggling with the reason behind what happened to her son.

"It matters," Valentina explained, "because of the ramifications. It can be like a stone thrown in a pond. The ripples that radiate from it can affect so many things."

Everyone was quiet. Perhaps thinking how this stone in this pond had changed lives as Valentina continued. "We've seen this sort of innocent mischance ruin covert operations before. We've seen it expose secrets."

Grimacing, she looked up at Jefferson. "We've questioned what we could have done differently each time."

"The answer, in the case of fate, chance, whatever you choose to call it," Marissa observed, directing her response to Jefferson's barely contained anger. "Is nothing."

"Marissa's right," Valentina agreed. "We could put a man from the Florida Keys in the wilds of Idaho, give him a new name, a new occupation, a new life where no one knew him. Then one day, one year, or ten years later, an old friend, an acquaintance, or a stranger who recognizes him could cross his path. And the danger he faced before will be as real as if the years in between had never happened."

Marta who had spoken little throughout the day, spoke again. "What mischance caused Menendez to seek us out and take Alejandro?" Once he was returned to her, she'd been content to hold the boy, to whisper to him as he clung to her. Now, she held him closer. "How could this place that seemed so safe be discovered so easily?"

"I don't know, Marta. We may never know," Valentina answered. "But be assured finding out will be our first priority."

Jefferson couldn't listen to any more. He couldn't stay closed in any longer. Snatching his hat from a hook by the door, he faced them. "Juan, Marta, I'm sorry this happened to Alejandro. I'm glad he's all right. But if you will excuse me, I need to see to the horses."

Turning, he opened the door. When Satan stood, obviously torn between his master and Marissa, Jefferson muttered, "Stay."

Stalking grimly away to the barn, he left a startled silence behind him.

He was working in the barn, finishing the last of a number of unnecessary, time-consuming, grueling chores when he felt her hand on his shoulder. Straightening from his task, his body taut, he tilted his head to stare at the ceiling and the loft. His chest rose and fell in uneven breaths as he heard Marissa call his name.

"Jefferson? Are you all right?" Worry trembled in her voice. "You left so abruptly I was concerned."

"That Menendez's men had injured me?" He wondered how she could worry about him when she had been the decoy. The target of one of Menendez's men in Jefferson Cade's wavering moment.

"Of course I worried," she admitted.

He faced her, his expression bleak as she stepped back. "I'm not hiding any hurt. I wasn't injured." He opened his left hand, revealing a nearly healed cut. "Not even this."

"Then what's wrong?" To assure herself he wasn't making light of some difficulty, she let her gaze rove over him and found only the haunted sadness she'd seen so many times before.

Though he had been working when she entered the barn with Satan at her heels, she recognized it as busy work for a troubled mind. The horses had long since been tended. Because his hair was still damp and he'd changed into the extra set of clothing he kept in the tack room, she knew he'd recently bathed in the stream.

Yet his mood hadn't changed. Jefferson was spoiling for a fight with someone. And that someone seemed to be himself.

"Juan and Marta have taken Alejandro home." She spoke casually, as if the Elias had only come for a visit. "Valentina took them in the truck. Then she'll touch base with Billy. Once this last is settled, she, Rick, and Ethan will be leaving."

He listened, as he watched her. She wore the pleated dress and her hair lay in damp disarray around her shoulders. The shampoo and soap Raven Canfield made of wildflowers rose from it in an intoxicating scent that made him want to kiss her. To learn for himself if the taste was as maddening as the fragrance.

Marissa was all he'd ever wanted. The only woman he'd ever needed. Now the bruise across her temple reminded him with sickening clarity that he'd almost lost her to the ricochet of a bullet.

Beneath his vivid stare and in his silence, Marissa continued as normally as possible. "All that's left are legalities. Valentina thinks we could be called to testify when the bodyguards come to trial. But who knows where or how long that will be. So, we're virtually free, Jefferson."

"Free?" He said the word as if it were a gift and a curse.

"Free to do what we want. To go where we want. Never looking over our shoulder."

"Will you go back to Argentina?"

The question astonished her. Where she might go wouldn't matter as much as with whom. "I'd like to go back. In fact I should, to make arrangements about the *estancia* and other family holdings. But only if you go with me."

"I can't go." There was no inflection in his tone. No life in his eyes. With the back of his hand he traced the purple line of the bruise that marred her face. "I have a way of failing the people I love. First my brother Adams, who spent years in prison for my mistake. Then, in the disgrace, my father. Now you."

Catching his fingers, fitting her palm to his, she kept their joined hands against her cheek. "You've never failed me."

"I made a mistake today. There was a moment…"

"We *all* had a moment. You, me. Rick, Ethan. Do you think Valentina made her shot without her own moment? Not doubt or anything that kept us from doing our part. Just that small second of thinking, what if?" Marissa took a step closer. Not close enough to touch him, but enough to make him stifle a groan. "What you did was save a child, Jefferson."

She kissed the backs of his fingers. "A child—and me."

His eyes closed. The scene playing eternally in his mind, Jefferson turned away. Back straight, shoulders taut, he stared through the barn door that led to the corral and the pasture. On a day that had wreaked havoc with all he believed of himself, bringing disorder to a finally ordered life, the canyon survived.

Through thousands of years, and countless changes, through cataclysm and in quiet times the land continued. The sun was setting. It would rise tomorrow.

As this day ended another would begin. Bringing with it the future. His future, to make of it what he would. If this new fear of the pain of loving and losing didn't cripple him. "Then," he muttered softly, "I lose either way."

A rustle of pleats stirred sweet memories, and the scent of wildflowers surrounded him only a faltering heartbeat before Marissa's gliding caress moved over his back.

A loving touch, worth all the pain and heartache time and fate would require of him.

"Jefferson." Slipping her arms around his waist, she rested her cheek against his broad back. "What is it? What troubles you? Let me help."

Then he was embracing her, holding her as if he would never let her go. His eyes were brilliant, the haunting shadows fading. His smile was tender and pensive at once as he hugged her to him so urgently all her breath was swept from her. His lips were pressed against her hair as he muttered, "I was afraid today. I wanted it to be me facing Menendez, but I knew it couldn't be. Not for Alejandro's sake. My mind knew you had to be the one, but my heart wouldn't listen. And I was so afraid it hurt. Dear God, how it hurt. Sacrificing my own life would have been easier than watching you walk toward that monster.

"Until today I didn't know loving could hurt so much. I keep hearing the bullet and seeing you fall, and God help me, I've never felt so helpless in my life. If it weren't for Satan…"

"Shh." With her fingertips she stopped the deluge. "My love, I know what it's like to watch the person who is your life go into danger. I know how frightening it is. And I know the greater the love, the greater the hurt." Stroking the line of his jaw, she cupped his cheek in her palm. Her dark gaze met his, holding him captive, daring him not to listen and believe. "But hurting doesn't stop us from loving. Not if it's real."

He wondered how he could ever deserve her. "Loving might tear out my heart. It might drive me mad. But it doesn't stop being love, does it?"

"Not unless we let it." Marissa's arms crept around his neck. "Your bedroom has a beautiful view of the canyon. The sun will be setting soon. Have you ever made love there at sunset?"

"Not yet." He laughed softly, a beautiful sound that was far too rare. "An oversight that can be corrected. If my lady's willing."

"Oh, she's willing. On the condition that we forget today, and file it away as a part of loving and growing stronger."

"Stronger," Jefferson repeated, knowing this day had been a lesson in strength, taught by Marissa.

With a kiss he took her in his arms. With another, he murmured, "But there's one more condition. A condition of my own."

"Anything," Marissa declared. "Because I trust you— with my life and with the lives of all I love."

"In that case, sweetheart, you've just agreed to marry me, to be my strength and my love for all time."

"No." She shook her head slowly. "Not agreed. Promised."

"And you always keep a promise."

"Always." With eyes closed she savored the rhythm of his stride. The stride that would take her to the bedroom where they would explore the marvelous, mysterious thing called love.

Early the next morning Jefferson was finishing the surprise he'd planned for Marissa, when the telephone in the bedroom rang. He'd stepped back to view his handiwork, when his bedroom door opened and Marissa appeared with Satan at her side.

"That was Billy." Sweeping her tousled hair from her face, with her back to the fireplace, she faced Jefferson. "The mystery of how Menendez found us has been unraveled."

"By Simon or Billy?" he asked.

"Actually, it was Cristal."

"Billy doesn't talk to Cristal if he can help it. Yell, yes," Jefferson amended. "Talk? Never."

"In whatever volume, the mystery's unraveled."

"Unravel it some more." Jefferson led her to the table, poured cups of coffee, then sat down. "Tell me."

"It was word of mouth, but considering all that followed, it can only be true."

"So?" Jefferson prompted, worrying the handle of his cup.

"Just before Paulo and my parents were to board the plane, the pilot asked for a mechanic to check a tire. Later that mechanic would remember there were only three passengers. He recalled overhearing that I was to join them later."

"Where did he recall this? To whom?" Jefferson wondered how something seen and heard in Argentina could lead to Arizona.

"He chose to talk in a bar, after there were rumors the plane had been found in a ravine. Perhaps he was drunk, or feeling boastful, but he added his gossip to the rest. Who knows who heard, or who repeated it. Our bad luck was that someone along the way was connected to Menendez."

"Makes sense," Jefferson agreed. The situation didn't seem so ludicrous in this light. "Any information brought to Menendez would be pursued by the bodyguards."

"Since I had disappeared, yet was not on the plane, the next logical step would be to look for me at my family's *estancia*." Marissa's expression grew somber. "From there the path led to Juan and his family. Our friendship was never a secret.

"Five minutes on the *estancia* and anyone might speak of our relationship. Because of the connection to Alejandro, Maria's mother would be targeted for questioning. Now, because of me, little Maria is missing part of a finger."

"That still leaves a gap between Argentina and Arizona, sweetheart. Perhaps you could explain it as Billy told it."

"I'm sure you know Billy had been trying to ferret out a drug ring with suspected contacts between the border and Silverton. It isn't inconceivable that the contact here was one of Menendez's men. A man familiar with the territory and the old mine."

"This is where Cristal comes in." Jefferson was a step ahead, but he wanted to hear it spelled out.

"Shortly after her visit to the Broken Spur, Cristal heard one of Billy's off-duty deputies talking out of turn. A new man on the force, trying to impress a lady. Cristal shut him up. Not because she understood the danger in what he was saying, but because she knew Billy Blackhawk's deputies were never to discuss business of any kind outside the office.

"Sadly, she didn't stop it before the deputy bragged about seeing the new folks from Argentina shopping in the feed store and hinting at a mystery involving them."

Jefferson pushed his cup away in disgust. "No doubt that bit of news went straight to one of Menendez's lackeys, too. Then, to Menendez himself. If only Cristal had known to speak up sooner. But there was no reason for her to think it was more than a harmless indiscretion."

"Regrettably, it wasn't until Billy brought Menendez's body and his men to town, and she heard what had happened to Alejandro that she realized the deputy's remark could have some bearing on case."

"Then Valentina was more right than we could know," Jefferson suggested. "A chance remark, or a chance encounter can undermine the most carefully laid plans."

"It could happen to anyone. This time it was us." Regret scored Marissa's face. "I couldn't stop what happened to Alejandro. But now that I'm wiser, I'll do everything I can to make sure it doesn't happen again. Neither to Alejandro, or Maria. I can't restore what she's lost. But I can make it up to her by ensuring her safety and giving her a better place to live.

"The *estancia* is mine. I can claim it now. With your help, I can make a difference in the lives of children like Maria."

"What about Juan and Marta, and Alejandro?" he asked.

"For selfish reasons, I hope they stay in this country. But if they return to Argentina, a share of the *estancia* will be theirs and, one day, Alejandro's."

"What about us, Marissa? Where will we be years from now?"

"I don't care, Jefferson, so long as we're together. If I have that, what else could I want?"

"Let me show you what I want." Offering his hand he

stood, waiting. When she rose, a puzzled look on her face, he led her to the fireplace. ''I want that.''

Marissa's gaze lifted to the mantel and the painting of a young girl on the edge of womanhood. A portrait of her, that even she could see had been painted through the eyes of love.

''When?'' she murmured when she could find her voice.

''I put it up this morning. You were too distracted by Billy's call to notice.''

''No, no.'' Her fingers tightened over his. ''I meant when did you paint this? I remember that you worked on wildlife drawings, then Eden's portrait for Adams. When I left Belle Terre, you were involved in a painting of Yancey. A surprise gift for his beach cottage. But I never had any idea you were doing this.''

''I didn't paint this in the lowcountry, Marissa. Or even when I first came to the Rafter B. It was here at the Broken Spur in my evenings alone that I began to paint again.''

''You did this from memory?''

''There were sketches.'' She would be surprised if she knew how often he'd drawn her through the years. He'd sketched her in the quiet times they were together. And later from memory. This work, which was to be an exorcism, he had painted from memory.

Proving he could never forget her.

''I didn't think anything could ever be as wonderful as the painting of Eden. But this…'' Bowing her head, she fought for control. When she looked at him again, there was delight in her eyes. ''I haven't the words to tell you.''

''I don't want the words, sweetheart. But someday, I want the little girl we never had. One who will grow up to be as courageous as the lady in the portrait.''

Marissa's face took on a warm glow. Her dark eyes were like black diamonds. And when Jefferson's someday came, she would tell him a child had been her third wish that day long ago in the swamp. Someday. But for now, they had this day. "It's over. Really over. We can have it all, love and a life together, without guilt, without fear."

The last of guilt and fear resolved, Jefferson caught her to him. "Starting now."

As he held her before the portrait, he knew Valentina was right, a chance remark or encounter could undermine the most carefully laid plans. But a chance remark and encounter could also put them aright again. "Thanks to Cristal."

Because she had reasons of her own to be thankful for both the wisdom and the example of so many wise women, Marissa agreed. "To Cristal, and all the women like her."

Marissa was working with the young mare that had officially become Bonita when the telephone in the tack room rang. Less than a week had passed since Menendez ceased to be a threat and she hadn't learned yet that all news needn't be bad news. Distracted from her routine, she glanced at Jefferson, who was putting away a mended bridle to answer the insistent summons.

She was dismounting when he reappeared. "Trouble?"

"I think maybe it's good news." Taking Bonita's reins and looping them over a rail, Jefferson wrapped his hand around Marissa's. "Let's give the horses a break and take a walk."

The grass was high and the stream full and glittering in the sun. It should have been a walk through a desert paradise, but Marissa was at the point of screaming when Jefferson stopped within the shade of a cottonwood and took her in his arms.

"That was Steve. They're coming home. Jakie's finished her courses early and wants to return to the ranch before school begins in Silverton."

''Will you go back to the Rafter B?'' Marissa asked the first question that came to mind.

''Sandy's assured me there's a place there for me. Steve said the same thing.'' Jefferson's gaze strayed over the canyon and the ranch Steve Cody built. ''But they've deliberately kept this as a small operation. I doubt they really want to change it.''

''What will you do? Where will you go?''

''I'd like to go to Belle Terre. I've been thinking about it for days.'' Smiling down at her, he asked, ''How would you like to be married in Eden's garden? And after that, look into pursuing your medical studies at the university? There's money I haven't touched, a gift from Adams. We could buy a horse farm. I could paint. The possibilities are endless.''

There was nothing Marissa wanted more than to see Jefferson at peace with himself, and with his brothers. Nothing except Jefferson, himself. But was this right for him? ''You can truly go home?''

''Yeah. I can go home now.'' Jefferson knew it was true. He could return to the land of his heart. For he'd learned a lot about loving, and sacrifice. About guilt and redemption.

Watching Marissa with Alejandro had taught him some sacrifices weren't truly sacrifices, but a deeper expression of love. Love that crippling guilt dishonored. ''There are some things I need to say to Adams. Most of all, I need to tell him what loving you has taught me.''

Looking up at him, Marissa saw that for the first time there were no haunted shadows darkening eyes as blue as a summer sky. In that moment, her happiness knew no limits, for she, too, had learned the difference between duty and honor and love.

The first had been her responsibility as a daughter. The

second, a promise kept. The last a gift surpassing all else. A gift shared and returned by Jefferson.

"Regrets, my love?" He questioned her thoughtfulness.

"I'll miss the canyon." Her gaze strayed over the familiar land. "And Juan and Marta, and Alejandro. But we can visit. So can they. Often. Or even come with us. But what about Satan?"

"My disobedient hound?" Jefferson lifted a teasing brow.

"Whose disobedience may have saved my life."

"He goes with us, everywhere. Always."

"Then how could I have regrets?" With smiling lips she kissed him. "Especially for loving you."

Her softly spoken words held the promise of a new life. From this day they would follow their hearts, together. And each day would be a celebration of a love that was the redemption of Jefferson Cade.

* * * * *

A COWBOY'S PROMISE

by
Anne McAllister

ANNE McALLISTER

RITA Award-winning author Anne McAllister fell in love with a cowboy when she was five years old. Tall, dark, handsome, lone-wolf types have appealed to her ever since. 'Me, for instance,' her university professor husband says. Well, yes. But even though she's been married to the man of her dreams for over thirty years, she still likes writing about those men of the West! And even though she may take a break from cowboy heroes now and then, she has lots more stories planned for them. She is always happy to hear from readers, and if you'd like, you can write to Anne at PO Box 3904, Bozeman, Montana 59772, USA. Please enclose an SAE with return postage. And you can visit her website at www.annemcallister.com and e-mail Anne your comments to anne@annemcallister.com

For my stepfather,
John J Perkins
(1917–2000)

Who taught me that love is thicker than blood

Prologue

They said that hearing was the last sense to go.

His hadn't gone. Yet.

But the light was getting brighter. He could see it, could see shapes in the distance—people—silhouetted in front of it. He tried to move closer.

"Hold him still, damn it!" The harsh voice came from a long way away.

"I'm trying! I'm trying!" That voice, too, barely penetrated his consciousness.

"C'mon! He's losin' a lot of blood. Must've took three bullets at least. Hurry up!"

"I'm moving as fast as I can!"

"Well, move faster! We don't get him there soon, he ain't gonna make it."

The light grew brighter, then dimmed. The voices muttered on, the noises grew harsher. He could hear metal on metal. Clanking. Jostling.

"Here. Just shove the door open. Give me that!"

"He's bleeding all over the place!"

"Press down, damn it!"

"I am!"

The light was brighter again. The faces clearer.

He could make out features. He could see his father.

Was that his father? That young smiling man? God, it had been years. He'd been three when the old man died. And his vague last memories of his father had not been of a happy man.

But he was happy now—with Charlie's mother, both of them smiling, their arms around each other and around Lucy, too. His mom had died when he was ten; his sister, five years later.

Luce, damn it, how could you have got yourself killed like that?

He moved closer into the light and tried to call out.

"We're losin' him!"

"I know! I know! Come on!"

Charlie barely heard the voices now. They didn't matter. He was trying to reach Lucy.

He had so much to tell her—about everything that had happened since she'd gone—about Joanna, her teacher, who had taken him on, had kicked his butt, determined not to let him die in the streets the way his sister had, about Chase, Joanna's husband, who had taught him how to be a man.

But before he could speak, he saw more faces.

He saw Chase and Joanna. He saw their children, Emerson, Alex and Annie, who had become like little brothers and sister to him.

Whoa. Wait a sec. *They* weren't dead! None of them! Then what—

Charlie looked around, puzzled.

He scanned the faces. He saw his best friend, Herbert,

from grammar school and DeShayne and Lopez, the guys he had hung with in high school, all still alive and kicking as far as he knew. He saw Gaby, his agent, who he'd spoken to last week, and his old friends Miles and Susan Cavanaugh and their sons, Patrick and James.

His gaze swept over them all. And moved on.

He was looking for one face.

One woman.

Where was she?

Cait!

He called her name. But no one replied.

Cait!

Everyone—his father, his mother, his sister, his friends—all stood silent and looked back at him blankly.

He reached them now, and the light was all around him. But he barely noticed. Instead of greeting his family, instead of throwing his arms around them in the joy of reunion, he pushed past them, wildly looking around.

Cait!

Silence. Emptiness.

She wasn't here.

He was going to die and she wasn't going to be a part of his eternity?

Of course she wasn't, he realized.

How could she be when he hadn't let her be a part of his life?

One

Abuk, Western Asia

The hospital wasn't there.

There was a pile of rubble instead.

The taxi driver who had brought him here shook his head. "I told you so."

At least Charlie guessed that was the meaning of the words the man was saying over and over. He'd given the driver the name of the hospital as soon as he'd limped out of the airport. And the driver had protested then.

"No, no. Can't go. Not there," he'd said over and over.

But Charlie had insisted. He hadn't come halfway around the world to be turned back three miles from his goal.

He hadn't realized then that "not there," meant the hospital itself.

The heat was suffocating, making him feel even dizzier

and weaker than he was. He'd left Los Angeles twenty odd hours ago, had killed time in Amsterdam and more in Istanbul before the long final flight into Abuk.

He was doing the whole trip against doctors' orders. A whole roomful of white-coated medicos had told him he wasn't ready for anything strenuous.

"You coded," one of them told him bluntly. "Clinically you were dead. You lost quarts of blood. You can barely walk. You aren't going to get better traipsing halfway around the world."

Yes, Charlie thought. He was.

He was doing the one thing that was going to make him really better at last. He was going to make up for lost time. He was going to find Cait.

The thought of Cait was what had got him through all the rehab he'd done so far.

"Where are the other hospitals?"

The driver gestured this way and that, and finally ended up pointing in two directions.

Charlie tried to remember which would be the more likely choice. He flipped through his pocket dictionary and found the word for *near*. Then he fished a wad of local notes out of his pocket and said it.

The driver nodded, pocketed the money happily, and off they jolted once more.

The city had changed in two years. The war that wasn't called a war had died down. When Charlie had been here last, it had been in full swing—sniping and strafing had been the order of the day.

No lines had been drawn. There were no clear "sides." You took your life in your hands whenever you ventured out. And you were as likely to have been killed by one faction as another. Misery had been everywhere.

It pretty much still was.

Two years ago Charlie had come to photograph it. It

was his job, and he did it well. He found pain and heartache and inhumanity wherever it existed, exposed it in
black-and-white, then showed it to the world.

For five years he'd done a spectacular job doing just
that. His photos had been hung from Paris to L.A. They'd
found their way into private collections and galleries all
over the world. His book of photo essays, *Inhumanity,*
which had contained, among other things, two sets of photos taken right here, had become a bestseller this past
spring while he was still in the hospital.

It was what damned near getting killed did for you.

"Nonsense," he remembered his agent Gabriela del
Castillo saying, her green eyes flashing angrily at his deliberate irreverence. "Your book is selling because it
touches people. You find the heart of things, Charlie. You
challenge the soul."

"And getting three bullets in me didn't hurt."

"Didn't hurt? They nearly killed you!" Gaby had been
furious about his being in the wrong place at the wrong
time when he'd got caught in that Middle-East crossfire.
"I worry about you."

"You should be glad," Charlie had maintained. "It
boosted sales."

"I'm not that mercenary," Gaby retorted. "Truly. I
worry. I don't know why you aren't dead."

Charlie knew.

Because he couldn't spend eternity without Cait.

He hadn't said so to Gaby. He hadn't said so to anyone.
He hadn't talked about it at all.

Talking about eternity and near-death experiences
wasn't something he did.

To Gaby and everyone else, Charlie Seeks Elk was a
gutsy, earthy, hard-nosed pragmatist, the embodiment of
the what-you-see-is-what-you-get guy. Down-to-earth realism was the name of his game. Charlie was the last man

on earth given to out-of-body experiences, to messages from the other side.

But the day he'd been shot—the day he'd coded—he had seen a bright light. He'd seen his family—all of them dead for years. He'd seen his friends, and knew the promise that they would spend eternity together. And frankly, he'd have been happy to join them.

But not if Cait wasn't there.

When he'd left her two years ago, turning his back on the idea of marriage and family, he'd done it for both their sakes. He'd felt strong, noble, independent—a man with a cause who couldn't be tied down.

But that was before he'd faced eternity—without the prospect of Cait.

It surprised him how instinctively he'd looked for her. He hadn't known he would. But he hadn't ever died before.

Since he had, he knew what mattered.

And he had to find Cait.

The driver whipped through semideserted avenues lined with rubble and burned-out buildings, heading back toward a more populated area of town. This part had been heavily populated when he'd been here. They drove right past the building where Charlie had rented a room, where he had taken Cait in his arms, where she had taken him into her body. There was nothing there now but two half walls and a pile of crumbling stucco. Charlie shut his eyes and prayed.

When he opened them again he saw a section of the street where the rubble had been cleared away. A foundation was being dug for a new building. The taxi driver was saying something, smiling, pointing and nodding.

Charlie caught a few words. *Peace. New. Hope.*

There was nothing there yet but a hole in the ground. But if you dared believe, it was a harbinger of hope, a belief in a future where buildings would be allowed to stand, where families would thrive again, where children would live unmaimed.

"Yes," he said. "Yes." And he leaned his head back against the sticky plastic upholstery of the car and hoped, too.

He hoped that at the next hospital, he'd find Cait.

But she wasn't there.

The health organization she worked for had pulled out, the director told him. "They come in during emergencies," the man said in heavily accented English, smiling at Charlie across the counter. "You see we are not emergent anymore."

Charlie wasn't seeing much of anything. He clung to the countertop to keep himself upright. His head was spinning. His leg throbbed.

"What about another hospital. She wouldn't be at another hospital here?"

"Not unless she left her job and stayed." The man shook his head. "You have to have a good reason to stay."

She might have had a reason. "What about the orphans?" Charlie asked urgently.

The man looked perplexed. "Orphans?"

"There were children at that hospital." Charlie's knuckles were white against the counter. "Kids who'd been hurt. Kids without families. Kids abandoned. If she'd wanted to adopt one…"

She *had* wanted to adopt one—a four-year-old girl with a shattered arm and the most expressive dark eyes Charlie had ever seen. Resi.

The director steepled his fingers. "I do not know of orphans." He pulled out a file and consulted it, then gave Charlie three addresses. "You will have to go there and check."

Clutching the piece of paper, Charlie left. He needed sleep. He needed pain medication.

More, he needed to find Cait.

He found another taxi. He gave the driver the addresses. They went from one orphanage to another. At each one Charlie described the little girl, Resi. At each he asked about the American nurse, Cait Blasingame. At all of them he was met with sad smiles and commiserations.

"No, I am sorry."

"No, no one like that here."

"No. We have never heard of them."

No Resi. No Cait.

For three days he stayed in Abuk and he searched. He went to every hospital, every clinic, every doctor's surgery he could find. He went to the consulate. He went to the newspapers. He went everywhere he could think of.

If Cait was here, he would find her.

In the end he was sick. In the end he was fevered. In the end he had to admit she was gone.

It had been a long shot, of course. He hadn't admitted that to himself before.

All the time he'd been recovering, he'd focused on getting well enough to go back to Abuk to find Cait, to say the words he'd never wanted to say before.

Marry me.

For three months he'd hoped and dreamed and planned. He had promised himself he would find her and he hadn't let himself think beyond that.

Now he was here and Cait wasn't.

Now what?

"So," Gaby stared down at him in his hospital bed, her expression a mixture of concern and irritation, "were they worth it?"

"Were what worth it?" Charlie didn't want company.

He'd told the nurse that. He had been turning away visitors since he'd ended up here a week ago after returning to L.A.

But Gaby never listened to nurses. Gaby was convinced she knew better than anyone. Now she loomed over him like a blond-haired avenging angel, ready to do mayhem. "The photos you had to go halfway around the world to take!"

Charlie turned his head toward the wall. "I didn't take any photos."

There was complete, stunned silence. Charlie lived to take photos. If he didn't take photos, Gaby used to say, he'd be dead.

Now, quietly, she asked, "So what did you go for, then?"

The old Charlie—the self-contained, fiercely independent Charlie—would have said, "Nothing." He would have stonewalled her the way he had stonewalled all attempts to invade his privacy for years.

But the new Charlie had a whole new perspective on life. Besides, he was so damn weak even now, after a full week of antibiotics and transfusions and hospital bed rest, that the stone wall was crumbling.

"I was trying to find someone," he muttered. His voice was low, and the words were hard to get out.

He hadn't said them to anyone. He hadn't even told his best friends, Chase and Joanna Whitelaw—the couple who had more or less become his surrogate parents when he was sixteen years old—about Cait.

He might have, but Chase and Joanna were gone.

Two weeks ago they had left for Europe for two months with their kids. It was a trip they'd been planning for a long time. Originally they'd planned to meet him in Athens. But that was before he'd got shot and sent home.

Then Joanna had been on the verge of canceling the whole trip. Charlie had argued against it.

He was home, he assured her. He was on the mend. He was fine! It wasn't merely that he wanted them to have the vacation they'd looked forward to for so long.

It was also that he'd wanted them gone so Joanna wouldn't fuss when he left to look for Cait.

They didn't know he had gone. They didn't know he was back. They didn't know he was in the hospital. And he had no intention of telling them.

But Gaby had caught him with his defenses down. If she'd bullied him, he might not have said any more, but Gaby knew when to bully and when to just wait. Now she waited. She pulled up a chair and sat beside the bed.

"Who matters that much?" Her voice was gentler than he'd ever heard it. She wrapped her fingers around his and gave a gentle squeeze.

He shook his head vaguely. "A friend," he said. "A woman I knew there. A nurse." He looked away. "Her name was Cait."

"Was?" There was a worried edge to Gaby's voice.

Charlie swallowed. "She's not dead. At least I don't think she is." God, he wouldn't let himself think anything like that! "She's just…gone."

"Gone where?"

"Don't know." He plucked at the coverlet, worrying it between his fingers. "She worked for one of those global medicine outfits, the ones who send personnel into war zones and disaster areas. It's still pretty much a disaster," he reflected, "but not an active one. So they've pulled out. I don't know where they are. Where she is."

"Have you asked?"

"Of course. I called from here. I might have had better luck if I'd stormed the headquarters. It was easy enough for them to tell me they don't give out that information.

Privacy, you know?'' His mouth twisted. He understood
their concerns, but it didn't help him.

"Do you have an address for her family?"

"No. She was from Montana. She used to talk about it
all the time. Used to call it 'the last best place.' I used to
tell her that was a slogan, and she said it was truth in
advertising.'' He smiled now at the thought.

In his mind he could still see Cait's own smile whenever
they'd had that teasing exchange:

"You should see it, Charlie,'' she would say. "You'd
love it.''

And he'd shake his head in protest. "No way. Not me.
I'm a city boy.''

But she'd persist, telling him stories about the ranch
where she'd grown up, about herding cattle and branding
calves, about seeing bears and coyotes and, once, she
thought, a wolf.

She told him about fishing in the creek and swimming
in the swimming hole and training her horse and tagging
along after her father or her older brother, Wes. And he
let her talk because he liked watching her face whenever
she told those stories. Her hazel eyes would get kind of
soft and misty, and she would smile a sort of faraway,
loving, gentle smile.

It was a childhood so unlike his own. Her memories
were happy ones, so very unlike his.

"What was it like where you grew up?" she'd asked
him time and again.

But Charlie had just shaken his head and lied. "I don't
remember.''

Now he found that he remembered her stories even better than he remembered the things that had really happened
to him.

"I'll look for her,'' Gaby said. "I'll find out where she
is. I'll get her to come and see you.''

"No!"

Gaby stared at him. "I thought you wanted to find her."

"I do, but...but I have to go to her." He knew that much. He would wait until hell froze over before Cait would ever come to him.

Gaby considered that. She considered him.

After the shooting, Gaby had come from Santa Fe to see him as soon as he'd been well enough to come back to Los Angeles.

He'd gone to his own apartment, refusing to stay at Chase and Joanna's, making it difficult for everyone, but needing the pretense that he was doing fine on his own.

Of course he hadn't been. Joanna had come and stayed with him. Or Chase had. Or one of the Cavanaughs. Patrick, who was fifteen now, and James, just turned thirteen, had even done their share of nursemaiding.

And then Gaby had come.

He remembered her sitting by his bed while he slept and, at other times, talking quietly, worriedly, with Chase and Joanna when they'd thought he couldn't hear. She'd been devoted on more than a business level, though Charlie had never asked for that.

Once, early in their professional relationship, in her straightforward way, Gaby had asked if he might someday be interested in more than that. In his own straightforward way, Charlie had said no. He knew she didn't mean an affair. Gaby was a marriage-minded woman. He had told her he wasn't ever getting married, that he would never care about any woman that way or that much.

She had taken him at his word. He wondered what she was thinking now, but he didn't wonder enough to ask.

He felt her hand squeeze his fingers.

"I'll look, Charlie," she said. "I'll be back to let you know what I find out."

* * *

Two days later, when he came in from physical therapy, Gaby was waiting for him.

"She's from rural Elmer, Montana," Gaby said without preamble. "That's in the Shields Valley. Daughter of Walter Blasingame, owner of the Rafter WB Ranch, acreage unreportable because apparently it's bad form to inquire." Gaby rolled her eyes. "She is presently nurse-midwife at a practice in Livingston. The nearest airport is Bozeman. If you want a place to stay, Brenna McCall has a cabin about half a mile from Blasingame's land."

Charlie just leaned on his crutches and stared.

Gaby smiled brightly and shrugged. "Anything else?"

"How did you do that?" He was shaking his head, amazed, his heart quickening in his chest. "She's there? In Montana? In Livingston?"

"Living with her father, Brenna says."

"You talked to *Brenna* about her?" It was one thing to bare his soul to Gaby. He didn't want the whole damn world knowing his business!

"I did not spill your guts," Gaby said indignantly. "I checked the Internet for Blasingames in Montana. When I found out where they were, I started checking each one. When it turned out that one of them lived near Brenna, it seemed foolish not to check. I know Brenna. I hung a show for her in my gallery last year. You know her. She does those fantastic watercolor, pen-and-ink cowboys?"

Charlie nodded vaguely. He didn't remember. He didn't care. He could only think about Cait. Gaby had found Cait!

"Thanks."

"You're welcome. You are not haring off, though," Gaby said firmly. "This time before you take off anywhere, you are going to be fit."

Charlie grinned. The world was brighter. Cait was in Montana. "Yeah, sure. Whatever you say."

* * *

"That's it, Milly! Oh, good. Oh, yes. That's right. Push. Keep going. Push, push, push!" Cait positioned herself to help ease the arrival of this new little person into the world. She could see lots of dark hair and a furrowed brow and then an entire fierce little face. She always loved this part, being there to witness the emergence of new life, to share in the first moments when a tiny new human being came into the world.

Milly Callahan, her fingers strangling those of her husband, Cash, was doing great. They were both doing great. "Just one more now," Cait said. "Whenever you're ready."

And moments later a blinking, black-haired baby boy entered the world.

"He's here!" Milly wept, her chin wavering, tears leaking down her cheeks and rolling into her ears.

"Ohmigod," Cash said, tears and joy mingling on his face. "Ohmigod. I've got a son! Can you believe it? God, Mil', look at him! He is so beautiful!"

They all were—scrawny, red and wet, there was nothing as beautiful as a newborn child. Cait, too, could have just sat and stared at him for hours, marveling at the miracle of life. But she had work to do, so it wasn't until all the afterbirth business was taken care of, the baby checked over and Milly, too, that she allowed herself a moment to savor the glow of the family before her.

The child, now named Cash James after his father and henceforth to be called C.J., was swaddled in a blue blanket and nestling in Milly's arms as he did his best to figure out this nursing stuff.

As he rooted and snuffled, Milly's gaze flicked worriedly between her son and Cait. "Am I doing this right?"

"You're doing fine," Cait assured her. "Here." She reached down and, cradling C.J.'s head, helped ease him to a slightly different angle so he could find the nipple.

"Ouch," Milly exclaimed as her son finally glommed on.

"Hey," Cash said with gruff tenderness to the baby, "you're not supposed to hurt your mom." He was sitting next to her on the edge of the bed, and he brushed a lock of hair off her cheek. "He already did hurt you," he said, the memories of Milly's labor obviously still fresh in his mind.

"He was worth it," Milly said fervently. She stroked the baby's soft cheek.

"They're always worth it," Cait said softly as she stood back and watched the new little family group.

She never delivered a baby that she didn't feel a pang of envy for what the parents had and she didn't.

She would, she assured herself. She was young enough yet. Twenty-nine wasn't that old. And both she and Steve wanted children.

Steve Carmichael. Her fiancé. The man she had been waiting for all her life.

They wanted the same things, she and Steve: home, family, children.

Three, she'd said, though Steve wasn't sure about that.

"How on earth will we have time for them?" he asked. "We can't even find time to get married."

He had a point. Steve was a cardiologist, presently practicing in Bozeman, but coming to Livingston two afternoons a week. In August he was taking a new job at a teaching hospital in Denver. Now he spent one week a month there getting established, making the transition.

Cait had demands on her time, as well. She was a nurse-midwife who not only worked with two physicians, but delivered babies, like C.J., on her own. She taught childbirth classes one night a week. And since her father's heart attack had brought her home late last summer, she'd been in charge of running the family ranch.

She'd expected her father to be back at it by now, but his recovery had been slower than anticipated. Always a vital, active man, Walt Blasingame now sat and stared out the window for hours. He had no energy, no enthusiasm. Cait tried to encourage him, run the ranch, and do her job. And, even though she'd hired a foreman this spring, she still didn't have much time for thinking about a wedding.

"Never mind," Steve said. "We'll get to it. I can always come back from Denver for a wedding. What matters is that we've found each other."

Amen to that, Cait thought. At last she had found the right man to marry.

Steve was solid, dependable, committed. He wanted exactly what she wanted—a refreshing change from the man she'd first set her heart on.

She barely spared him a thought anymore. Since she'd met Steve she had settled, relaxed, got her bearings once more. At last she felt as if her feet were on emotionally steady ground.

If there was a silver lining to the cloud that had been her father's heart attack, it was her coming home and finding Steve.

He thought so, too. "We're perfect together. We understand each other."

Only another medical professional could appreciate the emergencies, the unforeseen events that complicated life on a weekly and sometimes almost daily basis. Steve called and canceled dates because of someone's heart attack. She called and canceled dates because of someone's birth.

When they could, they enjoyed the time they had.

And when they finally had a family, Cait knew they would make things work.

She wouldn't have the ranch to worry about then. Either her father would be back running things or her brother,

Wes, would finally decide it was time to come home and do it, or—and she didn't like to think about this—the Rafter WB would be sold.

It wouldn't matter to her, she told herself. She'd be in Denver, anyway.

But the ranch was so much a part of her that she couldn't imagine it not being there to come home to.

It always had been.

She'd gone all over the world in the past seven years. She'd started at a prenatal clinic in Mexico. She had ended up staying to work as a nurse through one of the most devastating earthquakes to hit the region. After that, going back to Livingston to work had seemed almost a cop-out. There were so many other people and places who urgently needed medical aid.

If she, footloose and fancy-free, couldn't help out, who would?

So she'd spent the next seven years going from one disaster to another. Not just natural disasters, either. Some of them were man-made. Wars, to put it bluntly. Someone had to help. It might as well be her.

But in the back of her mind she'd always carried the ranch with her. She'd taken it out and talked about it, shared it with others, given them a taste of her home.

Once she'd dreamed about bringing them home.

One man.

One child.

She wouldn't let herself think about the man anymore.

She still thought about the child.

Resi.

The thought of the little orphaned girl who had wormed her way into Cait's heart made her throat tighten and an ache begin behind her eyes.

"Stop it!" she told herself sharply aloud. It wasn't productive, thinking about Resi. It wasn't even smart. There was nothing to be sad about. Everything had turned out for the best. Everything!

Cait had stopped counting the times she had assured herself of that.

The memories came back when she was tired, when she was vulnerable, when she saw families like the Callahans and knew how fortunate they were.

Now she finished washing up, dragged a brush through her hair and grabbed her tote bag. It was nine-thirty. She'd put in a full day before delivering C.J., and she still had to drive thirty odd miles and check with Gus Holt, the foreman, about how things were going at the ranch. But first she was going to see how the new family was doing.

The baby was sleeping in Milly's arms. Milly herself was dozing. Cash was sitting in the armchair by the bed, a stunned but blissful expression on his face. When Cait came into the room he looked up and grinned.

"I can't hardly catch my breath," he said, then gave a self-deprecating laugh. "I've seen calves born before. I know my birds an' bees. But that was a miracle tonight." He shook his head in amazement.

"It always is." Cait went over to the bed, and Milly opened her eyes to smile up at her. "You doing all right?"

Milly nodded. "Fine. Just fine." Her voice was a whisper. She brushed a gentle finger over C.J.'s soft hair. "Isn't he something?"

"He's something," Cait agreed. "Can I do anything else for you before I leave?"

Milly shook her head. "You've already done everything."

"Well, give me a call if you need anything. I'll be in tomorrow morning to check on you. The doctor will be by, too, just to check things out. You rest now. The nurse can put C.J. in the isolette for you." She nodded toward the one that had been wheeled into the room so C.J. and his mother wouldn't be separated. "You look like you could use some sleep, too," she said to Cash, who was still smiling his dazed, delighted grin.

"Go home and go to sleep now," Milly said to him.

Cash looked as if he was going to protest, but he didn't. "Yes, ma'am," he said. Then he bent down and dropped a light kiss on his son's head and another deeper more intense one on his wife's mouth. "God, Mil', I do love you," he said.

Cait, watching them, felt another stab of envy and swallowed the lump in her throat.

Someday, she promised herself, as she led the way and Cash followed her out, that would be her in the birthing suite. And it would be Steve kissing her and telling her he loved her and looking at her like that, with his heart in his eyes.

She and Cash walked toward the lobby together. When they reached it, he put his arm around her and gave her a hard hug. "God, Cait, I don't know how to thank you. I am the happiest, luckiest guy in the world."

Cait smiled. "Tonight, Cash," she said, "I'd have to agree with you. Just remember it a week from now when he's crying at 2:00 a.m."

He grinned and crossed his heart. "I promise."

They started toward the door when Joyce O'Meara, the receptionist, called, "Cait?"

"Go on," she said to Cash. "I'll see you tomorrow."

"Right. G'night. Thank you." He sketched her a quick salute, gave her a wink and sauntered out into the night.

"What is it?" she asked.

Joyce nodded toward the shadowy waiting room. "There's someone waiting to see you."

Please God, not someone in labor, Cait thought wearily. Smiling, she turned—and felt the bottom fall out of her world.

A lean dark man had hauled himself awkwardly out of a chair and stepped out of the shadows. The light fell on his blue-black hair and sharp, handsome, weather-beaten face.

"Charlie?"

Oh, God, no.

But it was. Charlie Seeks Elk in the flesh, right here, big as life, smiling that beautiful lopsided smile of his. "Hello, Cait."

Two

He didn't know what to say.

He'd driven all the way from California, had rehearsed his greeting at least a thousand times. And now, when he finally came face-to-face with her, the words stuck in his throat.

He just wanted to reach out to her, to put his arms around her and hang on. No one in his entire life had ever looked so good.

And so shocked.

And not exactly thrilled.

Charlie could read visuals better than most. It was, after all, what he did for a living. And he could read this visual with no problem at all.

Cait wasn't glad to see him. She looked, in fact, gut-punched.

She wetted her lips, but she didn't smile. She said his name again. "Charlie." Her fingers, one hand free, one hand clutching a tote bag, balled into fists.

He felt the first flicker of true apprehension since he'd fought his way back from eternity all those months ago. And he tried again. "I don't suppose you'd believe I was just in the neighborhood?"

"I don't suppose I would," she said coolly. She didn't look gut-punched now. The color in her cheeks, which had drained briefly, was coming back. She looked flushed and fit and absolutely wonderful.

"I wasn't," he said. "I came to see you."

The balled fist opened, and Cait tucked one hand into her pocket. The other strangled the handle of the tote. "I can't imagine why."

He didn't suppose she could. He took a deep breath and it was his turn to wet suddenly parched lips. He could feel a pulsing throb in his still-healing leg. It wasn't as steady as he would have wished. *He* wasn't as steady.

He rubbed a hand against taut muscles at the back of his neck. "Could we…go somewhere and talk?"

"What could we possibly have to say to each other?"

It was going to be harder than he thought. He shouldn't have been surprised, after all. And really, he wasn't. He hadn't been expecting a miracle. He'd had no illusions that she would take one look and throw her arms around him. He wasn't exactly the prodigal son.

He was the man who had left her without a word, had walked out in the middle of the night and had never come back—until now.

"I have some things to say," he said slowly and more steadily than he felt, "even if you don't. I wish you'd listen."

"Why should I?"

He looked straight at her. "I don't know."

Something flickered in her stubborn, unblinking gaze. Some tiny movement seemed to make her hesitate. She bit down on her lip and glanced around.

The receptionist was listening avidly and with no pretense about it. Charlie didn't care.

Obviously Cait did. One look at the woman's eager expression and Cait's lips pressed into a tight line. "Fine," she said curtly. "You can talk. There's a fast-food place not far from here. We can meet there for a cup of coffee."

She turned on her heel and headed for the door.

For a split second Charlie just watched her, drank in the sight of her—even the stiff, unyielding back of her. Then he strode after her, trying not to limp, aware of the receptionist's curious gaze.

Cait was waiting outside, keys in her hand. "You do have a car?" She barely looked back at him as she spoke.

He nodded. "Over there."

She didn't even glance where he had pointed. "That's my truck." She indicated an older full-size red Ford. "Follow me." She turned and started briskly away.

"Cait!"

She turned. "What?" Truck keys tapped impatiently against her thigh.

"I need—" He broke off. He couldn't explain. There were no explanations. Just need. A need that had been roiling desperately inside him since he'd looked around his eternity and discovered she wasn't there.

"What?" she said irritably.

He shouldn't. It was probably only going to make things worse. But he couldn't help it. Couldn't stop himself.

"Need this," he finished, and closed the gap between them, wrapped his arms around her and laid his lips on hers.

He was kissing Cait. Hungrily. Desperately. Like a drowning man opening to the gasp of air before he's swept away. He was holding Cait. He was knowing once more what it was like to have her in his arms, to wrap them around her, to fit her body to his, to mold them into one.

But her body wasn't fitting. It wasn't molding. She stood rigid and unbending, her arms stiff at her sides, her lips tightly shut.

Oh, hell. Oh, hell. Oh, hell.

And then, just as he was about to give up, he felt something—a softening, a warming—a kindling that was happening in spite of her determination that it should not. He could feel it.

And he thought, *Yes!*

And he dared to believe at last that things would be all right. She still cared. She loved him. She would take him back.

And then, abruptly, Cait pulled away from him. Her eyes were fierce and angry and brimming with pain.

"Ah, Cait," he said, still heartened in spite of the pain he saw there, certain he could heal it with the right words. "I didn't meant to hurt you."

She didn't move, barely even opened her lips. "Do you want that cup of coffee or not?"

Her voice was hard and clipped, but he believed. More, he could still taste just a hint of her, was still close enough that the scent of her—a scent that had always made even the worst of Abuk's nightmares go away—touched his nostrils.

How the hell had he ever managed to walk away from her?

How could he explain what he had done?

"I want the cup of coffee," he said. His throat ached.

"Then follow me." Her voice was cool, steady, at odds with the pain he'd seen in her eyes. She turned and walked ramrod straight to her truck.

She was shaking so badly that it took her three tries to get the key in the ignition. She finally got it when she grabbed her right hand in her left to steady it and jammed the key in and turned it on.

Then she gripped the steering wheel with both trembling hands and took deep, deep breaths.

Charlie! Here!

And even worse, kissing her!

Thank God she'd steeled herself the moment he'd taken her into his arms.

It hadn't been easy. He felt the same—hard and lean and warm. Maybe even a little harder and leaner than she remembered. He smelled the same. There was that hint of lime and leather and something indefinably Charlie.

The memories had swamped her, made her ache and need—and want things she knew she absolutely did not want at all.

She was done with him—just as he had been done with her.

When she'd awakened that morning in Abuk to find herself alone in bed, she'd simply assumed that Charlie had got a call that had taken him out on an early lead and she hadn't heard it. She worked twelve-hour days in conditions that no one should have to work in—and when she slept, she slept like a rock. She rarely heard Charlie's phone.

She hadn't been surprised to find him gone.

It had happened before. When you did what Charlie did for a living, you never knew when something would happen.

Something *had* happened.

She didn't realize until later that what had happened was that Charlie had walked out of her life.

Why?

She'd screamed the question. She'd cried it. She'd asked it a hundred times. And yet, if she opened herself to the silence, she already knew.

He hadn't loved her.

It was as simple and as stark as that.

She'd been fine to have an affair with, had been right there, ready and available for a desperate, passionate fling, the sort one had in the middle of a war zone where no one looked beyond today because tomorrow might never come.

The problem was that the night before Charlie had walked, Cait had dared to talk about tomorrow.

She had talked about *all* their tomorrows. She had talked about forever. Marriage. Family.

And when she'd awakened, he was gone.

And now, two years later, he was here…and he wanted to talk.

Cait didn't want to talk. She didn't want to listen.

Most of all, she didn't want to feel what she'd felt when he'd kissed her.

Damn him! It was over. Completely over!

And she was over him!

She had a new man now. A better man.

And she was going to tell him so.

She wished they had just "talked" in the hospital waiting room. She didn't want to drag this out any longer than necessary. But it was probably better, she thought, closing her eyes and praying for strength, that they did it somewhere else.

If they'd stayed at the hospital, Joyce would have heard every word.

Joyce was a good soul, but she knew Cait and she knew Steve—and a strange man and Cait Blasingame having a heart-to-heart in the hospital waiting room would give her lots of fodder for the gossip mill.

There would be plenty to talk about, anyway, simply because Charlie had showed up looking for her. And if Joyce had happened to glance outside and see that kiss…!

Cait didn't even want to think about that.

In her rearview mirror she saw a low-slung sports car—good God, was he driving a Porsche?—pull out of a stall, then come to idle close by. She could see Charlie behind the wheel, watching her, waiting for her.

"Do it," she told herself firmly. "You can do this. Talk to him. Walk away from him."

How hard could it be? It couldn't possibly be worse than being left in the middle of the night?

There were several fast-food joints not far from the hospital. She picked one where she hoped she wouldn't know anyone and parked just outside the door. She got out and waited as Charlie's car—it was, in fact, a silver Porsche!—glided to a stop alongside hers. Her fingers clenched involuntarily, and she consciously unfolded them and brushed them down the sides of her slacks.

The car door opened and Charlie got out. He moved as if he hurt. Cait looked away. She wouldn't ask. She didn't care. Her fingers curled tightly again.

"You look good," he said in that rough-silk voice of his as he came up to her.

"You don't," she said bluntly, making a point at looking him over now.

The light in the hospital had been soft, and it hadn't shown the new lines and hollows in his lean, gaunt face. They told her that the past two years had been hard ones. She knew about some of it—she'd seen the photos in his book.

Fool that she was, she'd bought it.

Resi, after all, was on the cover. She'd bought it because of Resi—because she had been a part of the poignant story of the life that Charlie had told in pictures.

That was the only reason. But of course she'd looked at it all. After he'd left Abuk she learned that he had gone to Africa, into an area that was, if possible, even more ravaged. The life his photos showed there had been much the same. Obviously, it had had its effects on him, too.

He was smiling at her now, but she noticed that it didn't reach his eyes. They were dark and serious.

"No," he said now, in reply to her blunt assessment of his looks, "I don't suppose I do." He held the door open, and she went in.

If Cait had ever let herself imagine seeing Charlie Seeks Elk again, it wouldn't have been beneath the glaring lights of a fast-food restaurant in Livingston, Montana, on a warm breezy summer night.

Charlie had never been inclined to come to Montana. He'd even teased her about her "country girl" life, though sometimes she thought he might actually have envied it just a little.

When she'd first met him she'd assumed he was, like many Indians she knew, born on a reservation from which he'd left to find a place in the world beyond it. He hadn't been, he'd told her.

"The L.A. kid, that's me. Born and bred." He'd gone on to tell her in a few brief, stark sentences about his childhood. His father had been born on a reservation, though Charlie didn't even know which tribe it belonged to. He'd left to join the army and, after his discharge, he'd stayed in L.A.

"What'd he have to go back to?" Charlie had said with a shrug. "Nothing for him there. Besides, he drank. He could drink anywhere."

He'd met Charlie's mother in L.A. where she worked as a secretary. "My mom's family were dust-bowl Okies, mostly Choctaw, on the rolls at least," he'd said. "But they left in the thirties. No future for them there."

They hadn't had much of a future in any case.

Charlie's parents had had barely eight years together before his father's drinking led him to have a fatal car accident. Charlie had been three, his sister, Lucy, eight. Their mother had worked hard. She'd done her best for them. In fact, she'd been so focused on providing for them that she had neglected her own health and missed the warning signs of diabetes until it was too late.

She'd died when Charlie was eleven. Lucy, at sixteen, decided she was old enough to take charge.

"Luce did her best," Charlie had told Cait late one night. They were lying in bed, listening to gunfire, and it was the only time he'd ever talked about his sister. "She just didn't know how hard it was going to be. She wouldn't get help, wouldn't ask. She was afraid they'd take me away from her." He'd lain silent for a long time, looking at the wall, not at Cait. The gunfire rattled on, and Charlie said tonelessly, "She got herself killed on the streets."

Cait looked at him now, remembering all that, resisting the memory.

Charlie was ordering two cups of coffee.

"Do you want anything else?" he asked. She shook her head. "One with milk," he told the spotty boy behind the counter.

She was surprised that he remembered how she took her coffee. She wished he hadn't.

While he was paying, she turned away and found a table on the far side of the room, grateful that she didn't know any of the few other patrons and didn't have to introduce him to anyone. Taking the bench seat, she slid in. She could see the room then. She could be the one who would sit protected with the wall at her back.

As if he understood, Charlie was smiling a little wryly as he came toward her. Unless she closed her eyes or deliberately looked away, Cait had to watch him cross the room.

He didn't move the way he used to. Charlie had always had a smooth, easy gait that had reminded her of a mountain lion on the prowl. He'd always been quick and lithe. "You move like a cat," she'd said once.

"An alley cat," Charlie had agreed.

Now his movements were much less graceful. He moved slowly and carefully, and there was a hesitation in his gait. Cait was certain that his caution owed less to the fact that he was carrying two full cups of coffee than that he had tangled with something bigger and stronger and tougher sometime in the past two years.

When he reached the table, he set one cup, a stirrer and three small half-and-half containers in front of her, then put his own down and took the seat opposite her. She saw him wince a little as he bent his leg to sit down.

"What happened?" She couldn't not ask, but she was glad her voice sounded cool and mostly indifferent when she did.

"I got shot."

It struck her as odd the way he said it. It wasn't offhand exactly, but the old Charlie would have made a joke of it.

"The bastards tried to blow me away," he would have said, and then he would have laughed at just one more brush with death.

But this Charlie wasn't laughing.

He peeled the top off his cup of coffee and sat with his hands wrapped around it. His fingers were laced together and his knuckles looked almost white with strain. Cait stared at them, then lifted her gaze to his eyes once more.

He closed his eyes for just a second and, with his fingers knit together like that, he almost looked as if he was praying.

Saying grace over a coffee cup? Cait thought. Charlie? Hardly.

Then he opened them again and took a breath. "That's why I'm here." His fingers clenched just a fraction. "Because I got shot." Another breath. His hands shifted a little on the cup. "Because I almost died. Actually—" that wry corner of his mouth lifted again "—I did die. Coded, I think the word is. I saw eternity." He stopped, but his eyes never left her face. "And you weren't there."

A group of teenagers across the room were laughing and arguing. The milk shake machine was whirring madly. There was the faint sound of the electronic voice from the drive-up saying something about taking an order, please.

And Charlie was talking about getting shot and dying and seeing eternity and her…*what?* Not being there?

Cait felt as if the world was spinning. The roar in her brain was deafening. She just stared. The pit of her stomach burned and she hadn't even yet drunk the coffee.

She wondered eventually if he expected a response. She couldn't imagine what one would be.

But apparently he didn't expect one, because after a moment's silence he went on. "I couldn't face eternity without you, so I came back."

"To life?" The words, thank God, came automatically and sarcastically and not without a certain measure of self-defensiveness.

But Charlie simply nodded. "Yes."

Cait shook her head. She reached for one of the half-and-half containers and, with trembling fingers, ripped the top off and dumped the contents into her cup. Then she did the same with the second and with the last. It was too much milk. She liked two, not three. She didn't care. She had to do something—and that was the only thing there was.

Agitated, she stirred the coffee. She didn't look at Charlie. But she could feel his eyes on her. Scrutinizing.

All of a sudden she was furiously angry. How dare he!

"Let me get this straight," she said finally, as evenly as she could. "You got shot. You died. And when you got to heaven or hell or wherever you went, I wasn't there so you came back?'' She was looking at him now. Her eyes were shooting daggers at him.

He didn't flinch. He looked, if anything, calmer. ''More or less. Yes. Of course, I didn't think I'd died. I knew I'd been shot. I got caught in a crossfire. Hit three times. I lost a lot of blood. I could hear them taking me to the hospital. Tony Sellers and another guy. I could hear them yelling at each other, and they must have finally got me to the hospital because all of a sudden it sounded less like streets and more like buildings. Gurneys. Metal. You know?''

He didn't wait for her reply but went on. ''And that's when I started seeing this light. It was really bright, like sunlight at the end of a tunnel. And then it started spreading out, like when the sun comes up, spilling light all over, and I began to see people.'' His eyes came back to meet hers for just a second.

Then they drifted away again and he was staring off into the middle distance. ''I saw my father,'' he said quietly, ''and my mother. And my sister.''

''Who are all dead,'' Cait said impatiently. He had told her once that he was the only one left in his whole family.

''And then I saw Chase and Joanna and their kids. And the Cavanaughs and the Craigs. You remember me talking about them?''

She nodded reluctantly. They were friends of the Whitelaws and, barring a total disaster, she was sure they weren't all dead.

''And my buddies from high school, Lopez and De-Shayne.'' Charlie smiled faintly. ''I even saw goofy old Herbert who could spit water through his front teeth. I saw a lot of other people.'' He paused and studied the tabletop for a long moment, then looked up once more. ''But I didn't see you.''

''Maybe I didn't get an invitation,'' Cait said tartly.

''You didn't.''

"Well, then…"

"Because I'd walked out on you."

"Tell me something I don't know."

"I love you."

Oh, God, no! Please, not that! Don't let him say that.

Cait's feet thumped, firm and flat on the floor, bracing her. She clutched the coffee cup so tightly that she was in danger of crushing it and sending coffee all over the table. "Don't," she said fiercely through her teeth. "Tell. Me. That."

"It's true."

"And that's why you left in the middle of the night?"

Charlie shook his head and raked a hand through his hair. "I didn't know it then. I didn't *want* to know it then," he corrected himself.

"How nice for you," Cait said bitterly. "Well, how about this—I don't want to know it now."

She tried to shove her chair back, realized she was sitting against the wall and couldn't shove anywhere. So, clumsily, she slid out the side of the bench and got to her feet. "I'm going home."

Charlie hauled himself awkwardly to his feet, too. "Cait, don't. Finish your coffee. Talk to me. God, I know it's weird. But it's true."

"It might be true, that doesn't matter. I don't have to listen to it!" She started toward the door.

He followed her, dogged her footsteps. "Look, Cait. I know I hurt you. Bad. I know that. I was wrong. I'm sorry."

She kept right on walking, head high, facing straight ahead. Not until she had gone out the door and reached her dad's old truck did she stop and turn to confront him. "Yes, well, I'm sorry, too. But that is over. It's finished. It's been *two years,* Charlie!"

"That's not a long time compared to eternity." His voice was quiet. Steady. Reasonable.

All the things she was not.

Cait folded her arms tightly across her breasts and shivered, anyway, feeling the cool night air knife down the back of her neck. She didn't want to turn and look at him, but she knew she had to, knew he wouldn't settle for less. So she turned. She stared straight into his eyes.

The best defense was a good offense. Wes had always taught her that.

"So what now, Charlie? Why are you here? What do you want?"

He seemed to balance lightly, not awkward at all now. Settled, cool. Like a gunfighter, she thought. Like a man in control.

"I want you to marry me, Cait."

She'd had to ask.

All the bright and shining dreams she'd once had—of the future, of the two of them, of a lifetime and an eternity spent together—rose up once more.

Ruthlessly she crushed them right back down.

"I'm already getting married, Charlie—to someone else."

A semi rumbled past above on the Interstate. The teenagers, still talking and laughing, jostled their way out of the restaurant and tumbled into a pair of pickup trucks and roared away.

He didn't move. He opened his mouth, but for a long moment no sound came out. Then at last he said, "You can't."

Red flashed before her eyes. "What do you mean, *I can't?* Who the hell are you to tell me what I can and can't do?"

He took a ragged breath. "I mean…you kissed me. You—"

"*You* kissed me, Charlie!"

"You responded!"

"No, I didn't!"

But damn it, yes, for just an instant she had. She crushed that thought, too. She hugged herself tighter.

"No, I didn't," she repeated with all the quiet force she could muster.

He just looked at her. "Cait." He said her name gently, cajolingly, persuasively.

She steeled herself against him. "No. I'm sorry you almost got killed, Charlie. I'm sorry you nearly died. I appreciate the fact that you 'missed' me in 'eternity.' But I'm marrying someone else."

"Who?"

"What difference does it make? You don't know him."

"Do you?"

"How dare you? How dare you come back into my life after two years and just assume that I'm going to jump into your arms? You hurt me, Charlie! You walked out! You left me cold and you never even said why! I *know* why. I'm not stupid. I figured it out. You didn't want anything more than an affair. You didn't want marriage. You didn't want a family. You didn't want what I wanted. You didn't love me."

"I—"

"You didn't love me," she repeated. She would *not* allow him to deny that! "And it hurt. I got past it, though. I'm over it. I have a life. I have a job. I have a fiancé. His name is Steve. He's a cardiologist. And yes, I know him. I also love him! And he's worth ten of you."

He didn't say a word. He let her wind down. And a smart thing for him, too, or she'd have steamrolled right over him.

"He probably is," Charlie said quietly. "But I love you.

And you love me, too. If you didn't—'' he rode right over her protest ''—you wouldn't have responded at all.''

''I can't help what you read into things, Charlie. You hear what you want to hear. You see what you want to see and nothing else. You always have.''

Her arrow hit home. She saw something flicker in his gaze. A muscle ticked in his jaw.

''I love you,'' he repeated. ''I was wrong to leave you. I was a fool.'' He still sounded calm, but the calm was edged with urgency now. His stare was intent. ''Don't compound it, Cait. Don't make the same mistake I did.''

''The only mistake I made, Charlie,'' she said with all the bravado she could muster, ''was two years ago, when I fell in love with you.''

''So,'' Gaby's voice trilled in his ear as he lay on the motel room bed staring at the ceiling. ''When's the wedding?''

''Very funny.'' His voice sounded raw even to his ears.

''Oh.'' Her tone changed at once. ''You talked to her?''

''Yes, I talked to her. And no, she doesn't want to marry me. She's marrying someone else.''

''Who?''

''Some guy named Steve. Some cardiologist. And now you know everything I know,'' Charlie said, still angry. ''So why don't you just drop it?''

There was a moment's pause. Then, ''Are you going to drop it?''

Charlie stared at the ceiling a long moment, seeing Cait with her arms tightly folded across her breasts, defending herself against him—or against herself? He hadn't imagined that momentary response. He was sure he hadn't. He knew Cait. He knew her body, the way it reacted, the way it loved.

But could he convince her?

Did he have any right to try?

Yes, of course he did. If she still loved him, she shouldn't be marrying someone else! It would be wrongheaded and downright dumb. She had to see that.

"No," he said at last. "No, I'm not dropping it."

It hadn't been easy to walk away from Cait the first time. He'd wanted to stay, but he'd been afraid of the commitment. Now he wasn't. Now he welcomed it.

He wasn't going to walk away a second time.

Not as long as he had any hope at all.

And he did have hope. For all that she'd denied still loving him, she still felt something—even if only for an instant.

Charlie was a photographer. He had built his life on moments caught in the blink of a shutter. That was what he'd felt in Cait's response.

He was willing to work with that.

"You said something about a cabin," he said to Gaby. "Some friend of yours?"

"Brenna McCall."

"Right. Would she rent it to me?"

"Are we talking a long siege here?"

"I don't know what we're talking. Will she rent it?"

"I can call her and ask. She offered it for a few nights already, if you recall."

Charlie hadn't been thinking about that then. He'd only been thinking about getting to Cait. Then he'd thought in the short term. Not now.

"I'd appreciate it," he said.

"Do you want me to tell her why? The *real* reason why," Gaby said, "or do you want me to blather on about you needing a place to regroup and take some pretty pictures? She knows you know Cait, but I didn't go into details."

"Let's keep it that way," Charlie said.

If she was engaged, he needed to move carefully. He didn't want to cause her embarrassment or pain. He simply wanted her back.

"Just tell her I want a change of pace. Tell her I'm working on my new vision."

Gaby chuckled. "What vision would that be?"

"I don't know. I'll tell you when I find it."

"I'll give her your phone number at the motel. I don't think it will be a problem. She won't be using the cabin herself for a while. She and Jed had another baby this spring, so she won't be going off to paint for a while. If you don't hear from her by tomorrow night, call me back."

"Will do. And, Gaby, thanks."

"Oh, I do this all the time for my clients, Charlie." She laughed. "I'll just be expecting you to name one of the girls after me."

One of the girls. Kids with Cait.

Scary thoughts. Notions that had sent him packing two years ago.

And now—Charlie stared at the ceiling some more—his dearest wish.

"Dr. Carmichael," the muttered voice was clearly sleep-fogged, and Cait felt immediately guilty for having called him so late.

"I'm sorry, Steve. I didn't realize what time it was." Now she looked at the clock and discovered it was almost two in the morning. "I'll let you go back to sleep."

"No. Don't hang up." He cleared his throat, yawned, then said, "What's up? Bad night?"

Sometimes they called each other when things were rough—when he lost a patient he was sure he'd be able to save, when she had a delivery that went wrong.

"No," Cait said hastily, because it wasn't—not like that, anyway. "I just...got lonesome."

Panic-stricken, more like. She'd trembled all the way home after her confrontation with Charlie. She'd taken deep breaths and tried to steady her racing pulse. She'd strangled the steering wheel trying to get an emotional grip.

It was the shock, she'd told herself. Seeing him would have been enough to set off heart palpitations. A proposal of marriage was the last thing she expected.

Or wanted.

She didn't need that! She didn't need him!

And so when she got home, she'd paced furiously, then she'd taken a long shower, hoping she'd be able to wash away the memories and the jumble of thoughts chasing each other through her mind.

But nothing had worked. Nothing had calmed her.

Nothing would, she realized, until she talked to Steve.

She needed to connect to the real man in her life, not the one who had just burst back onto the scene. Now she curled up in the armchair, tucked her robe around her and let the soft sleepy sound of Steve breathing settle her jangled nerves.

There was another yawn from Steve's end of the line. She heard him stretch. "Well, good." There was a hint of a smile in his still-sleepy voice. "I always like to talk to you. Even in the middle of the night. Is your dad okay?"

"Dad's okay. I'm just lonesome. Cash and Milly Callahan had their baby tonight."

"Ah." Steve smiled. "The hormones are responding."

"Maybe. Yes. That must be it." Better to think that than to think about Charlie.

She wondered if she should tell Steve about Charlie, then decided not to.

No man wanted to be awakened and told that his fiancée couldn't sleep because she couldn't stop thinking about the man she used to be in love with.

"Want to meet for breakfast?" he asked her. "I'm going to be in Livingston tomorrow. I don't have any appointments here in the morning. I could come over early. We could grab one of those egg and muffin things."

"I don't think so." There was no way she was going back to the place she'd just been with Charlie! "I have appointments in the morning. But how about tomorrow night? We could catch a movie?"

"If your beeper doesn't go off." She could hear the smile in his voice.

"Or if yours doesn't."

They chuckled together. Yes, Cait thought, hugging the notion to herself, they were definitely compatible.

"Okay. Movie it is." Steve yawned again. "Anything else?"

Just keep talking to me, Cait wanted to say. But she couldn't make Steve stay awake all night just to stop her thinking about. Charlie.

"No. I'm all right."

"You sure? Want me to come over?"

Cait laughed. It was a good sixty miles from Steve's place to hers. "No. It's okay. I just…thanks."

"Anytime," he promised. "See you tomorrow night. I'll call you."

"Yes," Cait said. "Please."

"G'night. Dream of me."

"Yes."

But she didn't. She dreamed of Charlie.

Three

————

Charlie got the cabin. He went up the next day with Brenna leading the way. They'd lent him her father, Otis's, old Suburban. It did gravel and dirt better than Charlie's car.

"You're sure you don't mind?" Charlie had asked.

"Oh, I think we'll manage," Jed had said with a sly smile in the direction of the Porsche.

They probably would. Charlie wasn't sure about himself.

Brenna had come up on horseback, bringing a mount she'd said he could pasture here and use in the hills. He hadn't been sure about that, but she'd insisted.

"You won't want to walk everywhere. Babe is easy. You'll like her."

She showed him how the generator worked. She pointed out the firewood pile in case he wanted a little warmth in the cool summer evenings. Then she stood on the porch, breathed deeply and said, "You'll love it here. Whatever you're looking for, you'll find it."

Charlie hoped she was right.

He dug in, barracked down, and told himself that just being in the vicinity was a start, that while he was here he'd think of a game plan, a way to convince Cait to fall into his arms.

He had no idea what he was getting himself into.

If Montana was the "last best place"—as many of its natives, its literature and its advertising campaigns would have you believe—it was also, in Charlie's mind, the strangest.

When Brenna left him, he was alone. Totally alone. He didn't think he'd ever been alone before in his life.

The sheer silence was unnerving.

Weird, he thought. Very very weird.

He walked around the cabin, admired the view across the Shields Valley toward what Brenna told him were the Crazy Mountains.

"Crazy?"

"They say an old woman went crazy from loneliness up there," she'd told him.

As afternoon turned into evening and evening into night and he still didn't see anyone else or hear anyone else, Charlie began to understand what she meant.

He had a hard time falling asleep that night. It was too quiet. He had too much time to think.

That's what he told himself.

But then he started thinking about Cait and remembering the stories she'd told about her home. He was here now.

He could hear the horse whickering. Some cows were lowing. There was an odd soft rushing sound he didn't recognize. It took him a while but he finally worked out what it was—the wind soughing through the pine trees.

He was here. In Cait's state. In the land she called home.

He didn't awaken until midday.

He'd never slept so soundly. He'd barely ever slept so long. It was the altitude, he told himself. But he didn't feel tired, he felt energized, curious about this new world he was inhabiting.

The first full day he spent at the cabin, he never saw another person. He never heard another person. He never talked to anyone.

The only things he heard were the whinnies of Babe, the horse, the cawing of a couple of jays, the occasional hoot of something that was probably an owl, the sound of his own footsteps as he moved around the small spartan cabin. And he heard the wind.

Sometimes it was the soft rushing sound he'd heard in the night. Sometimes it shifted and sawed through the trees. He went outside for a walk and heard it whistling through the long grass, saw the stalks bending in the breeze.

He began to hear the wind play an orchestra's worth of nature's instruments and found himself bewitched by every one. It almost seemed to talk to him.

And once he got past the strangeness, he liked hearing what it had to say.

In its whisper, he heard echoes of stories Cait had told of her childhood here. He remembered her talking about lying awake at night in a sleeping bag on the mountainside listening to the wind, and he had tried to imagine it.

Now he didn't have to imagine.

He could hear what she had heard.

The sounds and the memories of Cait's stories, of Cait herself, mingled together and exhilarated him.

They also grounded him—and challenged him. But it wasn't the desperate challenge he'd felt when she'd said she was engaged. It wasn't the frantic need to turn her head and argue with her to make her see she was wrong.

He couldn't make her see.

Like Chase said, he had to get himself balanced, get in harmony with this world in which he found himself, this world to which she belonged. He had to *be*.

Then, God willing, she would see for herself.

The first few days weren't easy. The old Charlie periodically wanted to rev his engine, go down the mountain and bulldoze his way back into Cait's life.

But the longer he stayed, the more he understood that bulldozing was out of place.

He remembered Chase once telling him about the time he'd met his father and had decided to stay on the Navajo reservation.

"It took some getting used to," he'd said with what Charlie imagined was his usual understatement. "But I needed it. I had to do it. I had to find out who I was."

That had surprised Charlie at the time. Chase had seemed pretty well sorted out to him. Now he understood that a man could look sorted out and still have pieces missing.

He'd come to find Cait, but he was starting to find himself, too.

At first Charlie didn't explore much. His leg bothered him every day. It was weak, and the ground was uneven. He saddled Babe and rode her a few times, but the two of them scared off the wildlife. And the longer he was there, the more Charlie wanted to see the animals that Cait had talked about. So he began leaving Babe behind and going out on his own.

He preferred hiking. It was easier to see, to stop, to listen.

This world was completely different from the one he knew. He might as well have been on another planet. Weaned on concrete and broken glass, window bars and concertina wire, Charlie now saw mountain peaks and prairie grasses, frolicking horses and ambling cattle.

He shot photo after photo, feeling like a kid in a candy store.

A lot of them were garden-variety calendar shots. Pretty pictures of the sort that he used to disdain. But where he once looked for despair and pain and inhumanity and, with his camera, trapped it, now he saw more.

His eye found beauty in the opening of a flower, in the soaring of a hawk, in the gathering bank of clouds that presaged a summer storm.

Now that he'd seen the "wilds" of Montana, he found another reason to be grateful he hadn't been killed four months ago—he not only wouldn't have had Cait, he'd have missed all this.

For a week Cait waited for the other shoe to drop.

She came around corners warily, always expecting to see Charlie. She picked up the phone nervously, sure that she would hear him there.

But days turned into a week without a sign of him. One week turned into two and he wasn't anywhere.

Not anywhere here.

She almost felt as if she'd dreamed the whole thing.

"What were you on about?" Steve had asked her. "Calling in the middle of the night like that?"

"You were right. It was just the Callahans' baby. I was thinking. That's all."

"Well, think about setting a wedding date, then," Steve said.

"Yes," Cait agreed. "I'll do that. Maybe this weekend we can—"

But just then Steve's beeper went off.

*   *   *

Each day Charlie moved a little farther afield. His leg got stronger.

He would always limp, the doctor had told him. But with each hike, his stamina improved, his muscles strengthened, and the next time he went out, he walked farther still.

He had rarely walked anywhere when he was back home. Why would he, when he had his Porsche?

The car had been one of his most fervent youthful dreams. Chase had had a Porsche when Charlie had first met him. It had been stolen and Charlie had found it, then helped Chase steal it back. It was the moment he and Chase had bonded, for real.

After that he'd deliberately patterned his life after Chase's. And when he could afford it, the Porsche was the first thing he bought.

He couldn't understand Chase selling his Porsche after he married Joanna. But just as Chase had moved beyond the Porsche to a more family oriented vehicle, so Charlie began to think for the first time that maybe the Porsche wasn't what he wanted anymore, either.

It certainly didn't do as well on country gravel as Otis's old Suburban.

A red Ford truck had a certain appeal, too.

So did Babe, though he didn't ride her much. He talked to her every night when he went down to the pasture to give her a sugar cube or two.

She was the only one he talked to.

He could have called anyone on his cell phone. He shut it off. If Gaby wanted to call, she could leave a message with Brenna and Jed.

He didn't want to be bothered. He had a new rhythm to his life.

The strangeness he'd found the first day didn't seem so strange a few days later. The quiet didn't even seem so quiet. Nature had sounds and rhythms all its own. It just took a different sort of hearing to pick them up.

Six months ago he'd have been drumming his fingers, itching to be moving, eager to get back to where the action was.

Now he liked this action.

He liked this place.

And even though he didn't see her, didn't talk to her, didn't even pretend to believe she wanted to see or talk to him again, he felt connected to Cait.

It was her stories that ran through his head as he went to sleep at night. Her words, her memories came back to him as he hiked the mountains during the day.

It was as if she was with him, walking beside him, sharing her home.

It was the knowledge that all this beauty was here waiting for her that kept her going, she'd once told him. If she'd thought the whole world was as strife-ridden and anguished as the part she saw every day, she had confessed one night, she couldn't have borne it.

Her memories had given her hope.

They gave him hope now—of a very different kind.

They gave him hope that all was not lost, that her rejection was not permanent, that her hurt could be assuaged and overcome.

She loved *him*.

"Hate to ask you, Caity," her father said, smiling vaguely at her from the armchair by the window. "I know it's your only day off."

"I don't mind," Cait said. "It's a nice break, checking cattle."

"You'll miss it if you go to Denver," her father said.

"When I go to Denver," Cait corrected. But then she admitted what he was getting at. "Yes, I will."

She loved the ranch, loved the rural work each season. "Maybe you should talk him into stayin' here."

She shook her head. "He wants to go someplace bigger. He wants to teach."

"What do you want, Caity?" Her father's pale-blue eyes watched her curiously.

Cait took a breath. "Him," she said firmly. "I want him."

It was a shock the first time he saw the bears.

Charlie hadn't ever seen a bear outside of a zoo. It was a little daunting to realize there was no barricade between him and the natural world.

It was fascinating, too.

He crouched behind a clump of scrub to watch them. There was a mother and two cubs along the side of the creek. The mother was poking at something. The cubs were watching. Then she waded in. They splashed. She gave them a hard, maternal look.

Charlie smothered a grin. He lifted his camera.

He began to shoot.

At first he didn't understand what he was seeing. Then he did. It was a lesson. How to catch a fish. Charlie shot half a dozen rolls, entranced. His leg throbbed, but he barely noticed.

First one cub, then the other took swipes at the water, splashing. Mother bear demonstrated again. One of the cubs fell in headfirst.

Charlie smothered a laugh.

He shifted, shot, reloaded. And finally got the moment of triumph on film, when one of the cubs came up with a fish about the size of his hand.

Mother bear looked approving, then turned her back and plodded away into the trees. The cubs splashed for a moment longer, then hurried after her.

And Charlie sat back for the first time in over an hour and realized he could barely bend his knee.

He swore and struggled to his feet. It was a hot afternoon, and flies buzzed around him. He swatted at them, but he didn't think about them. He thought about the bears.

He'd got some good shots. He could sense it. The feeling of exhilaration was back. The energy. If he could find them again tomorrow...

Considering the possibilities, he wasn't watching the ground. He didn't notice the loose rock until his foot hit it. His weak leg buckled and he tumbled. Years of quick thinking inspired him to tuck his body and roll, protecting his camera as he fell. He didn't manage to protect himself.

He crashed down the hillside until he hit a clump of brush.

Stunned, Charlie lay there, gathering his wits, tasting blood. Then slowly he hauled himself to a sitting position, breathing hard.

There was blood in his mouth from a split lip. His face was scratched. His shirt was ripped. He was dirty and scraped up, but he didn't think he'd done any serious damage. Thank God.

It suddenly occurred to him how on his own he really was.

Carefully he hauled himself to his feet. His leg buckled, and he grabbed for a handhold on a pine tree to steady himself. Gingerly he tested it again. It hurt. A lot.

He'd have to put ice on it when he got back to the cabin.

Except he didn't have any ice. The tiny generator-run refrigerator didn't have a freezer compartment.

Too bad. But he'd survive. He'd just hurt for a while.

Slowly, carefully, he turned and, watching what he was doing this time, once more started down.

It was when he heard the sound of a small creek that he had a brainstorm. The creeks up here were nothing but snowmelt. Not quite ice but close. He had learned that wading across one the first morning he'd been there.

On that same hike he'd passed another creek where a natural curve had created a water hole on the far side of one of the fence lines. It had looked like a nice place to take a dip, provided you didn't mind feeling like an ice cube. At the time he'd shuddered at the thought.

Now he didn't.

And even though he could see what looked like possible rain clouds gathering off to the west, he headed in that direction.

When he reached the fence, he gritted his teeth and ducked between the strands of barbwire, then laboriously climbed the hill that overlooked the water hole.

A black horse grazed beneath the cottonwoods, and a pile of clothes sat on a nearby rock. As he watched, a sleek dark head surfaced, and a slim naked body emerged from the water.

It wasn't a cowboy.

It was way too curvy for a cowboy.

Way too gorgeous.

Way too female.

Charlie stopped dead and stared at the naked woman coming out of the water toward him.

Then as he realized who it was, his heart caught in his throat.

What sort of sense of humor did God have?

Cait certainly didn't think it was funny when she walked out of the water hole, looked up and saw Charlie Seeks Elk!

She seriously considered plunging straight back in. She didn't because she refused to let Charlie know he had any effect on her.

In fact, she felt as if she had been run over by a truck.

"What are you doing here?" Then, "What happened to you?" she demanded as she got a look at his scratched, battered clothes and face. And all the while she was trying to get to her clothes.

Charlie unfortunately was in the way. He was grinning ear to ear, limping rapidly down the hill toward her, and apparently not even aware that he was bloody and battered.

"Stop that!" Cait snapped. She glared at his grinning face, furious, embarrassed and mostly willing him to turn around so she could go past him to get to where she'd left her clothes.

Of course he didn't.

"You could turn around," she said frostily. "It would be polite."

Charlie let out a half laugh. "Come on, Cait. You know better than that."

She did, unfortunately. So still steaming, she stalked past him, snatched up her shirt and yanked it on, not bothering with her bra.

She would have needed to dry off before putting that on, and she didn't want to expose herself any more than necessary. At least her shirt had long tails and would cover essentials. She should have known better than to come and take a swim. She wasn't a child anymore.

But today was her day off from the clinic, and she'd spent the entire day moving cattle. It made a change from teaching childbirth classes and seeing pregnant mothers and delivering babies, but she had been hot and tired when she'd finished.

Clouds behind the Bridgers looked as if they might bring rain eventually, but that would have been nowhere near as refreshing as a quick, cool dip.

It had been a spur of the moment decision to take a plunge. And obviously a huge mistake.

As soon as she had her shirt on and buttoned, she

stepped into her panties and dragged them on, then wriggled to get them up over her damp hips. All the while she was aware of Charlie watching her.

Once upon a time she'd liked his eyes on her. They'd made her feel desirable and sexy—and loved.

Now they just made her angry.

With her panties and shirt on and her jeans clutched in front of her, Cait felt covered enough to turn and fix him with a hard stare. "What are you doing? Why are you still here?"

Charlie nodded in the direction from which he'd come. "I'm staying at a place over the hill there. I'm renting a cabin from McCalls."

Cait didn't like the sound of that. "Why?"

"Well, I started because you're here."

She gaped. "You're *spying* on me?"

"Of course not. This was—" he grinned lopsidedly "—pure luck. I had to stay somewhere, didn't I?"

No, he didn't. He should have been long gone.

But before she could say so, he continued, "And Gaby knows Brenna. It's also for my work."

"Is there a war going on in Montana I haven't heard about?" she said sarcastically. From the look of him it seemed possible.

"You mean besides ours?"

"We don't have a war, Charlie. We don't have anything."

"We have a past."

"Exactly."

"And I want us to have a future."

"No."

"I'm not going to pressure you."

Oh, right. "Then what the hell are you doing here? And don't give me that crap about your work. You shoot wars, tragedies, devastation, pain."

"I'm not doin' that anymore."

"What are you doing? Sunsets? Wildflowers? Snow-capped mountain peaks?" she asked flippantly. Charlie had had no use for those kinds of photos when she'd known him.

But he didn't take offense. He said quite seriously. "I wasn't exactly sure, but I think today I might have hit on something. I got some good bears."

Cait stared. "Bears?"

"There were bears up by the creek. A mother and two cubs. She was teaching 'em how to fish."

She wouldn't have believed it if she hadn't seen it, but the look on Charlie's face at the memory of the bears was very like the eagerness he'd shown two years ago faced with a far different scene.

"And they attacked you?" she asked dryly.

He glanced down, almost surprised, as if his clothes belonged to someone else. "Not quite." He shrugged as if it didn't matter. "I fell." His grin quirked for a moment, then, as his gaze dropped and she saw him staring at her legs, the grin faded. He said abruptly, "Do you suppose you could put on those jeans?"

Could she put on her jeans?

As if she'd been standing here trying to seduce him by flaunting her nakedness! Cait felt as if she was burning up!

"By all means," she said through clenched teeth. But she made no move to do so, continuing to glare at him, waiting, until finally he got the point and, giving a negligent shrug, turned around.

Fortunately, the breeze had dried her legs a bit, making it easier for her to stuff first one and then the other into her jeans, which she then dragged up, zipped and snapped.

"There." She glared at his back until he turned around.

"I'm just a little susceptible," Charlie said, not at all repentant. "You remember."

Cait gritted her teeth because, damn it, she did remember. And she didn't want to. It was all too easy to remember when they had been able to heat each other's blood with a mere glance. "Well, I certainly don't want to provide any temptation."

Charlie's smile was rueful. "You don't have to try."

Cait felt her entire body warm under his gaze. "You should put something on that lip," she said gruffly.

Charlie dabbed vaguely at his mouth. "I will. It's why I came here. And I was going to soak my leg." He nodded toward the one he'd been favoring as he'd limped down the hill.

"Did you hurt it?" It was the nurse in her asking. She certainly wasn't asking because she cared.

"Maybe when I fell. It's not a big deal. But the doc always said to put ice on it. And I don't have any ice. But I remembered the water hole."

"I'll leave you to it, then." She bent to snag her boots and socks, then started toward her horse, relieved at the reprieve.

But before she'd got ten feet he called her name. "Cait!"

Reluctantly she turned back. "What?"

"Stay."

And watch him take off his jeans and soak his leg?

"Can't. I've got things to do," she said hastily.

He cocked his head, smiling at her. "You're afraid."

She was surprised there wasn't steam coming out of her ears. "Afraid? Of what?"

"Realizing you still love me…want me." The words were said softly, but the challenge was clearly there.

"If you're implying I can't resist your manly body, you are so wrong."

"Prove it."

Cait lifted her chin and said recklessly, "All right. I will.

Go ahead. Undress. Take your jeans off in front of me. See if I care.''

Slowly Charlie's hands went to his belt buckle and—damn him!—he began to do just that.

Charlie had never been self-conscious about his body before.

He'd never minded women studying him naked. While he personally didn't think men's bodies were nearly as impressive as women's, he'd always been proud of his lean, hard physique and the muscles that he could flex with ease.

He'd never even minded them tracing the nicks and gouges and scars from his rough-and-tumble past. They'd been badges of honor, signs of his toughness and determination to survive.

That was then.

Now it wasn't the same.

His body wasn't the same, he realized about the time he began to unbuckle his belt. It was no longer lithe and fit and supple. His wounded leg, with its angry red scar tissue and atrophied muscles was nothing to admire. On the contrary, the very sight of it would probably put Cait off. So would the scar on his chest.

A couple of years from now, they might look like badges of honor. Right now they looked like hell, and he realized that he didn't want to show them to anybody—much less the one woman in the world he wanted to impress.

Too bad you didn't think of that sooner, he mocked himself, because Cait, having taken his dare, was standing there, barefoot and unblinking, watching him.

His hands hesitated at the top of his zipper. He imagined opening it, then shoving his jeans down, and watching her look of shock and horror.

He imagined her comparing his body with that of her cardiologist boyfriend. Charlie couldn't believe the guy was a real hunk, but he probably wasn't a walking disaster, either.

Slowly his hands fell to his sides. He shook his head. "Never mind."

Cait did blink then. "Never mind?" She gaped. "Why?"

He shrugged irritably and jerked his head toward the sky behind her. "There's a storm brewing." The clouds creeping over the tops of the Bridgers were bigger and darker looking now. "You should get home."

Cait didn't even glance over her shoulder. "There was a storm brewing two minutes ago."

"Yeah, well, I forgot you would have to ride all that way. Open air. Tall object. Lightning strikes. It took a while, but I finally figured it out. I'm a city boy, remember? Go on now. Or you'll get soaked."

But Cait, damn her, didn't budge. She was regarding him closely. "Charlie, are you all right?"

"Of course I'm all right!" He glared at her. "Why wouldn't I be?"

"Your leg—"

"My leg's fine. I told you. I just had second thoughts. I know enough to get in out of the rain, even if you don't!"

When she still didn't move, he shrugged. "Well, fine, stand there. I don't care. Show's over. If you're not goin' home, that's your problem. I'm outa here."

He would have turned on his heel and stalked up the hill, but doing so would have sent him sprawling. Instead he carefully turned sideways and then sideways again, until he could head back the way he'd come.

As he climbed the slope he listened for the sound of her putting on her boots or her footsteps heading toward her horse. He didn't hear anything until he was close to the top of the hill.

Then she called out, "Show's over? Doesn't look to me like it even started!"

The trouble with being a nurse was you felt so *responsible*.

You saw someone hurting and you felt compelled to help.

If she were sane and sensible and *not* a nurse, Cait told herself, she would be home reading a book or playing cribbage with her father this evening instead of climbing the steps to the McCalls' cabin and banging on the door.

"It's open," Charlie's voice called from inside.

She turned the knob and gave the door a shove.

To say that he was surprised to see her would have been an understatement. He was lying on the bed, still wearing the dusty, torn jeans and shirt he'd been wearing this afternoon, and at the sight of her he sat up abruptly and said, "Well, hell."

"Nice to see you again, too," Cait said crisply. She stepped inside and shut the door behind her. One look at him told her she'd been right.

"You haven't even washed up," she accused him.

"Excuse me?"

Cait flipped a hand in his direction. "Look at you. You're a mess. Still. Don't they have running water up here? Of course they do. Then why didn't you use it? You shouldn't even be up here walking around on that leg. Sit on the edge of the bed and take your shirt and jeans off."

She didn't look in his direction when she spoke, instead rummaged in her duffel bag, then set out a plastic bottle of saline solution and some telfa pads and gauze, determined that her professional demeanor would distract from any telltale heat in her face.

"Take my—" Charlie began.

"Take your shirt and jeans off. I'll be right back." she said and hurried out the door.

She'd ridden home mortified at her afternoon encounter with Charlie at the swimming hole. But the longer she'd been home, the less she'd thought about her own mortification and the more she'd thought about Charlie instead.

He had clearly been ready to strip off in front of her, and then he'd abruptly changed his mind.

Why?

Obviously because it hurt too damn much, and he was self-conscious about it. Stupid man!

She'd told herself it served him right. But she was a nurse.

Concern had niggled at her all during dinner. Afterwards, she usually tried to get her father to play cribbage. Tonight he had looked surprised when she said she'd be back later, that she had to go back up on the range instead.

She had loaded up their cooler with ice, ice packs and flexible wraps, then tossed in her duffel with medical supplies and some nonprescription painkillers just in case.

"Somethin' wrong with one of the horses?" her father had asked

"One of the mules," Cait had muttered, which was close to the truth.

Now she got the cooler out of the back of her pickup, slammed the gate and lugged the cooler up the hill toward the cabin.

Charlie came to the door as she was climbing the steps. "For God's sake, Cait!" He hobbled to help her.

"I'm fine. Stay out of my way." She hauled the thing past him and set it on the floor. "There." She opened it, took out one of the ice packs and a thin cloth wrap, then straightened up and looked at him expectantly. "Jeans, Charlie," she reminded him.

"Cait," he said, voice strangled.

She lifted a brow. "Or maybe *you're* the one who's afraid?"

Their gazes met. Lightning seemed to flash, and Cait wondered if she had made a big mistake.

Charlie ground his teeth and, muttering, fumbled to unfasten his belt.

Cait clenched the ice pack, strove to look indifferent— and steeled herself for the sight of Charlie Seeks Elk unwrapped.

Four

It shouldn't have been like this.

It should have been him seducing her, them getting naked together. Not him shucking his clothes while Cait bustled around like some damned efficient nurse, setting out gauze and bandages and tapping her foot and looking like she had a hot date in half an hour—with Cardiology Man.

Okay, so she *was* a nurse.

She wasn't indifferent.

She'd loved him, for crying out loud! She'd stroked and touched his body in ways that had made his heart gallop and his body sing.

And now she was acting like he was a floor she'd been hired to scrub.

Yeah, well, let's see how long her indifference lasted.

Charlie tried not to think about his ugly leg or the scars on his chest and back as he pulled his shirt out of his jeans. He took his time, watching her all the while he unbuttoned it, then pulled it off and tossed it on the bed.

She didn't even glance his way. She was filling a plastic bag with ice and wrapping it in a cloth. She didn't even seem to notice the red scar on the front of his shoulder.

"You can put this on your leg," she said as she finished with the ice pack, "while I clean up your cuts."

"Don't you want to hold it on my leg, Cait?" He tried to put a little purr in his voice. Sometimes he used to tease her just to watch her blush.

But this time she simply said, "I'm sure you can manage. Then she glanced at her watch, not at him. "I'm meeting Steve for the late movie, so if we could hurry things along…"

Steve again. Damn Steve.

"Tell me about him," Charlie said. Not because he gave a damn, but it always helped to understand your competition.

Cait looked surprised. Then she hesitated a moment before she said, "He's tall, dark and handsome. He got his medical degree from Columbia. He's a cardiologist, like I told you. He's been practicing in Bozeman for the past four years, doing a little satellite work in Livingston. But he wants to teach and he's been asked to join a bigger practice in Denver, so he's going this August." She lifted her chin. "And I'll be going there this fall. After the wedding."

Charlie's eyes narrowed. "When's the wedding?"

"October 17. Before the snow. After shipping. Are you going to take those jeans off or not?" Cait demanded. She was tossing the ice pack back and forth between her hands, looking like she couldn't care less.

And all thoughts of "the competition" went right out of Charlie's head. Annoyed, goaded—and at the same time worried that she'd take one look at his leg and run—he shoved the jeans down his hips, then kicked them off and stood glaring at her as she finally looked his way.

"Pretty, isn't it?" His voice was gruff and defiant. He watched her face for signs of revulsion.

"Oh, Charlie." The words came involuntarily, he knew. And while he didn't want her pity, he was oddly grateful to see that she seemed to care.

Rather than running, in fact, she took a step closer. "Where exactly does it hurt?" she asked, and she put her hands on him. Her very cold hands.

Charlie almost jumped out of his boxer shorts. "Cripes, woman!"

But she ignored his protests. "Hush," she said, stroking his thigh gently. "Sit on the table."

He swallowed, willed his body to behave itself. Then he did as she said.

Cait began gently probing his leg, making *him* suck in his breath this time. And now that the initial shock had passed, he was breathless only partly because of the cold. He'd forgotten how good she smelled. Her hair was almost under his nose. The curve of her breast brushed his arm as she bent to study his leg. And her hands—cold though they were—were making him crazy.

"Here?" she said touching the knotted muscle. "I can feel the tension here."

"Mmm," Charlie stifled a moan.

"Sorry. Anywhere else?" She had her hand on his thigh, kneading it gently, then lifted it and slid her hand beneath, probing lightly.

The moan had nothing to do with his pain, and at her continued probing and stroking, Charlie very nearly moaned again. "Ah...um...yeah, there." His fingers clenched against the table. He shut his eyes and threw his head back.

The scent of her filled his nostrils. Juniper and sage and something indefinably Cait that even in the desert of Abuk spoke of Montana and reminded him now of the nights he'd held her in his arms.

They'd slept together in one narrow bed, Cait curled against him, exhausted from her long days at the hospital. Though he'd often been bushed, too, Charlie hadn't always slept. Sometimes he hadn't wanted to sleep. Sometimes he'd just lain awake and held her, storing up the moments, savoring them, convinced—and determined—that they were all he'd ever have.

God, he'd been a fool.

Now he was damned sure not settling for that. His heart knew it. His mind knew it. And his body very definitely knew it.

Cait must know it, too. Not many of a guy's secrets remained hidden in a pair of boxer shorts!

"Right. We'll need two."

"Two?" His head jerked; his eyes opened. He gaped.

She rolled her eyes. "Ice packs." She lifted his leg, slid the one ice pack under it, then went back to fill another.

"Oh." Charlie felt cold and bereft. His boxer shorts wavered. His body was in conflict. It wanted Cait. It didn't want more ice.

And then she was back, and naturally he got the ice.

"Hold this," she commanded. Then she put two fingers under his chin and lifted and turned his head so she could study his lip. "You could have washed at least."

"I drank whiskey," Charlie told her. "It's sterile."

Cait made a humphing sound. "Sit still." And she set to work.

She washed all his cuts and scratches with saline solution. She was brisk and efficient and not exactly gentle.

"Hey!" Charlie protested when it felt as if she were using elbow grease on a particularly dirty spot.

"Don't be a baby." And she scrubbed harder. "And stop groaning."

"I can't."

"I'm not scrubbing that hard!"

"The groans have nothing to do with scrubbing," Charlie told her, and was gratified to see the color rise in her cheeks. But, "Cait!" he protested when her scrubbing grew even more intense.

"There." She nodded her satisfaction when she'd scrubbed him down almost to the bone.

He touched his elbow gingerly. "Hurts worse now than it did when you started."

"But it won't get infected." She was cleaning up now, putting everything back in her duffel, then going to wash her hands.

Watching her taut shoulders and stiff back, Charlie was sure she wasn't as indifferent as she pretended. "Thank you, Cait," he said softly.

She had her hands under the water tap and she didn't turn around, but he saw her shoulders stiffen even more. "You're welcome."

He wished he dared go to her, put his hands on her shoulders and knead them gently. He used to do that when she got off work. And she would tip her head back and run her lips along the line of his jaw and make mmmmm sounds that set his hormones singing.

It was all he could do to stay where he was on the table. But he managed it.

She cleaned up and said, "Keep those ice packs on there twenty minutes at a time. Do it every few hours. I put in enough ice that you should have some until midday tomorrow."

"All right."

"Did the doctor give you stretching exercises?"

"Yes."

"Are you doing them?"

"Trying to."

"Do them."

"All right."

She looked at him narrowly, almost suspiciously.

Charlie smiled at her.

She averted her gaze and rubbed her hands on the sides of her jeans. "Fine," she said briskly. "I'll leave you to it."

The smile vanished. "And go to the movies with your fiancé."

"Yes."

He looked at her narrowly. "Going to sit in the back and neck with him?"

"Charlie!"

Her shocked face made him grin. "Sorry. I should know better. You'd never do a thing like that."

They had once gone to a political documentary in an old battered theatre in Abuk only so they could kiss in the back row because two of Charlie's journalist buddies happened to be sacked out in his apartment.

The sight of Cait's flaming face told him she remembered, too. He cocked his head and grinned at her.

"Goodbye, Charlie," she said through her teeth.

"Bye." He waited until she was going out the door. "Cait?"

She turned to look at him.

"Think of me."

"I think I'd like triplets," Mary Holt said the next afternoon. Cait was listening to her belly with a stethoscope, but staring off into space. "Or maybe quintuplets. That'd be fun, don't you think?"

"Hmm? Mmm, yeah. Sure," Cait said.

"All boys," Mary went on cheerfully. "Little hellions. Just like Gus. That'd be terrific."

"Yeah."

"And you can be their godmother and baby-sitter. Okay?"

Cait nodded absently. "Okay."

"You haven't heard a word I said."

At Mary's indignant accusation, Cait had the grace to blush. "I'm sorry. I was…listening to the heart beat."

"Only one?"

"You want more?"

"No. But I just told you I thought quints would be nice—all like Gus—and you agreed with me."

"Yikes." Cait shrugged guiltily.

Mary laughed. "My feelings exactly."

"He's a good foreman, though," Cait allowed. She'd hired Gus Holt this past winter right before he and Mary had tied the knot. He'd been apprehensive at first, worried that maybe for all his having grown up on a ranch, he wouldn't be up to the job.

But Cait had had faith in him. She'd seen how conscientious he'd been with Mary when she'd been pregnant. He hadn't known anything about expectant mothers, either, but he'd set out to learn.

"If you try as hard for the ranch as you did with Mary, you'll do fine," she'd told him.

And he had. He and Mary had moved into the old homestead on the Cutter place, which her father had bought a few years back. No one had lived there since and the house was almost falling down. But Gus and Mary had taken it on eagerly.

"It will be a great place to raise a family," Mary had said, seeing possibilities that were beyond Cait. In the past few months they had turned it into a home. And now they were going to have the family to enjoy it.

Mary was two and a half months along, bubbling, eager, and "only sick until noon," she reported ruefully.

"You're doing great," Cait told her now. "You look wonderful."

"You don't."

Cait blinked. "What?"

"You look worried." Mary sat up and pulled down her shirt. "Is it your dad?"

Cait shook her head. She made some notes on Mary's chart. "Dad's all right."

"Is it Steve?"

Cait looked up quickly. "What about Steve?"

Mary smiled. "Aha."

Cait set the pen on the counter and stuffed her hands in her pockets. "What do you mean, aha? Steve is fine," she said defensively.

"Or at least he was the last time you saw him," Mary said, disgusted.

"He's busy! *I'm* busy!"

"Busiest two people on earth," Mary said dryly. She stood up and adjusted her clothing, then laid a hand on Cait's arm. "Take time for each other. You need to. You're working too hard."

"I have to work hard. I've got the ranch as well as my practice and—"

"—as long as you're busy, you don't have to deal with the wedding."

"What?"

"You heard me. Maybe it's my imagination, but it looks to me like you're stalling."

"Stalling? I'm not stalling!"

"Well, you're not exactly rushing to the altar."

"Because we're not horny teenagers with stars in our eyes like some people."

Mary grimaced. "Point taken."

"I didn't mean that," Cait said hastily, remembering that Mary and Gus had been teenagers in love once upon a time. At least Mary had been. She'd had stars in her eyes, too. Gus had had cold feet. It had taken him nearly a dozen years to warm them up.

"Steve and I are adults," Cait said calmly. "We're waiting until the time is right. October isn't so far away."

"October?" Mary brightened. "You've set a date, then?"

"Yes. Well, sort of. I think." She'd picked a date out of the air when Charlie had asked her yesterday.

She didn't want him to think she was "stalling" like Mary did, and she knew he'd jump to that very conclusion if she admitted they didn't have a date carved in stone.

Besides, the more she thought about it, October 17 seemed as good a day as any.

It was, as she'd told Charlie, after shipping and before the snow flew—more or less. It would give Steve time to get settled in Denver and comfortable in his job, and it would give her time to breathe for a minute or two after the herd had been shipped. It would also give her time to wind down her practice and make sure her dad was really capable of running the place.

"When? Where? Can I help?" Mary was all eagerness.

"October 17," she said firmly. "We're still deciding where."

Steve would be delighted. He'd been eager to set a date since he'd given her a ring. She was the one who'd hesitated, worrying about her father mostly. How could she say she'd go to Denver when he was still so ill?

He wasn't *that* ill, Steve had maintained. He was taking advantage of her.

Cait had never believed that, but maybe Steve was right. In any case he'd be delighted when she told him tonight.

They were going to dinner. They hadn't gone to the movies last night. She'd called him when she got home from Charlie's to see if he wanted to. He might have, after all. Saying they were going had been for Charlie's benefit. And they could have, except he'd been on call and had had an emergency.

"Well, I'm glad you've got a date finally," Mary said. "I'll help."

"I think you'll have quite enough to do getting ready for this baby and teaching school."

"I might have a little free time. I'm not directing the Christmas pageant this year," Mary said. "I've already told Polly that. She seemed relieved," she added with a grin.

Last year Mary had not only directed Elmer's community Christmas pageant, but brought the house down by nearly delivering a baby in the middle of it.

"I suppose she would be," Cait said with a smile. "Who's she going to get?"

It was always a challenge finding a suck—er, volunteer—to take on Elmer's holiday extravaganza. Polly McMaster, Elmer's postmistress and long-suffering mayor, had to strong-arm someone into doing it. Last year she'd conned Mary, the community's newest and therefore most unsuspecting resident, into the job.

"It's a rite of passage," she'd told Mary. "You'll always belong once you've suf—er, done—it."

Mary had agreed, and she'd done it very well. She'd also cemented her place forever in Elmer folklore by her near delivery on stage. She'd made it to the hospital, but she'd also managed to convince Polly that pregnant pageant directors were probably not a good thing.

"Don't know who she'll get this year," Mary said. "Just breathe a sigh of relief that it won't be you."

It took Cait a moment to realize what Mary meant—that it couldn't possibly be her because she'd be gone.

She felt oddly bereft at the thought. She'd missed lots of Elmer's pageants over the years, but she'd remembered

the ones she'd seen as a kid with great fondness. She'd
told Resi about it. And Charlie.

She shoved away the thought. "Maybe we'll get back
for it, come see Dad for Christmas. It's not so far."

"That'd be wonderful," Mary said. "I hope so. Your
dad would be so happy. We'll take good care of him for
you." She put her hand on Cait's and gave it a squeeze.

"I know. Get Arlene to make you an appointment for a
month from now," she said as Mary started toward the
door.

Mary's face fell. "I just realized, you won't be here to
deliver the baby."

Cait smiled ruefully. "I know. I wish I could . Maybe
I—"

"No. You're not putting it off," Mary said flatly. "Between you and Steve, you'd let the entire state's medical
welfare dictate your wedding day."

"Hippocratic oath," Cait grinned.

"Whatever. You're not changing it. And I expect you
to let me know what you want me to do. Gus and I will
be happy to help. Anything at all. Don't hesitate to ask.
We owe you."

"Thanks."

But Cait imagined that even Gus might draw the line at
chasing Charlie out of town with a shotgun.

Charlie hesitated before he mounted the steps to the
broad porch that ran along the southeast side of the Blasingame ranch house.

He'd promised himself he wouldn't push Cait, and he
was on her doorstep less than twenty-four hours later. But
he was returning her ice cooler.

Returning the ice cooler wasn't pushing, was it? It was
being responsible. Adult. And she might need it.

Besides, he wanted to tell her about the bears. He'd

found them again today. Picking some kind of berries. It reminded him of that children's book *Blueberries for Sal* that he'd read over and over to Chase and Joanna's kids. He got some pictures their seven-year-old, Annie, would love.

Cait would love them, too.

He could hardly wait to tell her.

He left before the bears did this time. He'd been more careful to watch where he walked. His leg hurt, but it was better. Some better.

Maybe a little sore.

Maybe he could get Cait to put some more ice on it today.

He set the cooler on the porch and rapped on the back door. At least, he thought it was the back door. It also looked to be where all the activity took place. There were two pairs of boots by the door. Beside an old milk can and a stack of newspapers weighted down by a rock sat a box of veterinary supplies. Alongside them were some cans of motor oil, as if someone had been doing various chores and didn't quite finish.

Cait?

He didn't ever remember her expertise extending to car mechanics. But who knew?

He peered through the curtained glass of the door as best he could, looking for signs of life. It was dinnertime. He figured that was the best time to catch her home. But she didn't seem to be answering, and he hadn't seen her truck when he pulled in.

Maybe she was teaching a class tonight. Or maybe a baby was being born.

Or maybe she had another hot date with Cardiology Man.

Charlie gritted his teeth. He knocked again. Harder.

There was no response. He paced a small circle on the

porch, jammed his hands into his pockets, glowered at the shut door, then kicked the post by the steps.

Chase would tell him he was being too impatient, that he was "doing," not "being." But for Charlie, "being" was damned hard work.

He sighed and started to go back down the steps. He'd reached the bottom when he heard the door rattle open behind him.

He turned back, a smile and the words he'd planned forming on his lips—and dying there—at the sight of an older man.

"Help you?" In his jeans and faded plaid shirt he looked like a stereotype of a cowboy. His short, once dark hair was salty with gray now. His lined face was weatherbeaten, battered by the elements that doubtless made him appear older than he was. He looked like someone right out of those full-color cigarette ads. Except for the bedroom slippers he wore.

He looked tired. As if Charlie had woken him up. His eyes were flat and disinterested. They were blue, but they were the same shape as Cait's.

Charlie hadn't considered her old man. Of course he knew her father lived there, but he'd only been thinking about Cait.

Now he rethought quickly. What had Cait told him? Had she mentioned his name? And in what context? He couldn't imagine her having said anything positive. And he didn't want the old man having another heart attack on his account.

"Hi," he said, "I, uh, am a friend of Cait's. I've been staying at McCalls' and I was returning her cooler."

The old man looked at Charlie, then at the cooler, then said, "You cowboyin' for Otis an' Jed?"

Otis, Charlie knew, was Brenna McCall's father. He

shook his head. "Not...exactly. I'm a photographer. I'm just staying in their cabin."

The old man frowned. "You an artist?"

"Sort of. I don't do the same stuff. I do...*did*—" he corrected himself "—harsher subjects. Wars and urban violence. Inhumanity," he said awkwardly.

The old man's face lit up. "You're Charlie Seeks Elk?"

Taken aback by his suddenly beaming face and the quickening interest in his eyes, Charlie could only nod.

Cait's father, clearly delighted, was coming down the step, holding out a hand. "Caity said she knew you," he said, real animation in his voice for the first time, "but I didn't know she meant you were friends!" He grabbed Charlie's hand and pumped it up and down. "Mighty glad to meet you. Come on in."

Since he didn't let go of Charlie's hand as he went back up the steps, Charlie didn't have much choice. And since the old man was anything but ready to blow him away, Charlie went along quite happily.

"I'm Walt Blasingame, Cait's dad," the old man said, ushering Charlie into the kitchen and crushing his hand one last time before waving him toward a seat at the round oak table by the window.

"Pleased to meet you, Mr. Blasingame."

"Walt," the old man corrected. "Call me Walt."

"Walt." Charlie put a chair between himself and Cait's dad. "You say Cait...mentioned me?"

"She's got your book. *Inhumanity*. That's how I knew. How 'bout a cup of coffee? You want to stay for supper? Of course you do. Cait'd never forgive me if I let you leave without invitin' you for a meal." He was talking as much to himself as Charlie as he started running the water and filling the coffeemaker.

"She has my book?"

"Sure does. Damn fine book." Walt Blasingame

thumped the coffeepot down for emphasis. "You make a feller think."

"Er, thank you." Charlie couldn't help blinking at Cait's father's unexpected enthusiasm. Had he got it from Cait? Somehow Charlie doubted that.

"Sit down. Sit down," Walt Blasingame urged.

Charlie sat. He looked around the kitchen, feeling oddly as if he'd been here before.

Then he remembered that Cait had often talked about family meals right here at this table. He rubbed his finger along the edge and felt the tiny ridges that she once told him she'd carved to figure out a tricky math problem.

"My dad said to figure it out myself," she'd told him. "And when I did and he found out how, he tanned my backside."

The recollection made Charlie smile. The whole room made him smile. It was a warm, friendly sort of room. Homey. Comfortable. Different in style, but similar in feeling to the kitchen at Chase and Joanna's house.

Walt grabbed a cookie jar off the counter and dumped a pile of homemade oatmeal cookies on a plate, then stuck them in front of Charlie. "Help yourself. Where'd you come from? How come you're at the cabin? Ain't no wars in Montana. Not at the moment anyhow." He chuckled, then fixed Charlie with an avid look. "So what brung you?"

I came to marry your daughter.

Probably not the best place to start.

Charlie stalled, taking a cookie and biting off a chunk. It was ambrosial. When he'd finished it, he said, "I came from California. I'm just here for a while. A little R&R. Hadn't ever been to Montana before, and I remembered Cait talking about it…"

Walt beamed. "The last best place, that's what they call it. You like it?"

"Yeah," Charlie said, surprised at how true it was. "Yeah, I do."

"Good cookies, aren't they?" Walt poured two mugs full of strong black coffee and carried them to the table. "Cait made 'em. How'd you meet Cait?"

"I was taking some photos near the hospital where she worked."

"The one in Abuk?" Walt shook his head and grimaced. "She don't say much about it, but I reckon it was pretty bad." He sat down opposite Charlie and wrapped callused fingers around his coffee mug.

"It had its moments," Charlie allowed.

"I was in Vietnam. I know there are things you don't just toss into conversation, but...I'd like to understand a little more. She gets real quiet sometimes. An' I wonder if I can help. Will you tell me?"

"Er." Charlie swallowed. Tell him what, exactly? "What did you want to know?"

Walt pushed back his chair. "I'll get the book."

He came back moments later with an obviously well-read copy of *Inhumanity*. "Cait said she bought it 'cause of the little girl," he said. "But she don't want to look at it," he said. "Leastways, not when I'm around."

I wonder why, Charlie thought, mocking himself.

"Says she knew the little girl." Walt patted the cover picture of Resi with her sad wide eyes.

"Yeah." And for the first time in months, Charlie made himself look at Resi's picture. If it was possible to feel even more guilty than he did about what had happened between him and Cait, it was what he felt about Resi. He had betrayed her love, her trust, possibly her very life—to protect his own emotions.

"Lucky little gal," Walt said now.

"Lucky?"

"Well, not lucky in the first place," Walt qualified.

"Losin' her folks. Gettin' hurt like that. But in the end…''
He got a sort of sad, wistful smile on his face.

Charlie felt his heart skip. "In the end? What happened
in the end?''

Walt looked surprised. "You didn't know? Why she got
a new home! A new family. Somebody adopted her. One
of Cait's friends.''

Charlie stared. "One of— *Who?*''

Walt shrugged. "Dunno the name. Cait said it, but I
don't recall. Said she was one of the lucky ones.'' Walt
rubbed the side of his thumb over Resi's photo, and his
mouth twisted slightly. "Some of 'em ain't. People turn
their backs on 'em.''

"Yeah.'' Charlie felt hollow, and yet reprieved at the
same time. Like he'd been acquitted when he knew he was
guilty as charged.

Resi had been adopted? And Cait knew the family?

He tried to think who it might be.

Another one of the American medical staff? Her room-
mate, that girl from Tulsa, Jessie? That eye surgeon who
worked miracles on a daily basis? He had a hundred notions. All possible. But none had seemed likely when Cait
had suggested they marry and adopt her themselves.

Was Cait pleased now? She'd loved Resi, had wanted
her for her own.

Had wanted both him and Resi.

And it was his fault she didn't have her.

"Cait can tell you who, I reckon,'' Walt said. "Here,
now. Let me dish up dinner. Cait made stew an' it's keep-
in' warm. Don't usually feel much like eatin', myself. But
long as you're here…''

"Is Cait…teaching tonight? Or delivering a baby?''

"Don't think so,'' Walt said. He got out plates and put
half a loaf of bread on the table. "To mop up with,'' he
said. "She an' that doc were goin' out.''

"That doc? Her...fiancé?"

"Yep. Steve. Nice feller. Busier'n a one-armed paper-hanger. My Lord, he didn't hardly stop to say hello when he was doin' his rounds in the hospital. But he's a good doc. An' I reckon it's like that when so many folks are dependin' on you."

"I guess," Charlie said slowly. He'd wanted Walt to say Steve was a jerk.

"'Bout time they got a night to themselves," Walt said instead. "Too busy, the two of 'em, takin' care of everybody else." He eyed Charlie over the plate of stew he'd just put in front of him. "Reckon she went up last night and took care of you."

Charlie felt a faint heat in his face. "I got shot a few months back. Tore me up pretty bad. I fell yesterday. Ran into Cait afterward, and next thing I knew she was bringing me ice."

Walt smiled. "That's Caity. Wes, my boy, always used to call her Caity the Bandage Lady. She was forever patchin' him up when they were kids. Caity patches everybody up."

Charlie didn't want to hear that, either. He wanted to think she had done it because it was him.

"Eat up now," Walt said. "Then maybe you could tell me some about those pictures."

They ate in companionable silence. Cait's stew was wonderful—far better than anything he would have cooked for himself. When they finished eating they did up the dishes together and then he followed Walt into the pine-paneled living room to talk about the pictures.

Once more he had the sense of having been here before. Cait had talked about this room, too—about sprawling on the braided rug on the floor and watching cartoons on television, about building cabins with Lincoln logs by the fireplace, about the bookcases against the wall that her grandfather had built.

"My books were on the bottom shelf," she said. "And on winter days I used to sit in the chair by the fire and read them."

He could just imagine her there—a smaller, more freckled version of Cait curled in the leather armchair, deep in a book, her long dark hair in a braid that she nibbled on the end of during the exciting parts of the book.

Walt sat down on the sofa and Charlie took a seat next to him. He never minded talking about his photos, making his point. But this was different.

Walt opened the book to a photo of the devastation wrought by a grenade. "I saw buildings tore up like that," he said. His expression grew distant, his gaze far away.

This wasn't about Abuk, Charlie realized. The inhumanity was universal. It was Walt's way of dealing with all that he had seen.

They looked. They talked. Not so much in words, but in silences.

"There were children in Vietnam, too," Walt said. "Hurt same as that little girl you knew. Babies. Some of them soldiers weren't more than kids themselves."

Charlie stared at pictures he'd taken of soldiers who weren't more than kids. He hadn't been a whole lot more than a kid himself.

"Didn't know no more than kids," Walt was saying quietly. He stared unseeing out into the twilight. "Fella's scared he does some stupid things."

Yes. Yes, he sure as hell did. Charlie stared at Resi's sad, reproachful eyes and made himself confront the child and the reality he'd left behind.

In fact she, like Cait, had been in his heart ever since. He hadn't left her behind at all.

Then, in Walt's silence, he began to speak. Slowly.

"The first time I saw her," he said, swallowing past the sudden ache in his throat, "she wouldn't talk. She would only stare. And Cait brought me to see her because she thought I could do something. She thought I could help, that even if I couldn't help Resi, I could tell the world."

It all came back as he spoke—all the emotions, all the pain. Not just Resi's; everyone's. Abuk had been full of pain in those days. People lost. People hurting. People dying.

And yet, in midst of that pain, for a few isolated moments, there had been joy. Not just the joy of knowing Cait.

There had been joy with Resi, too.

No, there had been no words. But there had been growth. Eye contact. Her first wavering smile. Her tentative touch. And finally, the morning he found that tiny stuffed bear and brought it to her, the first words that broke a silence of God knew how long.

He could still feel her small trusting fingers curving around his. He could remember the light in her eyes when he walked into the room.

The light had flickered out early on that morning when he'd come to tell her that he had to leave.

Had to leave!

He stopped talking and just sat staring into space. He thought of all the things he'd done wrong. All the ways he'd tried so desperately to protect himself, to assure himself he was doing the right thing for all of them.

What a liar he'd been.

He didn't notice the tear that streaked his cheek. Or feel the muscle tick in his temple. Or hear Walt's quiet words.

Or wonder what they meant when the old man said, "I know. I know."

Five

Steve was thrilled at the news. "Well," he'd said. "Finally."

"It's all right?" Cait twisted her napkin nervously in her hands as she looked at him over the table at Sage's. "The date, I mean?"

Steve said, "Sure, fine." He grinned. "I'll shut off my beeper all day. Just kidding." He consulted his small day planner and did some mental figuring. "Perfect, as a matter of fact. I'll tell them I'll be gone a week. That way we can go on a quick honeymoon and I'll be back in time to fly out to Johannesburg for the conference on the twenty-sixth. Couldn't have planned it better myself. What inspired you?"

Somehow telling him about Charlie didn't seem like a particularly good idea.

"It was time," Cait said. "I mean, if we're going to do it, we ought to just do it. Right?" She gave him a brilliant smile.

"Absolutely." Steve reached across the table and gave her hand a squeeze. "That's great. You can come with me down to Denver the weekend after next and we can find a place to live."

Cait blinked. "What?"

"You come with me," Steve said. "For the weekend. Since we're actually going to do it this fall, wherever I am is going to be your place, too. No sense in me renting something for a couple of months and then us moving. You'd better come along, too."

Cait hadn't thought that far ahead. She also wasn't at all sure she should leave her father for a weekend. "We'll see," she said.

"Come on. Start planning now," Steve cajoled her, "and we can probably pull it off."

"I'll have to talk to my dad. Maybe we could take him with us?"

Steve didn't look extraordinarily thrilled at the idea, but he nodded. And the notion of taking her father along actually pleased Cait a great deal.

He needed something to cheer him up. Too many nights recently she had come home to find him sitting in his chair staring into space or, worse, looking through Charlie's book, dinner still slow-cooking away.

"Not hungry," he'd say when she remonstrated with him. "I'm not all that interested in eatin', Caity."

He wasn't interested in much these days.

"It would be great to take my dad along," she said eagerly now, and glanced at her watch. "I really ought to get going. I wasn't home last night, either. And I won't be tomorrow because of my birthing class. I should be there to eat with him more often."

"He's got to learn to cope sometime, Cait," Steve said. "He won't do things for himself if he knows you'll do them for him."

"It isn't a matter of doing it for him," Cait said, because she'd already done that, though Steve didn't know it. "It's a matter of keeping him company. He's all alone."

"Then he needs to invite people over. Get out. See his friends."

"Yes." Cait agreed completely. But agreeing and convincing her father to do it were two different things.

Brenna and Jed had invited him over several times. Unless Cait was there to go with him, he'd declined. Gus and Mary had invited him, too, but he hadn't gone. And he wouldn't invite anyone in.

Just last night she'd suggested he call Otis Jamison to come over and play cribbage while she was hauling the ice up to Charlie.

But Walt had said he was too tired. "Maybe another night," he'd said vaguely.

Cait lived in hope, but not much.

So she was surprised to drive into the yard that night and see Otis Jamison's old Suburban parked near the barn.

"Well, finally," she said, relieved. Maybe her going out last night and tonight was actually doing some good by forcing her father to seek out his friends if he wanted any companionship at all.

She opened the back door and went into the kitchen. A look around made her smile widen. Obviously he'd eaten. And had company for dinner, too. She could see that the slow cooker had been washed out and there were two sets of silverware and plates drying in the rack by the sink.

There were voices in the living room. She pushed open the door and breezed in. "Hi! You're still up! I'm so glad Ot—"

She stopped dead at the sight of Charlie.

Her father thumped his book down on the coffee table and looked up beaming. "Ah, Caity, look who's here!"

Charlie, who knew better than to beam, smiled determinedly as he got to his feet. "Hey. Out catching babies tonight?"

"What are you doing here?" Cait demanded.

Her father's eyes widened at her tone. "Caity! Where are your manners?"

Cait bit back the reply that sprang to her lips. "I'm just…surprised to see him here." She kept her accusing glare for Charlie, who was looking like innocence personified.

"I brought back your ice chest."

"You needn't have bothered."

"Well, I wanted to say thanks. And," he grinned faintly, "I was sort of hoping for more ice."

"Staying off your leg would do more good than coming clear over here."

"Can't do that. Gotta keep an eye on those bears. Besides, I am taking care of it. I watched where I was going today."

"Still—"

"I didn't wear it out. I had a good day. Took some shots of bears and berries." He grinned. "And then I brought the cooler back."

It all sounded very straightforward. But Cait didn't believe for a minute that was all there was to it. There was a look in Charlie's eyes that she recognized all too well. It was the same look he got whenever he'd been hot on the trail of good photos.

But she couldn't challenge him now—not with her father such an avid spectator.

"Well, thank you," she said grudgingly.

"I invited him to stay for supper," her father said cheerfully, looking brighter than she'd seen him in months. "Was sorry you missed him. But I asked him to stick around. Figured you'd want to see 'im. An' after we ate, we set out here an' talked."

Which sounded rather ominous. What had Charlie been telling her father? What had her father told Charlie?

"Well," she said briskly, "thank you for bringing the ice chest back. If you need some more I'll give you some and—"

"I'll live without it," Charlie said. "I really came to see you. To thank you." He was looking at her intently, so intently she had to look away.

Nervously she began to straighten the magazines on the coffee table. "You're welcome," she said. "But you didn't need to come all this way for that."

"It was the least I could do."

"No, it wasn't. You could have ignored me completely."

"Caity wouldn't do that. She'd never turn her back on a friend," her father said cheerfully. "Don't know why you didn't tell me where you were goin' last night," he said to her.

Cait lined up the magazines in precise rows. "It wasn't important."

"Not compared to your hot date," Charlie said.

Cait saw her father's eyes go wide. "Hot date?"

"Steve and I were going to see a movie," Cait told him, shooting Charlie an annoyed glance. "But Steve had an emergency, so I just came back here instead. We went out tonight," she said for Charlie's benefit.

His brows lifted and he glanced at the clock. "You're home early." The implication being that the date hadn't been all that hot.

"I thought Dad was alone," Cait said irritably. "Obviously, I was wrong. So thank you for staying and keeping him company. You don't have to hang around now."

Her father was positively sputtering at her rudeness.

Charlie seemed completely unfazed. "Oh, I enjoyed it. We had a good time. Besides, I sort of felt like I already knew you a little,'' he said to Walt. ''Cait told me a lot of stories.''

''Did she?'' Her father was smiling like the Cheshire Cat. Then he fixed his gaze on Cait. ''You,'' he accused, ''didn't tell me anything.''

''You were hardly in any shape to be entertained by my war stories when I got here. You were in Intensive Care.''

''Well, after,'' Walt grumbled. ''You sure never said anything much about this feller here.''

Cait didn't look at Charlie. She shrugged. ''I had nothing to say.'' Then she did glance at him and added dismissively, ''Charlie was in and out of my life so quickly.''

''And now I'm back,'' Charlie said.

''Briefly,'' Cait acknowledged. She yawned widely, doing nothing to mask it, hoping he would take the hint. When he didn't move, she said to her father, ''I'm tired. I think I'll turn in.''

Her father gave her a disapproving look, which Cait determinedly ignored. Instead she dropped a light kiss on his cheek, then turned to Charlie. ''Thank you for returning the cooler.''

''Have dinner with me tomorrow night.''

She stared for a split second. ''What?''

''Have dinner with me.'' He repeated the words she hadn't wanted to hear in the first place.

''No. Thank you.''

Her father looked shocked. ''Caity!''

''I've got things to do.''

''He's an old friend.''

''I'm teaching tomorrow night. My birthing class.''

''After your class,'' Charlie said, all accommodation.

''I don't finish until nine.''

''I'm allowed up after nine,'' Charlie said with gentle mockery, making her father chuckle and Cait furious.

''I'm engaged,'' she hissed at him.

"So? He won't let you have dinner with an old friend?"

"He doesn't have anything to say about it!"

"Well, then..." Charlie spread his hands. "Old friends need to catch up."

Friends? Cait looked at him skeptically.

"You're engaged. What else could we be?"

She glared at him. "Dad will be alone again and—"

"Enjoying every minute of it," her father cut in firmly. "You don't need to rush home on account of me, Caity girl. I'm feelin' fine."

Surprisingly he looked brighter, as if he'd taken a turn for the better, as if something had come along to inspire him.

Charlie?

Surely not!

"You might not be feeling good tomorrow night."

"Humph," her father snorted. "I reckon I'll survive. Quitcher fussin' and g'wan out with Charlie."

Quit her fussing? Cait gaped at him. Who had been demanding that she hover over him like a broody hen for months and months? Who had been saying he just wanted her around? Who had felt too poorly to be left alone?

Now he looked brighter than she'd seen him in ages. There was a hint of life and challenge in his eyes—as if he were daring her to have dinner with Charlie.

"Fine," she said shortly. "Be at the hospital at nine."

"If I come early can I check out your class?"

She blinked. "You want to watch a bunch of expectant mothers breathe and pant?"

"I like to see women pant." Charlie grinned, and her father smothered a chuckle.

"Come ahead then," Cait dared him. "I'll put you to work."

Charlie grinned. "I'll count on it."

* * *

Cait tossed and turned all night. It was because of the wedding, of course. She'd never planned a wedding before. She had so many things to think about. The wedding itself, the reception, the music, the flowers, her bridesmaids, the guest list.

Charlie.

She shoved the thought of him away. But, as persistent in her mind as he was in person, he came right back. "Fine," she muttered, crushing her pillow against her chest and staring at the ceiling. "I'll invite you. You can watch me marry Steve. You can eat your heart out."

Oh, yes. Sure he would.

She knew better. He was pushing her now because he thought he wanted her. If she ever said yes, she'd marry him, he'd turn and run so fast she'd be left staring at his dust.

Well, she wasn't going to say yes to Charlie. She'd already said yes to Steve. She just wished Charlie would go away and leave her alone.

She hadn't been thrilled to see him with her father tonight. She wasn't thrilled to know he was meeting her for dinner tonight. If she could have called him up and declined later, she would have. But the McCalls' cabin had no phone, and if he had a cellular, she didn't know his number.

So she spent the day hoping he wouldn't show up.

But at seven that evening he was standing outside the classroom, waiting, when Cait came around the corner.

The very sight of him caused that familiar quiver deep inside that she always felt when she saw Charlie. She used to think it meant she was in love with him. Now she knew better. It was just a hormonal response to a handsome man. It had nothing to do with love.

"You're early," she said.

"I'm interested."

"In a bunch of pregnant women?"

"And their teacher."

She felt her cheeks warm. "Don't, Charlie." She brushed past him to go into the classroom.

"I'm telling the truth, that's all."

"We're friends, remember? That's what you said. If you're changing the rules, you can leave right now."

He shrugged. "Fine, we're friends." He followed her to the front of the room and caught her hand before she could jerk it away. "We were always friends, Cait."

They had been. It was she who had wanted more, who had hoped for more, had thought they had more. She tugged to get her hand away from him, but he didn't let go, and she knew he wouldn't until she agreed with him.

"All right," she said, annoyed, "we're friends."

"Good. I thought maybe I could take some pictures."

"Of what?"

"Your students."

She stared at him to see if he was joking, but he seemed perfectly serious. "I've been doing a lot of moms these days. And kids." He glanced around. "Maybe a few dads, too. Relationships."

"Relationships?" Cait said doubtfully. That didn't sound like Charlie.

He nodded. "What you need to pass on. Connections. That sort of thing. What mama bear taught her young 'uns. I saw this elk with her calf this morning." A delighted grin lit his face. "Coolest thing." Then he looked a little embarrassed, as if his enthusiasm betrayed him. But finally he just shrugged. "I'm working it out as I go along. Photographing what interests me."

"Moms and kids?" Cait said, allowing herself to sound sarcastic.

"Yeah. I'm just gathering material. I'll look for the themes later."

"I thought you had a theme—inhumanity."

"Had," Charlie agreed, propping one hip against the edge of the counter that ran along beneath the windows. "But there's more to the world, thank God. More I need—*want*—to explore." He looked reflective for a moment, then continued. "I've seen enough inhumanity, God knows. I've helped other people see it. That's what my work was, what my book was. But after I got shot, well, I started thinking there was a lot of life I hadn't ever focused on. I'd only half lived. Gaby told me it was time to move on. She's right."

Cait was surprised at his sincerity. Still, it was hard to imagine Charlie doing mothers and babies. They were the opposite of everything he'd done before. Positive, not negative. Life affirming, not a record of death and destruction. Harbingers of hope, not despair. And they were usually settled.

Charlie had never been settled. She had seen that, in retrospect. He'd always been restless, eager to be moving, dashing here and there, intent on what was just over the next hill or in tomorrow's news.

"I'll ask my students if they mind," she said. "I'll introduce you to them and we'll see. We've got seven moms in all." She nodded toward the back of the room where they were beginning to congregate.

Most, of course, brought their husbands or boyfriends, but occasionally they brought a friend or a relative. After all, Mary had brought Gus before they were married or even really going together again. The birthing class had brought them together.

"And damn near frustrated the life out of me," Gus had told her ruefully not long ago. "But at the time it was the only way I could get my hands on her."

Cait had never thought of her class as an erotic experience before and had said so.

"It's all in the mind of the beholder," Gus had told her with a wink and a grin.

Cait was determined not to let any erotic thoughts cross her mind. She'd had plenty about Charlie in the past, but that was over. All her thoughts were for Steve now.

Charlie was just part of the furniture. He could hang around. She would even go to dinner with him. But that was as far as it would go.

Finally the last couple arrived—Angie Mayhew, barely seventeen and the youngest of the moms-to-be, came in with her coach and foster mother Maddie Fletcher, seventy-five if she was a day. Angie was looking her normally sulky self, but long-suffering Maddie was beaming as always.

"Sorry we're late," she apologized.

Angie kept on scowling until she saw Charlie, then her normally truculent expression changed and her gaze grew interested, speculative.

Cait felt an even greater than normal irritation with the girl. Putting it aside, she cleared her throat. "We have a visitor today, a friend of mine from California, Charlie Seeks Elk. Charlie is a professional photographer, and he's asked if you would allow him to take some photos of our session. I'm not exactly sure what he has in mind, so I'll let him explain what he wants to do."

If Charlie was surprised that she put him on the spot, he didn't give any indication. He looked up from tightening the lens on his camera and grinned that beguiling Charlie grin that, within minutes, had everyone eating out of his hand.

He used to take pictures of grim stuff, he told them. Misery and pain, he said, had been the hallmarks of his work. And then he'd seen the light. "I finally figured out that if I only focused on that, I was missing a big part of life," he told them, "the best part. I shot a lot of photos of death and dying. Now I'd like to look at the other side. So I'd like to take some photos here—of birth and getting ready for it. Unplanned. Unposed. If I get good ones, with your permission, I'll hang them in a show I'm doing down in Santa Fe next spring. What do you say?"

The women, except Angie, looked embarrassed, but nodded. Angie preened. Charlie, Cait could tell, noticed.

"Just ignore me," he said to all of them. "Listen to Cait and pretend I'm not here."

It was like telling them not to think of pink chickens, Cait thought. *Whatever you do, don't think of pink chickens!*

Charlie was the most noticeable pink chicken in the room. They eyed him warily out of the corners of their eyes. They glanced back over their shoulders to see where he was and what he was doing.

In fact, Charlie wasn't doing anything. He was holding his camera, but he wasn't shooting. He just held it easily in his hands and waited for Cait to start.

Cait was as self-conscious as her students. Maybe more so. But everything depended on her, so she began. This was the third week of the six-week course. The time of birth was getting close now. Several of the women were experiencing contractions. One had already been hospitalized overnight when labor had appeared imminent.

It was time to give them a view of what to expect instead of just talking about it. "We're going to look at a video first tonight," she told them. "A time lapse of labor and delivery so you know what to expect. You can see the breathing techniques in practice and watch for the transitions. It will help make some sort of sense of what we've been doing."

As she talked, she, too, flicked glance after glance in Charlie's direction, but he still wasn't moving, just listening. Everyone else—except Angie—had stopped turning around by this time.

She expected Charlie to wander off during the video or possibly shoot some low-light photos, but he never lifted his camera once. Instead, once the film started, he stayed right where he was, perched on the counter at the side of the room, and watched, entranced, as the on-screen labor progressed.

Everyone else watched the movie, too. Cait watched him.

She'd seen the movie already—about a dozen times. That was her excuse. There was also a little curiosity about Charlie's reaction. She'd seen him tender and gentle with Resi, but she knew better than anyone that he never really got involved. So it was a little surprising that he looked almost shaken when the video ended with the mother holding her brand-new child in her arms.

The other viewer who sat in complete silence was Angie. She looked scared to death.

About time, Cait thought.

The girl's cavalier attitude and general flippancy had irritated her from the start. Only the fact that Maddie had come with her, determinedly supportive and making up for Angie's general rudeness had convinced Cait to put up with her in the class.

"All right," she said after punching Rewind on the VCR. "Now that you've seen what you're in for, let's get to work again on some of the breathing techniques. Everyone get a mat."

Charlie began to move around the room, taking pictures as everyone got a mat. The pregnant women, grumbling and laughing at their own awkwardness, lowered themselves to the floor. Their coaches knelt beside them, all except Maddie who was moving a little slowly.

"It's these damned arthritic knees," she said with an

expression halfway between a grimace and a grin. "I'm not as young as I used to be."

Angie was looking impatient, not helping at all.

"Here," Charlie said to Maddie, dragging over a chair beside the mat where Angie sat. "You sit here."

"I'm supposed to help," Maddie protested.

"You can help from there," Charlie said firmly. "If you need anything done on the floor, I'll do it."

"She's supposed to put her hands on my belly," Angie informed him with a sly, speculative look.

Charlie just shrugged. "I can do that."

Angie brightened considerably, and Cait felt an unpleasant and unwanted shaft of annoyance spear her. She turned her back and began to start the breathing sequence. "Okay, everyone. Let's go."

She didn't think Charlie took another picture for the rest of the class, but he did manage to keep Angie focused on what she was supposed to be doing. Of course she was doing it to impress Charlie, but at least she was doing it. She had only come to the earlier classes because Maddie had insisted.

"I'm leading the horse to water," Maddie had told Cait privately. "God knows if she'll drink."

She would, Cait decided irritably, if Charlie was around to help her.

She tried not to notice them as she went around the room, helping out each couple who had questions. Naturally Angie didn't have any questions. Except for Charlie.

Even after the class was over and the mats put away, Angie was sticking close to Charlie, her expression equal parts lust and hero worship as she followed his every move with her eyes. Charlie was talking to Maddie, but he was smiling at Angie and resting a hand on her shoulder.

Cait grabbed the video out of the VCR and stuffed it in

her tote bag. Then she strode across the room. "I'm ready," she said bluntly.

Charlie turned his smile on her. "So am I."

She steeled herself against it, then turned to Maddie and Angie. "See you next week."

"Yes," Maddie said, then took Charlie's hand. "Thanks from my old knees."

Angie grabbed his other hand. "You're coming back next week, aren't you?" This from the girl who hadn't wanted to be there in the first place.

Charlie slanted a glance in Cait's direction. "If she'll let me."

Cait's jaw tightened, and she had to force herself to smile. "As long as you don't upset things."

"He won't!" Angie assured her eagerly. "He's a big help."

Cait raised her brows in a look of polite skepticism.

But Maddie smiled as she gave Cait's hand a squeeze. "He's a big help," she agreed.

Cait wasn't so sure about that. She knew all about being led on by Charlie Seeks Elk, who, even when he had no intention of doing so, had a disastrous effect on the opposite sex.

"Come on, Angie," Maddie said now. "We've got to get going."

"You're coming, right?" Angie insisted, looking imploringly at Charlie.

He gave a quick nod. "If it helps, I'll be here."

Satisfied for the moment at least, Angie left with Maddie, actually smiling for the first time since Cait had met her.

"Well, you've certainly made an impression on her," she said gruffly, leading the way out of the classroom and down the corridor.

Charlie fell into step beside her. "Nice to make an impression on someone."

"Just don't be leading her on."

"I don't lead women on."

"You might not try to. Sometimes it just happens. And Angie is susceptible."

"I've got the point," Charlie said. He paused. "Where's her man?"

Cait snorted. "He's not much of a man. He took off when he found out she was pregnant. Then her family kicked her out. She lived with a girlfriend for a while, then she started flirting with the girlfriend's boyfriend and got kicked out of there. She ended up in Bozeman and someone got hold of Martha Reese. Martha is a social worker. She got Maddie to take her in. Maddie's been bringing her here, trying to convince her to help herself and to take care of herself. She hasn't been exactly willing."

"I know the feeling," Charlie said with such quiet intensity that Cait looked sideways at him. His jaw was tight and there was a grim look in his eyes. She remembered what he'd told her about his own past and realized that he would feel a certain empathy for Angie.

"Then you realize how vulnerable she is."

Charlie nodded.

Cait hoped so. She didn't want to see Angie hurt further. The girl already had a big enough chip on her shoulder, and whatever Maddie and she and Martha had tried to do for her had fallen on deaf ears.

"Where do you want to go to eat?" Charlie asked when they reached the parking lot.

Cait had given that considerable thought. It had to be the right setting. She knew Charlie wouldn't settle for any of the fast-food places tonight, and she didn't want to go to a more expensive, intimate restaurant. That would make this look—and feel—too much like the date it wasn't.

"The Barrel," she told him. "It's a place to go with a friend."

"It's a bar," he protested.

"How do you know?" she said, surprised.

"I've been there." He didn't explain further, just scowled, then shrugged. "If that's what you want, let's go." He started toward the silver Porsche he had obviously traded for Otis's Suburban tonight.

But Cait wasn't riding in any Porsche with Charlie. "I'll meet you there."

He scowled again, but finally he nodded. "Suit yourself."

"Yes." Cait was determined she would.

The Barrel was noisy and cheerful. There were pool games going on in the back and a crowded bar up front. Many of the tables were filled, and Cait seemed to know a lot of people there. She stopped to talk to half a dozen, casually introducing him as a friend from L.A. whom she'd met overseas. It seemed to him she came down harder than necessary on the word *friend*.

Everybody nodded and said hello. One or two of the women looked at him with that sort of look that good-looking men come to recognize after a while. It said they were interested. And one or two of them were pretty enough to interest most men.

Not him.

"Come join us," one of them, a sweet-smiling brunette, invited.

Cait smiled. "Thanks. We'd love—"

"—to, but we've got some catching up to do." Charlie gave the woman a nod and a smile, took hold of Cait's arm and steered her right on past.

"How rude was that?" Cait muttered.

"I don't know. How rude was it?" Charlie found them

a relatively secluded table, pulled out the chair facing away from the room so she couldn't spend time looking for a little help from her friends, and waited until she had no alternative but to sit in the chair he held for her.

Like the gentleman he could be when he chose, he pushed it in for her and took the seat opposite. "There now. Isn't this nice?"

Cait looked as if she didn't know what to say to that.

Charlie was pleased. "I liked your class."

"Makes you want to run right out and have a baby, hmm?"

"Made me aware of how strong women are. I'd never seen a baby born before."

Chase had told him that, after his firstborn twins, Emerson and Alexander, arrived, if he'd known what *labor* really meant he would never have got Joanna pregnant.

Charlie, a clueless nineteen-year-old at the time, hadn't given it much thought. Sex was fun, that was all he knew. That it could be better when people loved each other, he'd supposed might be true. At least Chase and Joanna's relationship seemed to imply that it was. But the consequences for the woman had never really hit home until he watched that video tonight.

He couldn't quite imagine watching Cait go through that.

"It's hard work," he said, which was putting it mildly.

Cait nodded. "But it's only the start. Raising them is harder."

"Yeah." He smiled faintly. "Just ask mother bear."

"Did you see her again?"

He nodded. "This afternoon. Your dad showed me a good spying spot."

She looked startled. "My dad?"

"Yeah. He came by this morning just as I was leaving

to look for the bears again.'' He could tell that surprised her. ''Why? Don't you want us fraternizing?''

But she looked bewildered, not angry. ''I'm just…I can't imagine what he was doing up there.'' She shook her head. ''He's barely left the house since he got home from the hospital after his heart attack.''

''I thought that was last summer.''

''Last fall. He was in the hospital until early October. He came home right before round-up. He wasn't well enough to do that, and after round-up it was cold, and I didn't encourage him. I thought he'd start doing things again come spring. But he didn't. He's just been sitting at home staring out the window or…'' She paused and didn't finish the sentence. ''He actually came up to the cabin? Did he say what he was doing up there?''

''Came to check on some cattle, he said.''

Cait stared. ''He didn't drive his truck? He *rode?*'' Now she looked alarmed.

Charlie shrugged. ''He seemed to do all right. We rode up to some creek above your pasture and then we walked and—''

Her jaw sagged. ''He *walked?*''

''He's not at death's door, Cait!'' Charlie protested, but now he was starting to get worried, too.

''I need to call him,'' Cait said. ''To see if he's all right. Whatever did you say to him yesterday that would have made him do that?''

''What did *I* say to him?''

But she had jumped up and was heading for the phone, leaving Charlie to hurry after her.

Walt answered the phone. From the conversation, at first solicitous and concerned on Cait's end and finally terse, Charlie gathered that Walt had assured Cait that he was fine. ''I am not fussing!'' she protested. ''Fine. Goodbye.''

She got off the phone a few minutes later looking miffed

and perplexed both. "He acts like it was a perfectly normal thing for him to do," she muttered, heading back to their table.

Charlie shrugged. "Maybe it was."

But Cait was shaking her head. "To just get up after all these months and go see you to show you where he'd seen some bears?" Cait's eyes narrowed. "What did you talk about?"

"Bears."

"That's all?"

He thought about it. "My book," he added after a moment. "And Vietnam."

"He talked to you about Vietnam?"

"Yeah."

The waitress came over then and took their orders. When she left, Cait looked right at him and said, "He's never talked to anyone about Vietnam."

Charlie lifted his shoulders. "Sometimes it takes a while. You know as well as I do that what you see in places like that isn't something you come home and blab about."

Cait nodded. "Yes, but…" She paused. "But your book showed what it was like." She murmured the words, hesitated, then asked, "What did he say?"

"Just talked about how different everything was. The noises. The colors. How vivid it was. Like technicolor. Not the real world. Another world. Another universe."

Charlie had understood completely. Sometimes the places he'd been and the things he'd seen had seemed that way to him, too.

The waitress brought their beers and he wrapped a hand around his glass. "He talked about the people. Guys in his outfit. People who lived there. A teacher he'd met. He asked if I ever got close to the people where I worked."

Their eyes met, and there was no doubt they were both remembering how close they'd been.

Then abruptly Cait looked away. She picked up her glass and turned her head to stare across the room, to watch the pool players and the barmaids. The jukebox moaned a loved-'em-and-left-'em song.

Charlie ran his tongue over his lips. "We talked about Resi."

It seemed, for just an instant, as if there was the hard click of pool ball on pool ball—and then silence.

He laid his hands flat on the table and looked across it at her. "We haven't talked about Resi."

She swallowed. Her knuckles were white on her glass. She lifted her shoulders in a tiny shrug, as if doing any more than that would hurt too much. It hurt him to see it. He knew he deserved to be hurt.

"Why should we talk about Resi," she said evenly after a moment.

"Because she matters."

"To me."

"And to me, too. Though," he admitted, "I was afraid to let her matter too much."

She looked surprised, but she didn't say anything.

"Your dad says some friends of yours adopted her?"

Cait nodded. "Morse and his wife."

Charlie stared. "*Morse?* Morse Griffin? Mr. I'm-on-the-Next-Plane-Out-of-Here Griffin? Mr. Nothing-Touches-Me Griffin?"

"Resi touched him," Cait said simply.

He just sat there, stunned. Of all the people they'd known in Abuk who might have done such a thing, Morse Griffin was the last person Charlie would have expected to do it. Although he was married, Morse seemed to have had even itchier feet that Charlie had.

"Are they…is it…" He couldn't seem to find the words. "Are *you* all right with that?"

"Of course I'm all right with it," Cait said sharply. "Morse and Jeannie are good parents."

"Yeah, but…" His voice trailed off and he shook his head. "You wanted…"

"I wanted to adopt her. But I was single, and that wasn't going to fly. The government had certain requirements."

"Yeah. But Morse? I never would have figured." Charlie gave another disbelieving half laugh. "He didn't have a near-death experience, did he?"

"Not exactly." The waitress arrived then, bringing them steaks and salad. Cait waited until she had departed before continuing. "Part of Morse's being on the go all the time wasn't because he loved it so much. It was to avoid being home."

Charlie cocked a brow. "And now that they have Resi, that's all changed?" It didn't seem likely.

But Cait nodded. Her eyes softened. "Actually, yes." She smiled faintly. "Because he was finally able to give Jeannie what she wanted—a child."

Charlie stared. The song was a hard-driving Brooks and Dunn number now. Someone was whooping at the bar. He sat very still, thinking it through. "You mean…Jeannie wanted kids and…Morse couldn't have 'em?"

Cait folded her hands on the table. "Yes."

The implications of that took a moment to sink in. "Whoa."

"It happens," Cait said almost defensively. "It doesn't make him less of a man."

Intellectually Charlie agreed with her. But he *was* a man—and he could guess how the knowledge that he was shooting blanks would make Morse feel.

He sat back in his chair, took a breath and let it out

slowly. "A guy would have to come to terms with it," he said at last. "And it might take a while."

"It did. And I don't know that he would ever have considered adoption if it hadn't been Resi. But she was there…needing a home…and well, when you stopped coming in to see her, he started. It just sort of went from there."

Morse was the one he'd roped into grabbing his news van and taking him to the airport the morning he'd left. All the way there Morse had badgered him about where he was going, asking where on earth there was more devastation than they were seeing right there.

He'd thought Charlie was running *to* something, not away.

Finally at the airport he'd looked at Charlie narrowly and said, "There isn't anything urgent out there, is there?"

And Charlie had shrugged. "Just…gotta get away."

Morse had understood. Morse had stepped in. He'd done what Charlie couldn't do.

And he was now Resi's father.

"He never said," he muttered.

"It's not the sort of thing people talk about except to their nearest and dearest," Cait pointed out. "And sometimes not even then."

"Yeah." Charlie's steak was getting cold, and the waitress came and asked if everything was all right. He nodded and started to eat. It was good, he supposed. But he didn't taste it really. "Do you see them?" he asked finally.

Cait smiled. It was a little wistful, but not really unhappy. "I saw them in February. They adopted a baby boy. Travis Mark. They're very happy."

"Even Resi?"

"Resi most of all. She's done very well. She's almost seven now, you know. Starting second grade in the fall. A big girl, she told Morse and Jeannie, and tired of being an only child. She wanted a baby sister or brother.'' Cait's smile grew lopsided. ''She was ready to share. Travis is Resi's baby.''

Charlie could see tears in her eyes. He could feel them pricking behind the lids of his own. His throat squeezed shut on the steak he was trying to swallow. At least it saved him having to say something and the embarrassment of hearing his voice crack with emotion.

''So,'' Cait said finally, briskly, ''you did them a favor.''

''Yeah,'' Charlie said slowly.

It wasn't all that comforting a thought.

Six

She had handled it well. All of it.

She'd got through the birthing classes without letting Charlie see how aware of him she was. She'd survived last night's dinner at the Barrel very nicely. She'd even managed to talk about Resi with equanimity, stressing the positive aspects of her adoption. It was true, in fact, what she'd said when she told him he'd done them all a favor.

He'd done her a favor, too.

And she was determined to believe it.

"Earth to Ms. Blasingame." A teasing male voice infiltrated her consciousness above the hospital hub-bub that she routinely tuned out.

"Oh!" She glanced up from the paperwork she'd been staring at for the past ten minutes to see Steve grinning down at her. She shoved an escaping tendril of hair off her cheek and met his grin with a smile of her own. "Hi."

"Hi, yourself. Glad I caught you." He reached inside

his shirt pocket, pulled out a much-folded piece of paper and held it out to her. "Here."

Cait took it. "What's this?"

"Guest list. The start, anyway."

Cait, unfolding it, found her eyes widening. There were at least a hundred names. "The start?" she said when she had swallowed.

"Doctors at the hospitals here and in Bozeman. Their wives. Our office staff. A couple of the guys I play golf with… I figured, since we were getting sort of a late start, I should come up with something pretty quick. I talked to my mother last night. She has another hundred or so."

"Another…hundred?"

"That's not a problem, is it?"

"I, er, no. I just…hadn't given it a lot of thought." Frankly, thinking about it was terrifying. What did she know about planning a wedding?

"I'll help," Steve said. "And my mother said she'd fly out from Boston any time you want her to. She's thrilled. She was sure I was playing some sort of practical joke on her when I said we were getting married but could never come up with a date."

Cait had only met Steve's mother once. Carolyn Carmichael was The World's Most Organized Woman and she liked nothing better than to prove it by organizing people. Cait didn't need a human bulldozer right now, no matter how eager and well-intentioned she was.

"Um, thanks." Cait managed a bright smile. "Tell her I'll be in touch. I…need to check some things out first."

"Right." Steve dropped a kiss on her hair, started to leave, then turned back. "Don't worry about the rehearsal dinner."

"Rehearsal dinner?" Cait hadn't even considered one.

Steve grinned. "That's my responsibility, my mother says. We'll take care of that."

She probably already had, Cait thought glumly. "Well, good. Something I can take off my list," she said with all the cheer she could muster.

"I'll call you when I get a full list," Steve said. "And we can—"

Mercifully whatever they were going to be able to do was cut off when his beeper sounded.

"Gotta run. Talk to you later." He bent once more and gave her a swift kiss before hurrying off toward the operating room.

Cait sat in silence staring at the list in her hand. Where on earth was she going to find a place to put two hundred of Steve's nearest and dearest friends and relatives? What was she going to feed them? Where would they all stay? A thousand panicky questions reeled through her mind.

Cait was calm under fire. She had patched up disaster victims, delivered a baby under bomb threats, stitched up dozens of seriously wounded men. She was good at a lot of things.

Planning weddings obviously wasn't one of them.

Besides, an extravaganza of a wedding wasn't what she'd ever had in mind. She'd always envisioned a small intimate gathering—her closest friends, her father, her brother Wes, a few cousins, Chase and Joanna and the few people who mattered to Charlie—

Charlie?

Cait broke out in a cold sweat. No! Not Charlie.

Steve! Steve, whom she loved! Steve whom she was going to marry!

Charlie, indeed!

How could her mind have played such a trick on her?

Furious, she stuffed the paperwork into her bag and stood up, her hands clammy and shaking. She needed some fresh air, less stress, the opportunity to talk to someone who could set her on the right track, someone who understood about weddings, who could steer her straight.

As soon as her appointments for the day were over, she got in her truck and drove to Mary Holt's.

What was a foreman's wife for if you couldn't go dump wedding jitters on her? Besides, Mary had said she'd help, hadn't she?

But Mary, looking aghast at the list Cait handed her, said, "Two hundred people? That's out of my league. We'll call Poppy. And Milly. They'll know what to do. Poppy's a pro."

Poppy Nichols ran a florist shop in Livingston called Poppy's Garden. She was, thus, something of an expert on weddings, and Cait could see calling her.

But Milly?

"Wasn't it Milly's wedding that Cash crashed and slugged the usher?" Visions of Charlie pulling a stunt like that almost brought out a cold sweat.

"That was her *first* wedding," Mary said. "The one Cash stopped. The one where she married him went all right, I think."

"Still," Cait hedged, "maybe we should just call Poppy."

Mary laughed. "Worried you might jinx things? That someone might crash *your* wedding?"

"God forbid."

"We could screen them all for weapons before they came in the church." Mary laughed.

"I'm sure Steve's mother would be impressed by that."

"The point of the wedding, my dear, is not your mother-in-law. If you've got the right man, you don't need anything else."

Cait felt a sudden tightening in her chest. "What do you mean?"

Mary blinked at the vehemence of her question. "Don't

take it personally,'' she said with a laugh. ''I was only saying that the groom is the most important thing.''

''Well, of course,'' Cait said, laughing it off. But the tight feeling eased only slightly.

''Don't worry about his mother.'' Mary reached out and patted her arm. ''You'll do fine. If you're worried, stop by the Mini-mart on your way home.''

''The Mini-mart?'' Cait stopped there for bread and milk and eggs when she forgot to go to the grocery store. ''Why?''

''You can buy all the latest bridal magazines there. Read two or three of those and you'll be an expert. You'll know the best places to go on a honeymoon, the right number of courses to serve at a very formal affair, the proper wording for invitations. They'll tell you exactly what to do and when.''

''Truly?'' Cait's education had obviously been lacking. She'd never read a bridal magazine in her life.

Mary grinned and crossed her heart. ''You will find everything in them you need to know. And then some. I promise.''

Cait wondered if it would tell her how to forget the wrong man.

''Whitelaw.'' The voice was fuzzed. Either the connection or—

''Hey, it's me,'' Charlie said.

Chase groaned. ''You all right?'' His voice became suddenly rough and intense the minute he recognized Charlie's on the other end of the transatlantic call.

''I'm all right.''

''All in one piece? Not shot?''

''No.''

''Then do you know what the hell time it is?''

''Er. Sorry.'' It was early evening in Montana, which

would make it, what? Somewhere around four in the morning at the villa on Lake Como where they were staying for the week. "But…"

But not all that sorry. He'd been stewing ever since this afternoon.

Walt had come by again. He'd been moving some cattle and he'd stopped "to set a spell," he told Charlie. And then he'd begun muttering about Cait telling him he'd have to wear a morning suit at the wedding.

"Hell," he'd said. "Didn't even wear a morning suit at my own weddin'."

He'd talked about hundreds of people and Cait figuring only the town hall would be big enough to hold them all and how he was going to have to be Walter Francis Blasingame on the invitations and how there wasn't a soul in the county who'd know who that was.

"Always been Walt," he'd said. "Always." He'd snorted. "Not even my sainted ma called me Walter Francis."

It had all sounded very definite to Charlie—and his policy of letting Cait come to her senses in her own time was looking pretty disastrous. When Walt left he'd paced around the cabin wondering if he was doing the right thing by not just going in and grabbing Cait by the hair and hauling her off.

"I mean, they did it to the Sabine women, didn't they?" he asked Chase now.

"Um," Chase mumbled. "Not so sure that's a good idea, pal."

"Well, I've got to do something!"

"Hang on." Charlie heard him say something quietly and heard Joanna's muffled sleepy reply.

"Tell him I love him," he heard.

"She loves you," Chase said a moment later. "But then," he added grimly, "she's not talking to you at four-fifteen in the morning, standing on a balcony in her undershorts.''

Charlie smiled. "You're a good friend."

"I'm more than a friend."

"I know." He was the closest thing to a father Charlie had. He would have been Charlie's adopted father if Charlie had permitted it. He hadn't.

But Chase and Joanna hadn't let him turn away. They'd simply said, "Fine. You don't want to be a Whitelaw, that's okay. But you're still part of the family."

And despite his determination to hold himself aloof, he was.

"You're a good dad," Charlie said now.

There was a moment's silence. A long moment's silence.

Then, "Well, thanks," Chase said at last. "Now, let's see if I deserve the praise. What's up?"

"She's marryin' the wrong guy!"

"Not you, in other words," Chase said dryly.

"Not me. She's got bride magazines all over the house, according to her dad. She's talking about hundreds of people. Morning suits. Sit-down dinners."

"Tell me about it," Chase muttered, and Charlie remembered the event that had been shoved down his and Joanna's throats.

"Then you know how serious it is," Charlie said. "Nobody puts out that kind of effort and then backs out."

"Joanna did," Chase reminded him.

"What? Oh, God, yeah."

Charlie suddenly remembered that five years before Joanna and Chase were actually married, they had been engaged. They had gone through a huge society wedding right up to the vows and then Joanna had stopped.

She'd said, "I can't." She'd run off and left Chase to do the explaining.

Now Charlie cursed himself for bringing it up quite like that. "Sorry," he muttered.

"Don't be. It was educational," Chase said. "I learned from it. You can, too. The point is—you can't force someone to marry you. I wanted to marry Joanna. But when push came to shove, she didn't want to marry me."

"She was too young." Charlie remembered that.

"For whatever reason, she didn't want to do it. She felt pressured and she went along with it—up to a point. And then she balked. You don't want your lady doing that to you."

"No."

God, no. He didn't want that.

"So take my advice, don't push. Don't grab her by the hair, throw her over your shoulder and attempt to make her see things your way. You weren't ready two years ago," Chase reminded him.

"I am now."

"And she's not. That happened to me and Joanna, too. When she was finally ready, I wasn't. I had just discovered that everything I thought I knew about my family wasn't really true. I needed to find out who I was before I could commit. It isn't going to work if it isn't right for both of you."

"You're saying, just wait?" Charlie was appalled. "Don't do *anything?*"

"Just wait," Chase said, exactly the way Charlie wished he wouldn't. "If it's going to happen, it's going to happen. You have to trust."

"What if," Charlie finally voiced his biggest fear, "she's never ready?"

"God help you," said Chase.

It would have been harder if it hadn't been for Walt. He dropped by every day, inviting Charlie to accompany him while he rode out to check some cattle or mend some fence. Sometimes he wanted to show Charlie a good spot from which to look for wildlife. Sometimes he thought maybe Charlie would like to know how to rope a calf or use a running iron.

Sometimes he just wanted to talk.

Most days Walt talked. About the ranch. About his wife, Margie, who had died ten years before, about his kids, Wes and Cait, about his hopes, about his dreams, about the war.

In the end, Charlie realized, it always came back to the war. The places he saw, the experiences he had, the people he met, the impact it had on life as he had known it back home.

"Sorta got engaged before I went to 'Nam," he told Charlie one afternoon. "Me an' Margie were this close to gettin' hitched." He held his fingers half an inch apart. "But I told her we'd better wait. Didn't want her sittin' there waitin' for me if I went missin' or grievin' if I got blowed to bits."

From everything Walt had said about his wife, Charlie suspected that Margie would have grieved whether or not they'd been married had Walt been "blowed to bits." But he didn't say so. He just rode Babe alongside the older man as they checked the fence line. And he listened.

"There now," Walt said nodding toward a loose wire in the fence, then dismounting to fix it. "No, sir," he said, eyeballing the slack wire, "didn't want her sittin' around waitin' if anything happened. Told her so. An' she said, 'I'll wait, Walt. You know I'll wait.' Hand me the splicer," he said to Charlie.

By now Charlie knew what to do. He handed over the splicer. He'd been watching Walt mend fences for the past five days. It was like watching a skillful surgeon. With years of practice, Walt made it look like child's play.

The first time Charlie had tried it, he'd scratched himself

on the wire and dropped the pliers, and the wire had sagged when he was done.

"Walt had watched in silence, then let him try it again, showing him how until Charlie finally got it right.

But today Walt needed to do something with his hands, apparently. So Charlie watched and handed, and Walt did it himself, by rote, not even thinking about it.

"Met a lot of people there," he went on. "Women. Met this one lady schoolteacher. Pretty little thing. Sue, I called her. She wanted me to teach her English, said she wanted to come to the States sometime. Asked me all about it. I told her stories."

Like Cait had told him stories? Charlie wondered. Had this young Vietnamese woman been as enchanted with Walt's stories as he had been with Cait's?

"Talkin' about it made it some easier," Walt said, splicing new wire in with the old. "I liked talkin' to Sue. Made me a little less homesick. She was sweet and gentle—like Margie—and she laughed a lot. There we were in the middle of a war and sometimes she could still make me laugh." He shook his head, tested the wire, nodded his satisfaction and got back on his horse.

Charlie followed suit. They rode on.

"Sue was a sweet gal. And she was there. All I had from Margie was letters. Kept me from bein' homesick a little. But hell, sometimes it seemed like she was a million miles away. Reckon she must have thought that way about me, too. I figured she'd find someone else." He said the words more to himself than to Charlie.

They rode on. The breeze ruffled their shirtsleeves. The sun beat down on their backs.

"And then I got notice that I was gettin' some R&R," Walt told him. "A week in Hawaii, they said. Sounded like a week in heaven. I wrote Margie and told her she could meet me there." He slanted a wry smile in Charlie's direction. "You know, I really didn't reckon she would. I'd been gone a long time. She was just nineteen and damn pretty. Fellas were always sniffin' around. I figured she prob'ly had one and just hadn't told me 'cause of maybe makin' me walk in front of a bullet. I thought when I told her about Hawaii, I'd get a Dear John for sure."

The horses picked their way along the line of the fence as it rose over a hill and down the other side.

Walt shook his head. "But not from Margie. She wrote back, 'Name the day. Name the place. I'll be there.' An' five weeks later she was. R&R." He shook his head. "Hell of a thing."

Charlie understood what he meant. He'd been in a war zone one day and on a beach in Hawaii twenty-four hours later. It was mind-boggling. Unbelievable. It made you wonder what reality really was.

"We had six days. Sun an' sand an' each other. It didn't seem real. And yet it was more real than anything that had happened in 'Nam. She was real. We got married in Hawaii. First the honeymoon, then the weddin'." He smiled at the memory, and then the smile faded. "An' then I got back on a plane to Vietnam and she went home to Montana, and I didn't see her for another year."

"Must have been tough."

Walt smiled faintly. "You don't know the half of it."

The last thing Cait wanted to do was ask Charlie for a favor.

But Maddie Fletcher had called this morning, and now she didn't have any choice. Of course, he might not show up.

She'd told Maddie that. "I don't know if he'll even come to class. He might have got what he wanted." Photos, she meant, though she really didn't believe it much. It was just a subterfuge, just talk.

She knew· Charlie hadn't got what he said he really wanted—her.

"Well, if he does," Maddie· had persisted, "put it to him. Since he worked with Angie last week I've finally seen a spark of interest in her."

"Interest in Charlie," Cait translated and was still annoyed at the thought. It was purely on Angie's behalf, she told herself. She didn't want the girl getting all starry-eyed over a man who wasn't interested in her. Cait knew the feeling—had herself felt the humiliation of the consequences.

"Oh, absolutely," Maddie said with a smile in her voice. "But you learn, when you've been around kids like Angie as much as I have, to take any interest at all and go with it."

"You don't think it's…dangerous. I mean he's not interested in her."

"I know that," Maddie said. "I can see which way the wind blows."

Cait wondered which way Maddie thought the wind was blowing. But she refused to ask.

Maddie went on, "But if his being there, working with her, can get Angie involved, it will be good for the baby and good for her in the long run."

"But she'll expect—"

"You have to take things a step at a time, Cait," Maddie said. "We're not omniscient here. We can't play God. We can't see the end result. But we can do what we think best. In this case I think it's having Charlie work with Angie. And then we trust."

Trust Charlie?

Cait closed her eyes.

"So, would you ask him?" Maddie said after a moment. "I'd rather it was planned ahead of time."

Cait sighed. "If he shows up."

She still hoped he wouldn't. She hoped he'd got the point by now: that once upon a time she'd been interested in him enough to want to marry him—but he'd turned away, and now, when he said he was interested, she had, so to speak, other fish to fry.

No hard feelings. That was just the way it was.

She loved Steve. And all Charlie's persistence wasn't fazing her in the least. She didn't have time to even think about him. She was, with the help of a half a dozen bridal magazines, planning what her father had taken to calling "The Wedding That Ate Montana."

She had drawn up lists, called caterers, talked to Poppy about flowers, and had discussed with Polly McMaster renting the Elmer town hall. She had become a connoisseur of wedding invitations, formal and informal. She dreamed about ivory paper versus ash, rough edges versus smooth, italic versus bold. She chose type fonts in her sleep.

It was unutterably boring.

But it was better than dreaming about Charlie.

Why wasn't she dreaming about Steve? He was the man she loved, the man she was going to spend the rest of her life with, the man who had called just this afternoon to ask her to go to Denver with him this weekend to look for a place to live.

"It'd be great if you'd come," he said. "A whole weekend to ourselves."

It did sound great. But she didn't think she ought to leave her father that long, and she said so.

"He's going to be on his own when we get married," Steve reminded her.

"I know. I know. But he's just getting back on his feet. It's taken a while."

In fact, her father was progressing by leaps and bounds. He was riding again, checking cattle, mending fences, taking an interest in the ranch.

"He's doing stuff finally?" Steve said, obviously heartened. "When did this start?"

"A couple of weeks ago."

Ever since he'd met Charlie.

He was seeing way too much of Charlie. At first she'd attributed their encounters to Charlie turning up where her dad was. But from what her father said, that wasn't true. He was the one seeking out Charlie.

"Showed Charlie where I saw the bears last year," he said one day.

"Me 'n' Charlie rode up Hill Lake way," he said another. "I been showin' him how to mend fence."

Mend fence?

"You're teaching Charlie to mend fence?"

"He's turnin' into a fair hand," her father said. "Knows somethin' about horses. Learnin' about cattle. Quick study, he is."

What was going on? Why was Charlie turning himself into a cowboy? Why was her father taking such an interest in some tenderfoot urban photographer?

But she didn't ask, because she didn't want to know. She didn't want to talk about Charlie.

She hoped against hope that he wouldn't show up tonight. But she wasn't surprised to see him standing in the hallway waiting for her when she came around the corner.

He was leaning casually against the wall, his lean hard body looking relaxed and dangerous at the same time. He wore jeans and a long-sleeved blue chambray shirt—and boots, she noted now, irritated at how much he looked as if he belonged here. He straightened when he saw her coming, and she saw him wince just slightly as he shifted his weight onto his bad leg.

She didn't ask how it was. It was fine, she assured herself. He was riding with her father all day now. Besides, she didn't care.

He shoved a hand through the black hair which flopped onto his forehead. "Hey." He grinned. It was the standard Charlie Seeks Elk heart-melting grin. She was sure women all over the world had fallen at his feet because of that grin.

It was a good thing she was completely resistant.

"Hey, yourself." She pasted on her best pleasant smile and said, as she had rehearsed, "Maddie has a favor to ask. She wants you to continue to coach Angie."

Charlie cocked his head. "What does Angie want?"

"You in bed, I imagine," Cait said tartly. It was the bald-faced truth. She unlocked the door to the classroom, pushed it open and went in.

Charlie followed. "Well, don't worry," he said, an amused tone in his voice. "I'm a one-woman man."

Cait bristled at him. "Don't start, Charlie."

He spread his hands, still grinning. "I'm only saying."

"Well, I'm *not* worrying! Not about you and—" she floundered "—and anyone!" She took a deep breath. "If you agree to coach her," she said evenly, "I would just not want her reading more into it than you intend."

"She won't."

"How do you know?"

He shrugged. "Because I won't let her."

Like you didn't let me? Cait wanted to shout at him. But she twisted her fingers together and kept her thoughts to herself. "Fine," she said tersely. "Thank you."

Charlie nodded, still smiling. "You're welcome."

Charlie understood Angie.

He had *been* Angie. Tough. Angry. Defensive. Determined to put up barriers to shut people out before they could do the same to him.

So he wasn't surprised when she looked less than thrilled when he said he was going to be her coach. She just hunched her shoulders and feigned indifference. "Whatever," she said and turned away.

Charlie didn't take it personally.

It gave him a new focus for practicing patience. He just smiled and dug in.

He worked with Angie, he joked with her, teased her gently, charmed her. He got her to let him take pictures of her. And at the same time he got her to pay attention to what Cait was teaching them. He got her to really work on her breathing.

And when he showed interest in the book on baby care that Cait gave all the expectant moms, she actually picked it up and began to look through it.

But she wouldn't smile, even when he tried to cajole her into it.

"What is there to smile about?" she demanded.

"You're alive. You're healthy. You have people who care about you." His gaze flicked to Maddie who was sitting a few yards away.

Angie saw where he was looking and hunched her shoulders. "She has to," she said gruffly. "They pay her to."

"Sweetheart," Charlie said, "nobody could pay anybody enough money to compensate for the guff they take from kids like me and you."

Angie's eyes went wide with surprise, then shuttered immediately. "What do you mean, me and you?" she asked suspiciously.

"You work hard tonight, and I'll tell you all about how you and I are alike," Charlie promised.

"When?"

"I'll come out to Maddie's place. You can cook me dinner tomorrow night."

"I don't cook," Angie informed him.

Charlie smiled. "You will."

He waited for Cait after class. Everyone else left—even Angie, after making sure he had directions to Maddie's place for tomorrow night.

"If you want to come," she'd said offhand, as if she really didn't care. But he could see it in her—the tiniest flicker of hope followed at once by the wariness that any reliance she put on someone would come to naught.

"I'll be there," he promised her. It was nice to have someone actually looking forward to seeing him.

Cait certainly wasn't.

He reminded himself to be patient. To give her reason to trust him. He'd given her plenty of reason not to.

But it wasn't easy. If he was patient too long, it would be October 18 and Cait would be Mrs. Dr. Steve Whoever.

Charlie gritted his teeth.

"I thought you'd left." Cait came out of the room carrying her tote bag. When she saw him waiting, she pulled it up against her chest and wrapped her arms across it, holding it like a shield as she locked the door.

"I wanted to give you my cell phone number."

She put the keys back in her bag. "What for?"

"So you can call me when Angie goes into labor. I told her I'd be there."

"I'm sure Maddie expects to handle that." She started down the hall. "She only wanted you for the classes."

He fell into step alongside her. "Well, she's getting me for both. She knows it. We talked." He held out a slip of paper with the number on it. "I gave it to her, too. But she might lose it in the excitement of the moment."

Cait stepped sideways, as if the paper might bite. But when Charlie persisted, she took it ungraciously and stuck it in her bag. She kept right on walking.

"Missed you this week," Charlie said. "But your dad says you've been busy."

"Lots to do for the wedding."

Sheer provocation. He could hear it in her voice. Like waving a red flag in front of a bull.

Charlie almost charged. He could very nearly feel Chase grabbing him by the scruff of the neck and hauling him back.

He took a breath and said instead, "Your dad's been teaching me to cowboy."

"I heard. I'm sure that will be very useful."

"Sarcasm doesn't become you, Cait."

She made a huffing sound.

"And you're right, it might." If worse came to worst, he figured, he might be able to build a loop, lasso her, then haul her away from her prospective groom. He had the sense not to say that, though.

They kept walking all the way to the lobby. The red-headed receptionist looked up with interest as Cait said in a very businesslike tone, "Thank you for your help this evening."

Charlie grinned. "My pleasure. Always a pleasure to see you."

Her shoulders stiffened. "Charlie," she warned. "This is about Angie."

"No, it's not. It's about us."

"There is no *us!*"

The redhead looked very interested.

"You gonna keep on lying to yourself right up till your wedding day?"

He could almost hear her teeth grind. He certainly could see the sparks in her eyes. And if looks could kill he knew he'd be on the critical list.

"Why are you doing this?" she said, anguished.

"Because I love you. Because you love me."

The redhead was almost leaning across the desk.

"No. I don't!"

The redhead didn't even have to strain her ears to hear that. Her eyes widened. She looked amazed.

"Damn it!" Cait hissed. "Now look what you've done!"

"What *I've* done? You're the one shouting."

"Because you…because…!" Cait sputtered furiously.

"Because you still love me and you're afraid to admit it!" Then, determined to prove it, he pulled her against him, tote bag and all, and kissed her for all he was worth.

Seven

So much for following advice.

So much for patience.

So he'd blown it.

Big-time.

What the hell was he supposed to do?

A guy couldn't just stand there and let a woman make the biggest mistake of her life without trying to stop her, could he?

And she would do it, too, he was sure! Charlie thought as he paced around the small cabin, which seemed almost to rock with the force of his emotions. Damn it, she would! She would have marched right down the aisle and married the hot-shot cardiologist, if Charlie hadn't stepped in and made his point.

So he'd made it, God help him.

He'd thrown caution—and patience—to the wind.

He'd kissed her.

He'd *needed* to kiss her.

He'd been living off memories and dreams and one single kiss since he'd found her again a few weeks ago.

He'd felt her hands on his body, he'd smelled the scent of her skin and her hair, but he'd never touched her the way a lover touches the woman of his dreams. He'd watched her lips, had dreamed about them, had remembered all too well the soft temptation of them. And he'd needed them the way he needed air.

He flung himself on his back on the hard, narrow bunk and stared up at the ceiling. He still remembered them. He still tasted them, hours later.

And he'd be living on that kiss for God knew how long!

She had softened under his onslaught. She had yielded, had opened, had given for a second or maybe a few. Not long enough, that was certain.

And then she'd stiffened. Her whole body had gone rigid, and she'd given him a shove. "Damn you, Charlie!" she'd said, her eyes flashing fire.

And then she'd spun on her heel and run out of the lobby, leaving Charlie and the receptionist staring after her.

In the silence that followed, the receptionist looked back at him, her expression unreadable. "Did it help?" she asked.

Charlie doubted that.

Probably he'd just shown her what a jerk he was. Nothing she didn't already know.

"I've changed my mind," Cait said the second Steve picked up the phone. She was gripping it as though it was a life preserver in a stormy sea, which in fact she felt it was. "I'd love to come with you to Denver."

"Huh, wha—Cait?"

He sounded dazed and disoriented, and she realized that, oh, hell, she'd done it again.

A quick glance at the clock told her it was two in the morning. She had been pacing around her bedroom for hours—after the long shower she'd taken when she got home had done nothing to erase the memory of Charlie's mouth on hers. Not even when she'd turned the tap to pure blue cold had she been able to forget, to make her body deny its response.

She'd tried telling herself after the first time Charlie had kissed her that she'd responded because he'd surprised her. The shock of seeing him had simply caught her unaware.

But she'd seen him coming tonight.

She'd felt the electricity sizzling between them all evening, although she'd done her best to stay well away. She'd deliberately ignored Angie for most of the evening because Charlie was helping her. She didn't want to encourage him, she told herself.

She hadn't dared admit she was afraid.

Not of him.

Of herself. Of her response. Of the fact that despite her common sense and determined indifference, she had been unable to put her attraction to Charlie away. And his kiss had completely undermined her resolve. It had made her ache with desire, with longing, with need.

It made her furious with him—and with herself!

And if cold showers and willpower were not going to do it, she would have to call up reinforcements. And that meant calling Steve.

She hadn't even thought to look at the clock. Damn. When was she going to stop waking Steve out of a sound sleep?

"I'm sorry," she apologized. "I didn't realize it was so late. So early, I mean."

She heard him yawn. "Never mind. 'S okay. What happened? How come you changed your mind?"

"I just…thought about it some more." She rubbed her fist across her still-tingling lips. "And I decided you were right. That's where we're going to be. And Dad's going to have to be on his own sometime. He might as well start now."

"Amen," Steve said, then added, "Truly, it is for the best, Cait. He needs to get interested in things again. Interested in doing them."

"He's been getting better," she said. "Every day he's doing a little more." All of it, she thought, gritting her teeth, with Charlie.

"Then letting him be on his own now is an excellent idea," Steve said. "You'll probably come home and discover he's got a new lease on life."

"That would be good."

"It will be good for all of us." He yawned again. "I'm glad you're coming, Cait. I didn't want to find a place without you. It's going to be our place, after all."

"Right."

Yes, definitely. Our place. Denver. Mrs. Steve Carmichael. She said the words over in her head, trying to imprint them there. "Go back to sleep," she said at last. "I'm sorry I bothered you. I just wanted you to know I'm coming with you to Denver."

"Love you," Steve said. "Talk to you tomorrow."

"Love you, too," Cait parroted. She hung up after he did.

She was still pressing her fist to her lips.

The cell phone's ring jarred him out of a fitful sleep.

At first Charlie couldn't even identify the sound. He'd been dreaming of making love to Cait—slow, languorous love—and then something rang. Like a timer. Like a buzzer.

Like—

He jerked up, heart pounding, cursing the alarm clock that was depriving him of the only contact he had with her.

Only it stopped.

And then it rang again.

He groaned and, realizing at last what it was, fumbled in the darkness to find his jacket and the pocket in which he'd stuck the phone.

Dire thoughts ran through his mind. Panicky thoughts.

It had to be Chase—or Joanna.

Any news in the blackness of night would not be good.

He jammed the on button in the dark and barked into the phone. "What? What is it?"

"Charlie?" The voice was strained, female. But not Joanna, thank God.

He felt a moment's shock, then confusion, as he realized who it was. "Cait?"

"Angie's gone into labor."

Charlie was stupefied. "Labor? She's in labor? *Now?* But she's not due yet. She's not due for…for weeks!"

"Welcome to the real world," Cait said. Her tone was crisp and almost businesslike, but the hint of tension was still there. "Babies are on their own timetable, not ours."

"But—"

"You don't have to come. We can manage without you."

She could, no doubt. And she would prefer it that way. He was less sure about Angie.

Still, he felt a surge of panic at the thought of coaching the girl through her labor. What the hell did he know about labor? He'd only been to two lessons! He wasn't the father! He'd been there because of Cait, because of the photos, not because of Angie!

Not *at first* because of Angie.

But now...

He reached for his jeans. "I'll meet you at the hospital."

If he'd had second thoughts—and he had plenty all the way over the mountain track in Otis's old Suburban, all the way along the curving gravel road to the county highway, all the way into the hospital parking lot in Livingston, even down the corridor to the birthing room—they vanished the moment he walked in the door.

Angie was lying in the bed, halfway elevated. Her normally pale complexion now rivaled the white of the sheets. Her dark eyes were wide and scared.

"Charlie! It's not supposed to be happening now!" She practically jumped out of the bed into his arms. But she was hooked up to a monitor, and he got to her before she inadvertently detached herself as she hurled herself at him.

Gone was the tough facade, the indifference, the determined nonchalance. Her thin arms went hard around his middle and she pressed her face into the denim jacket he wore. He wrapped his arms around her, hugging her tightly, then removing one hand to stroke her spiky hair.

"Hey," he said gently, "it's okay. It's what we trained for."

He felt her head shake against his chest. "Not ready," she muttered. "Not yet."

"Yeah," he said, giving her one fierce squeeze before letting her go so he could step back from the bed and look down into her frightened eyes. "Well, kids never do what parents want them to, do they? Welcome to motherhood."

She blanched even whiter at his words. He put his finger under her chin and tipped it up. "You can do it, Ang. Just be the kind of mother you always wished you had."

He saw her swallow and nod. Something of the toughness returned. But not the hardness. She bit her lower lip.

"Hurting?" he asked. He'd seen a lot of pain, but he had never, except in the film Cait had shown them, seen a child born.

"Not...really," Angie said. "My back sort of aches. I wouldn't even think I was gonna have it but I woke up in a puddle. I thought I'd wet the bed. Maddie heard me get up, and she came in and said my water broke."

Charlie only vaguely knew the logistics of labor and delivery. But he had the notion that unlike contractions, which might stop, Angie's water breaking meant there was no turning back. "Well, then, I guess this fella wants to be born."

Angie licked her lips. "I guess."

There was the sound of footsteps behind him, and Maddie and Cait came into the room. Maddie looked delighted at the sight of him.

Cait flicked a glance his way, then focused her attention on Angie. "Let's see how you're doing," she said. Her voice was calm and gentle, just the way he remembered it in the hospital in Abuk. It was one of the things he'd always admired about her—the way she could shut out the chaos that had often reigned around them and give her complete support and attention to the patient in need.

Angie looked nervously at Charlie.

He gave her hand a squeeze. "I'll wait outside with Maddie. We'll be right here. We're going to see you through this, all of us."

"I'm so glad you came," Maddie said, taking his hand as they went into the corridor. "It was such a shock. She'd been doing regular chores all day, nothing she hadn't done any other day. And you saw her just tonight—yesterday," she corrected herself because it was now close to four in the morning. "She was fine." There was an urgency in her voice that made him realize she was looking for re-assurance.

He knew from what Walt had told him that Maddie and her husband, Ward, had taken in scads of foster kids over the years. They had devoted their lives and their ranch to helping kids who had hit a rough patch in their lives. Charlie knew she wouldn't want to think that something she had done had somehow caused Angie's premature labor.

"She was fine," he agreed. "You'll have to ask Cait, but it seems like it's just one of those things."

"Cait says that teenagers have more premature births."

"Do they have more trouble delivering?"

"I think they can." Maddie swiped a strand of gray-blond hair out of her eyes. "But Angie's healthy. She's strong." Now it was her turn to reassure him.

"She'll be fine," he agreed, as if it were a mantra, even as he prayed it would be true. "And so will the baby."

When Cait came out, her gaze went directly to Maddie. Charlie might as well not have been there. "She's doing well. Not having a lot of contractions yet, though she's dilating and the cervix is effaced. Still, it will be a while."

Maddie had questions for Cait. Charlie left them to it. He remembered his own time in the hospital all too well—and he knew what it was like to sit there, as the patient, while people talked about you outside the room. It had irritated him. He was pretty sure it would scare Angie.

She was still pale, but she looked a little less panicky now. "Cait says everything is coming along fine," she told him. There was a thready nervousness in her voice which implied that she wasn't sure Cait was right, but she was hoping.

"That's what she told us," Charlie said firmly. He came to stand right beside her, and when her hand moved restlessly on the sheet, he took it in his. Her fingers curved around his and clung.

They stayed like that for a long while. Neither spoke. Angie hung on. Charlie stayed where he was. His leg hurt. Every now and then he shifted his weight. But he never left, never gave her any indication that he was in pain.

When Maddie finally came in, she said briskly, "Get a chair, Charlie, and get one for me while you're at it."

When he did, she pulled the chair he brought over by the window away from the bed and took out her knitting. "This is supposed to be a baby blanket," she said, lifting the pastel bundle and settling it on her lap. "I'd better hurry. I've got a lot left to knit."

"You don't have to stay," Angie said to her.

Maddie looked up over her half glasses, startled. "And why wouldn't I stay?"

Angie flapped her hand vaguely. "You're tired…you've got the stock to take care of." She hesitated as if she might say more.

But Maddie forestalled her. "They're not more important than you," she said dismissingly. "I rang Taggart Jones before we left. He'll send some fellows over in the morning to see to things." She smiled. "It's the beauty of good neighbors. They come through for you."

Angie looked at Charlie. He could see in her face what she was thinking—that she'd never had neighbors like that. Until Chase and Joanna, neither had he.

He gave her hand a squeeze. "You've got 'em now," he said.

She smiled faintly, then pressed her hand—and his— against her abdomen. "Feel it?"

It was startling almost, the way it tightened like a drum skin right beneath his fingers. It made his eyes widen. "Whoa."

"Yeah." She ran her tongue over her lips. "You were gonna tell me…tomorrow…tonight," she corrected herself, "about you."

"Right." Charlie stretched and shifted again. "No time like the present. Besides, what else have we got to do?"

He wasn't used to talking about himself—wasn't comfortable doing so. The less people knew about him the better he liked it.

He'd only shared himself with Chase and Joanna and their family, the Cavanaughs and a few other close friends. He'd only shared part of himself with Cait.

He'd been too careful in those days, too wary of his own vulnerability. He hadn't wanted anyone to really know him. Cait had come as close as anyone, even though he'd held a lot back from her. He could see now why she didn't trust him.

How could you trust someone who didn't trust you?

Love meant sharing, he realized. It meant opening up and being vulnerable—at least to the people you loved.

He started to tell Angie. He didn't hold much back. It would be good practice, he thought, in case Cait ever let him talk to her again.

He told her about his father, about his mother, about Lucy. He told her about Chase and Joanna—how they'd pretty much saved his life.

"They wouldn't see it that way," he said. "But they don't know how close I came to falling right over the edge."

"Sometimes I think I'm falling over the edge," Angie whispered. Her eyes locked with his. Her lips were trembling.

He pressed her fingers between his. "You won't," he promised. "You won't if you don't let go. I won't let go of you."

But even as he promised, he knew the helplessness that Chase and Joanna must have felt. They had thrown him lifeline after lifeline when he'd been a teenager, but they'd never been able to make him hang on.

Ultimately he had to want to—he'd had to respond, to reach out to them.

He had—barely.

He'd been afraid to do more. He'd been afraid to let them adopt him.

What if they'd died like everyone else he'd ever loved? What if somehow it had been his fault?

That was, he realized, the reason he'd run from Cait. To save himself, yes—but also to save her and Resi.

Like he was somehow responsible for all the world's pain.

He wasn't. He could only do his best.

He gave Angie a lopsided grin as she tensed with another contraction.

"They're getting stronger, Charlie."

"Okay," he said, "let's go to work."

Five hours later it was time.

Cait checked on Angie frequently, but she didn't want to hover. It was her experience that laboring moms liked to have her nearby but not standing over them. It made them feel as though she was impatient and waiting to get on with it, and that it was their fault if nothing was happening.

And besides, there was Charlie.

Cait didn't want to be there with Charlie.

She hadn't wanted to call him. She hadn't wanted to see him. She'd told Angie they would do fine without him.

But Angie had insisted. "He said he'd help. He said he'd be here! He promised!" And with each sentence she grew more panicky and strident until Cait had had no choice but to call.

She didn't know if he'd come. She rather wished, for her own sake, that he wouldn't.

Of course he did.

She expected that he'd agreed to it so he could bother her some more, but it didn't take long for her to see she was wrong. She kept well away from him, of course. But for once he didn't pursue. His focus was entirely on Angie.

And before it was over, she had to admit it was a good thing he was there. He kept Angie steady. He kept her focused. He kept her calm. He talked to her almost nonstop in low, gentle tones that were so soft Cait couldn't really hear what he said even when she was in the room. And Angie listened intently to whatever it was he had to say.

When things began to speed up, when the contractions got stronger and labor more intense, he moved up behind Angie and let her grip his hands, all the while still talking to her, murmuring, steadying, encouraging, getting her to do what Cait needed her to do.

"I can't!" Angie cried at one point. "Oh, God! Oh, God! Oh, God!"

"Take it one breath at a time," Charlie said. "Work with me, Ang'."

And Cait could see their hands locked together, their gazes locked together. She could see in Charlie the man she'd once believed he could be—the man she'd wanted to marry.

But she had a baby to deliver. She couldn't let herself think about that.

"One more push, Angie," she said. "When you start to feel the contraction, go with it. Okay. Now. Push. Push!"

The girl grimaced, her sweat-streaked face red from exertion, her knuckles white from crushing Charlie's hands in hers. "I c-c-cannnn—I did!" she exclaimed as a wet squirming baby girl slid out into the world.

Cait caught her, held her, marveling as always at this miracle of new life, at the tiny perfectly formed fingers and toes, at the dark eyes that blinked at her.

Angie was crying, her body shaking with emotion and

exertion. Maddie was beaming. "Oh, isn't she lovely? Isn't she wonderful?"

And Charlie was just staring, an expression of awe on his face. Then he dropped a kiss on Angie's forehead. "Good for you, kid," he whispered.

Cait, watching, envied that kiss far more than she wanted to.

Denver.

She just had to get to Denver. That was what she told herself for the next twenty-four hours. Once she was in Denver—or even on the road—she would be looking toward the future, not the past. She would be seeing Steve, not Charlie.

And all would be well.

She kept telling herself that, counting the hours.

She wasn't sure exactly when she knew it wasn't going to work. Maybe she'd known before she ever set foot in Steve's car Friday night.

She'd jumped in eagerly enough, after giving her dad a hug and a kiss and the promise that she'd have lots to tell him Sunday night when they got back.

She'd refused to see the look of worry that had crossed his face. He was just concerned about himself, she told herself. He just wanted her to look after him forever. Well, she couldn't. If she needed to, he could move to Denver.

As for the weekend, she said blithely as she departed, "I'm sure Charlie will be checking in on you while I'm gone."

She was sure he would be. She'd asked him to. She'd made a point of telling him she was going when she'd seen him in Angie's room this afternoon.

She'd said, "Oh, by the way, if you could stop in and see Dad this weekend, that would be great."

He'd blinked. Then his eyes had widened and he'd

started to grin that heart-stopping Charlie grin, as if he
thought she'd changed her mind and was going the long
way round to say it.

So ruthlessly she'd gone right on. "Because Steve and
I are going to Denver tonight to look for a place to live."

The grin had died, and she'd been pleased. It was an
angry sort of pleased. She still felt angry.

"Who's Charlie?" Steve had asked.

"A new hand my dad hired," Cait said briefly. She was
angry about that, too. She'd been dumbfounded when her
father had announced that he was hiring Charlie.

"Hiring Charlie?" she'd said in stark disbelief. "For
what?"

"To help out."

"He's not a cowboy!"

"He can dig a post hole well as most," her father said
complacently. "And he's a damn good rider. He's got a
good eye. Comes from takin' pictures, I expect. Don't matter. A feller's gotta start somewhere."

Cait didn't see why Charlie had to start at all. He was
a photographer, for heaven's sake, not some two-bit cow-
puncher! He'd leave again in a few days. Please God he
would leave before she came back!

"You oughta be glad," her father said. "Gus said we
need more help. Hell, sweetheart, you been sayin' the same
thing yourself. Said you was overworked, you did. Needed
more time for the hospital and the babies."

"Yes, but—"

"So, I hired Charlie, and now you got it."

Hallelujah, Cait had thought grimly.

But then she pushed thoughts of Charlie out of her mind.
She breathed deeply. Steve stepped on the gas and they
drove away.

Cait watched the ranch recede in the rearview mirror

and then, resolutely, she looked ahead. She waited for the feeling of anticipation, of euphoria, to settle on her.

It didn't come.

Miles passed. They stopped in Billings and got a bite to eat, then forged on. The sun set behind them and they turned south on 25 and before long headed into Wyoming.

Steve talked about Denver, about the new practice he was going to be joining, about the hospitals he'd be working at, about what neighborhoods would be nearby and where they ought to look for a place to live.

Cait didn't say a word.

She thought—about her father, about how hardheaded he was, how almighty stubborn. She thought about Angie and her baby. They'd checked out of the hospital today to go home with Maddie.

Angie still didn't know what she was going to do. She needed to find Ryan, the baby's father and talk to him. Cait had made her an appointment with Martha, the social worker, who might be able to help. Cait had mumbled words about adoption, in case Angie wanted to think about that but was afraid people would think she wasn't brave enough to keep her baby.

"Sometimes it takes a braver person not to," Cait had said. "You have to decide what's right for you and for…Charlene."

Angie had named the baby after Charlie.

Even Charlie had tried to talk her out of it, but Angie had insisted. "She's *my* baby," she'd said fiercely. "I can call her whatever I want. Her name is Charlene."

But she called her Charlie. Cait had heard her. She'd cuddled the baby close and whispered, "I love you, Charlie," to her.

Cait wondered which of them she was really talking to—the man or the child.

She tried not to wonder much. She tried not to think about it. About him.

About Charlie.

But it was hard. The trip was long. She was only marginally interested in Steve's ramblings about his practice. She wasn't interested in Denver. She didn't care where they lived.

Charlie, too, had held the child. He'd stroked her soft cheek with his finger, a look of pure awe on his face, a smile flickering, barely suppressed as he'd said softly, "You're a darn sight better looking than me, kiddo."

She wasn't.

No one on earth was better looking than Charlie. At least not to Cait. No one could make her heart zing the way he could just by walking into a room.

Looks weren't everything, she reminded herself sharply. Looks really didn't matter at all.

But it wasn't only Charlie's looks, the devil's advocate in the other side of her brain pointed out.

She fought with it. She turned away from her thoughts and stared out into the blackness. Steve droned on.

Cait thought about Charlie.

She couldn't stop thinking about Charlie.

Not that night. Not the next day. Not when Steve took her around the hospitals where he'd be working or to meet the doctors with whom he would be practicing. She tried to remember their names, tried to smile and be polite and friendly. But she felt disastrously out of place. Like her body was here, but her mind and heart were somewhere else.

With Charlie.

Damn Charlie!

She didn't want to feel this way about Charlie. She didn't trust Charlie. He wanted her—he said he loved her—but what did that mean?

It meant he wanted her in his bed. He wanted to be in hers. He wanted what they'd had in Abuk.

He said he wanted eternity, forever with her—but how could she believe him?

And why should she want to?

She had Steve! She loved Steve!

But equally, she knew she couldn't marry Steve—not when she was as mixed up as this. But she couldn't just blurt it out.

It wasn't that she'd changed her mind—it was that she didn't know her mind! She only knew that she was a fool to be planning a huge wedding to one man when she couldn't get another one out of her head.

So she kept her peace. All day Saturday she smiled and nodded and listened to the doctors Steve introduced her to and the hospital administrators they met. She did the same with Annette, the real estate lady who showed them through half a dozen condos and an equal number of houses.

"What do you think?" Steve asked her.

"What do *you* think?" Cait countered.

"I want you to be happy," Steve said. "You decide."

The real estate lady looked at Cait expectantly.

Helplessly Cait shook her head. She couldn't blurt it out here, either. "I don't know. I think we need to…talk."

That night at dinner she tried to find the words to say what she felt. "I think we ought to…hold up a bit," she said at last.

"Hold up?" Steve looked mystified. "You mean about picking a place? Well, that's okay with me. You know that. I just thought you might not want to move twice. We can rent an apartment. I can call Annette back and—"

"I didn't mean about the place. I mean about the wedding."

Steve stopped, his fork halfway to his mouth, and stared at her. "The wedding?"

Cait shrugged helplessly. "I'm just…confused."

"About me?"

"No! Me! It's me," she said desperately. "Not you. It's just…I don't know what to do!"

Slowly Steve shook his head. Lines appeared above his brows. "About what?"

"About…life. About…love. About…what I want."

It sounded so stupid, so shallow. She felt like a child— a badly behaved, selfish child. But what else could she say? It was the truth.

"I've been so busy. I've been worried about my dad. I haven't had time to think. And now there's all this planning and I…just…I don't think I'm ready. Yet," she tacked on desperately.

"Ah." Steve's brow cleared. "Yet." He smiled a little. "Prewedding jitters."

"Yes!" Cait grasped the explanation eagerly. Then she shook her head. "Sort of." Because honesty required more than that. She didn't want to talk about Charlie, but she did want to let him know there was more to it than a few stray worries. "I'm sorry. I just…don't feel ready. And I can't get married until I do. Do you see?"

Why should he? She wasn't making sense!

But he nodded. "I think I do."

She pressed her lips together in a moue of self-disgust. "I'm sorry. I didn't realize until we came. Then it became so…real. I—" She stopped. Then she began to struggle to pull off her engagement ring. "Here. You shouldn't be stuck being engaged to a woman who doesn't know her own mind."

But he reached across the table and stilled her hands.

"No." He shook his head and his eyes, cool blue eyes, steady blue eyes, smiled faintly. "Wear it."

"But—"

"Wear it," Steve said. "I want you to. You'll get yourself sorted out. And maybe is better than no."

Eight

"**B**een thinkin'," Walt said as they pushed several dozen head of cattle across a hillside, heading for lower ground, "'bout Vietnam."

"Uh-huh." Charlie wasn't thinking about Vietnam. He didn't give a rat's ass about Vietnam.

It didn't matter to Walt, who was talking more to himself anyway. "Thinkin' 'bout people I knew. Wonderin' what happened to 'em. People I ain't seen in years, y'know? Some people I ain't never seen..." His voice trailed off.

Charlie didn't fill in the silence. He was barely listening. He had his own preoccupations—namely Walt's daughter, whom he had last seen yesterday afternoon.

She hadn't spared him a glance. She'd been in Angie's room to give her instructions and advice to help with the baby. She'd talked to Angie—and to Maddie. She hadn't said a word to him.

She hadn't spoken to him directly since she'd called him to tell him Angie was in labor three days ago. All her comments had been directed at other people, even when he was the one the message was aimed at.

"I bet you could use some ice chips," she'd said to Angie during labor.

Get the girl some ice, she'd meant, Charlie knew.

"A back rub would probably help you right now, wouldn't it?" she'd said to the girl at one point.

She'd meant, *Rub her back, you fool.*

When Angie had been leaving yesterday, he'd been there, too. Cait had been full of compliments and sage advice, and she'd told Angie how well she'd done and Maddie what a great help she was going to be over the next few days and weeks. And then she'd said, "If you need anything, give me a call. Except, this weekend you'd better ring Dr. Ferris because I'll be out of town."

"Where're you going?" Charlie had asked.

But she'd just said, "Bye. I'll try to drop over to the ranch to see you next week." And she'd walked out without a glance in his direction.

She'd gone to Denver, he now knew.

Walt had said so when he'd come by last evening to tell Charlie they were moving cattle today. "You oughta come eat supper with me," he'd said. "Caity'll be gone all weekend," he'd grumbled, "Her an' Steve gone down to Denver. To look for a house." He hadn't looked thrilled.

Charlie wasn't at all thrilled.

He'd barely slept a wink last night thinking about her spending the night with Steve. His mind had whirled with memories of his own nights with Cait. He'd relived every wondrous, tender, explosive moment. He'd ached with longing.

He'd been ready to chew nails when Walt had shown up this morning about six to head up to where they were going to move cattle. Walt hadn't looked much more rested than Charlie felt. His graying hair stuck out in tufts beneath the brim of his cowboy hat. He had a day's worth of stubble on his cheeks and a hollow look about his eyes.

"You feelin' all right?" Charlie asked him. He didn't need Walt having a heart attack on him in the back of beyond.

"Ain't been sleepin' too good. Been thinkin'," Walt had said.

He'd been talking about his thinking ever since. Charlie had let it go in one ear and out the other. It was Vietnam, Vietnam, Vietnam—stuff about making decisions and having regrets and wondering if you did the right thing.

Charlie had enough of his own questionable behavior to worry about. He didn't have time to spare on Walt's.

They moved the cattle. It was about the sort of work Charlie needed. Semi-mindless. Physical. Demanding at times, brainless at others. It kept him busy, but still gave him time to think about Cait. And since there was nothing he could do about her, it spared him bouncing off the walls of the cabin in frustration.

He thought he'd be able to sleep that night. The day's work had been demanding. He should have been dead on his feet. He declined Walt's invitation to stop for supper and then head on down to the Dew Drop for a little refreshment, figuring he'd grab a bite at the cabin, then sleep hard and deep. But he ended up pacing furiously instead.

He decided he'd had too much of his own company, so he got in Otis's Suburban and headed over to Brenna and Jed's. If they were surprised to see him turning up on their doorstep at nearly ten o'clock at night, they didn't say so.

"Ah, reinforcements," Brenna said, actually looking relieved. "Here." And she handed him a fussy baby.

The baby's name was Hank. He seemed big compared

to Angie's newborn. A person already—albeit an unhappy one. Charlie juggled him nervously. "What should I do?"

"Walk with him," Brenna said. "It's what we do."

She and Jed slumped wearily on the sofa and gave him grateful smiles. Otis and Tuck, watching a baseball game on television in the other room, looked around and gave him approving looks.

"Why not?" Charlie said. It was what he'd been doing back at the cabin. Jed got up and poured him a beer. Charlie held Hank in one hand and the beer in the other and he paced.

Something about his limping gait must have soothed the baby, because it wasn't long before Hank's head nestled against his shoulder. The sound of his wails softened, then disappeared altogether. It was replaced every once in a while by a sigh and a tiny hiccup.

"He's got the touch," Jed said in reverent tones.

Brenna nodded. "Can Hank go live at the cabin with you?"

Charlie laughed, causing the baby to stir and fret just a little before he slept once more. "I wouldn't mind," he said. "But I think he would."

Jed and Brenna exchanged looks.

"Nesting instinct got you?" Brenna asked.

Charlie shrugged. He wasn't admitting anything. He didn't need anybody's pity because the woman he wanted was in Denver with another man.

Brenna seemed to sense that. She didn't press. She just let him continue to pace until it was clear that Hank was down for the count. Then she led Charlie upstairs to the baby's bedroom. "Here's the test of true power," she said. "Can you ease him into bed without waking him up?"

"I used to be pretty good with my friends, Chase and Joanna's, kids." He'd lugged a colicky Emerson around a lot of nights.

"Novel way to keep a kid off the streets," Chase had said with a grin at the time.

But Charlie hadn't minded. It had made him feel needed. It had made him a part of things—even when he'd insisted he didn't want to be a part.

He realized now how foolish he'd been. He realized how he'd been fighting himself all these years. It was nice to have finally got it straightened out.

Pity that Cait didn't believe him.

He laid Hank in the crib, and the baby gave a tiny shudder, but his eyes stayed shut. He made a soft sucking sound as if he were dreaming of nursing. A faint smile curved his baby lips.

"You're a miracle worker," Brenna breathed.

And moments later when he accompanied her back downstairs, Jed looked at him with real respect. "A regular genius," he said.

Charlie stayed with them until after midnight. He talked with Brenna about her next show at Gaby's which was coming up in the fall. He talked to Jed and Otis about the cattle he and Walt had moved today. He talked to Tuck about the Porsche and admired some of the drawings Tuck had done of it.

It was a whole lot better than rattling around the cabin by himself, worrying himself sick about Cait and Steve in some Denver motel room. He liked the company and the conversation. He felt comfortable. At home.

He wanted...

He wanted to stay.

Not simply at Jed and Brenna's. Not at Jed and Brenna's at all, really. But in Elmer. In the valley. Here. In this community. With these people.

With Cait.

"Getting tired?" Brenna said, smothering a yawn.

And Charlie, startled, realized how late it was and how

early Jed would have to be up in the morning—how early Walt would expect to see him—and how much he had overstayed his welcome.

He scrambled to his feet. "Hey! I'm sorry. I wasn't thinking. I just—" He shrugged, a little embarrassed at how he'd settled in.

"Glad to have you. Wish you'd come down sooner," Brenna said. "But I know you had your own priorities." She took his hand and gave it a squeeze. She was smiling at him.

Had Gaby told her why he'd really come?

Suddenly he didn't care. "Thanks," he said to all of them—and meant it from the bottom of his heart.

He slept.

Fitfully.

He dreamed.

Desperately.

He woke.

Haggardly.

Sunday was even worse. Walt woke him up when he finally fell asleep at dawn.

"Uh, right. I'm gettin' up," he mumbled, only to have Walt tell him he wasn't coming today, that he had things to do at home.

"Don't mean you can lie abed all day," the old man said. "Just that I trust you to do it yourself," he said. "Just ride that fence line along near the water hole."

It was a vote of confidence, of course. Walt believed in him. Another time Charlie would have been gratified by the news.

Today he could have used the company. Riding fence was far less demanding than moving the cattle. Far less interesting, too. And without Walt there to drone on about Vietnam, naturally all his thoughts were of Cait.

She would be back today. He would go down tomorrow and see her. And if she said she and Steve had put a down payment on a house, what was he going to do?

Was he going to battle all the way to the altar? Was he going to fight to make her love him? Or was he going to beat a tactful retreat?

They weren't questions he wanted to consider.

He didn't believe in retreats.

But he didn't believe in making Cait's life miserable, either.

He itched to call Chase and talk it over. But since he hadn't really followed the advice Chase had given him the last time they'd talked, he didn't think calling again and confessing he'd done the opposite would net him any stars for good behavior now.

Besides, whatever Chase said would probably be right— just as what he'd said last time was undoubtedly right. And Charlie would probably do it wrong. Again.

But he was beginning to get the idea that there were some things a guy had to work out for himself. Convincing the woman he loved that he did indeed love her was obviously one of them.

He finished with the fence about five in the afternoon and rode back to the cabin, passing the water hole as he went.

He didn't stop. He didn't need any more reminders. And even though he was hot and tired and his leg ached, he didn't even consider taking a dip.

He unloaded the pack horse, put away the wire and posts he'd taken along, then unsaddled his own horse and turned them both out to graze. He didn't even have to think about it anymore. Handling horses and fencing material was getting to be second nature now. The silence didn't bother him now. In fact it didn't seem all that quiet. There were birds. Grasshoppers. The rustle of the breeze blowing through the trees.

There were a lot of people in the world who wouldn't believe this was Charlie Seeks Elk if they could see him now. But he knew it was a good fit. A better fit for the man he'd become than going back to cover wars would be.

Yes, he could get used to this.

He could love it and never leave it.

If only he had Cait.

It was dusk when Charlie heard Walt's truck.

He was making coffee and, given Walt's unerring instincts and love of java, figured that the old man must have heard him pop the vacuum seal on the new can. Well, good. He could use the company. He hadn't spoken to a soul since Walt had rung this morning.

Maybe Cait was back. Maybe Walt had news. Charlie felt his insides clench. He got out a second mug, set it on the table and stepped out on the porch.

Behind him, over the Bridgers, the last light was fading. From the east the truck rounded the bend, and Charlie could see its headlights bouncing as it navigated the dirt track. He stood, one hand braced on the porch support and waited.

Finally the truck pulled up alongside where he'd left Otis's Suburban, and the engine shut off. The door opened.

"Coffee's on," Charlie called down. "You must have ears like an elephant," he added as a figure emerged and the truck door shut.

"Thank you very much," a decidedly female voice dryly replied.

Charlie's stomach did a complete flip.

"Cait?"

* * *

This was a bad idea.

A very bad idea.

An idea born of desperation and agitation and not much else.

But it was the only idea Cait had—so she had gone with it.

And now the time for backing out was past. The minute she'd driven through the gate and started up the hill, she knew she'd reached the point of no return.

He'd hear her coming. He'd be waiting. Expecting someone. She couldn't just turn around and head back down.

Well, she could, but she wouldn't let herself.

She'd lived in limbo too long. It was beginning to feel like hell. And she had to resolve things one way or the other. She couldn't go on like this.

It was Charlie's fault, she reasoned. So it was Charlie who was going to have to help resolve it.

Now she took a deep breath and walked resolutely toward him. "Yes," she said. "It's me."

She was close enough now that she could see the glint of his grin.

Don't, she thought. *Please, Charlie, don't!*

She didn't want him to be happy, to be glad to see her, to virtually welcome her with open arms.

"Hey," he said, still grinning. But when she didn't smile in return, gradually his grin began to fade. His brows drew together. "What happened? Did something happen to Walt?"

"What? No. No, of course not. I—" She raked a hand through her hair. She'd raked her hands through her hair a hundred times in the past hour, it seemed. "He's not even home. I don't know where he is."

And she was glad of it. It meant he was getting out,

doing things, having a life. And it meant she didn't have to tell him about her weekend in Denver with Steve. She didn't want to talk about it—or about Steve—or anything else for that matter, until she had things settled in her mind.

"Then…what?" Charlie was looking worried now. Good. She was tired of being the only one whose life was spinning out of control.

She stuck her hands in the pockets of her jeans and debated how to begin. Just baldly blurt it out? Work it into the conversation?

"I'll have that coffee," she decided abruptly. Maybe if she had a few moments to think things out…

Charlie blinked, then nodded. "Right. Come on in."

He went back inside, leaving her to follow.

The room seemed even smaller now than the last time she had come, when she had brought him the ice. Then it had been Charlie filling it. Now all she seemed to see was the bed. She jerked her gaze away from it.

Charlie was pouring two mugs of coffee. In his jeans and a navy-blue long-sleeved shirt, his black hair flopping forward onto his forehead, he looked healthy and handsome and comfortable in his surroundings. He looked as if he fit in, as if he was at home, as if this *was* his home.

Last time she'd thought how out of place he seemed here, but not now. The cabin had his mark on it—and it seemed to have made a mark on him.

It surprised her.

It disturbed her. She'd wanted him to hate it, to leave it. To go away.

He was adding a dollop of milk to one of the mugs. Hers. And then he carried it over to her. "Here you go."

"Thank you." She was careful that their fingers didn't touch. The mug was hot, but it gave her something to hang on to while she got her bearings.

Charlie had his bearings. He looked relaxed, one hip

propped against the sinkboard as he took a sip of coffee and regarded her over the top of the mug.

Cait studied the coffee in her own mug. Then she looked around the room. She shifted her weight from one foot to the other, breathed deeply and tried to find the right words. There were no right words. There was only the deed.

She looked up at last. "I want to go to bed with you."

So much for Charlie looking relaxed. His heels hit the floor with a thud, and he stood up straight so quickly that the coffee in his mug slopped onto his hand. He blinked rapidly, and a tide of color darkened his cheeks.

He opened his mouth, but it took a second or two for him to respond. It was as if she'd knocked the breath right out of him, which she supposed she had.

And then he said, "Yes," and started to grin. It was a warm grin, a wonderful grin. A grin of relief and joy.

Cait couldn't look at it. She gripped the mug between her palms and began to pace, shaking her head. "I didn't mean that," she muttered.

Behind her Charlie sucked in a breath. "What did you mean?" His voice was quiet. Without even looking she knew the grin was gone.

She didn't turn around until she reached the far wall and was forced to. Then she stopped and turned and lifted her shoulders irritably. "I meant that we need to sort things out...clear the air."

Charlie stared at her. "Sort what out? Clear what air?"

"Between us!" Cait shoved one hand through her hair this time. "Between us! It's making me nuts. I can't...I can't think! I can't make sense of things! I tried to find a house with Steve this weekend and I...I kept thinking about *you!*"

"What a shame," Charlie said dryly.

"It is," Cait said, frantic. "It's wrong! I shouldn't be feeling this way when I'm marrying someone else!"

"Or maybe you shouldn't be marrying someone else."

Damn him for being so bloody rational!

"I don't know what I should be doing!" She was almost shouting now. "Don't you see?"

She didn't wait to find out whether he saw or not. She went back to pacing again, almost knocking over one of the chairs. Charlie reached out and snagged it out of her way. She took a deep, steadying breath, then stopped and faced him again.

"I told Steve we couldn't get married the way I'm feeling right now. I told him I needed to clear my head. And this is the only way I can think to do it."

"By going to bed with me?"

"By getting you out of my system," she agreed. "And it can help you, too!"

"Really?" Charlie lifted a brow.

"Yes," she insisted. "It will get me out of your system, too."

He just looked at her.

It was what he'd wanted, damn it! It was *all* he'd wanted two years ago!

And here she was, standing in front of him offering it to him—offering *herself* to him—no strings attached.

Take me to bed.

How much more blatant could she be?

And Charlie shook his head. A faint rueful smile touched one corner of his mouth for just a moment, then it disappeared.

"I don't want you out of my system, Cait," he told her quietly. "I love you. So, thanks, but the answer is no."

Nine

He needed his head examined!

For crying out loud, she'd just flat-out offered to go to bed with him—and he'd said no.

Like he hadn't wanted to! Like it hadn't been the very thing he'd been hoping for and dreaming of since he'd come back from his encounter with eternity.

He had hoped for it. He had dreamed of it. Had prayed for it.

But not like this.

He understood now the old adage, ''Be careful what you pray for,'' because when she stood right there and baldly offered it to him, he couldn't take it.

It wasn't enough.

He didn't want only Cait's body in his bed. He didn't want merely the softness of her skin against the roughness of his. He didn't want just sweet murmurs and shaking passion.

He wanted love.

God help him, he wanted her love.

But that wasn't what she was offering, and he knew it. So they had stood and stared at each other for what seemed like another eternity, but which could only have been a few seconds.

And then—when Charlie said no…thank you, but no— she'd turned on her heel and walked away.

And now he stood staring at her taillights as the truck hurtled down the hill. He braced one hand against the porch post, gripping it so hard he felt his nails dig into the wood.

"Damn it!" The words were wrung from him.

They broke—a harsh ugly painful sound echoing exactly the way he felt since the moment of his refusal when he'd watched the color drain from her face.

She'd blinked her astonishment—and her hurt—then carefully, oh, so carefully, she'd set her coffee mug down on the table, turned and walked out the door.

For at least ten seconds Charlie had stayed right where he was. Frozen. Not just immobile, but literally cold as ice from the inside out.

Then he'd heard the truck door open and slam shut. He heard the engine kick over, sputter and die. Then the key ground in the ignition and the engine growled to life again.

The sound had moved him. He reached the top of the steps in time to see her jerk the truck into reverse and back it around. He was conscious of her overrevving the engine. He knew she was angry as hell.

He just didn't know what he could do about it.

So he said, "Damn it," again. Then he took a breath. Short, shallow, all he was capable of—and he let it out.

"You can't do anything about it," he said quietly into the darkness.

Around the bend, the taillights disappeared. The sound of the truck grew fainter.

He waited. He listened. But in a few minutes, even straining, Charlie couldn't hear it anymore.

In the silence he stood alone.

Slowly he let go of the post, unbent his knuckles and saw his hand begin to shake. He balled it into a fist and jammed it into his pocket. His throat started to thicken and ache, and he swallowed desperately. His eyes began to burn and he shut them. He clamped his teeth together to trap and swallow the sound of pain. He stood there, rigid, fighting it.

But it was a fight he wasn't going to win.

It was over.

He'd been as honest as he could be.

She'd walked away.

So much for bad ideas.

Such a bad idea it was positively off the charts!

Anger, pain, mortification, humiliation.

Cait felt all of the above—and knew she deserved every one.

The emotions had come in waves. Anger first. She couldn't believe he'd said no. *Thanks, but no.* Like she'd offered him a piece of pie for dessert. Calm and almost dismissive. But polite.

God, yes! He was so freaking polite!

No, thank you, Ms. Blasingame, I don't want to go to bed with you. Her face could still burn just thinking about it.

The mortification and humiliation were in a dead heat for second.

The last time Charlie had, in effect, turned her down, he'd done it without saying a word. He'd simply got up in the middle of the night and left.

She hadn't figured it out right away. The realization that he hadn't just left for the moment, but for life, was gradual. And painful. And mortifying.

She'd felt such a fool.

She couldn't imagine ever feeling like a bigger one.

But she did now.

This time, like an idiot, she'd spelled it out. She'd flat-out offered her body to him—and he'd rejected her.

When would she ever learn?

No, that wasn't right. She had learned!

And then there was the pain.

It was the pain of rejection first. Then the pain of embarrassment and humiliation. Those were the feelings of pain that had propelled her out of the cabin, into the truck and down the hill. Those were the feelings that had roiled in her heart and in her soul and in her mind as she berated herself for her foolishness. Those were the feelings that kept her awake and pacing all night. Those were the feelings that wouldn't even let her face her father.

She heard him come in, but she pretended to be asleep.

She couldn't answer questions about her weekend in Denver. Her weekend in Denver seemed a million years ago!

And she couldn't tell him about tonight. She couldn't talk about Charlie to her father, who thought the sun rose and set on him.

So she huddled in the darkness of her room and relived the stomach-grinding humiliation of her evening with Charlie over and over and over.

She beat on her pillow. She punched and hammered it, then clutched it against her belly and wrapped herself around it.

And she wept.

For her foolishness. For her needs. For wanting a man she didn't want to want.

Then, as night slid into the first rays of dawn, the tears subsided and she lay silent and still and stared at the ceiling. And she realized that her foolishness was even greater than she'd thought it was.

Charlie hadn't refused to make love with her tonight to embarrass her or to humiliate her or even to hurt her.

He hadn't taken her to bed because he really did love her—and he hadn't been willing to settle for less.

Her lips trembled. Her vision blurred, and the tears came again.

But this time Cait wept for an even greater foolishness—for not believing him.

"You look like hell," Steve said when she finally tracked him down late Monday afternoon.

She hadn't had a chance before. She'd lain awake until dawn, aching and crying for herself—her foolishness—and for the man she'd lost by denying feelings she'd been afraid to have.

There was no reason to keep Steve's ring now. No sense in holding out the slightest bit of hope for them. But just as she was thinking she might call him, her phone had rung and it had been one of her patients telling her that she was in labor.

Cait had never felt less like doing her job. But she hauled herself up and headed for Livingston. She'd find Steve later. But between Lucy's labor and delivery and the patients she had appointments with at the office, she barely had a chance to think.

That was a good thing—as the only thoughts she had were of Charlie—and of what a fool she'd been. Well, she had the answer to her question now.

She was no longer confused about why she was thinking about Charlie when she was determined to marry Steve.

It was because she still loved him.

Charlie had been right and she'd been wrong. Terribly terribly wrong.

She knew that now—for all the good it would do her.

"I feel like hell," she told Steve frankly when she finally saw him. She tried to smile, but her mouth didn't seem to be working.

"What happened? It's not your dad?"

Everyone thought everything was her dad. But Charlie had helped him out of whatever depression he'd been in.

"It's not my dad," Cait said. "It's me." And this time she really did wiggle the ring off her finger and put it in his palm. "I can't marry you."

"Ever?"

She nodded, just once. "I can't."

"What did I—" he began but she cut him off.

"It's not you. It's me. And someone else," she added, needing to be honest because Joyce had seen that kiss. Joyce had heard her argue with Charlie. And she didn't want Steve hearing things she hadn't had the guts to tell him.

Steve looked at her. "Who?"

"A man I used to know. A man I thought I was over—and wasn't."

"And he came back for you?"

"He tried," Cait said. "I turned him down. But then I realized—"

Steve made a face. "And now you're going with him."

Cait shook her head. "No. Now I'm quite sure he won't want me."

"Then—"

"No. I don't love you the way I ought to. Seeing him again made me realize that. I would only make you unhappy. I'm sorry."

Steve smiled wryly. "Yeah. Me, too." He hesitated, then went on. "Though I'm not exactly surprised."

He didn't look exactly heartbroken, either. In fact, he looked almost relieved. Or maybe, Cait thought, she was just indulging in wishful thinking. She didn't want to ask what he meant. She'd behaved badly enough already. So she just looked at him and hoped he would explain.

"You kept making up excuses not to go to bed with me."

Cait shut her eyes. If she hadn't already used up her lifetime supply of mortification, she could have wallowed in it here. She ducked her head and shifted from one foot to the other. "I didn't mean…"

But she couldn't finish because obviously she *had* "meant"…or her body had. It had apparently realized what her mind had not—that Steve was not for her.

"I'm glad I'm moving to Denver," he said frankly.

"Yes," she agreed, looking up at last. "And I'm sure you'll meet someone there. Someone better for you. More suited. Someone who loves you the way you deserve to be loved."

Before he could answer, his beeper went off. He smiled a little ruefully, then actually laughed as hers went off ten seconds later.

He tucked the ring in his pocket, then reached out and gave her hand a squeeze. "Take care of yourself, Cait."

She clung for half a second, then let him go. "I will. You, too."

He turned and headed for emergency. She watched him go, knowing she'd done one right thing at last. Steve had his whole future ahead of him, and he would meet someone far better than she was. His future was bright.

Hers seemed endlessly bleak.

"I'm amazed. No, I'm not amazed," Gaby said as she studied the slides Charlie had spread out on the light box. "I mean, I knew you'd find something wonderful. And I knew you said mothers and children, bears and babies, but I never thought…'' She lifted her gaze and her eyes shone. ''They're brilliant, Charlie. They're just wonderful.''

''Uh-huh.''

Some of them had promise, he was willing to admit. The series on the mother bear and her cubs was strong. He'd done some good stuff on a horse and foal, too. And he had some he liked of Angie and the baby.

He'd taken quite a few of Brenna and her bunch while he was there. Those girls of hers, Neile and Shannon, were shot stealers, for certain. And he'd done a whole series of Brenna with Jed's nephew Tuck. He saw echoes of his own relationship with Joanna. Brenna was the closest thing to a mother Tuck had, and his devotion was clear.

They were both artists, and Charlie had taken lots of shots of them working, talking together, studying a subject, then working again. He'd taken other shots as well—of Brenna and Tuck on horseback, of Brenna and Tuck doing dishes, of Brenna sitting in the passenger seat of his Porsche and Tuck behind the wheel, pleased as punch to be driving her to town in such a vehicle.

But perhaps his favorite shot of all was one of the whole family around the dinner table—Jed, Brenna, Otis, Tuck, Neile, Shannon and Hank. Three generations. A complete mix: Brenna's father, Jed's nephew, her child by her first marriage, the two they'd had together. Laughing, arguing, talking.

Family.

Loving. Caring. Supporting.

It made him ache just to look at it.

It was what he'd always wanted—even when he'd been afraid to reach out for it—first with Chase and Joanna, then with Cait.

Yes, he'd finally come to his senses. But with Cait the hurt had been too deep, and he'd left it too late.

There was a moral there somewhere. Charlie saw it staring him in the face.

He regretted leaving Montana, he was grateful for Brenna's offer to come back whenever he wanted and he said maybe someday he would.

After all, Cait wouldn't be there. She'd be safe in Denver with Steve. Or if she didn't marry Steve, she'd find someone else. Someone who got it right the first time.

Not him.

"We can hang a show next week," Gaby said now, eyes shining.

"What!" That was impossible. Shows took months to set up. Charlie stared at her, mouth open.

She laughed. "Not a full-scale, all-out, one-man band sort of show. But I've got a show opening next week—Nathan Wolfe. You know Nathan. He does those fantastic arctic photos. Animals. Birds. He's got some wonderful polar bears. What you have here could blend in." She was warming to the notion, he could see it in her eyes. "Your own audience will find you, anyway, but since you've moved on in your interests, you're going to want people to know where you've gone. Nathan's audience would be a natural."

"Nathan won't be thrilled." A man didn't happily share a one-man show.

But Gaby disagreed. "I think he might. He's been a bit distracted lately." She shook her head. "He keeps muttering about having other things on his mind. Like he thinks I don't? Anyway, he hasn't given me all I need to really go big with this, so if we hung some of yours—just a couple of series even—you'd fill my walls and you'd be doing him a favor."

"I don't know…"

Gaby, of course, took that as a yes. She was already picking the slides she wanted to use.

And Charlie didn't have the energy to argue with her.

He didn't have any energy at all.

He had come back home two days ago, and he'd done nothing since he got here except stare at the ocean.

It didn't have the soothing effect it usually had. It was too…flat.

He still liked the horizon, but he didn't like it flat anymore. He needed a little high relief. He needed mountains. Towering pines. Icy, running creeks.

Southern California felt alien to him. He'd never been so aware of the pollution, the noise, the buildings, the cars. There were so many people. Too many people.

And not one of them was Cait.

It always came back to Cait.

He had to stop thinking about her. He had to get past it. He'd given it his best shot. There was nothing else he could have done.

You could have gone to bed with her one last time, he told himself. If he had, at least he would have had the memory. But maybe that would have been worse.

He tried to tell himself it would have been worse. Sometimes he believed it. He needed to stop thinking about it.

"Fine," he said heavily to Gaby now. "Do it. I'll help."

Maybe it would distract him, occupy him, force him to get on with his life.

She finished picking the slides she wanted. Then she went into his kitchen and made them both a cup of coffee. When she had poured it, she sat down, and for the first time she looked at him and studied him as closely as she'd studied his slides.

"You're not happy."

"No."

Her eyes softened. Her expression saddened. "The woman in Montana…"

"Is still in Montana," he said flatly. "And I'm here."

"Ah, Charlie." Her eyes reflected his misery.

He shook it off. "I'll get over it."

She touched his cheek. "Of course, Charlie. Someday you will."

She would get over it—over *him*.

She had to. She had no choice. It wasn't as if she could go running after him now. She'd made her bed, as her father would say. She would have to lie in it.

And she did. Miserably. Night after night. With all the memories of what might have been.

Every day Cait dragged herself out to work. She saw patients. She helped mothers and fathers bring babies into the world. And when she had the slightest bit of energy left, she threw herself into work on the ranch.

They needed her help since Charlie had gone.

She wasn't surprised to hear that he had.

Her father was.

"Thought he was comin' into his own," he'd said, shaking his head when he'd told her. "Told him he had the makin's of a pretty fine hand."

"He's a photographer, Dad. He has a job to do."

"He was doin' it here," Walt groused. But then he stopped, straightened up and squared his shoulders. "Glad he came," he said. "Made me think about things I hadn't thought about in years."

Cait wasn't really listening. She was thinking about Charlie as always.

She was completely shocked, then, to come home from work a few days later to find her father packing a bag.

"Dad?" She stopped at the doorway to his room and stared at him.

He jumped as if she'd surprised him. Then a fleeting embarrassed smile flickered over his face. "Oh, Caity. You're home, then."

"I'm home. Are you…leaving? Taking a trip?"

She'd encouraged him to get out, to do things, to bounce back from the heart attack, to find new interests if the ranch wasn't enough. But he'd never said he was going away.

Had he?

She'd been in such an emotional funk since the night she'd had her encounter with Charlie that she didn't hear half of what anyone said. "What are you doing?" she asked him.

"I wouldn't have left without telling you," he said now, folding a shirt and laying it in the bag.

"Well, good." She tried a smile. "Of course you wouldn't. Are you taking one of those weekends to Las Vegas? Going to see Aunt Rachel in Seattle?" Please, God, don't let him be going to California to visit Charlie.

He straightened up and faced her squarely. "Vietnam."

She was conscious of her jaw falling open and her eyes widening a lot. Vietnam? No, she was quite sure now—he'd never told her that.

"But…why?"

"Now that's somethin' we need to talk about." He left the bag sitting on his bed and crossed the room to her. "Come sit down. I want to tell you a story."

An army story?

Her father had never been one of those guys who spent hours talking about his experiences in the military. He didn't live in the past. It was over, finished. Whenever she and Wes had asked him about those days, after they had heard about Vietnam from their friends or their friends' dads or they had seen something on television, he'd brushed them off.

"It's over," he'd always said brusquely. "Time now to move on."

Of course his sentiment was shared by a lot of people.

For one reason or another, many did not want to look back at what had happened in Vietnam. Her father had simply been one of them.

Until now.

Now he told her his story.

Cait knew some of it. Her mother had told her about their long-distance love affair. "I wanted to get married before he left," she'd told Cait. "But Walt wouldn't do it. He said he didn't want to leave a widow. And he said I was too young, that I might meet someone else. As if I would." She'd shaken her head and laughed at the chance of that.

Cait had understood. Her father was still, at sixty, a handsome man. And when he wanted to he could charm the ladies. But the only woman he'd ever looked at, as long as Margie was alive, was her mother.

"Margie was so young," he told Cait now. She sat on the sofa where he'd steered her while he paced back and forth. "A child. Nineteen, for heaven's sake. And she thought the world rose and set on me. She never knew anyone else! She never," he reflected, "wanted to know."

He paused and ran his fingers over his short, salt-and-pepper hair. "I thought we should wait. War's unpredictable. I didn't want her tied to me. We wrote letters. She was a lifeline to the world I knew. I loved her for it. I loved her," he said more firmly. "But I was surprised when she actually came to Hawaii for my R&R."

That part Cait had heard about. She knew lots of stories about the whirlwind week her parents had spent together on Oahu. Her mother had told her time and again, her eyes shining, of how exciting it was to see her father again, to touch him, to hold him.

"Of course she came," she said now. "Why wouldn't she?"

"Lots of women didn't," her father said. "Guys went,

hoping…and their girls weren't there. I was all ready to have the same thing happen to me. I couldn't believe it when I got off the bus at Fort DeRussey, and she was actually there."

"She loved you, Dad. She would never have gone with anyone else."

"I know that now. I knew it in Hawaii. I didn't know it before."

Cait stared at him, not quite following.

He didn't say anything for a long moment. Then he sighed and spoke, his voice low. "I met a woman in Vietnam. A teacher. Before I met your mother in Hawaii. Before we got married. This teacher spoke some English. She wanted to learn more." He rubbed a hand against the back of his head. "She asked me to teach her." He stared away out the window again.

Cait didn't have to guess what had happened next.

She remembered Abuk. She remembered Charlie. She knew exactly what could happen. It had happened to her.

"Her name was Sue. Well, actually it was somethin' I never could pronounce," her father said ruefully, "so I called her Sue. She was a fine woman. And I…I—" He stopped and shook his head, unable to say the words.

"And you fell in love with her."

He twisted his head to look at her. "I don't know if I loved her or not," her father said, surprising her. "I liked her. I liked her a hell of a lot. I might have even thought I loved her. She was sweet, funny, generous. Very kind to a homesick American guy. But then I went to Hawaii, and I saw your mother again and there was no comparison. That was love, Caity. That was my future. And when I went back, married, I looked up Sue first thing and I told her so."

He turned away again. Stood still as a statue. And Cait contemplated him. She tried to envision her father as a

young man in a foreign country, finding solace with another woman. She could see that. She imagined even her
mother might have understood. They hadn't been married,
after all. And once they'd got married, he'd presumably
ended it with this Sue.

"And you never saw her again?"

He shook his head. "I told her we couldn't."

"And now you're going back to look for her?"

"Not for her, Caity. She's gone. She died several years
later. Right at the end of the war."

"But then…?" She didn't understand.

A ghost of a sad smile touched his mouth. "There was
a child."

Cait couldn't move.

She was glad she was sitting down. She stared at her
father as if she'd never seen him before.

A child?

Her father and this Vietnamese teacher, this woman
called Sue, had a…*child?*

There was another Blasingame halfway across the
world? A half brother or sister of hers and Wes's? A sib-
ling she had never known?

Never even heard of?

She tried to bend her mind around this. "All these
years…" Her voice trailed off, her mind whirling. "A
child?"

Her father nodded. "A child."

"Did Mom…?"

He knew what she was asking. "No. No one knew. I
never said."

"But—"

"Life is full of choices, Caity. We make them, sometimes on the spur of the moment, sometimes with a lot of
thought. But we make them—and then we go on. We do
the best we can with what we've made. It's what I tried

to do.'' He sighed. "I didn't know Sue was pregnant when I left for Hawaii. Had no idea. Hadn't even considered the possibility, fool that I was. I didn't find out until I came back and told her I was married.''

"Oh, God.''

Her father sighed. "Yes. Oh, God. I was pretty well poleaxed when she said. I didn't even want to believe her. But I did.'' He studied the tops of his boots, then lifted his gaze and looked straight at her.

"But you didn't see…you never knew your—'' Cait couldn't even finish a sentence.

"No. I let it go.''

"You never—''

He shook his head adamantly. "No. I might have been able to try to get the child. I might have been able to claim it and have brought it to the States. Some guys had kids there and did that. I didn't. Sue wanted to keep the baby. She said so. And I…I didn't push. I was afraid to hurt your mother. I didn't know what she'd say. I was afraid to…rock the boat. Afraid to take the risk.'' He sighed and slumped a little then, as if the decision weighed him down.

"But why now?'' Cait asked.

"Because when I had that heart attack last fall, I had a lot of time to think.''

That's what he'd been thinking about? That's what had made him so pensive and withdrawn?

"And I thought I could die without ever having known him…or her. Because I wouldn't take a risk.'' He shook his head. "I'm not saying I was wrong in the first place, Cait. Maybe I was. Maybe I was selfish. I was damn sure scared. So I made the choice I thought was right—and I went on. I didn't look back.''

She tried to think back over all the years of her life, all the years her father had lived keeping this inside him, tried to imagine what it must have been like for him to walk away from this child he would never know.

"But I'm looking now," he said. "It was your little gal that made me start thinkin' I needed to look."

Cait started. "My little gal?"

"The one in Charlie's book. The little girl in the hospital. The little girl who lost everything in the war. Seein' her made me think. It made me feel guilty, and like I needed to know. I talked to Charlie."

"Charlie knows?"

"Charlie and I have talked. Not about my…my child. About kids. About risk. About war. About life. About dyin'."

Cait nodded. Yes, Charlie knew about dying. Her throat grew tight. Her eyes blurred.

"Reckon I might never know," Walt went on resolutely. "It might be impossible. There might be too little to go on, it might be way too late. But I don't want to die without tryin', Cait." His pale-blue eyes met hers. "I don't want to die without tryin' to find 'im. Eternity is a long long time."

As usual Gaby pulled out all the stops.

The night of the opening, the sangria flowed and the champagne corks popped. Critics and journalists drifted along with art patrons who had more money in their checking accounts than Charlie would earn in a lifetime, casually consuming trays full of Santa Fe's trendiest hors d'oeuvres while they wandered through Sombra Y Sol's gallery rooms, murmuring and discussing the photos, Nathan's and his.

It was Nathan's show, of course. Nathan would be the one the critics praised or scorned. He was the one whose work they would buy or walk away from. He would live or die by the results of it.

But Nathan barely seemed to care.

He was distracted. Preoccupied. Forgetful.

"We're lucky he even remembered to show up," Gaby muttered, glaring at him. "At least he could have dressed for the occasion!"

Nathan was wearing jeans and an open-necked shirt. He was standing with the same half-full glass of champagne that Gaby had handed him an hour ago. He looked startled when one of Santa Fe's biggest art patrons came up to talk to him. Watching, Gaby groaned.

"He'll be all right," Charlie said.

"Will he?" Gaby didn't look optimistic. "He's about as bad as you were a few months back. Couldn't follow a three-word sentence from beginning to end."

Well, yes, Charlie could do that now—if he worked at it.

He'd been working at it. He'd been trying hard. Working his butt off to help Gaby get the show hung. Determined to take his mind off Cait.

It was true what he'd told her—that he didn't want to get her out of his system. But he had to function.

If he wasn't going to have her in his life, he still had to live. He'd come back to Santa Fe with Gaby the day after she'd proposed the show to him. He'd been working flat-out ever since. It was how he coped.

But it wasn't easy.

His mind could still drift away in the middle of a conversation. He could still see a flash of dark hair in the other room, and if the light caught it just the right way, he would still whip his head around to see if it might be her. Some voices had nearly the same timbre as hers. Some laughs were almost, but not quite, as genuine and delighted.

Some woman someday would probably come close.

But no other woman was Cait.

He'd hoped Joanna and Chase would say something encouraging, something that would give him hope.

He'd gone to see them as soon as he'd got home. He'd walked straight into their house and put his arms around both of them and said right out, "Thank you for everything. For being there. For…loving me."

It hadn't even been hard to say it, though he'd thought it might.

And the looks on their faces—the joy, the tenderness, the love—had made him wish he'd had the courage to say it, and to believe in it, years ago.

They loved him. They told him so. But they hadn't held out hope for him with regard to Cait.

Joanna had hugged him and told him with maternal ferocity that Cait was crazy. Chase had clapped an arm around his shoulders and said, "It's hell, man. I've been there."

He had. But at least Chase had found his way back.

Eventually, Charlie reminded himself, years later Joanna had found him again.

So maybe…

But thinking things like that was the way to drive himself nuts.

"Ah," Gaby said, patting his hand and craning her neck to look past dozens of gallery lurkers and patrons, "your family's arrived."

And Charlie looked around, following her gaze, eager to catch a glimpse of Joanna's red curls and Chase's raven hair. He'd told them they didn't have to come.

"It's not a big deal," he'd said. "Not a one-man show or anything."

"It's your show," Chase had said.

"It's a big deal," Joanna had said. "We're all coming."

That meant they were bringing the kids, too. He was glad. For all that he'd said they didn't have to come, he was glad they had. He'd looked forward all week to them coming. He wanted them all here.

Now he could hear seven-year-old Annie's high-pitched voice saying, "Look, Daddy. Look! There's Charlie's bears!" And he saw her tug Chase to see the bears Charlie had told her about, but not before Chase had nodded backward toward the rest who were following him.

Charlie spotted the ten-year-old twins, Emerson and Alex. They waved to him, gave him a thumb's-up, then made a beeline for the punch bowl and the food.

Then he saw Joanna. She caught his eye and smiled, then drew someone else forward.

Cait.

Charlie stared. The noise faded. The clink of glasses, the clatter of trays, soft comments, raucous laughter, droning opinions—all of it—vanished. The only thing Charlie could hear was the roar of blood in his veins.

Cait?

Here?

He blinked, disbelieving. But when he looked again she was still there. Looking straight at him. There was a warmth, a tenderness, a hope in her eyes that he remembered from the days she had first loved him.

It was the expression he'd looked for on the day he'd been shot, when he'd sought her out in the crowd of people in the light. The day she hadn't been there.

And now she was here.

He felt a deep, fierce ache in his throat. He felt his body begin to tremble.

"Charlie!" Gaby's voice sounded a million miles away. "You're spilling that champagne!" Then her gaze seemed to follow his and she said quietly, "Oh. I see."

He felt her grab the glass out of his fingers and take him by the hand and pull him across the room, through the throng of people to where Joanna stood with Cait.

She didn't say anything when she got him there. And he didn't, either.

He couldn't. He didn't know what to say.

Cait did. She wasn't smiling as she looked at him. Her eyes were brimming. "Forgive me?"

"For what?"

Her lips trembled. "For being a fool. For doubting you. For being afraid."

He was the one who was afraid now—afraid he was hearing things, seeing things—afraid to believe.

"Afraid of what?' His voice sounded rusty.

"Of loving you. I do," she said, and it sounded like a vow. "Oh, God, Charlie, I do! And I believe you love me, too!"

A pinch-faced critic stepped between him and Cait. "I've been looking for you, Mr. Seeks Elk. We need to discuss this unpredictable highly irregular turnabout in your work."

"I—"

Cait was looking at him, her heart in her eyes.

"You are the one who did those stunning post-urban chaos photos, are you not?"

"I—"

Her fingers reached out tentatively past the critic to touch his. His wrapped tightly around hers, and he gave her his own heart, though she'd had it all along.

"I find the departure astonishing," the critic rabbited on, regarding Charlie over his spectacles with blatant disapproval. "And not a little disconcerting. I wonder how you can move so rapidly from such brutal realism to this…this…tender, hopeful…" He said the words as if they were epithets.

"I—"

"Can't," Gaby finished for him firmly as she took the

man by the arm and drew him away. "But I'm his agent and I'll be happy to talk to you."

The critic was only slightly mollified. He shot a look over his shoulder at Charlie and Cait.

Gaby made shooing motions at them with her hands. "Go on," she mouthed. "Go." Then she tucked her arm into the critic's and led him away to see the mothers and the babies—the bears and the horses and the humans.

"How do you account for this astonishing development?" the critic demanded.

"Well," Gaby said, "I think it all began when he saw the light."

He had her in his bed.

He had her in his arms.

Just as, for so long, he'd had her in his heart.

He couldn't believe it. He'd had to keep stopping on the walk back to the apartment just to touch her, to kiss her, to reassure himself that she was really here.

"I'm here," she'd said. "I'm here." But there was such wonder in her voice, that he guessed she didn't mind reassuring herself, too.

"I was so wrong," she told him when they went inside and shut the door. She wrapped her arms around herself, hugging herself tightly, fiercely, shaking her head, and then she looked up at him anguished. "I'm sorry. I do love you."

And all Charlie could think to tell her was the truth. "I love you, too."

Then he wrapped her in his arms and held her close. He didn't kiss her this time. He just held her—felt the warmth of her body melt the ice that had held his heart so long, felt the gentle touch of her hands against his back, felt them press him closer. Felt their two hearts begin to beat as one.

"How did you...Chase...Joanna?"

"I went to find you. You were gone. So I went to find them. Joanna wasn't all that thrilled to see me. She told me a few home truths." Cait smiled a little ruefully. "And I deserved every one of them."

"Joanna can be a little fierce," Charlie said, smiling as he stroked her cheek.

"She loves you."

"Yes."

"I love you, too. I don't want to get you out of my system, either, Charlie," she whispered. "I understand about eternity now."

His hand stilled and he looked deep into her eyes. "Do you?"

She kissed him. "Oh, yes."

He took her to bed then and he loved her.

His body ached for release. But he made himself go slow. He stroked her skin. He kissed the line of her jaw, the slope of her breasts, their peaks and the valley between. He moved over her, touching and brushing. His hands shook. His body trembled. He reined it in.

He was making memories. He was storing up pieces of eternity.

Until finally Cait wrapped her arms around him and drew him down and into her warmth. He felt her body clench and heard her cry out. And he closed his eyes and saw the light—and gave himself up to their love—and to her.

They had more than time now.

Their love went beyond.

Charlie had never seen snow.

"Never seen snow?" Cait had been astonished when he'd told her that. It had been September then. They'd come back to the ranch from their honeymoon in Jamaica to find two inches of snow on the ground.

He'd shaken his head. "Never." And he'd scooped it up in his hand, oddly surprised when it felt so cold. He'd tried packing it into a snowball, but it hadn't worked. He wasn't skilled at it. Something else he'd had to learn.

Now it was December. He could mend a fence now. He could spot black leg and scours. He could make a snowball. And a snowman. And he could shovel it for hours.

"Never saw so much snow in my life," he muttered as he stood with his arms around his wife and watched a blizzard of white flakes swirl around outside.

"You haven't seen much snow," Cait reminded him, laughing. "Remember?"

"I've seen enough," Charlie said darkly. "Seen one snowball, you've seen 'em all."

"Think so, do you?" Cait challenged.

"You bet." He tugged her toward the door. "Want to have a little snowball fight?"

"You just want to show off, now that Tuck and Jed have taught you all they know," Cait said.

"Well, yeah."

And he wanted to go outside and roll around with her. Actually he wanted to go to bed and roll around with her, but it was only two in the afternoon, and Walt would look askance if they disappeared upstairs.

They were living at Walt's for the moment, deciding whether they would build or if Walt would. He'd come back from Vietnam with leads, but so far nothing had turned up. They were waiting. Hoping.

"I'm a little nervous," he conceded.

"It's worth the nerves," Charlie told him. If he hadn't gone back after what he'd left behind, he wouldn't be here now. He wouldn't have Cait.

"Just a few snowballs?" he said now, grinning at her.

Cait shook her head. "Can't. We have obligations. *You* have obligations."

The Elmer Christmas pageant, she meant. When he'd married Cait, Polly McMaster had let them have the town hall for the reception rent free, with one string attached—Charlie would direct the town's Christmas pageant.

"She won't expect me to come today! It's dumping out there."

"Haven't you ever heard the old adage, the show must go on?" Cait teased.

"But—"

"Come on. The sooner we get there, the sooner we'll get home."

It wasn't true, but Charlie wasn't going to argue. He'd have his way with her sooner or later—and anticipating it was almost as sweet.

It snowed the rest of the afternoon. It snowed into the evening. It didn't matter. Everyone within ten square miles of Elmer, Montana, attended—as they always did. No one got stuck in the ditch. No one delivered a baby on stage. Charlene, whom he'd cast as the babe in the manger, never whimpered, Angie whom he had coerced into playing Mary, actually sparkled. And when it was over, he was quick enough to avoid getting stuck bringing home all the rabbits that had doubled as livestock in the manger.

Grinning as they went out to their truck, Cait told him he was learning.

He laughed. "Yeah, I guess I am."

Sometimes he thought he had so much to learn about life and about love that he would never touch the surface of it. Sometimes at night he woke up and just lay looking at the love of his life and marveling that he'd been given another chance.

Sometimes she would wake to find him lying there and, wordlessly, she would understand and wrap him in her

arms. She would love him—and he would love her—and
they would come together, two hearts, two hopes, two
souls made one.

They would do that tonight.

But first they ate a late supper. Then he helped Walt
with the chores, and while Cait brushed out her hair, he
called Chase and Joanna and regaled them with the tale of
his directorial triumph. Then she finished and turned to
smile at him, a look of such love in her eyes that his heart
seemed to catch in his throat.

"Gotta go," he muttered to Chase. "Take care. Love
you all," he said to Joanna.

Then he hung up and took his wife in his arms.

Outside the snow continued to fall. Inside they were safe
and warm. Cait drew him down with her onto the bed. She
kissed him.

"Remember once," she said, "when we were in bed
and I started talking about love and marriage and family."

"The first time, you mean?"

She nodded.

"I remember."

"And you were scared."

"Yeah."

"And now you're not?"

"You'd better believe I'm not," he vowed. "Marrying
you is the best thing that ever happened to me. I promise
you that."

"And the rest?" Cait persisted.

"What do you mean? Love? You know I love you.
Family?" The light suddenly dawned. It glimmered. Or it
could have been that tears were blurring it. "Caity?"

She laughed and rolled together with him on the bed,
and he held her gently, reverently, and heard words he'd
never thought he wanted to hear and knew now were his
greatest joy.

''August first more or less,'' his wife the midwife told him, ''you're going to be a father.''

* * * * *

SILHOUETTE®
DESIRE™ 2 IN 1

AVAILABLE FROM 18TH OCTOBER 2002

WHEN JAYNE MET ERIK Elizabeth Bevarly

20 Amber Court

Jayne Pembroke hadn't planned a marriage-of-convenience to millionaire playboy Erik Randolph. He set her heart racing; but was it a good thing to fall in love...with her own husband?

SOME KIND OF INCREDIBLE Katherine Garbera

20 Amber Court

When her gorgeous boss, Nicholas Camden, made love to Lila Maxwell, right there in his office, she wondered if that night of passion could be the start of a lifetime commitment...

BILLIONAIRE BACHELORS: RYAN
Anne Marie Winston

The Baby Bank

Ryan Shaughnessy married his best friend, Jessie Reilly, to save her from the sperm bank! But did Jessie see him as *more* than just the father of her twin babies?

JACOB'S PROPOSAL Eileen Wilks

Tall, Dark & Eligible

Jacob West needed a wife to secure his inheritance and Claire McGuire was the perfect in-name-only bride. But she awoke a deep passionate possessiveness in him. Had the powerful tycoon been overpowered...by love?

DR DANGEROUS Kristi Gold

Marrying an MD

Injured doctor Jared Granger hated being a patient! That was, until he found himself in the healing hands of physical therapist, Brooke Lewis—part seductress, part saint and *all* woman.

THE MD COURTS HIS NURSE Meagan McKinney

Matched in Montana

Dr John Saville suspected that Nurse Rebecca O'Reilly's saucy defiance hid a secret innocence--and desire. Would he resist the ultimate temptation—or surrender and claim Rebecca, now...and forever?

1002/51a

AVAILABLE FROM 18TH OCTOBER 2002

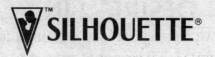

Sensation™

Passionate, dramatic, thrilling romances

CAPTURING CLEO Linda Winstead Jones
HOT AS ICE Merline Lovelace
RETURN OF THE PRODIGAL SON Ruth Langan
BORN IN SECRET Kylie Brant
THE RENEGADE STEALS A LADY Vickie Taylor
PROMISES, PROMISES Shelley Cooper

Special Edition™

Vivid, satisfying romances full of family, life and love

SURPRISE, DOC! YOU'RE A DADDY! Jacqueline Diamond
COURTING THE ENEMY Sherryl Woods
THE MARRIAGE CONSPIRACY Christine Rimmer
SHELTER IN A SOLDIER'S ARMS Susan Mallery
SOLUTION: MARRIAGE Barbara Benedict
BABY BE MINE Victoria Pade

Superromance™

*Enjoy the drama, explore the emotions,
experience the relationship*

JUST AROUND THE CORNER Tara Taylor Quinn
ACCIDENTALLY YOURS Rebecca Winters
LAST-MINUTE MARRIAGE Marisa Carroll
BABY BUSINESS Brenda Novak

Intrigue™

Danger, deception and suspense

SECRETS IN SILENCE Gayle Wilson
SECRET SANCTUARY Amanda Stevens
SOLITARY SOLDIER Debra Webb
IN HIS SAFEKEEPING Shawna Delacorte

1002/51b

DELIVERED BY
Christmas

Linda Howard
Joan Hohl   Sandra Steffen

Available from 18th October 2002

1102/128/SH41

THE COLTONS

FAMILY   PRIVILEGE   POWER

BOOK FOUR
THE DOCTOR DELIVERS
JUDY CHRISTENBERRY

Burdened by fame and family secrets,
Liza Colton seeks refuge in Saratoga Springs.
Meeting Dr Nick Hathaway makes her
feel whole again, but poisoned by his past,
the cynical doctor cannot see her for
who she really is.

Until one night of passion changed everything.

Available from 18th October 2002

COL/RTL/4

SHERRYL WOODS

about that man

It was going to be a long, hot summer...

On sale 18th October 2002

Available at most branches of WH Smith,
Tesco, Martins, Borders, Eason, Sainsbury's
and most good paperback bookshops.

SILHOUETTE®
DESIRE™

welcomes you to

20 AMBER COURT

*Where four women work together,
share an address...and confide in each
other as they fall in love!*

November 2002
WHEN JAYNE MET ERIK
by Elizabeth Bevarly

&

SOME KIND OF INCREDIBLE
by Katherine Garbera

December 2002
THE BACHELORETTE
by Kate Little

&

RISQUÉ BUSINESS
by Anne Marie Winston

1102/SH/LC44

SILHOUETTE®

DESIRE™

proudly presents

TALL, DARK & ELIGIBLE

Eileen Wilks

brings us three sexy, powerful,
exceptionally wealthy brothers...

Will three convenient marriages lead
to love for these bachelors?

NOVEMBER 2002
JACOB'S PROPOSAL

DECEMBER 2002
LUKE'S PROMISE

JANUARY 2003
MICHAEL'S TEMPTATION

1102/SH/LC46

SILHOUETTE® SENSATION™

proudly presents

Ruth Langan's

fabulous new mini-series

THE LASSITER LAW

Lives — and hearts — are on the line when the Lassiters pledge to uphold the law at any cost

BY HONOUR BOUND
October 2002

RETURN OF THE PRODIGAL SON
November 2002

BANNING'S WOMAN
December 2002

HIS FATHER'S SON
January 2003

1002/SH/LC43

SILHOUETTE®

proudly presents

five wonderful, warm stories from bestselling author

SHERRYL WOODS

The Calamity Janes

Five unique women share a lifetime of friendship!

DO YOU TAKE THIS REBEL?

Silhouette Special Edition
October 2002

COURTING THE ENEMY

Silhouette Special Edition
November 2002

TO CATCH A THIEF

Silhouette Special Edition
December 2002

THE CALAMITY JANES

Silhouette Superromance
January 2003

WRANGLING THE REDHEAD

Silhouette Special Edition
February 2003

1002/SH/LC42

SILHOUETTE® INTRIGUE™

proudly presents

MORIAH'S LANDING

Where evil looms,
but love conquers all!

An unknown force is about to irrevocably change the lives of four young women—and the men captivated by their spell.

1 FREE

book and a surprise gift!

We would like to take this opportunity to thank you for reading this Silhouette® book by offering you the chance to take ANOTHER specially selected title from the Desire™ series absolutely FREE! We're also making this offer to introduce you to the benefits of the Reader Service™—

 ★ FREE home delivery
 ★ FREE gifts and competitions
 ★ FREE monthly Newsletter
 ★ Exclusive Reader Service discount
 ★ Books available before they're in the shops

Accepting this FREE book and gift places you under no obligation to buy, you may cancel at any time, even after receiving your free shipment. Simply complete your details below and return the entire page to the address below. *You don't even need a stamp!*

YES! Please send me 1 free Desire book and a surprise gift. I understand that unless you hear from me, I will receive 2 superb new titles every month for just £4.99 each, postage and packing free. I am under no obligation to purchase any books and may cancel my subscription at any time. The free book and gift will be mine to keep in any case.

D2ZEA

Ms/Mrs/Miss/Mr ....Initials.................................
                                                            BLOCK CAPITALS PLEASE
Surname ....
Address ....
....
....Postcode..............................

Send this whole page to:
UK: FREEPOST CN81, Croydon, CR9 3WZ
EIRE: PO Box 4546, Kilcock, County Kildare (stamp required)